THE LAND
OF DREAMS

MINNESOTA TRILOGY

The Land of Dreams
Only the Dead
The Ravens

THE LAND OF DREAMS

VIDAR SUNDSTØL

Translated by TIINA NUNNALLY

MINNESOTA TRILOGY 1

University of Minnesota Press
Minneapolis

This translation has been published with the financial support of NORLA (Norwegian Literature Abroad, Fiction and Nonfiction).

Published by the University of Minnesota Press
111 Third Avenue South, Suite 290
Minneapolis, MN 55401-2520
http://www.upress.umn.edu

LIBRARY OF CONGRESS CATALOGING-IN-PUBLICATION DATA
Sundstøl, Vidar, 1963–
[Drømmenes land. English]
The land of dreams / Vidar Sundstol ; translated by Tiina Nunnally.
(Minnesota Trilogy; 1)
Translated from Norwegian to English.
Originally published in Norwegian as Drømmenes land.
ISBN 978-0-8166-8940-8 (hc)
ISBN 978-0-8166-8941-5 (pb)
1. Sundstøl, Vidar, 1963–—Translations into English. I. Nunnally, Tiina, 1952– translator. II. Title.
PT8952.29.U53D7613 2013
839.82'38—dc23
                      2013027215

Printed in the United States of America on acid-free paper

The University of Minnesota is an equal-opportunity educator and employer.

20 19 18 17 16 15 14 13   10 9 8 7 6 5 4 3 2 1

1

THE LAKE GLITTERED IN THE SUNLIGHT. Seemingly endless, far in the distance it merged with the sky.

It was early morning, with hardly any traffic. A black Jeep Cherokee was on its way south along the lake. The driver was wearing sunglasses because of the sharp morning light. On the passenger seat lay a copy of the weekly *Cook County News-Herald*, an almost empty bag of Old Dutch potato chips, and a Minnesota Vikings cap. A photo of a dark-haired boy who was missing his front teeth was taped to the middle of the steering wheel.

The road would soon fill up with tourists in SUVs and RVs, but for now he had it almost to himself. The few people he met were locals on their way to work. They greeted each other as they did every morning. He knew who their ancestors were, and where they had come from. He knew the names of the towns and districts in Sweden and Norway where their families had lived for centuries, before someone had finally come up with the liberating idea of emigrating to the New World. But right now he wasn't thinking about any of this. He was thinking about whether he should call his brother down in Two Harbors or whether it was too early. It was actually always too early to call Andy. Too early or too late. He couldn't remember the last time he'd done it. Maybe before deer season last fall, which was seven or eight months ago now. But today he had a special reason for phoning him. Even so, he was reluctant to make the call.

Those were the sorts of things the man in the black Jeep was thinking about on this particular morning.

He passed the junkyard of the local scrap dealer, a veritable landscape of wrecked cars on the right side of the road, and continued down the hill toward the center of Tofte. There stood the Bluefin Bay Resort, in all its morning silence, right on the bay. A few yards from the modern-looking building, with its angles and glass facades, were the remains of the old wharf sticking up out of the water. Only the five stone pilings were left. In their partially collapsed state, they looked like the vertebrae of a broken spine, as if just below the surface there might be the skeleton of some huge ancient monster. At the same time the pilings seemed ridiculously small in comparison to the big resort that had been built a few years back.

He'd seen it all a thousand times before. This morning was no different from all the other sunlit summer mornings when he'd come driving down the hill toward Tofte. He drove past the Bluefin, Mary Jane's yarn shop, the post office, the church, the AmericInn Motel, and the gas station. And with that he left the center of Tofte behind. Ahead of him the road stretched out straight as an arrow, lined with birches on either side. Between the white tree trunks on the left he caught a glimpse of the lake. Halfway down the long, straight stretch of road was a sign pointing to the right: "Superior National Forest. Tofte Ranger District."

The station, which looked a little like a military base, consisted of several low, brown-painted buildings with lawns and asphalt pathways in between. He used the driveway reserved for employees and parked under the big birch tree. There was a car he hadn't seen before, and he guessed that it belonged to the new station chief.

The receptionist, Mary Berglund, and a man he didn't recognize were standing on either side of the counter and talking when he came in. Between them stood two paper cups holding steaming coffee. Up near the ceiling a stuffed bald eagle floated from almost invisible strings. A snowy owl perched on a branch. On the wall behind the counter Mary Berglund had hung up a dream catcher. It was a cheap, mass-produced one, and yet it was intended to be a tribute to the local American Indian population, a sign that their culture was also respected by the U.S. Forest Service. Over by the public entrance stood a big wolf with its tongue hanging out.

"Good morning, Lance," said Mary, a woman in her sixties wearing glasses and sporting a permanent.

The stranger, whom he immediately pegged as the new ranger,

2

turned around and looked at him with an open and inquisitive expression.

"Lance Hansen?" the man said.

He nodded.

"John Zimmerman, district ranger," said the stranger, thrusting out his hand.

They shook hands. Zimmerman's handshake was firm and quick.

"Coffee?" He nodded toward the coffee machine, which stood on a table behind the information counter.

"Sure, thanks," said Lance.

Mary Berglund took a paper cup from the holder, poured the coffee, and set it on the counter. "Lance is our local genealogist," she told Zimmerman.

"Is that right?" He didn't sound particularly interested.

"It's just a hobby," said Lance. He took a sip, but the coffee was too hot, so he set the cup down. "What about you?" he said. "Where are you from?"

"My last posting was Kentucky. Daniel Boone National Forest."

"But you're not originally from the South, are you?" said Lance.

"No, I'm from back east. Born and raised in Massachusetts."

Zimmerman was a lean, suntanned man around fifty, and he made Lance feel flabby and heavy. The two of them were wearing identical khaki uniforms, with green slacks and sand-colored shirts. The only difference was their name badges, which said, respectively, "District Ranger," and "Law Enforcement Officer." Plus the fact that Lance was armed. He wore a pistol in a holster on his right hip.

"I'm sorry I haven't been by to say hello before now," said Lance. "Normally I'm in the office at least once a week, but great weather like this brings a lot of folks to the woods. I've been going full-tilt from morning till night."

"Anything special?"

"Just the usual. Brawls and boozing at a couple of campgrounds. Reckless driving. Illegal fishing. Welcome to the North Shore," he added.

"Thanks," said Zimmerman. "So what's on the program this morning?"

As a police officer, Lance didn't like being asked what he was working on. But since this was his first meeting with Zimmerman, he gave as detailed an answer as he could. "Someone may have put up a tent illegally over by Baraga's Cross. I got word of it yesterday but didn't have time to do anything about it. I'm going out to see if they're still there."

"So the cross is on federal property?" asked the ranger.

"Yes, it is."

"I didn't know that," said Zimmerman. "I guess I've got a lot to learn."

"It's a huge area," said Lance. "I've worked here for over twenty years now, and there are still parts of the forest I've never seen. It's a whole world of its own."

He took a cautious sip of the coffee. And then another. Mostly just to be polite. Then he set the cup back down on the counter.

"Well, I'd better get going," he said.

He headed down the basement stairs, which were under a wall mural showing a wolf pack in a blizzard. In the downstairs corridor he waved to the ladies in the office cubicles, as he always did when he walked past their door. He noticed the gentle face of his childhood friend Becky Tofte. Then he went into his own small office.

His job consisted primarily of making sure that people didn't dump large quantities of garbage in remote areas, that no one did any hot-rodding on the desolate roads, and that people didn't fish without a license, even though it was a hopeless battle, considering how large the area was. Sometimes people got lost, and he had to organize a search party. Or someone might set up camp in an area that was off-limits. In the Boundary Waters Canoe Area Wilderness, tents could only be pitched in campsites designated by the U.S. Forest Service. So his job didn't exactly involve high drama. But occasionally he did have to investigate real crimes, such as illegal logging. Twice he'd also come across methamphetamine labs in the woods.

Because of the investigative nature of his job, strictly speaking he wasn't supposed to answer Zimmerman's question about what was on the program for the day. At any rate that was how Lance Hansen interpreted his role as a police officer working for the U.S. Forest Service. His position was somewhat scorned by law enforcement officers who had more urgent types of assignments—which meant most of them. Lance was a "forest cop." But he had no desire to get shot or to shoot anyone else, and for that reason he thought his job was far more preferable to walking a beat in some place like Duluth or Minneapolis.

He took the keys to his service vehicle from the hook on the wall. For a moment he paused, wondering whether he should call his brother now, but he decided against it. If he'd remembered to call him last night, he might have saved himself a trip down to the lake to check on those tourists. He'd been planning to phone him as soon as he got back from Duluth, but instead he'd turned on the TV and stretched out on the sofa. When he woke up a couple of hours later, dazed with sleep, he had forgotten all about the phone call. Now he might as well drive down there and check on things himself.

HE PARKED HIS SERVICE VEHICLE at the end of the road and got out. It was 7:28. In front of him stretched Lake Superior. There was nothing to see but light and water and sky—no opposite shore on which to fix his eyes, just the illusory meeting of sky and the surface of the water far off in the distance. The site where the tent had been spotted was a couple of hundred yards north of where he stood. An alert woman had called to report that someone had illegally pitched a tent down by the lake. He tried to catch sight of anyone over there, but the birch trees stood too close together. As he turned around to get his binoculars from the truck, he noticed a shoe lying on the path that led to Baraga's Cross.

He went over to the shoe. It looked brand-new, a white running shoe. It looked as if someone had simply stepped out of it, and when he examined the ground more closely, he discovered that he was right. That was exactly what had happened. About eighteen inches in front of the shoe he saw the print of a bare foot that had skidded on the path, which was damp with morning dew. He also saw a handprint, which showed that the individual had fallen. But the person hadn't put the shoe back on. Lance wondered what would make someone leave an almost-new running shoe behind. Even though the reported campsite was in the opposite direction, he picked up the shoe and followed the path through the dense birch underbrush.

Soon he emerged from the thicket. In front of him the Cross River calmly flowed down to the lake. A few miles farther south, smoke was pouring out of the tall stacks of the coal-powered electrical plant at Taconite Harbor. At the very tip of the point stood the cross. Someone was sitting on the other side of it. A bare leg was sticking out. Lance had sat there many times himself. It was a great place to sit, with support for your back and a view of the lake. As usual, withered flowers and burned-out tea light candles were visible at the base of the cross.

He began walking across the rocks toward the cross, still carrying the shoe in one hand. As he approached, he saw more of the leg that was sticking out. It seemed to be bare all the way up. He also noticed something that looked like dried blood on the thigh.

When he was almost there, standing in the shadow of the towering stone cross that was more than ten feet tall, he unfastened the flap on his holster and put his right hand on his service weapon. Then he quickly stepped to the side. The man was naked, except for a white running shoe on his right foot. His hands, thighs, and stomach were smeared with blood that had dried long ago and turned dark. His eyes were closed, his lips slightly parted.

Lance cleared his throat. "Sir?" he said cautiously. The face below him didn't move. "I'm a police officer. Can you hear me?" He was speaking louder now, but still got no response.

At that instant a wave of fear surged through him. He spun around, ready to draw his gun, but no one was there. He stood there with his hand on the gun hilt, breathing fast and loud. In his other hand he still held the white running shoe. When he heard a sound behind him, he spun around again, but the naked man hadn't moved.

"Can you hear me?" he shouted. His voice sounded strained.

Now the man opened his eyes, but he didn't look up. He merely stared off into space in the direction of Lake Superior. Lance noticed that there was also dried blood on his curly blond hair.

Suddenly the man emitted a long-drawn-out wail of despair.

"Are you hurt?" asked Lance. In spite of all the blood, he couldn't see any wounds. He squatted down next to the man. "What happened?"

The man drew his thighs up toward his chest in a protective gesture and wrapped his arms around his legs. He sat there like that, with his forehead resting on his knees as he rocked gently back and forth. Lance was about to put a hand on the man's back to reassure him, but he stopped himself. The man's nakedness made him shy.

"Are you hurt?" he repeated.

Finally the naked man said something, but it was impossible

6

to make out his words, because he spoke with his mouth pressed between his knees, in a voice that sounded shattered. After listening intently for several seconds, Lance realized that the man was speaking a foreign language. And the longer he listened, the more convinced he became that he knew which language it was, because he recognized the intonation. Suddenly he heard quite clearly the word *"kjærlighet."* This was one of the few words of his forefathers' language that Lance actually knew. He remembered hearing that there were Norwegian tourists in the area. This man was apparently one of them.

The man raised his head and looked him straight in the eye. Lance noticed that his face seemed young and unfinished. His eyes were narrowed and red, and he had three bloody fingerprints on his forehead, under his blond bangs.

"Love," the man said suddenly in English. Just that one word. And then he repeated it. "Love . . ." Whispering, hoarse and insistent, as if it summarized and explained everything, as he continued to stare into the eyes of Lance Hansen.

"Are you Norwegian?" asked Lance, without getting a reply.

Now the man caught sight of the running shoe Lance was still holding in his left hand. With great effort he began hauling himself to his feet. It was obvious that he'd been sitting there for a long time, and his muscles had gotten stiff. Finally he was standing upright, with the red hair of his groin level with Lance's face.

Lance quickly stood up as well. "Where are your clothes?" he asked, but the man merely shook his head and started across the rocks toward the path that led to the parking area. He limped along, naked and wearing only one shoe with the laces untied. His butt was as white as chalk compared to the rest of his body.

"Wait a minute," said Lance.

The man stopped. Lance went over to him and squatted down. He held out the white running shoe. The Norwegian obediently stuck his left foot into it. By putting his finger in the heel, Lance managed to get the shoe on the man's foot. Then he tied the laces of both shoes. As he did this, he glanced nervously around, worried that someone might see what he was doing, but no one was there.

"Where are your clothes?" he asked, but again received no reply.

As they walked along the shadow-filled path through the birches, heading for the parking lot, Lance once again put his hand on the holster of his gun. The naked man in front of him couldn't possibly be armed, but he still had the feeling of imminent danger. Something was wrong, something more than the fact that a completely naked, blood-spattered man was walking in front of him on the path. There wasn't so much as a scratch on his body, at least as far as Lance could tell. But all that blood must have come from somewhere, he thought to himself. As soon as the idea appeared in his mind, he realized that the man was covered with someone else's blood.

And it occurred to him that the man must have killed someone.

Up ahead he saw the parking area with his mint-green pickup. He needed to contact the sheriff and call for backup. When they came out into the sunlight shining over the blacktop, Lance could see the slightly wavering mirror image of himself and the naked man in the polished surface of the truck. The man made no sign of pausing at the vehicle. Instead, he seemed determined to keep going across the parking lot and into the woods on the other side. When Lance grabbed his arm from behind to stop him, the man doubled over and tried to protect his head with his free arm, as if he thought he was being attacked.

"Stay here!" shouted Lance. "Don't move!"

He let go of the man's arm and walked the few yards over to the pickup, opened the door, and got in. He was just about to reach for the radio to call for backup when he saw the naked man running in loping strides across the parking area. And before he could get out of the truck, the man had dashed into the woods and disappeared.

Lance ran after him, but he was not a light or agile man, and there was no trail here, just dense birch woods. He plowed his way forward as best he could, but he saw no sign of the naked man. After a while he stopped to listen, but there was nothing to hear. He was going to have trouble explaining how he could have let a naked, unarmed man get away. A man who was a possible murder suspect. Lance took his gun out of the holster and held it out in front of him as he used his left hand to push aside the branches. The whole time he felt that at any second someone might leap at him from the dense forest.

Now the insects started pestering him. Blackflies buzzed around his lips and nose, trying to land in the corners of his mouth. He spat and blew to fend them off, swatting at them with his free hand, but more and more of them appeared. Soon there were so many that he could hear a steady buzzing. It was hard to breathe without getting flies in his mouth, so he breathed through his nose. Sweat ran into his eyes and made it difficult for him to see clearly. Finally he had to stop. He wiped the sweat from his forehead with his shirtsleeve and looked around. Between the birch trees on his right he caught sight of a tent no more than twenty yards away. Beyond the tent glittered the lake. This must be the tent that the woman had called to report.

Lance studied the woods around him. The whole time he held the gun ready in his right hand. Suddenly he saw the man lying on his stomach in the underbrush, just a few yards away. He could see only one leg and his white butt. Lance wondered whether he was about to be lured into a trap. He noticed that the man's shoelaces had come untied again. To reach the man he would have to crouch down and stoop to make it through the dense thicket. When he saw the rest of the naked man, he realized where all the flies had come from. A black swarming mass covered the man's head, or rather what used to be his head. Lance took a step forward. The flies rose up and it felt like the whole swarm flew at his face. With his left hand Lance covered his mouth and nose as he stared down at the mess of hair and blood and bone. He knew that he ought to look away, but he couldn't. He just stared. Was he looking at teeth? Yes, a row of white teeth was visible inside the bashed head. And yet the man was lying on his stomach. Lance failed to reconcile what he saw with the fact that the man couldn't have been lying there for more than a couple of minutes. There was something settled about the way he was lying, as if the forest floor had already begun to absorb him. Lance tried desperately to understand what had happened.

At that moment he heard a sound. He spun around. A couple of yards away stood the naked man, staring at him with a rigid expression of horror on his face. He was standing there, yet at the same time he lay dead in the underbrush behind Lance, who suddenly knew what was going on. He knew where all the blood on the man's body had come from. With his gun raised, Lance made his way through the foliage as he used his left hand to unfasten the handcuffs from his belt. This time he was going to do things properly.

"Turn around and get down on your knees!" he said. But the man made no sign of obeying the order. He just kept staring at Lance, with that same rigid expression of terror.

"Turn around!" shouted Lance. He didn't really know why he was shouting, because the man was completely defenseless. "Okay, turn around and get down on your knees," he said, forcing himself to speak calmly.

Instead the man sat down right there on the forest floor. Again he drew his thighs up toward his chest in a protective position, wrapped his arms around his legs, and began rocking gently back and forth, exactly as he had done when he was sitting against Baraga's Cross.

2

ON THAT MORNING Bill Eggum, the short, fat sheriff of Cook County, Minnesota, had only two months left on active duty. He was sitting in his police car, listening to a *Car Talk* CD. Standing on the rocks all the way out by the lake were Lance Hansen and Sparky Redmeyer. They were talking. Seven police officers, meaning practically the entire police force of Cook County, had assembled in the parking lot. Most of them were standing around their vehicles, not doing anything useful. The call that had come in that morning sounded desperate and incoherent, indicating that U.S. Forest Service officer Lance Hansen was in serious trouble out at Baraga's Cross. So they had rushed out with blue lights flashing and sirens wailing full-blast, all the way from Grand Marais and farther south. When they arrived and found Hansen with a man who was wearing nothing more than handcuffs and white running shoes, the sight sparked a certain amount of amusement. But it didn't last long. The sight of the corpse had prompted two of the officers to throw up. The sheriff had seen his share of shattered skulls in his career, usually in connection with car accidents, but he'd never seen anything like this.

While he listened to the two hosts on *Car Talk* trying to calm a woman who claimed she'd seen a real live snake loose in her car, the sheriff wondered what Hansen and Redmeyer were talking about. Barely two hours had passed since Lance had discovered the body of a murdered man. Was that what Hansen and Redmeyer were discussing as they stood there, off by themselves on the rocks, a bit

11

blurry-looking in the sharp glare of the lake? I wonder if Hansen has anyone he can talk to when something drastic like this happens? thought Sheriff Eggum. Does he have anyone in his life at all? Or is the past the only thing that concerns him? He looked at Lance again and wondered what it was that drove him in his untiring efforts to preserve the history of Cook County. Eggum had once seen with his own eyes the impressive archives that Lance kept in his house. Officially the archives belonged to the local historical society, but no one considered them anything but Hansen's own property. The sheriff thought that regardless of his motivation, Lance must have something he himself lacked. Something no one else in the whole area possessed. Sheriff Eggum had no idea what that "something" could be, but he thought it might be what made Lance Hansen such a loner.

Then he pushed all those thoughts aside. Lance wasn't his responsibility, after all. He felt he had things under control now. The crime scene had been cordoned off. Not far from the tent they'd found the canoe belonging to the two Norwegians. The surviving man, who was still in no condition to be questioned, had been transported to the hospital in Duluth. According to the doctor, the other man had died sometime between one and four o'clock in the morning. A team of homicide investigators was already on its way north from St. Paul. Bill Eggum had done his job; now it was just a matter of waiting for the experts.

He chuckled as one of the hosts on *Car Talk* suggested that the caller should sell her car to an animal lover. He was in a good mood, in spite of the grisly murder they had just discovered. Only two months from now his retirement would begin, and then he was thinking of spending as little time as possible with his wife. Not that he wasn't fond of her; on the contrary, she was a wonderful woman, and he didn't know what he would do without her. That was why he was worried about Lance, who had no one to talk to about difficult matters like this. Crystal Eggum had always been the only person the sheriff could confide in. He was able to tell her what an awful toll it took on him to see young people who'd been killed in car wrecks. Or his thoughts about all the domestic violence he'd been forced to witness. Crystal was a fabulous woman. Even so, he was looking forward to being alone for days on end in the little cabin over by Dumbbell Lake. Just him and his fishing gear. And a radio so he could listen to *Car Talk*. Finally he was going to have time to fish as much as he liked. He hadn't done that since he was a kid, which was close to fifty years ago. It's actually been more like a fifty-year interruption, he thought. A boy goes out fishing and has a lot of fun, and then suddenly one day his whole boring adult life starts up, with all its obligations. Fifty years later the interruption is finally over, and he can go back to fishing again.

Most of this boring period of time Bill Eggum had spent on the police force—the past twenty-five years as sheriff of Cook County. Not a single murder had been committed in all those twenty-five years. Until now. He didn't really know what to make of it. Murder by an unknown perpetrator. Although the other Norwegian was most likely the guilty party. It probably wasn't any more complicated than that. Even so, here he sat, waiting for a team of homicide detectives from St. Paul. No matter what, this was the biggest case of his career, and he wanted everything to be looking good for the detectives when they arrived. They would see that the sheriff of Cook County knew how to handle the situation.

He cast another glance at the bunch of officers chatting in the sunshine of the parking lot. It was about time to send most of them home. But just as he was about to open the car door, his cell phone rang. It was the man from the Bureau of Criminal Apprehension in St. Paul. He claimed there was some confusion about the information that Eggum had supplied when he called in the murder. A police officer working for the Forest Service had found the victim, was that right? Yes, that was right, Eggum told him. And since they were in Cook County, this officer must work for Superior National Forest, right? Yes, he did. But did this mean that the crime scene was located inside the borders of the forest? the man asked. Eggum had to admit that he hadn't thought about that. The man said that he'd better start thinking about it *now*.

The sheriff squeezed his fat body out of the car and irritably yelled for Lance Hansen, who was still standing out on the rocks with Sparky Redmeyer. Both men turned around. Eggum shouted for Lance to come over. The rest of the officers who were gathered in the parking area looked at Eggum with interest.

"It's been a busy morning up here," he apologized to the man in St. Paul. "Okay, here comes the guy who found the body."

Lance stopped a few feet away and ran his fingers through his straight, sandy-colored hair. "What's up?" he said.

"Do you know whether the crime scene is on federal land?" asked the sheriff.

"Yes, it is."

"Okay, I heard that," said the man on the phone. "And federal land means federal agents," he went on, as if the sheriff wouldn't realize this himself. "So this is a matter for the FBI, not us. I'll see that they're informed. Try to be good hosts to them."

Eggum swore quietly as he ended the conversation. "The FBI has jurisdiction," he said. Lance didn't look particularly interested, but the sheriff's deputies, who were lounging around the police cars, seemed amused by their boss's blunder.

"All right, people!" Eggum shouted. "Time to make yourselves useful! Redmeyer and Jones will stay here with me. The rest of you can head out. Go back to whatever you were doing before we were called out. If you were doing anything at all, that is."

A couple of the men laughed, but then realized this was no time for amusement. Five of the officers got into three cars, and soon the small procession slowly began making its way up narrow Baraga Cross Road and disappeared. Remaining were Sheriff Eggum, Sparky Redmeyer, Mike Jones, and Lance Hansen.

"Well, what do you know," said the youngest officer, Mike Jones.

"You can say that again," said Bill Eggum.

"A murder," said Redmeyer. "A murder in Cook County."

The others nodded somberly.

"Has this ever happened before?" asked young Jones, turning to the sheriff.

"Not on my watch as sheriff, at any rate," said Eggum. "Lance, you probably know whether there's ever been a murder here before."

Lance shook his head. "Not as far as I know," he said. "But it seems strange," he added. "This couldn't be the first murder in Cook County, could it?"

"Why not?" said Sparky Redmeyer.

"Why not? Well . . . don't you think it would be strange if it was?"

"No," said Redmeyer. "It would be even stranger if this turned out *not* to be the first murder in these parts."

Lance pointed toward the crime scene among the birch trees. "So you think this is the first one?"

"Yes," said Redmeyer. "You said yourself that you've never heard of any other murder happening around here. Wouldn't you know about it? You, with all your journals and old documents?"

Lance shook his head. "No," he said. "Or rather, yes . . . but no . . . no, that can't possibly be true."

Sheriff Eggum cleared his throat. "Right now none of that is important," he said. "What's important is who bashed in the skull of the canoeist from the old country? That's something we're going to let the FBI figure out."

"When do you think they'll get here?" asked Sparky.

"Well, let's see," said Eggum. He lifted his hat and scratched his bald scalp. "Sometime this afternoon, I'd guess."

"Would you mind if I took off?" asked Lance. "I should write up my report as soon as possible."

The sheriff gave him an awkward pat on the shoulder. "You go ahead," he said. "You've done a terrific job today."

Lance made a noise that sounded like an amused snort. "Well, see you guys," he said, and walked over to his pickup.

The other three watched him go. He got in and closed the door, leaning his left elbow on the frame of the open window. As he started the truck, Sheriff Eggum set off running. His short, stout body moved much faster than anyone would have believed possible; there was something almost unnatural about it. Redmeyer and Jones snickered. When Eggum reached the pickup, he stuck his flushed face in the window.

"Hansen," he panted.

"Yes?" said Lance.

The sheriff's gaze shifted. "What a way to start the day, huh?"

Lance nodded.

"If there's anything . . . ," the sheriff went on, but he clearly had no idea how to finish the sentence. "If there's anything, all you have to do is . . . you just have to . . . this has been a tough go-round."

"I'm really fine," Lance reassured him.

"Okay, I just wanted to . . . just in case."

"Thanks, but I'm really okay."

"All right, good, we'll leave it at that," said Eggum as he straightened up. He rapped his knuckles twice on the roof of the truck, as if knocking on wood. Then he turned on his heel and walked away.

3

WHEN LANCE GOT BACK TO THE RANGER STATION, he made it only as far as the bottom of the basement stairs before he realized that everyone already knew what had happened. He didn't feel like asking how they'd found out. Tofte was one of those places where people called to tell you to get better before you even knew you were under the weather.

Deb Larson, the head accountant, was standing in the doorway to the office area. She was just standing there, gawking. A moment later Becky Tofte appeared behind her. Then Peggy Winters popped up. Three frightened yet inquisitive faces stared at him from the doorway.

Lance gave them a nod and then attempted to continue down the corridor to his own small office, as if it were a normal day. But it was no use. Becky grabbed his arm with both hands and held on tight. Even though he'd known her all his life, he found it embarrassing to stand there like that, held in her grip.

"Poor Lance," she whispered several times.

He realized that for now he might as well give up any idea of writing his report. He had no choice but to follow them into the office area. There he had to tell them all about what had gone on that morning, from the time he said good-bye to Zimmerman and Mary Berglund until the moment he returned.

As he talked, new people kept showing up in the basement. Many of them Lance didn't know, including young summer hires from Minneapolis and St. Paul, plus additional firefighters who had been sent south from Alaska because of the high fire danger in Minnesota that summer. But most he'd known for years.

Since more people kept joining the group, he had to tell the story several times. Finally there were nearly thirty people gathered in the room, and the sole topic of conversation was the dramatic events that had just occurred over near Baraga's Cross. No one could agree on who the guilty party might be. Some thought the Norwegian had killed his companion, plain and simple. Others were convinced someone had tried to murder both men but succeeded in killing only one. Mary Berglund, the receptionist, thought it had something to do with drugs, though she couldn't explain any further. Becky Tofte said she didn't believe for a minute that a Norwegian would kill a fellow countryman, which brought a laugh from John Zimmerman. And then there was the fact that both men had been naked. One of the guys from Alaska thought that was the strangest thing of all. Two men running around naked in the woods!

The whole station was feeling the effects of the extraordinary circumstances. Only Mary was still doing any work. She ran up and down the stairs to check if any tourists had appeared, in need of information. Soon she was able to inform the group that news of the murder had reached the media. "It's on the radio—everybody knows about it now!" she shouted, her cheeks flushed.

Zimmerman said he'd go upstairs and personally handle any contact with the public. Right after he left the room, they heard him pause on the stairs to speak to someone. Lance recognized his brother's voice.

"He's down there," he heard Zimmerman say, and a moment later Andy Hansen appeared in the doorway.

Several of those present knew him well and said hi. He was a thin, sinewy man in his early forties. Like his taller and heavier brother, he was starting to lose his hair. But unlike Lance, who always made sure to comb his hair smoothly back, Andy wore his hair long, as if trimmed with a bowl on his head. He had on worn jeans and a faded T-shirt that said "Twins Baseball" on the front.

"So, Lance," he said, looking at his brother, who was two years older. "How are you doing?"

Lance shrugged. "Things are great," he said.

It had been more than six months since he'd last spoken to his brother. The fact that Andy had dropped by now to find out how he was doing could mean only one thing. His younger brother always behaved in a concerned and brotherly fashion when he wanted something from Lance. It had always been that way. He wondered what it was this time, but at the moment the only thing he could think of was the image of the dead man. That naked male body with his skull bashed in. And the row of white teeth in the midst of all that red.

"A murder, huh?" said Andy.

Lance mumbled a reply. The two of them were standing next to the wall as conversations continued to swirl all around them.

"I heard about it on the radio on my way down from the cabin," his brother went on. "They said the dead man was found by a forest cop, so I put two and two together. I've been out at the cabin since yesterday afternoon. Went out in the boat and fished until midnight. Nice and quiet, didn't see a soul up there. It's so unreal to think that a murder was committed near the lake. Do they know who did it, or anything?"

"How should I know?" replied Lance. "I've got nothing to do with the investigation."

"No, I guess not," said Andy. "So you're okay?"

"Of course I'm okay." He was beginning to feel stressed with his brother in the room. That gaunt, pinched face of his. The feeling that he wanted something. "Of course I am," he repeated.

"Well, I'd better head home now," said Andy. "I just wanted to check on how my brother was doing."

He said this loud enough for everyone to hear.

As Andy turned to go, Richie Smith, who was in charge of road construction and maintenance, had a word with him about a logging job he'd recently contracted to do. Something about which roads he could use. Andy Hansen was one of the most frequently hired logging contractors in this part of the Superior National Forest.

As Andy was leaving, he ran into Sparky Redmeyer in the doorway. The two men nodded to each other. Then Redmeyer asked if he could speak to Lance.

He went out into the hall with Redmeyer. Andy had stopped halfway up the stairs. He smiled at them, giving no sign of continuing on his way.

"See you later, Andy," said Redmeyer in a loud, rude voice. Andy reluctantly went up the stairs and disappeared.

"What is it?" asked Lance.

"A message from the FBI. They just arrived. They want to talk to you tomorrow."

"Okay. Where?"

"At Bluefin Bay. That's where they're staying during the investigation. I'm supposed to be their chauffeur and local guide. They want you to come by before eleven."

4

THE HOUSE WAS ABOVE THE HIGHWAY, at the end of the road on a small hill. Lance stood at the living room window, looking out. Down the road was a big wooden building painted red. That was Isak Hansen's hardware store, the only one between Two Harbors and Grand Marais. There you could buy everything from nuts and bolts to down jackets and work boots to refrigerators and slalom skis.

About a hundred yards below the road was the lake. It filled most of the view, but it was rare that Lance actually *looked* at it. The lake was just there, much like snow was there in the wintertime.

He'd already been standing at the window for quite a while. He'd seen his cousin, Rick Hansen, lock up the shop and drive off. Rick was the son of Eddy Hansen, who was the brother of Lance's father, Oscar.

They were both dead now, Eddy and Oscar. The hardware dealer and the policeman, sons of the carpenter Isak Hansen, who had emigrated from Norway in 1929. By the time Isak retired in 1974, he had not only built a successful hardware business, he was also responsible for an impressive number of houses that were constructed in the area after his arrival. From Grand Marais in the north to Duluth in the south, there were many houses along the North Shore that Lance's grandfather had built. Houses in which people continued to live out their lives. All sorts of people. Good and not so good. And some who were downright bad.

It was a splendid legacy to have left behind. There was something decent and respectable about it, Lance thought. Isak had built houses for people to live in, and a hardware store where they could buy nuts and bolts.

And here stood his grandson on a summer evening approximately eighty years after Isak came to America. A truly fine summer evening. The traffic was bumper to bumper down on Highway 61. Folks were on their way back south, headed for the Twin Cities of Minneapolis and St. Paul. He wondered how many of those people had heard about the murder by now. Personally he couldn't bear to hear any more about it, so he'd switched off the radio and TV.

He still hadn't started shaking.

That was something he'd noticed when he phoned the sheriff to ask for backup. I'm not shaking, he'd thought in surprise as he looked at his hands. All day long he'd prepared himself for the shaking to begin. Some sort of reaction had to set in, he'd thought.

Again he pictured the shattered skull and the row of gleaming white teeth.

Several times afterward, while he was in the parking lot along with the Cook County police, he'd had a strong urge to go back into the birch woods to have another look at the corpse. He'd been on the verge of asking Eggum for permission to do just that, but realized how odd the request would sound. He couldn't exactly tell the sheriff that he felt as if the terrible sight in there belonged to him, Lance Hansen, and not to anyone else. Or that he had a certain proprietary right, which was diminished every time someone else looked at the dead man and wrote down something in a black notebook, or took photographs of the corpse.

He didn't know why he was thinking like this. He stood at the window, waiting for his body to start shaking. It just didn't seem right for him to go to bed, as if nothing had happened. To wake up in the morning and leave for work as usual, stopping by the Bluefin Bay Resort to answer a few questions. After that, would the whole thing be over?

He turned around. The living room was neat and tidy in an impersonal, almost sterile kind of way. There were no pillows or blankets on the dark leather sofa, nor on the recliner or the easy chair with the floral upholstery. The latest issue of *TV Guide* was the only thing on the coffee table. A few kids' movies were stacked up on the floor next to the TV and DVD player. On the dining table stood a green plant that might easily be mistaken for real, and a plate holding two oranges and an apple.

A row of framed photographs hung on the light-colored paneling on the walls. One of them was a bigger version of the picture in his old Jeep. A dark-haired boy, maybe seven years old, with a big smile that showed he was missing his front teeth. In another photo Lance was seated on a snowmobile in a glittering winter landscape, and on his lap sat the same boy, although younger, maybe four. Both were bundled up like Arctic explorers, and they were smiling at the photographer. A third picture showed the little boy alone. He was proudly holding up a fish the size of a grown man's index finger. His eyes glowed red from the flash. Only a few long, pale reeds stuck out of the darkness surrounding him.

Lance went out to the hall and paused for a moment under a photo of him and his brother kneeling on either side of a big buck lying dead in the marsh, with a river in the background. Each held a rifle in one hand and had wrapped the fingers of the other hand around one of the eight points of the antlers.

He went into his home office where the desk was covered with so much paperwork that not a single clear space was visible. Unlike the living room, here the walls held only one photograph. It was an old black-and-white picture of thirty or forty people, both adults and children, who had obviously posed for the photograph on the deck of a large ship. In the background on the right, smoke was pouring out of a big stack. In the lower right-hand corner someone had written in black ink: "Duluth, October 3, 1902."

One wall of the room was covered from floor to ceiling with shelves holding binders, books, and file folders. This was the archive collection belonging to the Cook County Historical Society. Lance had been a member since he was a teenager, and he was still head of the organization. At least in name, although strictly speaking there was no longer any need for anyone to head the group. The only other active member was a teacher from Grand Marais High School who had moved to Minneapolis three years ago. There were still three or four people who paid the modest annual dues, but the last time Lance had called a meeting, no one showed up. Formally the Cook County Historical Society still existed, and it was listed in the phone book, with Lance Hansen's phone number. Nowadays he had in his possession all of the society's archival materials, which had largely been accumulated by Olga Soderberg, a teacher who had devoted her adult life to preserving the brief history of Cook County for posterity. She was the one who had founded the historical society. When she died in 1980, there was never any doubt as to who would take over. By then young Lance had already become Soderberg's favorite.

Now he was a forty-six-year-old divorced cop.

And he needed to write a report about the murder. Previously, the most dramatic cases he'd ever been part of involved a couple of labs producing methamphetamine. That sort of thing could be dangerous, of course, but both times everything had gone just fine.

He started with the day before, when he'd received word that somebody had pitched a tent near Baraga's Cross. He also wrote down a brief summary of what had prevented him from checking out the complaint at once. But soon his thoughts returned to the question that Mike Jones had asked in the parking lot. When was the last time a murder had been committed in Cook County? He thought about it but couldn't come up with anything. Was it really possible that not a single murder had occurred here since 1874, when Cook County was established? At least he couldn't recall having read or heard mention of any such thing. But what about before Cook County was established, when the area was still part of Lake County? Or even further back in time, before Minnesota became a state in 1858? Lance was aware that the wilderness the Scandinavians had encountered when they arrived here at the end of the nineteenth century had already been exploited commercially by white men for the previous two hundred years or so. But the heyday of the fur trade was long over by the time the first Norwegians and Swedes built their primitive log cabins in the area. Practically the only things remaining from the French voyageurs were the portages that led from one body of water to another, or to circumvent waterfalls and rapids, where they'd been forced to carry their canoes and cargoes of provisions and precious pelts. Murders must have occurred among such men. And among the Ojibwe Indians. But there were no written sources from so far back in time. Cook County got its first newspaper in 1891, and there were police reports and court documents back to 1881, but from earlier eras the sources were few and not at all reliable.

By now Lance had completely forgotten about writing his

report. He got up and went over to the archives. Taking up one whole shelf were numerous binders containing printouts from microfilms of old newspapers. The collection included most issues of the *Grand Marais Pioneer*, which was published from 1891 until 1895, as well as every single issue of its successor, the *Cook County Herald*. Sometime between the world wars the name was changed to the *Cook County News-Herald*. It was still published every Friday, and Lance always read the paper with great interest. The archive also contained a large collection of police reports and court documents from the period 1881 to 1930, which Olga Soderberg had gone through and then copied when the police department cleared out its files before moving out of the old courthouse in Grand Marais in 1974.

There were also private diaries in the collection, including one belonging to Lance's own family—the so-called French diary, or "Nanette's diary." It was from his mother's side of the family. They had lived in the United States since 1888, when Lance's great-grandfather, Knut Olson from Tofte on the island of Halsnøy, had come to the North Shore. That was where he settled, at the place that was today called Tofte. Back then the only inhabitants were the Ojibwe. He soon married a French Canadian woman, and they had nine children, one of whom would father Lance's mother.

So it was Knut Olson's French Canadian wife, Nanette, who had left the diary. Occasionally Lance would be overcome with emotion as he held the diary in his hands, even though he'd never read a word of it, for the simple reason that he didn't know French. He couldn't be certain, but he assumed that no one except his great-grandmother had ever read the diary. Presumably the Olsons had spoken some form of English to each other. It seemed unlikely that Knut Olson from Halsnøy in Norway would have spoken French. And maybe that had been an added incentive for Nanette to keep a diary, since she knew that no one could read what she wrote. Her mother tongue provided a sort of refuge for her, deep in the wilderness. Maybe that's how it was, thought Lance.

But Nanette's diary probably couldn't answer his question about any past murders in Cook County. He knew that plenty of people had died sudden, brutal deaths up here. From mining accidents, gunshot wounds, drownings. But murder?

At the same time, almost as if it were happening in a different part of his brain, he was thinking that it wasn't normal to be so obsessed with this particular subject. I should be focusing on the report, he thought sensibly. I should be helping the FBI solve the case as quickly as possible. Yet that didn't stop him from searching the shelves.

Finally he pulled out two thick binders and dumped them onto the desk. One of them was labeled *The Pioneer 1891–93*, and the other *The Pioneer 1894–95*. The labels were written in Olga Soderberg's old-fashioned schoolmarm script. The files inside the binders were photocopies from microfilm housed in the library of the University of Minnesota in Duluth.

Lance opened the first binder and began leafing through the pages.

As was the practice among small country newspapers of that era, most of the column space in the *Grand Marais Pioneer* was taken up with syndicated stories in the vein of "romantic serials," as well as travel descriptions from exotic climes. But there were also notices announcing religious meetings, firefighting exercises for the volunteer fire brigade, meetings of the homemakers' club, and the arrival and departure of the steamship *Dixon*.

He quickly paged through the material. Occasionally he would stop to read one of the few and always extremely brief news reports. For instance, on June 26, 1891: *Mr. McNamara from South Dakota, who suffers from unusually bad hay fever, arrived in Grand Marais on board the "Dixon" this week to continue the tradition he established many years ago of spending a couple of months here during the summer.*

The first inklings of today's tourism, thought Lance.

Or on October 28 of the same year: *We have acquired two new shops this week, as a result of the government's annual payments to the Indians. The peddlers arrived in Grand Marais from Two Harbors on Tuesday evening with a large supply of dry goods, which they hope to get rid of at exorbitant prices.*

At last, as he was making his way through the 1892 issues, Lance came upon something that caught his interest. Specifically from April 3. Under the headline "Where is Swamper?," he read the following: *Swamper Caribou, the well-known Indian from Grand Marais, has been missing for more than two weeks now. It was Swamper's brother, Joe Caribou, who reported this during a visit to the* Pioneer's *offices. All of the Ojibwe in the area are very upset by his disappearance, since Swamper Caribou is so highly regarded by the tribe, and it would surprise us to hear anyone disagree when we say that we white folks hold him in the same high regard. According to his brother, Swamper Caribou disappeared from his hunting cabin near the mouth of the Cross River at the time of the last full moon, meaning in the early morning hours of March 16. The* Pioneer *joins Joe Caribou in wishing fervently that his brother will soon reappear and prove to be in the same good health as always.*

Lance had heard about Swamper Caribou, a medicine man who sometimes also helped the whites in Grand Marais, since back then it could take days before a proper doctor was able to make the trip from Duluth. He knew the Ojibwe told many ghost stories about the medicine man's spirit, which was apparently still roaming restlessly around the lake, because Swamper Caribou had never been seen again. At least not in the flesh.

He could very well have been murdered, thought Lance. Although the Indian could just as easily have died as the result of some sort of accident. He could have drowned, with his body vanishing into the lake. Or he could have been accidentally shot. But in theory, at least, he could have been murdered.

Lance continued to go through the 1892 issues of the *Grand Marais Pioneer,* scanning more announcements about church services and firefighting exercises and the arrival and departure of the steamship *Dixon.* He nearly missed the brief notice from September 2.

Corpse discovered, it said, almost hidden at the bottom of the page. *Last week a body was found in the lake, not far from the mouth of the Manitou River. Due to the sorry state of the remains, it was impossible to determine the man's identity.*

That was all.

Lance thought it was unbelievable that the missing Swamper Caribou wasn't mentioned, since it seemed entirely plausible that the body of the medicine man had now been found. How far was it from the mouth of the Cross River, where he disappeared, to the mouth of the Manitou River? Maybe ten miles. Couldn't the current have carried a body that far in six months' time? It seemed possible.

So why wasn't Swamper Caribou mentioned? It was difficult to answer that question, since the article provided very little information. Maybe it was the body of a white man, and the editor of the *Grand Marais Pioneer*, who wrote these news articles himself, had taken it for granted that his readers would know this. But it said that "the sorry state of the remains" made it impossible to identify the dead man. Presumably they could tell from the clothing that it was a man, but otherwise they were unable to say who he was. So why not come to the logical conclusion that it might be the body of the medicine man, since he hadn't been found? In the article about Swamper, the editor had sounded as though he personally liked the missing Indian. Could the second article have been written by a different editor?

Lance got up and again went over to the archive shelves, taking down a binder containing only a few pages. These were lists of the individuals who had held various positions in Cook County over the years, including the job of newspaper editor. He soon found what he was looking for: *Albert DeLacy Wood, 1891 to July 1892; Chris Murphy, July 1892 to October 1894.*

Albert DeLacy Wood, who was the first editor of the *Grand Marais Pioneer*, had left the position in July 1892, after Swamper Caribou disappeared. In early September, when the body was found near the Manitou River, the new editor had been in Grand Marais for little more than a month. He might not have known about Swamper's disappearance, or maybe he thought that one less Indian was not worth mentioning.

In any case, the whole story contributed nothing to Lance's search for a murder. He thought it most likely that the Indian had died in a drowning accident. That is, if the body found near Manitou River was, in fact, Swamper Caribou.

He wondered whether he should start reading the police reports and court documents from the period 1895 to 1905, when the John Schroeder Lumber Company ran what was still the biggest logging operation on the North Shore. At its peak, the company employed more than a thousand men, who were quartered in barracks in a camp that had two saloons and a whorehouse where the men could rapidly be relieved of their wages.

But Lance didn't feel like reading the documents right now. It was nine forty, and he still hadn't written more than a few lines of his report. He needed to finish it before morning. And besides, it would help him to formulate his answers before his meeting with the FBI.

He looked at the brief paragraph that he'd written so far. At one fifteen he'd received a call from a woman who had seen a tent down by the lake, not far from Baraga's Cross. She and a male companion had been out in a boat at the time. It was illegal to pitch a tent outside the U.S. Forest Service designated camp areas, which did not include that particular spot. But Lance hadn't had a chance to check it out, since he was all the way up at Gunflint Lake when he got the call. He was busy checking on fishing licenses, and that took up the rest of his workday. Afterward he went home to shower and change his clothes before setting off on the almost two-hour drive to Duluth to visit his mother in the nursing home where she now lived. When he got back, around ten, he stretched out on the sofa and promptly fell asleep. There was nothing else to report about yesterday.

Or was there?

He realized that by now he'd had enough of sitting in the cramped office. With a heavy sigh he got up and went out to the hall, where he put on his shoes and his Vikings cap.

THE MOON WAS ABOUT A DAY SHORT OF BEING FULL. A gleaming streak of moonlight extended from the horizon almost all the way to the tips of his shoes. It was so wide that it splintered into thousands of tiny flashes glinting off the waves in front of him. On both sides of the moonlight the water was a deep purple that was almost black. He stood there, looking out across the lake without really seeing it.

And what was there actually to see? Only a vast void and this shimmering moonlight path. That was Lake Superior at the moment. In addition to the faint gurgling sound that seemed to envelop him.

Many of Lance's ancestors had spent their lives on this lake after coming here from Norway. They had made their living from logging, fishing, mining, boatbuilding, home construction, or whatever else might put a few dollars in their pockets and food on the table. And they had survived. Most of their descendants, including Lance, were people who largely subsisted just one notch above poverty. And they never moved much beyond that. Sometimes he thought the pioneers had sacrificed much more than the value of the average way of life in America.

Take Thormod Olson, for example, the nephew of Knut Olson,

who had married the French Canadian Nanette. Thormod was fifteen when he arrived in the New World all alone. He had first traveled by ship from Bergen to Hull, where he boarded a train for Liverpool. Then by ship from Liverpool to New York. From there he went by train and stagecoach through the United States and Canada to Duluth. And he did all that without knowing more than a smattering of English words. When he finally reached Duluth, he still had ahead of him the eighty-mile trip up to his uncle's pioneer cabin at the base of Carlton Peak, where the little community of Tofte is located today. At the time, winter was just giving way to spring, and his uncle had made arrangements for him to be given lodging in the house of an acquaintance in Duluth so that young Thormod would have someplace to live while he waited for the ice to melt from the Lake Superior coastline. Then he'd be able to take the steamship *Dixon* up to Carlton Peak. But the fifteen-year-old had no intention of sitting around in a room in town. Equipped with a pair of snowshoes, he began hiking north along the coast. In the light of the moon he was even able to continue his trek at night. A couple of days after Thormod set out from Duluth, there was a knock on the door of the small log cabin near Carlton Peak. When Knut Olson opened it, his fifteen-year-old nephew fell into the room, stiff as a board. The boy was completely shrouded in a coating of ice, which shattered into a thousand pieces when he hit the floor.

To save time, he had walked on the frozen lake, crossing many of the bays between Duluth and Carlton Peak. Then on the last night he had fallen through the ice. It was bitterly cold, and it really shouldn't have been possible to survive a night in the woods after taking a plunge in the frigid water. At least that was what Lance had always heard. But young Thormod did survive, although he was nearly dead. His uncle and Nanette saved his life and nursed him back to health.

Lance had heard this story countless times as he was growing up. It was the primordial myth in his family. "That's the stuff we're made of," his father the policeman had once told him, even though he himself had no blood relationship to Thormod.

Today there were, in fact, descendants of Thormod Olson living in large parts of Minnesota, and undoubtedly in other states as well. But as far as Lance knew, none of them had ever done anything that was particularly noteworthy. Yet it seemed highly unlikely that young Thormod would have given a single thought to any possible descendants on that night when he was fighting for his life.

Lance stood there gazing out at the same lake in which Thormod had nearly drowned before even beginning his life in America. He himself had lived his whole life near the lake. His father, Oscar Hansen, had been on the Duluth police force. Lance and Andy had grown up in that steep-sloped city near the westernmost point of Lake Superior.

He thought about how his brother's presence at the ranger station had somehow seemed to him the last straw, although he had no idea why. He felt as if he could handle everything else that he'd been through during the day, but not the fact that Andy had shown up.

He should have called him when he got back from Duluth last night, after visiting their mother in the nursing home. He remembered now that he'd even thought about phoning him this morning but decided it was too early to do that. Then he'd found the naked man and discovered the murder, and he'd forgotten all about his brother, who had turned off the highway and driven down to Baraga Cross Road.

"Good Lord . . . ," he whispered.

It was on the previous evening that Lance had come driving north from Duluth. When he approached the turnoff to Baraga's Cross, he saw his brother take the exit from the highway.

Now he remembered Andy's words from earlier in the day: "I've been out at the cabin since yesterday afternoon. Went out in the boat and fished until midnight."

But it was his brother's car that he'd seen, a white Chevy Blazer with a red door on the right-hand side. Inside he'd clearly seen Andy's gaunt, pinched face. And the car had disappeared down Baraga Cross Road.

IT WAS AFTER MIDNIGHT. The North Shore was cloaked in darkness. In small communities like Tofte and Lutsen, all the inhabitants were now asleep. They had to get up early the next morning, Thursday. They were hardworking people with ordinary lives, and they seldom encountered any big surprises. They watched TV in the evening. The women had their knitting clubs, the men went on fishing trips. On the weekend they might drive to Duluth to shop at the mall. Maybe they'd take the kids to see a movie before they made the two-hour drive back north along the shoreline.

But on this day something unexpected had happened.

By now almost everyone had heard about the murder near Baraga's Cross. And it had probably been on their mind before they fell asleep, since now there was a murderer among them. They thought about their children. The children thought about their parents. Maybe some people also thought about the cross. Baraga's Cross. Maybe they pictured it standing there near the lake.

In the house on the ridge above Isak Hansen's hardware store Lance lay in bed with his eyes closed, feeling sleep approaching like a wave rolling toward shore, and the shore was himself and his thoughts. For a moment his thoughts were almost obliterated by the wave.

Then the teeth reappeared and he gave a start. Those white teeth in the mass of blood and hair. He wasn't scared, but he couldn't get rid of the image of those teeth. Just as he couldn't get rid of the thought of Andy driving down Baraga Cross Road. There couldn't possibly be any connection between the two things. Between his brother and the gruesome image of the dead man. But what was Andy doing at the cross so late at night? And why had he lied about it?

It seemed to Lance like a waking dream. The thought made him smile as he lay there. His last dream had been seven years ago. In that dream he was walking along the bottom of Lake Superior. He could breathe underwater, and it was as easy to walk as on land. The bottom sloped downward as he moved. In places he had to climb over steep cliffs. But the light never faded beyond dusk down there; it never got completely dark. Finally he reached the deepest spot in the lake. There it was very bright. The water was as clear as air, and just as easy to move through. All around him were huge icebergs, shimmering blue. The ground beneath his feet was solid ice. It was a world of ice down there, and so cold that it felt like the marrow in his bones was turning to slush. He was sure he'd never be able to reach the surface again.

But then he woke up, cold and sweating. Next to him lay Mary, sleeping calmly. It was dawn on a summer day. Outside the window, behind the drawn curtains, he could hear a bird singing.

Lance got out of bed and crept through the dimly lit room, over to the baby's crib. He could just barely make out the tiny head resting on the pillow. He leaned down and listened. He stood like that, bending over the crib until he was sure the boy was breathing.

He still recalled every detail so clearly. He even remembered that the bird singing outside the window was a white-throated sparrow.

Since that day he hadn't dreamed at all. Of course he'd read that everybody dreams, whether they're aware of it or not, but what does it mean to dream if you're not aware of it? The only dreams that count are those you remember having. And Lance hadn't had a single dream in more than seven years. He was absolutely sure of it, because for a long time he'd hoped that he would dream about the bottom of Lake Superior again. There was something enticing about that deep, ice-cold, shimmering blue place. So when he woke up in the morning, he always tried to recall whether he'd dreamed of anything in the night. But he soon realized that he was having no dreams whatsoever, and that was when he stopped waiting for a new dream about the bottom of the lake and began instead to wait for any type of dream at all. But none came. Not even a sense that he'd dreamed of something but quickly forgotten it.

Lance had never told anyone about this. It was too strange, almost unreal. He wasn't like other people. Some had lots of dreams, while others dreamed only once in a while, but Lance never dreamed at all. For him, sleep was merely a nothingness that repeated itself every night. Always the same deep, dreamless sleep. And now it came washing over him. His thoughts were a shore where something had been written in the sand, but now the words were erased by the waves.

5

Just before eleven on the following morning, Lance knocked on the door of the conference room in the Bluefin Bay Resort. He heard footsteps approaching, and then the door opened. A younger man stood there.

"FBI?" Lance hesitantly asked.

"Yes."

"I was asked to . . . I was the one who found the body."

"Of course. Come in."

The man closed the door behind them and then held out his hand. "Bob Lecuyer," he said. "I'm in charge of the investigation."

"Lance Hansen."

Lecuyer went over to the long conference table in the middle of the room. A lot of documents were spread out on the table, along with several newspapers. He sat down in front of an open laptop.

"Have a seat."

Lance sat down across from him. It looked like Lecuyer was busy reading something on the computer screen. He reminded Lance of a bank teller. Close-cropped dark hair, light-blue shirt, wristwatch, wedding ring, and at least ten years younger than himself.

After a moment Lecuyer looked up. "Are you some sort of local historian?" he asked.

"Not really. I have an archive, but . . ."

"Exactly. So you're the local historian. And that means you must know more about this place than most people."

"Just things about the past. That's all I know about."

"But that could be interesting too. We never know until we get started. I'm sure you know how it is. You're a police officer, aren't you?"

"That's right."

"So, shall we begin?"

Lance nodded.

Lecuyer leaned back, clasping his hands behind his head. "Tell me *everything*," he said.

AN HOUR LATER Lance was on his way to Sawbill Lake, where his cousin Gary Hansen had a canoe rental business. He usually dropped by to have a chat with Gary about once a week. He really should have gone out to Grouse Creek to check on a couple of teenagers who had apparently been riding their off-road four-wheelers outside the marked trails. All part of a typical workday for Lance Hansen. But his meeting with Lecuyer had made him uneasy. He'd answered the FBI man's questions as accurately as he could, but when he was asked whether he knew of any suspicious activity occurring in the area around Baraga's Cross, he had emphatically shaken his head and said no. And yet he knew a car had driven down Baraga Cross Road just before ten o'clock on Tuesday evening, meaning only a few hours before the murder. He also knew the driver of the car had shown up at the Tofte ranger station on the following day, claiming that he'd been at Lost Lake all night.

As Lance sat there in the conference room, he pictured once again the shattered skull. The teeth. The tufts of hair. And he pictured his brother. Those two images belonged to two different worlds, which for some inexplicable reason were on the verge of colliding. But one thing he did know: it was up to him to prevent it from happening.

The part of Superior National Forest that is a protected wilderness area begins at Sawbill Lake. A boundary passes through the entire forest. North of that line, no motorized vehicles are permitted, and not even the tiniest hut can be built. There isn't a single foot of roadway, and all hunting is forbidden. In vast sections, the trees haven't been cut in close to a hundred years. In fact, some parts have never been logged at all. The entire area would have been inaccessible if it weren't for the water—and the canoe. That ingenious, simple vessel that from time immemorial had carried human beings through these woods.

Lance got out of his car in the parking lot in front of North-woods Outfitters, run by his cousin Gary. There were plenty of other cars in the lot. He saw Gary in full swing, instructing some first-time paddlers on how to lift a canoe onto their shoulders.

Lance gave him a wave and went into the shop, where it was possible to buy everything from matches to a six-man tent. He looked at some books that were for sale: *Birding Minnesota, Minnesota's Geology, The Complete Idiot's Guide to Canoeing and Kayaking, The Singing Wilderness.*

It looked as if there were about a dozen seasonal employees hired for the summer. His cousin's business was clearly booming. Most of the young people seemed to be from the Twin Cities and had come here more because of the proximity to the wilderness than for the paltry wages Gary was paying them. Eco-youths, Lance thought to himself. Not that he had any negative associations with that term, just an impression of a group of kids who had a certain look about them and a certain set of opinions. Plus they were all wearing the blue T-shirts with the Northwoods Outfitters logo. They seemed so agile and lightweight as they slipped between the shelves and racks filled with gear. Lance felt heavy and torpid in comparison.

After a few minutes Gary appeared. "Hi. Need a canoe?" he said.

Lance smiled. "No, I just thought I'd drop by, since I was in the neighborhood."

He could see that his cousin was busy and not real happy about being interrupted. One of the young girls in a blue T-shirt was waving and calling his name. Lance wouldn't have minded having a girl like that waving at him.

"Okay, I'll be right there. Excuse me a minute, Lance."

Lance looked around. One of the young shop clerks caught sight of him and came over.

"Can I help you?" he asked.

"No, thanks," said Lance. But then he thought of something. "Well, actually, there *is* something." He pointed at his name badge, which said *Law Enforcement Officer.*

The young guy in the blue T-shirt nodded eagerly. "Is this about the murder?" he asked.

"So you've heard about it?"

"Sure I've heard about it. That's all people are talking about. They came in here, you know. I remember them."

"The two Norwegians?"

"Yep. They knew a lot about canoes. Real pros. And nice too. It's so awful, what happened," he said.

"Tell me, did you happen to notice anything else besides the fact that they seemed nice and were real pros?"

The young guy paused to consider the question. Then he shook his head. "No, I just got the impression that they were very experienced canoeists. And they seemed to be in a really good mood. In fact, they were positively *beaming.*"

"Beaming?" Lance repeated in surprise.

"Yeah, that's right. They were beaming."

"Hmm . . . Do you know where they were headed?"

"No, but they were gone for two nights."

"And when was this?"

"Last week. They left on Tuesday and came back on Thursday."

"Did you get the impression that they'd already been here for a while? That they'd be leaving soon?"

"I remember they said something about Finland. You know, that town down the road. I think they'd spent some time there. They thought it was a fun name. A fun place too."

"Hmm . . . ," said Lance. "Tell me, how can you be so sure we're talking about the same Norwegians?"

"How many young Norwegian men do you see around here?" the clerk replied. "Besides, they said they were going to spend the last part of their trip paddling on Lake Superior. So we were positive those were the same guys, when we heard the news on the radio."

"I see," said Lance. "Well, thanks for the info. I suppose you need to get back to work?"

"I probably should. Did you want to buy anything?"

"Actually, I do. Do you still sell sandwiches here?"

"Yeah, we do."

"Can I get a ham and cheese?"

"Ham and cheese it is."

Lance watched the guy go over to the café area, which consisted of a counter with a cash register and a few tables.

While he was waiting, his cousin Gary reappeared. "I've got a few minutes now," he said. "Should we sit outside and have a cup of coffee?"

....

AFTER HE GOT HIS SANDWICH, Lance went out the back door of the building. Gary was already sitting at a table with a pot of coffee and a sandwich in front of him. The same young brunette who had called him earlier was there, talking to him. Lance noticed that she was standing very close. It almost looked as if her hip was touching Gary's shoulder. When they caught sight of Lance, they abruptly ended the conversation, and the brunette turned on her heel and walked away.

"Come and sit down," called Gary.

Lance went over to the table and sat down.

"How's business?" he asked.

"Can't complain," said Gary as he filled their coffee cups.

There was a real hustle and bustle all around them. Couples and groups were constantly showing up to rent canoes. Kids were shouting, dogs were barking. Tourism was the new lifeblood for the entire Arrowhead area. These crowds also represented the majority of the public that Lance Hansen dealt with on a daily basis.

"It's a helluva thing, that murder," said Gary. "And to think you were the one to find the body. Was it bad?"

"I could have done without it."

"They were here, you know. Those Norwegians."

"That's what I heard. Did you talk to them?"

"No, I just heard about them from some of the staff."

For a while they ate in silence. Lance wondered whether his cousin had something going on with the young brunette. Gary's wife, Barb Hansen, was a good friend of his, and he didn't know how he was going to act around them in the future if he found out Gary was cheating on her. He sincerely hoped he was mistaken. But then he remembered how close the brunette had been standing.

"How's it going with Inga?" Gary asked suddenly.

"Pretty good, thanks," replied Lance. "I went to see her at the nursing home the day before yesterday. She asked about you, in fact. You and Barb. Wondered how the two of you were doing." Lance peered at his cousin over the rim of his coffee cup.

Gary cleared his throat. "The two of us? We're fine." He met Lance's eye as he set his cup down.

"How long have you guys been married, anyway?" asked Lance.

Gary looked away. "Twenty-four years," he said.

"Silver wedding anniversary coming up, then. Has it really been that long?"

His cousin nodded.

"I remember your wedding like it was yesterday," Lance went on. "Good Lord, you were so young!"

Gary just sat there, looking past him without saying a word.

"Do you remember how drunk Chad Aakre got?"

Gary nodded and smiled, but it was a distant, melancholy sort of smile, the kind provoked by the thought of happier times that had long since passed.

The two cousins sat there with their cups of coffee and half-eaten sandwiches, silently staring ahead at the end of County Road 2. The road was usually just called the Sawbill Trail, after the original path that had once been the only accessible route. It was made sometime in the 1870s by the first pioneers in the area who were first-generation Americans. Men who were driven by dreams of gold and silver, although no significant amounts of precious metals were ever found. But it was the energy from those dreams, long since relinquished and forgotten, that was the reason County Road 2 even existed.

"I don't know . . . I guess we're all getting older," said Gary, looking at his cousin again.

Lance wondered if this was meant to be the answer to his question. Because he thought that he had, in fact, asked a question. In his own way he was asking Gary whether he was having an affair with the young brunette. But he couldn't really tell whether Gary had answered him or not. If he had, what then was his answer? Lance thought that in good faith he couldn't do any more digging. A person's private life was just that: private.

"So how is . . . Do you see much of Andy lately?" Gary went on.

The mention of his brother's name felt like a cold jolt in Lance's stomach. He was trying to think of something natural and noncommittal to say when he was saved by the ringing of his cell phone.

It was his mother, Inga Hansen.

When Gary realized who was calling, he mimed the words "Say hi from me," and then got up and went inside the shop.

Inga Hansen had just heard that her elder son was the one who had found the murder victim the day before at Baraga's Cross. She was worried about how he was doing.

"Did you get any sleep, my boy?" she asked. "You didn't have nightmares, did you?"

"I'm perfectly fine, Mom," he said. "I'm a police officer. I can handle things like that."

"Oh, right, of course," exclaimed his mother in the nursing home in Duluth. "Just don't forget that you're talking to a policeman's widow. So tell me how you're really doing. And be honest."

Lance sighed in resignation. "I'm not exactly sure, but I think I'm fine. You shouldn't worry so much."

"You're not as tough as you think," said his mother.

"You're probably right about that."

"Do you really think there's anyone who knows you better than I do?"

They went on talking like that for several minutes, exchanging reassurances and sympathetic complaints. Finally Lance promised to visit her that evening, even though he'd just seen her two days earlier. She wanted to make sure he was okay, as she said.

As soon as he finished talking to his mother, Lance got up and headed for the parking lot. When he looked over his shoulder, he caught a glimpse of Gary inside the shop talking to the brunette. Suddenly laughter suffused her whole face—an open, youthful kind of laughter. It was undeniably a lovely sight.

6

DULUTH IS LOCATED AT THE WESTERNMOST TIP of Lake Superior, where the St. Louis River runs into the lake. That's as far west as you can go on the Great Lakes of North America. It's the point where the world's largest freshwater lake system ends. But of course you could also say it's the point where it begins, and that it ends where the St. Lawrence River pours out into the Atlantic Ocean near Quebec City in Canada, half a continent away.

Where he was sitting in room 22 in Lakeview Nursing Home, Lance Hansen was approximately at the midpoint of the North American continent. To the east were the five Great Lakes: Superior, Huron, Michigan, Erie, and Ontario. To the west were the Great Plains, and beyond them the Rocky Mountains. To the north the boreal forests stretched all the way up to the tundra. Barely two hours' drive away, beneath the bridges of the Twin Cities, the Mississippi River flowed southward. With its numerous tributaries and tributaries of tributaries, the river resembled a great tree made of water, with its roots in the Gulf of Mexico and its sparse crown sticking all the way north into Minnesota.

From his mother's room he had a view of the steep-sloped city where he'd grown up. The roofs of the Victorian houses lining the slope. The tops of the big oaks and maples growing in neglected gaps between the houses. Farther down was the town's business district, with modern glass-and-steel structures mixed with elegant art deco buildings. The smokestack of Fitger's Brewery stuck up like a signaling index finger. Beyond it Lance could see the structure that

40

more than anything else had become the symbol of Duluth—the Aerial Lift Bridge, which was over a hundred years old. Even from a distance of several miles you can see the big steel construction looming above the entrance to the harbor when you come driving south along the North Shore. It looks like an enormous steel gateway, and when a ship needs to pass, the bridge is simply lifted up under the top span, high overhead.

At the moment the bridge was being lowered. Lance and his mother had been watching a ship pass through. How many times had they done just that? From their house on Fifth Avenue they had also had a view of the harbor and the Aerial Bridge.

"There used to be more ships going through," said Inga Hansen.

"It probably varies from year to year," replied Lance.

There were coffee cups and a tray of cookies on the table between them. On the wall hung a series of photographs. Baby pictures of her sons. High school photos. Andy and Tammy's wedding picture. Lance's class at the police academy in Minneapolis. Her own wedding picture. Her husband in uniform. And the same photo that hung in Lance's home office, showing a group of people, both adults and children, posing on the deck of a ship. On this one someone had also written in black ink "Duluth, October 3, 1902" in the right-hand corner. There were also baby pictures of Andy's daughter, Chrissy. She had a faraway, dreamy look in her eye—something that Lance had never noticed before.

"But I remember sometimes counting thirty lifts in one day. The most I've seen since I've been here is twelve. Twelve!" his mother said, as if she could hardly believe it.

Lance wondered if this was how she spent her days, sitting here and waiting for the old bridge to be raised. He thought that he ought to take her for a drive along the North Shore so she could see all the places she loved. She was seventy-four and could easily live another ten years, maybe more, but he could see how fast she was aging these days. Only a couple of years ago it had been a very slow process, but all of a sudden it was speeding up, and he was starting to realize that it wouldn't be long before she too would die. His father had been dead for seven years. There sat his mother with her white hair, and soon both of his parents would be gone.

They had already talked about all the family members, what everyone was up to lately, and now they were just sitting together without saying much. Lance was always disinclined to leave once he sat down in his mother's room. He liked sitting there and looking out the window. It reminded him of his childhood and youth, since the view was almost the same as he'd had from his boyhood room. And his mother was the same, even though she seemed to be on a steady decline. Fewer things claimed her attention. But now it was almost eight o'clock, and he couldn't stay any longer.

"I think Chrissy looks like an angel in that picture," his mother said. She was looking at the most recent photo of her granddaughter, taken about a year ago.

Lance took a closer look at the picture, studying the strange expression that he hadn't noticed before. Maybe it was simply because she was discovering something new about herself. That's how her life is right now, he thought. And that's how it's going to continue for many more years to come. A constant discovery of new things. Both good and bad.

"An angel from Two Harbors," Inga went on.

That made him laugh.

"But don't you see it?" exclaimed his mother, laughing too. "She looks like an angel!"

"Sure, but Two Harbors is a long way from heaven."

"Don't say that," she told him.

That was where his parents had lived the first year of their marriage. Lance knew that. He looked at the picture of Chrissy again. It had to be her hair that was making Inga think of an angel. Her blond hair was like a halo around her head. "All right, that's what we'll call her, then," he said. "An angel from Two Harbors."

At that moment his cell phone rang. He apologized and then took the call. It was Sparky Redmeyer. Lance could tell at once that he wanted to ask a favor. "Is there something I can do for you?" he said.

"As you know, I'm working for the FBI now," said Redmeyer.

That's one way of putting it, thought Lance. "Yeah. So I hear."

"But tonight there's something I've got to do that's going to make it difficult. So I was wondering if you might do me a favor."

"And what's that?"

"Well, you see, I'm supposed to pick up a police officer at the airport in Duluth tonight. A homicide detective from Norway. And then I have to drive him up to Tofte, to the Bluefin Bay."

"And?"

"Well, it turns out that my wife is going to be away overnight, with her knitting club. I promised to stay home with the kids, but I forgot all about it."

"Aha! And you'd rather lie to the FBI than disappoint your wife. Is that it?"

"You know my wife, don't you?" said Redmeyer.

"So you're wondering if I could pick up the Norwegian for you?"

"You'd be doing me a big favor. I can't ask just anybody, you know. It has to be a police officer."

"Sure. That's fine, Sparky. I'm actually in Duluth right now."

"Really?"

"Uh-huh. I'm over at Lakeview, visiting my mother. When does his plane arrive?"

"It gets in at eight thirty."

"Jesus Christ! It's already eight!"

"I was going to give him a call and ask him to wait at the airport," said Redmeyer.

"Hmm . . . Sounds like you're having a stressful night."

"You don't know the half of it. But don't tell Laura, okay? And it'd be great if you could get the Norwegian detective to say that I was the one who picked him up, if anyone asks. Do you think you could do that?"

"Sure, sure. Relax, Sparky. I'll take care of it. Now go send Laura off with her knitting club."

"Great! Thanks a lot, Lance. I owe you big-time."

"Wait a minute," said Lance. "How will I find this Norwegian?"

"Oh, that's right, I almost forgot. His name is Nyland: n-y-l-a-n-d. You'll have to make a sign with his name on it, and then he'll be able to find you."

When he finally ended the call, his mother held up the palm of her hand toward him. "Spare me," she said. "I know everything there is to know about policemen and personal lives and jobs and all of that."

Lance smiled.

"So you're going to pick up a Norwegian at the airport?"

"Yeah. Someone who's supposed to help the FBI investigate the murder."

He realized instantly that he didn't feel like talking about the murder again. His mother had begun asking about it the minute he stepped in the door. He told her that he was perfectly fine and that he'd put the whole case out of his mind. He assumed she didn't believe him, but in the end she relented and switched to talking about the family instead. Now he could sense she was on the verge of asking him a new round of questions about the murder. He had to find another subject to conclude his visit.

His gaze fell on the group photograph from 1902. The boat was the steamship *America*, docked in Duluth. On deck stood a large share of the population from Tofte on Halsnøy in Norway, posing for the photo. After sending a steady stream of letters from America over a period of fourteen years, the pioneer Knut Olson—Lance's great-grandfather who had left for the United States in 1888— had finally managed to persuade family members and neighbors to follow. It took fourteen years for the sober-minded fishermen and farmers to leave behind everything they'd ever known. Until that time, only one person had followed Knut across the Atlantic: his sister's son, Thormod Olson, the boy who fell through the ice.

"There we all are," said Lance.

"Hmm?" said his mother.

He nodded at the photo. "There we all are, standing on the deck of the old *America*." He knew his mother loved to talk about this subject.

"Yes, there we are. Soon we'll see the North Shore for the very first time. Can you imagine what it must have looked like?"

"No highways," said Lance. "No roads at all, except for the cart track that ended at Two Harbors. A few houses in small clearings along the coast. Huge scars in the landscape from the logging that was going on, and camps that housed hundreds of lumberjacks. A small cluster of buildings at the base of Carlton Peak when they arrived at last. The new Tofte."

"And all the hard work that awaited them," his mother sighed.

"But don't you think they also had a feeling of freedom?"

"Oh, of course. Here it didn't matter where you came from, only where you were headed, and how hard you were willing to work to get there. Just think of Thormod Olson," she said.

Lance knew that Thormod had died the way he had lived, as a poor fisherman, but he didn't say anything.

"One night ten years before that picture was taken, young Thormod fell through the ice," his mother began.

Lance had no idea how many times he'd heard this story.

"There was a full moon, so he continued his trek through the night," she went on. "He walked across the ice from one bay to the next. You know how cold March nights can be. But Thormod kept on going and managed to make it all the way to Great-Grandfather's house. Just imagine the strength of will it must have required to manage such a feat."

Lance was pleased to see how interested she seemed in the topic.

"We can thank all of them for everything we do from the time we wake up in the morning until we fall asleep at night," she said. "Those pioneers, all of those forgotten men and women."

"Uh-huh," said Lance absentmindedly. "You're certainly right about that." He noticed that the Aerial Bridge had started to rise. "The bridge is going up again," he said.

They sat in silence as they watched the old ritual that they'd seen so many times before. The body of the bridge rose all the way up to the crosspiece, the ship glided through the gateway of steel, and then the body of the bridge was lowered once again.

Lance looked at the picture of Chrissy, the angel from Two Harbors. Then at the picture of the folks from Tofte posing on the deck of the *America* in October 1902. A crowd of black-clad, somber-looking Norwegians in the New World.

And ten years earlier Thormod Olson had fallen through the ice. In 1892, to be precise.

"Did you say it happened on a March night?" he asked.

His mother gave him a puzzled look.

"Did you say that it was on a March night that Thormod fell through the ice?"

"That's what I've always heard, at any rate."

"A March night in 1892?"

"Yes."

"Near the mouth of the Cross River, right?"

"That's right."

"And there was a full moon?"

"There must have been, since he was able to keep walking at night."

"Sure," said Lance. "Of course . . ."

He sat there staring out at the city where he'd grown up as he nodded a bit at his own thoughts. If his mother was right about Thormod walking across the ice under a full moon in March 1892, it meant that it happened at the same time as the disappearance of the Indian, Swamper Caribou. He remembered clearly the words of the article published in the *Grand Marais Pioneer:* "Swamper Caribou disappeared from his hunting cabin near the mouth of the Cross River at the time of the last full moon, meaning in the early morning hours of March 16."

7

EIRIK NYLAND LOOKED AT THE BAGS AND SUITCASES slowly revolving in the glare of the terminal lights. It was sixteen hours since he'd climbed into his car to drive to the airport. He'd crossed seven time zones, and it actually should have been early the next morning, but here it was still evening. And not more than half past eight. He felt like he'd been partially erased, as if important files on his hard drive had been deleted. Inside his temples a headache was brewing, and soon it would begin to swell and explode against the inside of his skull if he didn't do something to stop it.

The passengers who had arrived on the forty-five-minute flight from Minneapolis stood around the luggage carousel on which suitcases, bags, and backpacks were circling. He heard people mentioning names, times, and appointments, but he had no idea what any of them were referring to. He studied their body language and clothing, their glasses, watches, and wedding rings—all indications of personal lives beyond this building where these people happened to be gathered. Outside the big windows he saw the typical airport landscape. A few low buildings. The passenger plane in which they had just arrived. Farther away a fighter jet was coming in for a landing. A forklift was moving slowly across the runway.

In spite of the typical and anonymous scene that characterizes every airport, he had a distinct awareness that he was in the United States. Even in this small airport in Minnesota, he had the feeling of a smooth, carefully structured surface concealing a violent energy underneath.

Finally his suitcase emerged from the chute. He waited until it was right in front of him and then reached out to lift it off the belt. Then he headed for the exit along with several other passengers.

In the arrivals hall a small crowd was waiting. Someone was supposed to pick him up, but he couldn't see anyone who looked like a representative from the FBI. He was prepared to call the number he'd been given in case there was a problem, but suddenly he caught sight of someone holding up a piece of cardboard on which was written "NYLAND."

He stopped and set down his suitcase.

The two men looked at each other.

The American held out his hand. "Welcome to Minnesota," he said. "I'm Lance Hansen, and I'm here to drive you to your hotel in Tofte."

"Eirik Nyland," said the Norwegian.

BELOW THEM LAY DULUTH. The evening light still shone on the top of the tallest buildings down there. The rest were shrouded in the encroaching dusk. They drove down the steep streets, through neighborhoods with Victorian houses that had undoubtedly once looked quite presentable but were now in a state of disrepair. People were sitting on the steps and porches, watching the traffic. Several little girls were playing hopscotch on the sidewalk.

Nyland actually hadn't had the slightest desire to assist the Americans with their investigation of the murder of Georg Lofthus. He was supposed to be spending next week at the cabin near Lillesand with his wife and daughters, but that probably wasn't going to happen. In spite of this, along with the jet lag and the incipient headache, he felt a boyish glee about being in a new place. He'd been to the States many times, but never to Minnesota.

"Is it okay if I open the window?" he asked.

"Of course," said Lance.

The air was filled with the smells of deep-fried food and gasoline, asphalt beginning to cool after a hot summer day, a faint whiff of coal from the big coal depots in the harbor area, malt from Fitger's Brewery, exhaust fumes, and freshly made coffee, as well as a deeply entrenched underlying smell of freshwater coming from the lake itself. For Eirik Nyland it was all just one, undifferentiated odor, but he liked it, and he could easily tell that it had a distinctive quality that set it apart from the smell of other cities he'd visited.

"A fine-looking town," he said.

They had now left the steep hill behind and were stopped at a traffic light.

"I grew up here," said Lance.

The light changed from red to green. They drove through the intersection and turned in to a gas station.

"Best city in the world, if you ask me."

At the gas station Eirik Nyland bought some Excedrin for his headache, a bottle of Chippewa mineral water, and the latest issue of the *Duluth News Tribune.* Lance bought a bag of Old Dutch potato chips, a Diet Coke, and several little heart-shaped Dove chocolates.

"Do you see that cloud?" asked Lance as they came out. He pointed to the north.

Nyland saw a boomerang-shaped cloud that looked like it was cast out of some sort of synthetic material. It was dark gray, and inside he thought he saw a faint greenish sheen, but he wasn't sure.

"What does it mean?" he asked.

"Bad weather," said Lance, and they got back in the Jeep.

As they drove out of Duluth, Nyland opened the newspaper and began leafing through it. In a moment he found what he was looking for. "Murder at Baraga's Cross," said the headline. "The police find no trace of a third person present at the crime scene where a Norwegian canoeist was murdered," he read. He skimmed the article, which strongly implied that Bjørn Hauglie must have killed his friend.

"What is this Baraga's Cross?" Nyland asked when he was done reading.

"It's a cross put up near the lake just south of Tofte," said Lance.

"Why is it called Baraga's Cross?"

"Frederic Baraga was a priest who risked his life to help the Indians in the area when they were stricken by the plague. He tried to cross the lake in a small boat, but midway across he was caught by a sudden storm. He almost didn't make it. He ended up near the mouth of the Cross River, which of course wasn't the name of the river back then. It got its name after Baraga put up the cross to show his gratitude at having survived the storm. Apparently it was just a small wooden cross. Later it was replaced by a big stone cross, which stands at exactly the same place."

"And it was near this cross that the dead man was found?"

"No. That was where I found the man who survived. He was sitting there, naked and bloody. Afterward I found the dead man a few hundred yards away, near their tent."

It occurred to Eirik Nyland that he hadn't bothered to find out who exactly this Lance Hansen was.

"So you were the one who found the body?" he asked in surprise.

"Yup."

"But I thought you worked for the FBI."

Lance snorted with laughter. "Yeah, well, that was sort of the intention," he said.

"So you're actually from the local police force?"

"I'm what is often referred to as a *forest cop*. Which means an ordinary police officer with a slightly unusual jurisdiction. In my case, the Superior National Forest."

"What exactly is that? I saw it mentioned in the fax that I got."

"It's a big forested area that comes under the auspices of the federal authorities," said Lance. "There are lots of areas like it in this country. The U.S. Forest Service is in charge of operations and administration for these properties. They also have a separate division that handles law enforcement, and that's where I work. We're regular police officers with regular police training."

"What did you do when you found the man who'd been murdered?"

"I contacted the Cook County sheriff, who then asked for assistance from the FBI, since the crime scene is located on federal land."

They drove in silence for a while. So far Nyland had seen only a few glimpses of the lake, because this section of the road was a short distance away from the shore. It was a little disappointing, since he'd been looking forward to seeing Lake Superior.

Shortly after passing a sign that said "Two Harbors, population 3,613," he saw to his astonishment that there was a big fiberglass figure of a rooster next to the road. It had a red comb and yellow feet. Next he saw an even bigger figure, well over ten feet tall, of some sort of frontier type with a cap on his head. He stood there leaning on a canoe paddle. The figure, which also looked like it was made of fiberglass, stood outside what appeared to be a laundromat. He couldn't figure out what the point of the rooster and the frontiersman could be, but he noticed that Highway 61 had now become Seventh Avenue in Two Harbors. Once again he felt a boyish glee at discovering completely new places. He saw a couple of car lots with long rows of pickup trucks and SUVs, the local liquor store, a Vietnamese restaurant, several teenagers hanging out at the Dairy Queen, and a couple of big RVs parked at the curb. A woman was smoking as she stood on a porch facing the street. Lance honked and waved at her.

"That's my sister-in-law, Tammy," he said. "My brother and his family live in that house."

They passed a church and yet another car lot, and then Seventh Avenue turned into Highway 61 again. They had left Two Harbors behind. Nyland had the impression of a small, run-down, and not especially thriving community.

"So where do you live?" he asked.

"A place called Lutsen, just north of Tofte."

"What did you say it's called?"

"Lutsen. L-u-t-s-e-n. Named after someplace in Europe where the Swedes once won a big battle long ago."

"Founded by Swedes, I assume?"

"That's right. By Charles Nelson in 1885. He was one of the first Scandinavian pioneers to come to the North Shore—the shoreline area that we're driving along right now."

"Sounds like you know a lot about the history of the area," said Nyland.

"I've been interested in it since I was a teenager. Genealogy and local historical events. All four of my grandparents were Norwegian. One of them was even *from* Norway. My grandfather Isak Hansen."

"And where was he from?"

"A place called Levanger."

Nyland noticed that Lance's pronunciation of the Norwegian name was very good.

"And you said you have three other Norwegian grandparents?"

"That's right. Two were born here, but of Norwegian stock. One came here from Norway as an infant."

It was now 9:10. It had grown significantly darker in a matter of only a few minutes. Now the road was running along the lake, just as Nyland had pictured. He stared at the dark water off to the right. So this was Lake Superior. On the other side of the road he saw mostly forest. There was a Norwegian flag attached to a mailbox near a side road leading into the woods.

"Have you ever been to Norway?" he asked.

"No, I'm afraid not. But one day, maybe."

At that moment the first big raindrops struck the windshield with audible splats. Only seconds later the rain was coming down with amazing force. In fact, they could hardly see through the water cascading down the windshield. The sound of the rain hammering on the roof of the car was so loud that Nyland had to raise his voice to be heard.

"When did they come over from Norway? Your ancestors, I mean," he practically shouted.

Lance had slowed down and was leaning forward, staring hard to see through the pelting rain.

"My paternal grandfather, Isak Hansen, came here from Norway in 1929. He was a carpenter. He married a girl who was born in Norway but came to the States at the age of one. On my mother's side of the family . . . Now, let's see . . . One of my great-grandparents came here back in 1888. He was the first person in my family to immigrate to America. Knut Olson from Tofte on Halsnøy. He married a Canadian woman. French Canadian, actually. Her name was Nanette. They were my mother's paternal grandparents. Then in October 1902 a whole boatload of immigrants arrived from Halsnøy, including two young people who ended up getting married, and they became the parents of my maternal grandmother. So there you have it. That's how they all got here."

"And your whole family has stayed in this area ever since?"

"Yes, most of us live in what's called the Arrowhead region."

"And what's that?"

"The section of Minnesota that's squeezed in between Lake Superior and the Canadian border. On the map it looks a little like an arrowhead. Hence the name."

The force of the rain ratcheted up another couple of notches. Nyland wasn't normally a nervous type of person, but he thought the situation was starting to get dangerous. The beams from the headlights reached only a few yards before being drowned out by the torrents of rain. And occasionally, out of the mud-colored darkness, cars would suddenly appear only a few yards away. He felt an urge to tell Lance to pull over, but he thought that might be going a bit too far.

"Do you often have weather like this?" he asked.

"Fairly often," replied Lance. "The whole region around the Great Lakes is like this. Sudden, violent storms. Luckily they usually don't last long. It has to do with the topography. No mountain ranges to block the air masses, either to the north or the south. Just flat plains. Warm air from the Gulf of Mexico forces its way up here, and then meets cold air from the Canadian Arctic. And they slam together."

"Like now?"

"This is just light entertainment."

Nyland glanced at Lance Hansen, who was leaning as far forward as possible while the wipers slapped frantically back and forth with little effect. Every time they saw another vehicle, Nyland felt a brief stab of anxiety. He told himself it was just the jet lag. It's already tomorrow in Oslo, he thought. This was both the wrong day and the wrong continent.

Suddenly he remembered the bottle of Gammel Opland that he had in his suitcase. Some of his colleagues had given him the idea: "You can't arrive empty-handed when you're going to Minnesota from the old country! The Norwegian Americans are still crazy about lutefisk and aquavit," they'd told him. "It doesn't matter that it's too early for Christmas." So Nyland had bought a bottle of Gammel Opland but decided to drop the idea of bringing any lutefisk. Right now he had a strong urge to open the bottle as soon as he got to the hotel and take a good slug of the liquor himself. At the same time he felt an almost devil-may-care joy in the whole situation and this strange drive—as if he were steadily heading deeper into something that was not merely an unfamiliar landscape. But what exactly did he mean by that? Everything was so different from what he'd imagined. He'd expected to have an efficient introductory meeting with the well-oiled machinery of the FBI. Instead, he was sitting here in this old Jeep with Lance Hansen in one of the worst rainstorms he'd ever experienced.

A bluish, shimmering light filled the car, giving Lance's hands on the steering wheel a cadaverous appearance. Then the moment was shattered by what sounded like the boom of cannons in the surrounding darkness. Another flash of light, and this time he saw the actual lightning bolt, a trembling spear of energy that pierced the rain-pelted surface of the suddenly illuminated lake.

"Would you still call this just light entertainment?" asked Nyland.

At that instant lightning struck again, and an electrically lit interlaced pattern, like the map of a complex river delta, spread out across the sky in front of them before collapsing with a deafening boom.

Nyland laughed. He heard Lance laughing too. He didn't know why; he just couldn't help it.

Soon he glimpsed the outline of large buildings and installations through the darkness on the right side of the road. He was about to ask what they were when lightning lit up the entire area. Before the light faded, more lightning struck, and then twice more—a series of four lightning bolts so close together that there was hardly any intervening darkness. During these few seconds he saw an area containing big, hangarlike buildings, cranes, conveyor belts, enormous steel structures reaching over the lake through the darkness, and an entire landscape of black pyramid shapes, which he took to be piles of coal, gleaming like wet asphalt in the rain and glare from the lightning. If was as if someone had pulled aside a curtain that had concealed another world, and then all of a sudden the curtain again fell into place. Only the afterglow from the lightning remained on his retinas.

"Silver Bay," said Lance. "Did you see the big black piles? That's taconite. Millions of pellets the size of marbles. They contain a strongly magnetic type of iron. Low-grade ore is transported by rail from the mines that are many miles inland. Silver Bay is where the taconite is processed into pellets and shipped. Lightning always strikes those taconite mounds."

The rain was still coming down hard. Once in a while they were surprised by the sight of a car emerging from the darkness right in front of them. Lightning continued to flash over the desolate landscape. Since the sound of thunder had no mountainsides to bounce off, it crashed like it would on the open sea. Yet Nyland noticed something stirring inside him, as if a tightly wound spring had been released. He sank back in his seat, surrendering to the darkness and rain and thunder and jet lag, and to this road with the lake on one side and the forest on the other. He was tired. Maybe he'd be able to sleep tonight after all. It would be good if he could save the aquavit for another occasion. And preferably share it with some Americans.

He thought, as he had so many times during the past twenty-four hours, that strangely enough he knew absolutely nothing about this region, even though he'd been to the States a dozen times and believed that he had a fairly good understanding of the country. But he drew a complete blank when it came to this state where, he'd been told, the people loved aquavit and lutefisk.

He saw a sign that said "Finland," and a moment later they passed through the intersection that was clearly the turnoff to that particular area.

"That's Finland, the small town where the two Norwegians were staying," Lance told him. "What I mean is, I think they were staying somewhere else during the days leading up to the murder."

"Are you involved in the investigation?" asked Nyland.

"No, but my cousin runs a canoe-rental company. And one of his employees told me that he'd talked to the two Norwegians when they came in to rent a canoe. He got the impression that they'd been staying for a while in Finland. But as I said, I have nothing to do with the investigation, so don't give too much weight to what I say."

"Did you tell the investigators about this?"

"What do you mean?"

"The fact that the Norwegians had rented a canoe from your cousin."

"No, I didn't find out about that until after they interviewed me."

"When was the interview?"

"This morning. I talked to my cousin afterward."

"I'll make a note of that when we get to the hotel. So you won't have to give it another thought."

"Do you think it might be important?"

"I doubt it. But we're dealing with a murder case, and you never want to give the impression of holding anything back."

This brief exchange was enough to arouse Eirik Nyland's curiosity. Here he sat with the man who had discovered the body. He had him all to himself and didn't have to share whatever he might find out with the FBI, if he didn't want to. It was always impossible to say how this type of collaboration might develop. So it might be useful to obtain some information that the American authorities weren't yet aware of.

"Do you think Bjørn Hauglie killed Georg Lofthus?" he asked. "What was your initial impression? I mean, when you found Hauglie."

"I thought he was dead. That was my first impression."

"Why's that?"

"Because of all the blood. He was completely smeared with blood. And he was also just sitting there, without moving a muscle."

"When did you realize that he wasn't dead after all?"

"When he started talking."

"What did he say?"

"At first it sounded like gibberish, but then I realized that he was speaking Norwegian. I've heard people speak Norwegian countless times. We often have Norwegians visiting the area. They come here to see their relatives. And I know a few words of the language too. Suddenly I recognized the word *kjærlighet*. And then he repeated the same word in English. He looked me in the eye and said 'love.' In fact, he repeated it several times."

"Did you tell the FBI about this?"

"Of course. I told Bob Lecuyer everything I knew."

"Good. But do you think Hauglie killed Georg Lofthus? What if you had to bet a large sum of money on it? Did he do it, or didn't he?"

"I'd probably bet that he *didn't* do it."

"Why's that?"

"He was clearly in a state of shock. But it seemed to me the shock had been caused by an outside force, so to speak. As if he'd *seen* something gruesome—not that he'd *done* something terrible. Do you know what I mean?"

"I agree that there's a definite difference. But if Hauglie didn't do it, who did?"

Lance paused to consider the question. "Someone who can't stand the sight of naked men?" he ventured.

"Why do you think they were both naked?" asked Nyland.

"Hmm . . . well, do you think they might have been . . . what should I say? Lovers?"

Nyland noticed that Lance seemed embarrassed by the subject.

"Georg Lofthus was going to be married in September, so I doubt he was gay," he replied.

"Hmm . . . ," said Lance, and then repeated it. "Hmm."

"What is it?" asked Nyland.

"I don't know, but I was just thinking that . . . Hauglie seemed awfully young to me. Do you know how old he is?"

"Twenty-one."

"What about Lofthus?"

"Twenty."

"Isn't it a little unusual to get married when you're only twenty? I mean, in this day and age."

"I suppose so," said Nyland. "But I don't see what that has to do with him getting killed."

"No, but it might say something about who he was. What sort of person gets married at the young age of twenty?"

"Someone who's naive," replied Nyland.

"Sure, but aren't all twenty-year-olds naive?"

"What about an *extremely* naive person?"

Lance Hansen laughed. "It's possible," he said. "Maybe we're talking about the murder of an extremely naive person."

"Did you know that they were Christians?" asked Nyland.

"No. But is that significant?"

"It might have a certain impact on how early a person gets married. They belonged to a Christian youth community that requires everyone to take a vow not to have sex before marriage."

"Is that right?"

Lance took out one of the little heart-shaped chocolates he'd bought at the gas station in Duluth. He handed it to Nyland and then took another one out of the paper bag for himself.

"What should I do with the wrapper?" asked Nyland.

"Just toss it on the floor, but first read what it says on the inside."

Lance switched on the overhead light, held up the chocolate wrapper, and studied it intently before dropping it on the floor.

Nyland smoothed out his own wrapper. " 'Savor every second of it,' " he read aloud. "Of what?" he immediately asked.

"Of your stay on the North Shore?" suggested Lance.

"Savor every second of yet another murder investigation," Nyland said sarcastically.

For a while neither of them spoke. The rain was tapering off, and the lightning flashes were no longer as frequent. There was also more time between the lightning and the following roll of thunder. Nyland thought about the strange boomerang-shaped cloud he'd seen when he was at the gas station in Duluth. That must be what they had just passed under.

Soon they came to a turnoff on the right-hand side of the road.

Lance slowed down and pointed. "That's where it happened. Down there," he said.

Nyland saw the sign that said, "Baraga's Cross."

"It's probably too dark right now, or we could drive down and take a look," said Lance.

"Definitely too dark. Besides, I'm sure I'll be seeing the crime scene tomorrow."

Lance stepped on the gas again, and they quickly left behind the turnoff to Baraga's Cross.

"Well, here's the Tofte ranger station," he said a short time later.

Nyland saw something that looked like a military encampment in the dark to the left of the road. "So this is where you work?" he said.

"Partly," Lance told him. "Mostly I work out of my car. And here comes the impressive center of Tofte," he added.

Lights were on in the gas station and a few other buildings at the end of the long clearing.

"Named after Tofte on Halsnøy."

They drove past the gas station and the church. Then Lance slowed to a crawl and turned onto a road that led down to a big, modern-looking building.

A well-lit sign proclaimed "Bluefin Bay."

Lance parked the Jeep. They got out and stretched their legs. Eirik Nyland was feeling stiff and creaky after all the traveling he'd done. The rain had stopped, the air smelled fresh and good. He could hear the lapping of the waves from the lake right below the parking area. Lance opened the back, took out Nyland's suitcase, and set it down on the rain-soaked asphalt.

"Well, thanks for picking me up," said Nyland. "It was a nice drive. And dramatic," he added.

"No problem," said Lance. "And if there's anything . . . if there's anything you want to know . . . just give me a call."

He took his wallet from his back pocket and handed Nyland his card. The two men shook hands.

"By the way," said Lance, "could I ask you a small favor?"

"Of course."

"Somebody else was actually supposed to pick you up at the airport tonight. Someone from the local police force. He's on loan to the FBI, as a sort of gofer. But something came up so he couldn't drive to Duluth, some family matter. He's a little scared of his wife, you see. And he doesn't really want to tell that to the FBI."

Eirik Nyland laughed. "Okay, if they ask me, it was this other guy who met me at the airport and drove me here. Right?"

"We'd really appreciate it. Both of us," said Lance. "I mean, both Redmeyer and I."

"Redmeyer," said Nyland, memorizing the name. "And what's his first name?"

"Sparky," said Lance.

"All right. He was the one who picked me up at the airport."

8

EIRIK NYLAND was sitting in one of the two easy chairs in Bjørn Hauglie's hospital room. In the other sat the man he'd be working with here, FBI agent Bob Lecuyer. He looked to be in his thirties. A man not given to grand gestures, and Nyland respected that.

Bjørn Hauglie was sitting on the bed. He was suntanned and muscular, with sun-bleached blond hair. A tape recorder was on a small table between the two police officers and the bed. It had not yet been turned on.

"Do you think they'll keep you here long?" asked Nyland in Norwegian.

"In a hospital? Why would they do that?" replied Hauglie.

"Well, you've suffered a huge shock, of course. So I thought it might be good for you to . . . get some rest for a while."

"No. I want to go back home as soon as possible. Can you help with that?"

"The best thing you can do to get back to Norway is to answer our questions and provide as many details as possible."

Hauglie nodded.

"So let's get started. It would be better if we could conduct the interview in English. Most of it, at least. For the sake of my colleague from the FBI."

"That's fine with me."

"All right," said Nyland, turning to Lecuyer. "We're going to do it in English, and then Bjørn and I will have a talk in Norwegian, if that's okay with you."

"Fine." Lecuyer leaned forward and switched on the tape recorder. Then he went through the litany of introductory facts. Time, place, who was present. His pronunciation of Bjørn Hauglie's name was so American-sounding that Nyland had to stifle a laugh.

"First of all, could you tell us what you and Georg Lofthus were doing in Cook County, Minnesota? It's a long way from home for you," said Lecuyer.

"We were . . . canoeing."

"That's all?"

"Yes."

"Why did you choose Cook County?"

"It's one of the best canoeing areas in the world. Famous among canoeists."

"Were you and Georg part of an international canoeing community?"

"I suppose you might say that."

"Did you often travel abroad?"

"No. We once went to Sweden. Otherwise this was our first trip abroad. But we meet a lot of foreign canoeists who come to the west coast of Norway. So we practically grew up with that type of community all around us."

"But you didn't seek out the canoeing community here in Minnesota?"

"No."

"And you didn't meet anyone here that you'd met before?"

"No one."

"Tell me, did the two of you come straight here, or did you go to other places in the United States first?"

"We came straight here. We flew to Minneapolis. Then to Duluth. We rented a car and drove to . . . er . . . Finland."

With a glance Bob Lecuyer invited Eirik Nyland to continue the interview.

"How long were you in Finland?" asked Nyland.

"That depends whether . . . I mean, we spent most of our time canoeing in the wilderness, you know. Over the course of two weeks we took three different canoe trips. And we slept in a tent at night, of course. But we used Finland as a sort of base camp for those two weeks."

"Where did you stay when you were in Finland?" Nyland continued.

"At the Blue Moose Motel."

"But when Georg was killed, you were staying at a motel on Highway 61, weren't you?"

"Yes. The Whispering Pines."

"Why did you decide to stay there?"

"We didn't think we could leave Minnesota without canoeing on Lake Superior, and—"

"Tell me one thing," Lecuyer said, interrupting. "While you were staying in Finland . . . while you were taking those three different canoe trips that you mentioned . . . meaning, before you moved to the Whispering Pines . . . what sort of people did you have contact with? You must have met plenty of people in two weeks' time. Did anyone seem suspicious? Did you have a run-in with anyone?"

"We spent most of our time in the canoe. Just Georg and me. And you don't meet a lot of people like that. Occasionally we'd see other canoeists, of course, but there was nothing . . . nobody acted suspicious. Just pleasant people."

"Did you go into any bars or restaurants?"

"Not very often, but once in a while."

"Did you meet anyone there? Anyone you remember in particular?"

"We talked with a few people . . . especially about Norway. Folks up here seem very interested in everything Norwegian."

"Yes, I've noticed that too," said Nyland.

"But you didn't run into anybody suspicious the whole time you've been here in the States?" asked Lecuyer.

Bjørn Hauglie shook his head.

"All right. Let's move on to when Georg was killed. Would you say that everything was going the way the two of you had planned?" said Nyland.

"Definitely. Things were actually going better than we'd ever dared hope. The worst calamity we had was wet socks and a couple of small cuts on our fingers."

"What were your plans after you'd been canoeing on Lake Superior?" asked Lecuyer.

"We were . . . we were going . . . *home.*" Hauglie's voice suddenly faded. As if all energy had deserted him. He seemed to be fighting back tears.

The two police officers studied him in silence. Finally Lecuyer said, "Do you want to take a break? We don't have to ask all the questions in one session."

Hauglie shook his head. "No, that's okay. Let's just get it over with."

Lecuyer glanced at his Norwegian colleague.

"All right," said Nyland. "So we've gotten to the time when you moved to the Whispering Pines Motel so you could go canoeing on Lake Superior before you went home. But first, there's something I've been wondering about. What sort of relationship did you and Georg Lofthus have?"

"We were best friends."

"Were you friends for a long time?"

"Ever since grade school."

"And you grew up in the same place, am I right?"

"Yes, that's right."

"A small town. I've done a bit of homework in advance, you see. Talked to a few people in Norway." He noticed that Hauglie shifted position. "And from what I understand, you both moved to Bergen two years ago. Is that right?"

"Yes. To study at the university."

"And you lived together?"

"Yes, we shared a small apartment. It's really expensive to live in Bergen."

"Sure. And is it true that Georg Lofthus was going to get married in September?"

Hauglie buried his face in his hands. Nyland heard what sounded like sobs.

"Is this something that's especially difficult for you to talk about?" he asked.

Hauglie raised his head, sniffling. Then attempted a smile. "No. The whole thing is just so . . . it's all so . . ."

"All right," said Lecuyer. "So you make plans for this big canoeing adventure. And you go ahead with things, without encountering any major setbacks. But then you want to go canoeing on Lake Superior before you leave, right?"

Hauglie nodded.

"Let's see now. Today is Friday, the twenty-seventh. And this was on . . . Monday, right?"

"Yes."

"The twenty-third, right? Monday the twenty-third?"

"Yes," Hauglie repeated in a low voice.

"And what happens? What do you do on that Monday?"

"We check in at the Whispering Pines. Then we rent a canoe and go out on the lake for a while. When we get back to the motel, we decide to make one last canoe trip on the following day. One last overnight outing in Minnesota."

"But before we get to that," said Lecuyer, "who did you have contact with at Whispering Pines?"

"Nobody."

"But you must have talked to someone. What about when you checked in, for example?"

"The desk clerk was really the only person we talked to."

"What can you tell us about him?"

"The clerk? Nothing. What about him?"

"Did he say or do anything unusual? Was there anything special about him?"

Hauglie shook his head. "Nothing at all. He was a completely ordinary motel clerk."

"Not too nosy, or anything?"

"No, not at all."

"And you never got the impression that he was keeping his eye on you?"

"No. Why are you asking all these questions about the motel clerk?"

"Fine. Let's go on. The next day you set off for your last canoeing trip. On Tuesday, the twenty-fourth of June. What time of day did you leave?"

"We checked out around noon. We left a lot of our stuff there and booked a room for Wednesday night. But we . . . we never got to use it. Where are our things, by the way?"

"We have them. We'll be going through everything, but you'll get all of your belongings back. I promise you that. Let's not think about that right now. Try to focus on Tuesday, the twenty-fourth of June. It's about midday, and you and Georg are checking out of the Whispering Pines Motel. What do you do then?"

"We get in the canoe and paddle north along the shore."

"Does anything special happen along the way? Do you run into any kind of problems?"

"No. Everything is great, just like the rest of our vacation."

For a moment no one spoke, and then Eirik Nyland took over. "Did you go ashore anywhere?" he asked.

"Yes, at a couple of places. Just to take a break. We stretched out on the rocks and relaxed."

"Did you meet anyone when you were taking these breaks?"

"No."

"Did you see anyone at all? When you went ashore, I mean."

"No, not a soul."

"When you made camp . . . Why did you choose that particular spot?"

"Well, we just thought it was about time we pitched our tent. And besides, we'd noticed the cross. There's a big cross there, on the point. We thought there was something special about it. Something appealing. We're both . . . we *were* both Christians, so it seemed right to set up our camp near the cross."

"Baraga's Cross," said Lecuyer.

"What?"

"That's what it's called. Baraga's Cross."

"Oh."

"What time was it when you went ashore?" Nyland continued.

"It was between seven thirty and eight, I think."

"Okay. So you go ashore near Baraga's Cross," said Lecuyer. "What happens next?"

"We set up camp. Pitch our tent."

"By the way, why didn't you set up camp right next to the cross? Your tent was a couple of hundred yards away."

"Well . . . you're only allowed to set up camp in designated areas. Places that are marked with a sign. They're all on the map too. But there wasn't any place like that nearby. Since we were camping illegally, we pitched our tent inside the dense birch forest instead of out there, near the cross, where somebody might see it."

"As it happens, someone did notice your tent," said Lecuyer. "The police officer who found you works for the U.S. Forest Service. He came out there because of a tip they'd received about an illegal campsite. Apparently somebody saw the tent from a boat out on the lake. So what did the two of you do for the rest of the evening?"

"We set up the tent. Then we cooked dinner and ate it."

"Did you drink any alcohol?"

"Yes, as a matter of fact. A bottle of red wine. We'd bought the wine to share on a special occasion. And since it was our last night in Minnesota . . . But we didn't drink the whole bottle."

"So the two of you weren't drunk?"

"No, far from it."

"Okay, then. What did you do after dinner?"

"We decided to take the canoe out on the lake again."

"Really? Wasn't it dark?"

"Sure, but the moonlight was beautiful."

"What time was this?"

"From ten to eleven thirty, I think. Plus or minus a little."

"So you went back to your campsite at around eleven thirty?"

"About that time."

"What did you do next?"

"We went to bed."

"Did you fall asleep immediately, or did you lie awake for a while?"

"We lay awake and finished off the red wine. Then we must have fallen asleep . . . because when I woke up, Georg wasn't there."

"There's something I've been wondering about," said Eirik Nyland. "You were naked when you were found. The body of Georg Lofthus was too. Did you sleep together naked?"

"We didn't sleep *together*. We each had our own sleeping bag. But it's true that we usually slept in the nude. We'd been best friends since grade school. We swam naked and we slept naked. Everything was completely . . . relaxed between the two of us."

"Up to the time when you fell asleep," said Bob Lecuyer, "did you hear or see anyone else at any time? I'm sure you realize that this is particularly important."

"No. We could faintly hear the traffic up on the highway. Just a distant rushing sound from the cars. But nothing else. No voices or anything like that."

"So nothing suspicious happened before you both fell asleep that night?"

"Absolutely nothing."

"Tell us about what happened when you woke up," said Nyland. "Do you know what time it was?"

"It was a few minutes past five. I remember that clearly. I woke up because I needed to take a piss. When I saw that Georg was gone, I thought he must have left the tent for the same reason. I put on my shoes and went outside."

"But otherwise you were naked?" said Lecuyer.

"Yes. I just had on my shoes. After I took a leak, I stood there waiting for Georg to show up. It was already daylight, so he might have gone a short distance into the woods. But he didn't come back. So I started shouting his name. That didn't do any good either. Then I walked farther into the woods . . . not far, maybe twenty or thirty yards . . . and that's where I found Georg. That's where he was lying . . ."

Hauglie was staring straight ahead, without saying another word. It looked like he was running out of steam.

"Can you tell us specifically what you did when you found Georg?" said Nyland. "Both Lecuyer and I know what Lofthus looked like when you found him. We realize that this is extremely stressful for you. Let's just focus on your physical movements. What exactly did you do?"

"I lay down next to him."

"You lay down on the ground?"

"Yes. I lay down and put my arms around him. Talked to him. He was my best friend. The best friend I've ever had. I couldn't just let him lie there, all alone in the woods . . . in a foreign country."

"But at some point you must have gone over to the cross," Nyland continued.

"Yes. It suddenly occurred to me that somebody had *done* this to Georg. So then I . . . panicked. I was completely terrified. And I just started running."

"You ran straight to the cross?"

"I guess so."

"And that's where you stayed?"

"I'm a Christian. I have accepted Jesus Christ as my savior. It was the only place that I felt safe. The cross protected me. I firmly believe that. Otherwise I'd be dead too."

"Did you stay sitting there next to the cross the whole time until the police officer found you?"

"Yes."

"I think we're about done here," said Bob Lecuyer. "But there's one last question I need to ask you. Who do you think killed your friend?"

Bjørn Hauglie merely shook his head.

LATER THAT DAY Eirik Nyland was sitting next to the big picture window in conference room number two at the Bluefin Bay Resort, checking the Norwegian newspapers on his laptop. The three largest papers had the story on the front page, although it was obvious that as of yet they had very little information to report because the headlines were bigger than the actual articles:

"BODY OF NAKED NORWEGIAN CANOEIST FOUND IN MINNESOTA"
"BRUTAL MURDER OF NORWEGIAN TOURIST"
"NAKED MAN KILLED IN NORWEGIAN-AMERICAN COMMUNITY"

The newspapers also contained articles about Minnesota, the Midwest, and Norwegian Americans—all of them probably gleaned from Wikipedia.

Nyland was still thinking about how Bjørn Hauglie shook his head when Lecuyer asked him who might have killed his friend. He couldn't get that image out of his mind. There are lots of different ways to shake your head, he thought. And this was one way that he'd seen before. It signified a person who no longer believed that the world was turning as it should. That Friday would be followed by Saturday. That the sun would come up tomorrow too. That the whole thing wasn't just a dream.

It was three o'clock in the afternoon. Behind him he could hear a screeching and popping sound coming from the loudspeakers. A young woman who was in charge of conference arrangements at the Bluefin Bay was testing the microphones and sound equipment for the press conference that would be held in an hour. Occasionally she exchanged a few words with Lecuyer, who was standing next to the fax machine. He'd been there for a while now. The autopsy report from Duluth was supposed to be ready this afternoon. That was what Lecuyer was waiting for.

The conference room was on the second floor, with a view of the small bay, which Nyland assumed had given the hotel its name. A trim white sailboat was anchored nearby. On the other side of the bay a road headed up the slope toward a shop and an auto junkyard.

Right outside the hotel he could see some partially collapsed stone structures sticking out of the water. He wondered if they were the remains of an old dock.

Nyland turned around in his chair. "What do you think we'll learn from the autopsy report?" he asked.

"The preliminary autopsy report," said Lecuyer. "Probably not much. We'll have to wait until the samples taken from the crime scene have been analyzed. If we're lucky, they might give us a few leads. But they're being analyzed at an institute in Chicago, and the lab is really backed up. So I'm afraid it's going to take some time. At least a week, I'd guess."

"What do you think the samples might show?"

"Well, they're testing the blood that was found on Hauglie. Plus the blood that was spattered on the tree trunks. We can always hope that the perpetrator left behind some sort of biological traces."

"What do you think the murder weapon was?"

"I've rarely seen anybody killed with such force. Maybe an ax handle. Or a baseball bat. We've done a search of the lake and the river, but didn't find anything."

"Have we received any tips?"

"Two," said Lecuyer. "Anonymous, of course. You know how it is in small towns. Old grudges. Suspicion and gossip. But we're checking them out, of course. My assistant, Jason Fries, is working on one of the tips today. Out at the local Indian reservation. The other one has to do with the clerk at the Whispering Pines Motel, where the guys were staying. An anonymous woman claimed that the clerk is known to spy on the guests, and that he's a suspicious type, in general. That's why I pressured Hauglie a bit to tell us about him. I don't put much faith in the claim, but we do have to question him. After all, he was one of the last people to see Lofthus alive. And no matter what, we need to visit the motel ASAP."

"So no witnesses?" asked Nyland.

"No. Just the police officer who found the body and arrested Hauglie."

"Oh, right. Lance Hansen. So what's your opinion of him?"

Bob Lecuyer rubbed his chin as if tugging on a nonexistent beard.

"I don't know," he said. "On the one hand he gave us a detailed explanation that sounds perfectly reasonable."

"And yet . . . ," said Nyland.

Lecuyer smiled. "And yet I have a feeling that he's keeping something back. I don't know why, but sometimes you just get a gut feeling, you know? But it's quite possible that I'm mistaken, so don't take what I just said too seriously."

At that moment the fax machine started up. Nyland placed his laptop on the floor, then got up and went over to join Lecuyer, who was intently reading the paper that was coming out.

"Would you mind giving us some privacy for a moment?" he said to the young woman who worked for the hotel. She left without a word, closing the door behind her.

"What is it?" asked Nyland.

"Guess what our friend had in his stomach."

Nyland thought for a moment. "Red wine, at least."

"Right. Plus the remains of his last meal, consisting of beef and rice."

"Okay. What else?"

"Semen." Lecuyer had a pleased little smile on his face. "And this was the guy who was going to be getting married soon," he said.

"So Bjørn Hauglie had a motive," said Nyland.

"A classic motive. Jealousy."

Eirik Nyland paused to consider this. Then he said, "What are you planning to do with this information? I mean, with regard to the press conference."

"Nothing. We're keeping this news to ourselves for now," said Lecuyer.

9

DRIVING NORTH ON HIGHWAY 61, Lance Hansen heard a brief portion of the FBI's press conference on the car radio. It was ten after six, and the conference had evidently been recorded earlier. He hadn't even known they were planning to hold a press conference. Now he heard Bob Lecuyer say they hadn't yet made any arrests in the case. When asked whether Bjørn Hauglie was a suspect, Lecuyer replied that his only status was that of a witness.

"But do you have any indications whatsoever that anyone else besides those two Norwegians was at Baraga's Cross on that night?" asked a female journalist.

"I can't comment on that," said Lecuyer. Then he added that they were waiting for the lab analysis of the blood that had been found at the crime scene, and they hoped this report would provide new angles to the case.

The radio announcer then said, "The Norwegian police officer Eirik Nyland, who is in Cook County to assist the FBI and the local police, had the following to say about the extraordinary circumstances of investigating the murder of a Norwegian in the area that is sometimes jokingly called the 'Scandinavian Riviera'":

"First of all, this is a tragic case . . . as is every homicide," said Nyland, speaking with a typically British accent. "But the fact that this happened in Minnesota . . . I don't know, but maybe the public will be especially eager to help us solve the murder of a young man from the old country . . . or at any rate what many Minnesotans consider to be the old country."

And with that the broadcast segment came to an end. Lance regretted having missed the press conference when it was broadcast live on the radio a couple of hours earlier.

He drove through Grand Marais, the county seat of Cook County and a small town of approximately 1,400 permanent inhabitants, with almost as many vacationers in the summertime. He was thinking about what the female reporter had asked. Was there anything to indicate that someone else besides the two Norwegians had been at the scene of the crime that night? Nobody knew that Andy Hansen from Two Harbors had driven down Baraga Cross Road at about 9:30 p.m.— just a few hours before the murder. I wonder how Andy is feeling now, thought Lance. But it was impossible to imagine, since he had no idea what his brother had been doing down by the cross, or why he'd found it necessary to lie about his whereabouts. The question of how he was now feeling depended, of course, on what he'd been up to that particular night. For a moment the worst possible scenario crossed Lance's mind, and again he pictured that shattered skull. He had exactly the same feeling as he'd had in the hours immediately after discovering the murder—the feeling that something that belonged to him alone was about to be taken away from him. He'd noticed it right after he heard Lecuyer and Nyland talking about the murder on the radio. As if it now belonged to everybody, and yet for a few dizzying minutes it had belonged solely to Lance Hansen. That unreal sight in the birch underbrush. The tufts of hair. The sharp little fragments of bone. The teeth. The buzzing of the flies.

I still haven't started shaking, he thought.

Then he thought about Andy again. Why couldn't he have asked him outright what he was doing near the cross on that night? Tell him that lying was a risky business for someone on the periphery of a homicide investigation. He might be drawn into the very center of it. And once a person ended up there, it was often too late to admit that he had lied. At that point there might be no choice but to continue lying, and in the long run he could end up being convicted of a crime that he hadn't committed. As his brother, this was what Lance should say to Andy. As his big brother and a police officer. He should do it to protect Andy, but he knew that he wouldn't. It must be because I'm scared of the truth, he thought. More than anything, I'm afraid of hearing what Andy was really doing over there.

He drove past Hovland, where many of the buildings were in various stages of disrepair. Pretty soon nobody will be living in Hovland anymore, he thought.

In the summer of 1888 Ole Brunes and Nils Eliasen each built a small log cabin on either side of the Flute Reed River. Soon afterward their families came from Duluth to join them. A total of twelve people lived in those two cabins during the first winter. Twelve people, snowed in near the Great Lake, with Indians their only neighbors. A few years later they had a post office, school, church, boatbuilding business, and telephone exchange.

What dreams those people must have had, thought Lance. People who with their own hands had built a local community from scratch, in the midst of the darkest forest. And soon there would be nobody left who remembered that anyone had ever lived here.

The forest was taking on a more and more uniform appearance. Thin, wind-ravaged firs stood close together to create a vast darkness, the beginning of the real boreal forests that extend in a belt around the entire Northern Hemisphere, primarily through Russia and Canada, but with an offshoot stretching into the States on the northern shore of Lake Superior.

After a while he crossed the bridge over Reservation River, and on the other side he passed the sign announcing that he now found himself on the Grand Portage Indian Reservation. Nothing looked any different on this side of the boundary. It was the same evergreen forest, the same bare, rocky beaches, just like on the rest of the North Shore. Between the huge expanse of the lake and the massive, dark forests people live out their lives as best they can along Highway 61. That's what the world looks like between Duluth to the south and the Canadian border to the north. And this world continues on in exactly the same way after you cross the boundary into the Indian reservation. The same road, the same lake, the same woods. But Lance knew all too well what the conditions were like in this small community, and for that reason he always felt as if he was entering another world when he drove onto reservation land.

He turned off from the main road and drove toward the village of Grand Portage, the location of the reservation's administrative office, along with its tribal casino. He passed the school and the local grocery store, then headed down a narrow road toward the lake, past the home of Willy and Nancy Dupree. He had to remind himself that it was now just Willy's house, since Nancy had been dead for almost two years. He would have liked to visit Willy, but he could never bring himself to stop there.

At last he turned into a driveway in front of the ocher-colored house where his ex-wife had lived for the past three years; he parked between the propane tank and her old Toyota.

Then he sat in the Jeep and waited for the front door to open. He still had the same feeling of failure every time he sat here like this. It didn't help that three years had passed. Or that this was something countless other people did too. He was like so many others who sat like this, waiting outside a house they never entered. That fact actually made matters worse. Because it had been so easy for him to think that he would never be like those men who parked outside, usually on a Friday afternoon, and waited for the front door to open. But here he was again, just as he was every second Friday, the year round.

At that moment the door opened, and there they stood, both of them. He was wearing his little backpack. She leaned down and kissed the boy on the cheek. As he ran down the stairs, she gave Lance a brief smile. But it was a smile offered with the necessary restraint.

UNTIL HE TURNED THIRTY-SEVEN, Lance Hansen was more interested in the past than the future. Early on he realized that the most diverse events and relationships could be gleaned from the darkness of the past, to become part of the more or less complex web called "history." This was something he discovered as a teenager, through his close friendship with Olga Soderberg, the founder of the Cook County Historical Society. The future, on the other hand, comprised a different sort of darkness and could not be studied the way the past could. Quite simply, the future did not hold a particularly strong appeal for him.

He completed his training as a police officer at a young age. After that he first spent a couple of years working with the police force in Duluth. When the job with the U.S. Forest Service became available, he decided to apply, mostly because then he'd be able to move to Cook County. That was something that seemed natural to him, since it was the area where most of his ancestors had lived after emigrating from Norway. He viewed his own parents' decision to live in Duluth as something of an aberration.

He got the job, and after renting a house in Grand Marais for a couple of years, he bought a piece of land for a cheap price from his uncle Eddy. There he built a house on the top of the hill above Isak Hansen's hardware store, where his paternal grandfather had settled when he arrived in the United States in 1929.

But aside from these basic and very necessary things—finding a job and a place to live—he'd really had no relationship with the future. His life proceeded in the here and now, but his gaze was always looking back. The future was nothing more than days that came and went, one after the other.

Only once did he ever fall seriously in love—with Debbie Ahonen from Finland. Debbie was a tall, slender blonde who was desired by many men. In the end a police officer won her, but unfortunately for Lance, he was not that policeman. Yet before that happened, Lance had enjoyed several months of happiness that surpassed everything he'd previously experienced. There was something cool and indifferent about Debbie's facial features that made her irresistible. Being allowed to see that apparently distant young woman surrender gave Lance a sense of manhood that he'd never known before. After spending a night with Debbie, he walked differently; he noticed it himself. His gait became more like a swagger, as if he owned the ground under his feet. But then one day Debbie told him that she'd fallen in love. "Finally I'm in love too," she said. And at that moment he realized his feelings had never been reciprocated.

Debbie and her new policeman moved to California, but Lance met her one last time before she left. She said the thought of escaping Minnesota made her feel as giddy as a schoolgirl. Lance had never seen her like that before.

It took him almost a year to get over his broken heart. But the realization that she had never loved him, and the memory of that moment when she said as much to his face, had caused such a deep wound that he never entirely recovered. Even today, more than twenty years later, he could still feel a trace of the sting in his heart.

After Debbie Ahonen departed, Lance carried on his life much as he'd done before their brief relationship had started. The only difference was that he became even more actively involved with local history and genealogy, and he took on more overtime hours.

Basically he wanted to have as little free time as possible. Free time just made him more aware of how lonely he was. Because even though he had relatives on the North Shore and in Duluth, he was still very much alone. Besides, when he was working he didn't think as often about the hurtful words Debbie had said.

That was Lance Hansen's life for twelve years, a life in which the future held no meaning, existing only as the days that came and went.

But just before he turned thirty-seven, everything changed.

IN 1854 THE CHIPPEWA INDIANS, many of whom prefer to call themselves "Ojibwe" or "Anishinaabe," ceded the area of land that today makes up the northeastern part of Minnesota. All they had left were six small reservations. But at the same time, they retained extensive rights to hunt, trap, and fish outside reservation land. This led to conflicts between the Ojibwe and the white immigrants, who steadily increased in number as the nineteenth century drew to a close. In the twentieth century the conflicts increased. It was never a matter of violent clashes, but rather a long series of disagreements and individual legal cases having to do with the hunting of moose, the trapping of marten, and the commercial fishing for freshwater herring along the shores of Lake Superior.

At the end of the 1980s, as a result of the mutual wishes of both parties for a more codified relationship, the Tri-Band Authority was established. Its name was later changed to the 1854 Treaty Authority, which represents the Grand Portage and Bois Forte bands in the territory ceded under the Treaty of 1854. Its purpose is to manage, in an intertribal manner, the Ojibwe rights to hunt, trap, and fish beyond the boundaries of the reservations.

As a police officer with the U.S. Forest Service, Lance Hansen had often dealt with the 1854 Treaty Authority, and he regularly attended the meetings with its representatives. At one such meeting, shortly before his thirty-seventh birthday, a lecture was going to be held about the old clan system of the Ojibwe, and Lance thought it sounded very interesting.

When he arrived, he was immediately introduced to the speaker, Mary Dupree, almost twelve years younger than him and a teacher from Grand Portage. Her father, Willy Dupree, was a member of the Cook County Historical Society. He wasn't particularly active, but Lance had met him several times, and he liked him.

Now it turned out that he liked his daughter even more. The feeling was mutual, and they soon began going out together, often to the Gunflint Tavern in Grand Marais. Lance would drink mineral water with dinner while Mary had a glass of wine. Then he would drive her home to Grand Portage, where she lived on the second floor of her parents' home.

She was a slight, not very tall young woman—the exact opposite of Lance in terms of physical build. She wore her black hair cut short in a boyish style, and Lance never tired of looking at her sensitive face, which was so full of expression and yet so calm at the same time. She also had the most beautifully slender neck that he'd ever seen. Lance wanted nothing more than to spend all his time with her.

So they frequently had dinner at the Gunflint Tavern, and sometimes at the Angry Trout restaurant. On such evenings, after driving Mary back to her parents' house in Grand Portage and saying good night in the car, Lance would notice a strange feeling come over him as he drove south along the lake. It was in the spring and summer that the beginning phase of their relationship unfolded. The evenings were long and bright, the lake and the sky merging in a hallucinatory way so that it was impossible to see where one ended and the other began. The humidity from that enormous expanse of water filled the air with a delicate mist, and in the mist floated shades of yellow, pink, and blue, like watercolors, all of them illuminated by the evening sun hovering low in the sky. After the sun sank below the horizon, the colors darkened to violet and black.

Being a man in love, Lance found the landscape more beautiful than ever as he looked at the lake, the dark forest, the road gently winding along the shore, and the vast expanse of sky above it all. And as he drove, aware of the lake in a way he'd never noticed before, a feeling intermittently came over him that he'd been here much longer than the thirty-seven years that had passed since he was born at St. Luke's Hospital in Duluth. He actually did think of his own history as beginning in 1888, when Knut Olson arrived in the area. But that was all in his imagination, a consciously chosen way of perceiving himself in relation to his surroundings. This feeling, on the other hand, was something that suddenly flooded over him, a sense of being tied to this landscape with bonds that stretched so far back in time that his personal history lost all importance. His family's history too. As if something inside him recognized this landscape, especially the lake, in an entirely different way than he'd ever acknowledged before. A sense of belonging, aside from everything that had to do with the wave of immigration, the Norwegians who had scratched out a permanent settlement on this shore, his ancestors.

Later on this feeling would desert him, as if it had never existed at all, but during that first spring and summer, when his relationship with Mary was in its earliest phase and their shared opportunities hadn't yet begun to dwindle, Lance Hansen was present on Lake Superior in a way that he'd never experienced. When he drove south along Highway 61 on evenings like that, he felt the lake wasn't just outside the car window, it was also inside him. Not exactly in his thoughts, but rather *behind* his thoughts, or *underneath* them— something slower and more lasting that resembled a soundless monologue and was perhaps one of the most important things that made up the man who was Lance Hansen. The lake had managed to seep inside him, as if Mary Dupree had unleashed an invisible spring tide.

ON HER FATHER'S SIDE she was descended from Chief Espagnol, who is mentioned in a few written sources from the first half of the eighteenth century. So Lance liked to think of her as a "chieftain's daughter," even though he knew that was sheer nonsense. Willy was anything but a chieftain. He was the former postmaster of Grand Portage, now retired and a fanatical bingo player. Yet there was something about the way Mary talked and moved that gave her a certain dignity, Lance thought.

At the time when Espagnol, who supposedly also had Spanish blood, was chief of the Grand Portage area, the Ojibwe had already had contact with the whites for more than 150 years. As early as the 1660s, Frenchmen were making their first forays along the shores of Lake Superior. They came from Montreal, the primitive capital in the French king's sparsely populated North American colony. A small town on the great St. Lawrence River. They knew almost nothing about what lay beyond Lake Erie, but they'd heard rumors from

the Indians about a water so vast that it had no end. Some Frenchmen thought this meant it must be an ocean. At that time they were
searching for a waterway from the Atlantic to the Pacific through
the interior of North America.

The first daredevils returned without having found the Pacific,
but their canoes were fully loaded with valuable furs they'd bought
from the Indians along the shores of the newly discovered lake.
What they had hoped would be the Pacific Ocean turned out to be
what the Indians called "Kitchi-Gami," or the "big water." Soon the
Frenchmen would start calling it "Lac Supérieur."

The fur trade was enormously profitable. It involved acquiring
pelts by giving the Indians in exchange woolen blankets, rifles, gun-
powder, axes and knives made of metal, cooking pots, cloth, tobacco, alcohol, and other things the indigenous inhabitants soon felt
they could not do without. It was so profitable that strict regula-
tions were instituted. The Frenchmen considered the entire region
surrounding the North American Great Lakes to be in the Crown's
possession, and it was decided that whoever wished to buy so much
as an ermine pelt from the Indians must first purchase a license
from the French king. These licenses were expensive, and they also
required holders to pay a tax to the king of France on any eventual
profits. So it wasn't surprising that a number of men headed west
without obtaining a license. They were risking long years of impris-
onment, but the opportunities for making a killing were tremen-
dous. If only they could manage to avoid getting caught, there was
always a greedy merchant in Montreal who was more than willing to
buy their wares, since his own earnings would be even greater once
he exported the furs to Europe. There they would be used to make
expensive hats and cloaks for the aristocracy.

Many of the illegal fur traders ended up staying in the wilderness. Some stayed because a lengthy prison sentence was the only
thing awaiting them back home. Others simply discovered that they
preferred the world of the Indians to the life they had left behind.
One important reason for this was presumably the fact that many
of these illegal fur traders came from impoverished circumstances
in the feudal society of France. Among the Indians, with their more
egalitarian culture, these Frenchmen were often welcomed.

In the earliest stage of the fur trading, between 1670 and 1730,
close to a thousand such Frenchmen or French Canadians were

living among the Indians in the forests along Lake Superior. They married Indian women and had children with them. It's a fact that many of them renounced Christianity and instead embraced the Indians' religion. Some of them became medicine men and dealt in matters that would have gotten them burned at the stake if they had returned to the outposts of European civilization on the St. Lawrence River.

Yet most of the men who carried on fur trading did so legally, and the number of traders increased rapidly during the 1700s, in keeping with the rise in profit that could be accumulated after each expedition.

But there were those who continued to search for a waterway from the Great Lakes to the Pacific Ocean. For instance, a certain Pierre de La Vérendrye. In 1729 he saw something he'd long dreamed of—a map made by the Indians, showing a waterway leading west from Lake Superior. La Vérendrye believed this had to be the route to the Pacific that he'd long been searching for. The reason no white man had yet discovered this route was that the river, our present-day Pigeon River, plunges down toward Lake Superior via several huge waterfalls. In addition, the terrain is largely so inaccessible that it would never occur to anyone to try to make their way west by means of that particular river—the Nantouagan, as the Indians called it. That was true until La Vérendrye had a glimpse of the map an Indian had drawn on a large piece of birch bark. After that he was initiated into the secret that up to that time had existed like a hidden key to the vast new trapping areas in the northwest. The secret was a nine-mile-long route overland, from a position on the lake to Fort Charlotte on the Pigeon River, upstream from its highest waterfall. This was the longest of the countless routes used by the Ojibwe to carry their canoes overland. That was why they called it Kitchi Onigaming, the great portage, or in French, *le grand portage.*

La Vérendrye never found the route to the Pacific Ocean, but his discovery opened up enormous areas for trade. Soon the trading houses in Montreal started sending their men west via Grand Portage, and the most legendary epoch in the history of the fur trade had begun. Deep within the trackless American wilderness, Grand Portage was from 1730 until 1802 the center and hub of an economic system that extended all the way to cities such as London, Paris, and Moscow.

Grand Portage was of major importance, and not only because the route from Lake Superior to the hunting grounds started there. But the distance from these hunting grounds to the city of Montreal was so great that no one could make it there and back before the ice, which had released its hold on the lakes and rivers, began once more to set in. Which meant that it was easy enough to paddle the distance one way. But to maintain continuity in the fur trade, the men also needed to make it back to the hunting grounds before winter, and that proved impossible. They were able to cover half the distance, from Montreal to Grand Portage, and then back to Montreal. Or they could make their way to Grand Portage from the hunting grounds in the northwest and then return.

In other words, the operation had to be handled in two parts, and Grand Portage, the big Ojibwe portage area halfway along the route, became its hub.

The men who had spent the winter deep in the wilderness, where they had traded their European goods for furs the Indians brought them, would load up their canoes as soon as the ice melted and start paddling with their precious cargo through the lakes and rivers. It took weeks for them to reach the place where the portage began, across from the huge waterfall on the Pigeon River. There they would leave their canoes and cargo—under the watchful eye of guards, of course—and walk the nine miles down to the trading post to meet up with colleagues who had already arrived from their own winter quarters.

At the trading post they would also meet the players in the other half of the operation—the men who brought the European goods from Montreal. Every summer a constant stream of thirty-six-foot canoes, which could carry up to four tons and were usually paddled by ten men, would arrive. They brought with them rifles, woolen blankets, glass beads, tobacco, whiskey, cooking pots, axes, knives, and cotton fabric to Grand Portage. All of these wares would then be transported onward by canoe to the wilderness by the same men who had paddled their cargoes of furs to the meeting place, after the goods had been carried up those nine miles. The European goods were the currency they possessed to trade with the Indians during the coming winter. The second group, those who had brought the goods from Montreal, then took over the large loads of furs and paddled with them back to the trading houses in the city on the St. Lawrence River.

But first they spent two weeks in August conducting business, drinking, and brawling. This annual event, the so-called rendez-vous, was the very engine driving the whole system.

As the fur trade continued to expand, and especially after 1763, when France had to surrender all of its North American possessions to England and the British interests formed the North West Company, the presence of white people became more and more permanent.

The North West Company constructed a large building that was called the Great Hall, which hosted splendid parties for the company's owners, who increasingly came to Grand Portage. Their voyageurs would bring them in canoes loaded with all sorts of luxury items the gentlemen needed in order to spend several weeks in the wild. Eventually they also held their annual board meetings there.

The Great Hall stood behind a protective palisade made of sharp-tipped poles sixteen feet high, and in the evening the sounds of Celtic music could be heard, produced by fiddles, flutes, and bag-pipes. The North West Company was owned in part by Scottish businessmen. There, surrounded by the vast American wilderness, they ate steaks and drank imported wine and liquor while they dis-cussed the price of furs in London and Moscow, as well as the fash-ions of Paris.

Outside the Great Hall, beyond the sixteen-foot-high palisade, was the territory of *les voyageurs.* That was the name given to the men who traveled by canoe on one of the halves of the route—both those who paddled from Montreal and back to the city, and those who spent the winter in the forests. But the two groups always kept a certain distance between them. Each had its own camp. Those who stayed the winter had more contact with the Indians than the other whites, and they spoke their own dialect, which was a blend of French and various Indian languages. Most were pro forma Catho-lics, but it was a type of Catholicism that was heavily influenced by the Indians' spiritual world, in which dreams played a central role. The Ojibwe, for instance, made dream catchers that were meant to capture bad dreams before they made their way to the sleeper. French fur traders were presumably the first white men to see these magical objects. Many of them also practiced Indian medicine. And they often defied the rigid racial segregation that was prevalent at the time. Many had Indian wives and children waiting for them in the wilderness of the northwest. This group was dubbed *les gens du nord*—the men of the north.

The other group, those who paddled their canoes on the route between Montreal and Grand Portage, were called *les mangeurs de lard,* or the pork eaters, because they were always eating salt pork. The pork eaters were the ones who carried all the goods those nine miles up to where the men from the north had beached their canoes. The goods were packed in parcels weighing ninety pounds each, and most of the men would carry two of these parcels each time they walked that precipitous nine-mile portage. They carried everything by using leather straps that were fastened around their heads. This was something they had learned from the Indian women, who used this method for carrying all of their families' belongings from one encampment to the next. After carrying the goods up the slope, the men had to carry equally heavy loads of furs back down to the trading post. Most of these *mangeurs de lard* were poor farmers from villages outside Montreal. For them the trip to Grand Portage and back brought much-needed extra income to a way of life in which hunger was never far away.

The two groups—*les gens du nord* and *les mangeurs de lard*— never trusted one another. They often fought and maligned each other, but they were all so-called voyageurs, the canoe-paddling adventurers of the fur trade, with their own songs and stories told around the campfires. The voyageur culture continued to be French Indian, even after France lost all its possessions in North America and the North West Company took over the fur trade. In 1798, when the company was at the height of its power, it employed 50 bookkeepers, 71 interpreters, 35 guides, and 1,120 voyageurs. And nearly all of its activities were centered on the Ojibwe Kitchi Onigaming, or Grand Portage.

Because of the American Revolution and the subsequent war, the British finally had to leave this lucrative hub. They set up a new post, Fort William, about forty miles north of the border between Canada and the United States, at the place where Thunder Bay is located today. Not until 1803 did the North West Company finally leave Grand Portage for good, after having accumulated a spectacular profit over a period of several decades.

But the fur trade was dying out. This was partially because of the new fashions in Europe, but even more because the beaver

(*Castor canadensis*), which had always been the most important catch for trappers, had been practically eradicated. And it hadn't taken more than a century to achieve. The last remaining beaver populations lived so far to the west that it was no longer profitable to trap and transport them.

And what about the Indians? Some family members had lived near Kitchi Onigaming long before the Frenchmen arrived, and of course they wouldn't leave their old lands just because the white man's trading operations collapsed. They had their winter encampments in the forests, where they hunted moose and other game. In the spring, when the sap rose, they moved to their traditional sugar bush, where they tapped maple trees for sap to make syrup. Summer was the time for fishing, and they spent their days on the lake.

But their world had changed, nevertheless. The Ojibwe had become dependent on things they couldn't produce themselves, and this meant a fundamental change in their way of thinking and living.

And besides, the white people never left Grand Portage entirely. At least one trader always lived there, a man who ran a primitive trading post. During a transition period in the 1830s, the wealthy capitalist John Jacob Astor injected money into a fishing project on Lake Superior's northern shore, and a fish-processing plant was built on the remains of the Great Hall. For a while more than a hundred Ojibwe were employed in this large fishing operation, but in 1837 a financial crash put a halt to the project.

And yet Astor's investments seemed like a portent of what was soon to come. Gone was the fur trade's motley assemblage of mixed-race interpreters, bookkeepers whose hands were black with ink, medicine men who had grown up in Marseille, voyageurs with wives and children waiting for them in birchbark tepees near a river that didn't exist on any map. Gone were the voyageurs' romantic songs and the Celtic strains from the Great Hall. Gone were the dairy cows, the pigs waiting to be slaughtered, and the crates of Portuguese wine. Gone were the European Crowns' colorful flags and banners, the uniforms and drums, and cries of "God Save the King!"

Instead, something entirely different was approaching. Something that would redefine the land itself. The time of treaties was approaching. Legal provisos, signatures, and maps. Rivers and mountains and valleys were given new names. The flowers too. And the birds and fish. Everything had a new name, and the names were written down in books. And the world as it actually existed was erased and conjured into a dark spirit world.

What was approaching was the modern nation of the United States.

In 1854, after being subjected to increasing pressure for several years, the Ojibwe—or the Chippewa, as the whites called them—yielded to the demands of the U.S. government and ceded the entire region that today comprises the northeastern corner of Minnesota. All the tribe had left were six small reservations, annual payments of $19,000 for twenty years, plus a one-time bonus, to be paid in various goods.

The agreement was duly signed by the government representatives, Messieurs Gilbert, Harriman, and Smith, while the Ojibwe envoys had to make do with setting an "X" next to their names, since they did not know how to write.

They were men with names like Little Marten, Black Cloud, Otter, Eagle, Little Reindeer, Old Man, Youth, Lone Man, Northern Feather, Bear's Heart, Clear Sky, White Thunderer, and He Who Carries the Voice.

They exist in the memories of posterity by virtue of the names that were preserved on a piece of paper—the same paper that put an end to their world. Only their names are there. The men themselves disappeared, sometimes into a world of alcoholic dreams. A world of their children sent to boarding schools, and secondhand clothing from white homes; the forced planting of cabbage, mining work, ridges that resembled dead porcupines after they'd been logged, top hats, prison cells, and huge steam locomotives that carried logs and iron ore through the forests.

The Ojibwe were subjected to a campaign whose goal was to wipe out even the smallest sign of Indian culture and to turn them all into civilized Christians. It meant schools in which the language was English, and the pupils were forbidden to speak Ojibwe. Black-clad Catholic priests arrived in boats from the other side of the lake; a church was built. It meant agriculture. Orchards. It meant square houses with tarpaper roofs. Few Ojibwe would live in birchbark dwellings any longer. The government representatives even drew up a town plan according to the European model, with straight streets and a small town square. The ugly, primitive houses were then built, following this plan, which can perhaps be traced even today in the street layout in the center of Grand Portage.

This assimilation campaign sought to force the Ojibwe tribe and its way of life to its knees in a matter of a couple of decades.

Then came the immigrants. At first it was solitary men who arrived, dreaming of gold and silver. But starting in 1880 a steady stream of Scandinavians poured in. Norwegian fishermen began fishing commercially, on a scale the Ojibwe had never before seen. The Swede Charles Nelson opened a hotel at the mouth of the Poplar River and christened the entire place Lutsen, to commemorate the death of the heroic King Gustaf II Adolf at the battle of Lützen in Germany.

By the end of the nineteenth century, the virgin forests of northeastern Minnesota were rapidly disappearing. Then came the roads. In the mid-1920s the first road for automobiles was constructed from Duluth to Thunder Bay in Canada. And the cars came jolting along. The population increased, more tourists arrived. Airports were built. More white streaks appeared in the great sky above Lake Superior, stretching from one horizon to the other.

And one day at the end of the twentieth century, the policeman named Lance Hansen, descendant of Norwegian immigrants, drove along the lake with a strong feeling that he'd been there much longer than the thirty-seven years that had passed since he was born at St. Luke's Hospital in Duluth. He even had a sense that he'd been there long before his ancestors arrived as immigrants. And he knew this was all because of the young Ojibwe woman from Grand Portage.

They were married the following summer in Zoar Lutheran Church in Tofte. The wedding celebration was held in the Tofte town hall. It was one of the last times Lance saw his father feeling healthy. A few months later he found out he was suffering from brain cancer. But on that evening he stood behind the building talking to the bride's father, the gray-haired Ojibwe named Willy Dupree, retired postmaster of Grand Portage. Both men had been drinking moderately, and there they stood, talking and laughing, and it looked as if they had always known each other.

10

THE DAY AFTER Lecuyer and Nyland held the press conference, Lance Hansen and his son went to the Great Lakes Aquarium in Duluth. Lance had been wanting to take Jimmy there for a long time, but until now he hadn't thought the boy was old enough to get much out of it.

It was another hot and cloudless day. As soon as they walked in the door, the first thing Jimmy wanted was more ice cream. Lance went over to the stand, the whole time keeping an eye on his son, who was standing a few yards away, leaning against the big pillars that supported the glass roof of the aquarium. It was the boy's second ice cream of the day, even though it was only a little past noon. Lance was determined not to be one of those weekend fathers who try to compensate for their absence by stuffing the child with ice cream and sodas and animated movies. But the heat outside was nearly tropical, and the boy probably needed something to help him cool off. Besides, he'd brought Jimmy here to the aquarium, which was anything but an attempt to coddle him. This was a place for learning!

Holding the ice cream in one hand and gripping his father's hand with the other, Jimmy began looking around. The aquarium's three huge fish tanks occupied the central portion of the building. They were rather like elevator shafts made of glass, except that instead of containing elevators and people, they were filled with water and fish. This meant that the midsection of the building was open all the way up to the glass roof high overhead. Surrounding these tanks were exhibition areas on two levels, with wide stairs leading upward. From the floor above, people were leaning over the railings to look down at the crowds on the ground floor, including Lance and Jimmy.

"Wow, otters!" cried Jimmy, tugging on his father's hand. He'd caught sight of the otter exhibit, an artificial cove behind a wall of glass, fifteen to eighteen feet wide and twice as much in height, with water that was constantly trickling and running down the slope to the small but deep pool below. A couple of otters were floating on their backs in the water. Another was lying on a ledge jutting out from the slope and seemed to be asleep. When they got closer, they could see that the slumbering otter had stuffed his paw in his mouth, as if sucking on a pacifier.

As they stood there, looking at the sleeping otter and the other two in the water, a fourth animal suddenly peeked out from a hole partway up the incline.

"Look, Dad!" said Jimmy.

At that moment the otter came out to slide on its belly down the slippery wet slope, landing in the pool with a big splash. Jimmy shrieked with glee as he involuntarily took a step back so as not to get drenched, although of course the water got only as far as the glass wall in front of them.

Lance put his hand on his son's shoulder. Jimmy looked up at his father. The boy's face under the Minnesota Vikings cap displayed such undisguised joy that Lance felt an urge to lift him up and hug him tight.

Jimmy shrugged off his father's hand and pounded on the glass.

"No, don't do that," Lance told him.

"I just want to wave good-bye to them before we leave," said Jimmy.

"That's okay, but don't hit the glass. You might scare them."

"But I want them to *see* that I'm waving," Jimmy said, now a bit uncertain.

"Oh, they see you, all right. Don't worry about that."

"No, they don't," said Jimmy, pointing.

Lance saw that he was right. The otters weren't the least bit interested in the people on the other side of the glass wall.

"Well, they won't know what you mean when you wave to them," he said. "They have their own otter language."

"Really?" Now Jimmy was interested. "They can talk?"

"Uh-huh. They make otter sounds. And they make otter signals with their paws. But they don't understand human signals. For instance, they wouldn't know what to make of it if you wave."

"So what do they think it means?"

"I don't really know. Maybe it means 'I've got to pee' in otter language."

Jimmy sputtered with laughter.

"Tell me again how you say otter in Ojibwe," said Lance.

"Nigig," relied his son promptly without even pausing to think.

"You're so smart. Are they teaching you the language in school now?"

Jimmy nodded.

"Do you like it?"

The boy shrugged. "It's okay."

"Do you like school?"

Jimmy gave his father an exasperated look.

"Oh, right. Sorry," said Lance. "School is boring. I should know that. Besides, you're on summer vacation."

Crowds of people were swarming around them. There was a steady hum of voices. He wondered which things they could skip, because there was way too much to see and do. They'd never be able to cover everything in one day.

He regretted waiting so long to come back here. It had to be almost nine years since his last visit to the aquarium. Together with Mary, at the very beginning. Since then so many new exhibits and attractions had been added that he hardly recognized the place. What he did remember was the special atmosphere in the large building—all the sounds and voices, a sudden splash from somewhere, children hooting with enthusiasm. And the constant, bubbling sound of oxygen being pumped into all the surrounding tanks. Plus the light filtering through the glass roof high overhead. All of it made him feel as if he were underwater.

He suddenly recalled the dream that he'd had long ago in which he was walking on the bottom of the lake. Could it have been their visit to the aquarium that had gotten mixed in with his dream that night?

"What's an eagle called?" he asked his son. They were standing in front of a bald eagle that was perched on a tree stump behind a glass wall, regarding them with a stern expression.

"Migizi," said Jimmy. The eagle shook its head when he said the word.

Again he tapped on the glass, but more cautiously this time, using the knuckle of his little finger.

"Hi," Jimmy said in a low voice. He pressed the palm of his hand flat against the glass in greeting, but the eagle didn't react.

"His name is Birdie," said Lance, reading the fact sheet on the wall.

"I do know how to read, Dad."

"Sorry."

"Why was the eagle found on a golf course?" asked Jimmy after reading the sign.

"Well, it says that the bird fell out of the nest before he learned to fly. So the nest must have been near a golf course."

"Do they have golf courses in Alaska?"

"Of course they do."

Jimmy didn't seem convinced.

"But why is the eagle here if he was found in Alaska?"

"I don't really know," said Lance. "Maybe it's not that easy to find a home for a big bird like an eagle."

"Do they have aquariums in Alaska?"

"I'm sure they do."

"So why isn't the bird living there?"

Lance had to laugh. "You're sure full of questions today," he said.

Suddenly the eagle shot out a long, white spray of excrement.

Jimmy burst out laughing as he pointed. "Look at that doo-doo!" he cried.

"Uh-huh," said Lance. "Eagles have to take a crap once in a while too, you know."

"But the doo-doo is white!"

"That's how it is with all birds."

The boy thought about that. "Ducks too?" he asked.

"What?"

"Is duck doo-doo white?"

"Yeah. I guess it is," said Lance.

"So why doesn't the water turn white from all the duck doo-doo?"

"What do you mean?"

"When there are lots and lots of ducks in the water, why doesn't the water turn totally white from the doo-doo?"

"Jeez, I don't know. Maybe they wait to go until they're on land," said Lance. He could tell that he needed to get his son to think about something else. "Shall we go and have a look at the big fish tanks now?"

"Yes!" exclaimed Jimmy eagerly. "See you later, Birdie!" He waved to the eagle, which sat there motionless behind the glass wall.

On their way to the tanks, Lance threw away the rest of Jimmy's ice cream, took a paper napkin out of his pocket, and wiped off his son's mouth. As he stood there, leaning over the boy, he realized suddenly how much he missed the small daily routines. It was now three years since he'd lived in the same house with his son. And Jimmy had already started school. Before Lance knew it, he'd be in college in Duluth or the Twin Cities. And the only part of his son's childhood that he would have shared was every other weekend like this one.

They reached the three big fish tanks, which extended from floor to roof, two stories high, rather like gigantic test tubes. Jimmy tipped his head back to look up. Lance did too. High overhead they could see daylight through the glass roof. Above them swam scores of fish, although most of them were actually not moving. They were hovering there in the water, their streamlined shapes dark and glistening silver. Occasionally one of them would flap its fins and dart away. Lance soon noticed that there was a system to how the fish were distributed. Various types dominated different levels in the tanks. The fish at the very top were just dark shadows high above. And they were big fish, at least six to nine pounds. Trout and salmon. He also saw a couple of eels and plenty of smaller fish that he couldn't identify.

"Look, Dad!" cried Jimmy. He was pointing at something right in front of them, at the bottom of the tank.

"Look under that log."

There were lots of tree stumps on the bottom of the tank. Quite a few rocks too. Made to resemble a natural habitat.

And then Lance caught sight of the big fish lying next to a log, not moving at all. It looked like it was almost as long as Jimmy was tall. Its head was strangely compressed, so that its mouth almost looked like a duck's bill, and from its lips hung several long thread-like protuberances.

"That's a sturgeon," said Lance.

"Look, there's another one!" Jimmy pointed. "To the right of that big rock over there."

And then he saw another one. And a fourth. None of the fish moved. They were resting at the very bottom of the tank that must have been a good sixty-five feet deep. Black shapes against a black bottom. Strange, prehistoric-looking fish. Occasionally one of them would open its mouth slightly, but that was all. Otherwise they didn't budge.

"Are there fish like that in the lake?" Jimmy was almost whispering now.

"Yes, but there aren't many of them left," Lance told him. "In the old days tons of sturgeon were caught farther north. Near Hovland, for example."

"They're sure *big*," said the boy.

"Uh-huh. And they can get huge."

"Have you ever fished for sturgeon, Dad?"

"No, I don't think I have. But your grandfather might have."

"You think so?"

"I don't know, but you can ask him."

Lance raised his head to look up through all the water that was held in place by those thin but strong walls of glass. He imagined them standing next to each other on the bottom of Lake Superior, father and son, and it felt as if that was where they belonged, enveloped by the lake. He pictured the bottom of a canoe gliding above them. Paddles were dipped into the water and pulled out again, quietly and rhythmically, soundlessly propelling the canoe forward. Then he sensed the presence of ice and knew where he was. He had been here before. Not far away was a cold and shimmering blue world. The deepest spot in the lake. His thoughts and will were being pulled in that direction, toward the great icebergs that he couldn't yet see, although he knew they were very close by. He wished he could stand on that same icy lake bottom and once again see the wondrously beautiful underwater world.

But then he happened to think about Jimmy, and he took a step back. His son was still staring at the sturgeons resting on the bottom of the tank. Lance put his hand on the boy's shoulder. Jimmy turned his head and smiled up at his father. He was missing several teeth. Lance found the sight of those gaps in his mouth disturbing. At the same time he couldn't take his eyes off them.

"What's wrong?" asked Jimmy.

"I was just looking at your teeth. You've really lost a lot of them."

"Do you know what I do with them?"

"No, what?"

"I put them in a tin can and save them. I'll show them to you next time."

Lance suddenly felt a wave of nausea come over him at the thought of his son's teeth lying inside a tin can.

"What's wrong now?" asked Jimmy.

"Nothing," said Lance. "Why don't we go upstairs and check out what's up there?"

Jimmy nodded, but he still looked a bit skeptical. Lance was worried that he might have upset the boy. He took his hand. Together father and son moved away from the big fish tanks and climbed the stairs to the second floor. Jimmy discovered at once that what he really wanted to do was lean over the railing and look down at the crowds on the floor below, at the very spot where they had just been standing.

Lance had been looking forward to showing Jimmy the big model of the lakes, which was in the next room. Built on the surface of a large table, it was a scale model of the five Great Lakes and the surrounding terrain—from the St. Louis River, which runs into Lake Superior in the west, to the St. Lawrence River, which flows out of Lake Ontario in the east. Then the river runs through the former French hub in North America, past the cities of Montreal and Quebec, before it finally empties its huge load of freshwater into the Atlantic Ocean. The model also showed the various canals and locks that ships had to pass through in order to make it all the way from the sea to Lake Superior. That was one of the things he remembered from the time he visited the aquarium with Mary nine years ago. He still recalled how she had reached across the table to point at the St. Mary River, that short, shallow stretch of river connecting Lake Superior with Lake Huron. There, near the town of Sault Ste. Marie, the shipping traffic passes through an enormous system of locks. As they stood there, she had told him about the incredibly abundant fishing the Ojibwe had enjoyed at that spot long ago. She gave such a vivid account of those days, as all the while her slender hand hovered over the St. Mary River.

Even though he remembered that scene so clearly, there was

something unreal about the fact that he, Lance Hansen, had actually stood here in this room together with Mary, the woman he had loved so much. He wondered whether he would ever be in love like that again.

But before he could think any more about his failed love life, Jimmy grabbed his hand and began pulling at him. "Let's go over there," he said eagerly. "I want to look at the axes!"

He'd caught sight of some glass display cases that held old flint axes, spears, and arrowheads. These were artifacts belonging to cultures that preceded the Ojibwe. There were objects that were several thousand years old, all discovered in the area around Grand Portage. On the wall at the other end of the room hung an Ojibwe birchbark canoe.

Jimmy held up an imaginary bow and soundlessly shot an invisible arrow through the room. "Pow!" he said, as if it had struck a target in the distance. "Can I have another ice cream?"

"No, you've already had two. That's enough. No more ice cream today. But maybe we should eat the lunch we brought along. Are you hungry?"

Jimmy shook his head.

"Okay, do you want to stay here a little while longer?"

He nodded.

"What would you most like to see?"

The boy thought for a moment. "Crocodiles," he said.

Lance laughed. "The aquarium only has fish and animals that live in the Great Lakes. Crocodiles live in Africa."

He noticed that Jimmy was starting to get restless and was losing interest. He'd probably been expecting too much—it would be hard for a seven-year-old to take in everything in a place like this. But before they left, he wanted to show Jimmy the impressive view from the veranda.

"Come with me," he said. "Let's go out on the veranda over there."

"Why?" said Jimmy, sounding reluctant.

"There's a huge, superpowerful pair of binoculars out there. You might be able to see all the way to Grand Portage."

Jimmy gave him a dubious look.

"You don't believe me?" said Lance. "Come with me and I'll show you."

They made their way past the other visitors and went out to the veranda, which faced northeast. Here too there was a big crowd, and they had to wait awhile for their turn at the binoculars. Finally Lance was able to put the required three quarters in the coin slot.

"Here," he said. "Take a look and see if your grandfather is out in his boat."

"Grandpa can't go out in his boat anymore. He's too old," said Jimmy, in his most precocious voice. Then he stepped forward to peer through the big binoculars.

As Lance stood there looking at his son, it occurred to him that in a sense Baraga's Cross provided a link between the murder of the young Norwegian and the mystery of the medicine man's disappearance more than a hundred years ago. The cross had stood there since 1846, albeit in three different versions. Was it starting to take on a new meaning for him? Previously he had viewed it as a historical landmark and local tourist attraction. A destination for a Sunday outing. Barbecues and sunbathing. Listening to the clamor of kids running around and playing. Watching the water from the Cross River calmly flowing into the lake. Just one place among many—that was what Baraga's Cross had always been. On a par with the giant potholes in the Cascade River, the magnetic boulders near Gunflint Lake, or Artists' Point at Grand Marais, where pioneers and early tourists had carved their names into the soft hillside, often including the date and year.

Lance suddenly felt very alone. He realized that Baraga's Cross would continue to be that sort of place for everybody else here on the North Shore. He was the only one for whom it had started to take on new meaning. Because he was the only one who knew about both of the unsolved mysteries connected to the place. Of course, by now everyone had heard about the murder of Georg Lofthus. But only Lance knew that the medicine man Swamper Caribou had disappeared without a trace from his hunting cabin near the mouth of the Cross River on the same night that fifteen-year-old Thormod Olson almost lost his life.

What really happened on that March night in 1892? According to the version Lance had always heard, Thormod fell through the ice and nearly drowned in the frigid water. Then he had survived a night in the woods with the temperature well below freezing. That's the kind of stuff we're made of, he thought. But now the convergence, in both time and space, between that story and the medicine man's disappearance had sown doubt in his mind. And he knew his suspicions would continue to grow until he eventually figured out what happened. Lance realized that he must be the first person in his family ever to doubt the story. The family's primordial myth.

He looked at Jimmy, who was still staring northeast through the big binoculars. For a moment he questioned what he'd just been thinking. Maybe he was imagining things as a result of his recent traumatic experience. It hadn't made his hands shake, but instead maybe it had undermined his sense of judgment. Lance looked at his son standing there, the back of his boyish neck so tender and vulnerable. And he thought that he had to do everything in his power to uncover the truth about those stories. Jimmy shouldn't have to grow up surrounded by lies and deception.

I need to find out what Andy was doing that night at the cross, Lance thought.

THEY WERE DONE EATING. The empty ice chest stood open on the bench beside Lance. He was keeping an eye on his son, who was playing with a remote-controlled truck on the brick pathways in the park. Occasionally someone would stop to watch the toy for a moment. Usually older men. They seemed to be enjoying the sight of the little monster truck racing across the bricks, making an energetic buzzing sound.

Leif Erikson Park was looking its most beautiful, with all the rose beds blooming in glorious colors. There were probably more than a hundred different varieties of roses, which the Duluth Garden Flower Society maintained with both diligence and expertise so that the rose garden in Leif Erikson Park was actually considered a tourist attraction.

From the bench Lance had a view of the innermost western tip of the lake. On the other side was the town of Superior, Wisconsin. A long bridge connected the two cities.

He thought about how he'd felt like he was standing at the bottom of the lake a short time ago, and recalled the sensation of being on his way back to the cold world of ice that he'd once seen in a dream. He didn't want to think about what that might mean.

Behind him stood the statue of Leif Erikson, erected by the

Norwegian League in 1956, and beyond the statue, on the other side of the street, was St. Luke's Hospital, where both he and Jimmy had been born.

He looked at his son again. Half Ojibwe, with a drop of Spanish blood from Chief Espagnol, and a few French genes from Lance's French Canadian great-grandmother, Nanette. The other half was Norwegian American. Immigrant fishermen from Halsnøy in Norway. Jimmy Hansen was a genuine son of the North Shore. He was a descendant of both those who had come here from somewhere else and those who were already here when the immigrants arrived.

Lance got up and began packing away the few lunch items that remained on the bench. It was time to head for Lakeview to visit Jimmy's grandmother. That would complete the three items on the agenda for today's Duluth expedition: the aquarium, lunch in Leif Erikson Park, and visiting Grandmother. Tomorrow he had to drive Jimmy back to Grand Portage, but tonight they would have a barbecue outdoors, just the two of them.

He called to his son. Jimmy began walking along the brick path toward the bench where his father stood, keeping the toy monster truck going the whole time. It raced along in front of him as if to guide the way. Finally it stopped when it ran into the toe of Lance's shoe, buzzing like an insect.

11

ON MONDAY, JUNE 30, around lunchtime, Eirik Nyland and the FBI agent Jason Fries drove into the parking lot in front of the Whispering Pines Motel. Fries was in his late twenties, with dozens of tiny scars on his face, which Nyland assumed must have come from acne. He was Bob Lecuyer's assistant.

"So what's your opinion about the tip we got?" asked Nyland. An anonymous woman had called the FBI, claiming that the motel clerk was generally a suspicious type who liked to spy on the guests.

"Probably bullshit," snorted Fries. "Do you really think the clerk would have followed those two Norwegians all the way out to Baraga's Cross, and then beat one of them to a pulp? Doesn't sound very likely. Let's hope the guy has an alibi so we can stop thinking about him. It's probably just somebody who has a grudge against him. The same thing happened when I was out at the Indian reservation. That was on Friday, when you and Lecuyer were in Duluth to interview the Norwegian. Did you know there's a reservation near here?"

"I think Lecuyer mentioned it . . . and that you had gone out there."

"I had to go see a guy with a police record. A typical small-time crook. Some minor drug arrests. Drunk driving. He had an alibi, but he told me, 'I've got bad friends, and my *enemies* are even worse. Plenty of people are going to cheer if I get locked up for life.' That's just the way things are. In small communities like this, there's always somebody who's got a beef against somebody else. And they're the ones who usually call in these kinds of tips."

Fries got out of the car, and Nyland followed. The motel was an L-shaped building with long rows of reddish-brown doors. A gilded room number on each door. Identical orange curtains at all the windows. The office was at the end of the short leg of the L; a big metal sign that said "Whispering Pines Motel" was screwed to the wall next to the door. The logo was two stylized pine trees.

They went inside. The man behind the counter looked up from his newspaper. He had a dark, nicely trimmed beard and looked to be around fifty. He was wearing a cap with the words "Whispering Pines Motel."

"Welcome. Can I help you?"

Jason Fries placed both hands on the counter, as if taking possession, and said, "Are you Garry Yuhala?"

The man nodded. His name badge said Garry Yuhala.

Nyland wondered whether it was a Finnish name. Right across from the motel was the road that led to the community of Finland. He remembered that Lance Hansen had mentioned that as they drove up here on Thursday.

Fries held up his ID and introduced both himself and his Norwegian colleague. "We're investigating the murder that was committed near Baraga's Cross," he said. "The two Norwegians stayed here before they set off on their last canoe trip. Isn't that right?"

"Yup," said Yuhala.

"How would you describe them?"

"You mean what did they look like?"

"No, we know what they look like," said Fries. "What I want to know is what sort of guys would you say they were?"

"What sort? Hmm . . . I don't really know. They were just staying here. I don't talk to the guests much."

"So you're not interested in what the guests might be doing?" Nyland interjected.

"I run a motel," said Yuhala. "The only thing I care about is whether the guests pay the bill and don't wreck anything."

"What about immoral activities?" asked Fries.

Yuhala laughed. "It's none of my business what grown-ups do behind closed doors."

"But to get back to the Norwegians," said Fries, "how would you describe them?"

"I didn't really talk to them while they were here. What do you want me to say?"

"Was there any indication that they might not be getting along? Did they have any arguments?"

"No, not at all. Nothing like that."

"So where were you on the night that Georg Lofthus was killed?" asked Nyland.

"I was here until midnight. After that I left for home and went to bed."

"What time did you get home?" asked Fries.

"About a quarter past twelve."

"Is there anyone who could confirm that?" asked Nyland.

"Yes, my wife."

"Anybody else?" asked Fries.

"No. I think the kid was asleep. One of the neighbors might have seen me getting home."

"Okay," said Fries. He handed the clerk his card. "If you happen to think of anything that might be of interest to us . . ."

Yuhala nodded and slipped the card into his shirt pocket.

"Christ, I almost forgot!" he suddenly exclaimed. "Wait just a minute." He dashed out the door but was back in seconds. "Here," he said when he reappeared. "They left this behind. And I assume I should give it to you." He was holding what looked like a Bible.

"Is it in Norwegian?" asked Nyland.

"Some language I can't read, at any rate," said Yuhala.

"Let me see." Nyland took the dark-green, leather-bound Bible and opened it. On the title page was an inscription written in an elegant, old-fashioned hand: "To our dear Georg on his Confirmation day. From Grandmother and Grandfather (1 Tim 4:4)."

For a moment Nyland pictured in his mind a white-painted church. A spring day in Vestlandet, maybe no more than five years ago. The grandparents in attendance to see their grandson confirmed.

"What does it say?" asked Fries.

"It's a dedication from his grandparents. The Bible belonged to the dead man. A confirmation gift."

"Isn't that a Bible verse in the parentheses?" Fries went on.

"Yes. First Timothy chapter four, verse four," murmured Nyland hesitantly as he ran his fingertip over the table of contents. "Paul's first letter to Timothy," he said in Norwegian, which made Yuhala raise his eyebrows in bewilderment.

"Is there anything else you haven't told us?" asked Fries.

"No, that's it," said Yuhala calmly.

They said good-bye to the clerk and left. Nyland carried the Bible. He had stuck his finger inside, to mark the place. When they were back in the car and about to put on their seatbelts, Fries said, "So what exactly does it say, that Bible verse?"

Nyland opened the Bible and read the quote first in Norwegian and then translated into English. "For everything created by God is good, and nothing is to be rejected, if it is received with thanksgiving."

"Hmm. And you said it was from his grandparents?"

"Yes."

"It doesn't tell me much," said Fries.

"Me neither," said Nyland. "But it must have meant something, or why would they include it in the inscription?"

12

THAT SAME DAY Lance Hansen was on his way to Two Harbors to visit his brother. He didn't know what to think about the fact that Andy had been in the vicinity of the crime scene on the night in question. Maybe he'd be able to find out something by talking with him in person.

As Lance drove, he plucked a heart-shaped Dove chocolate out of the bag and carefully peeled off the thin foil wrapper with his fingernails before he stuffed the chocolate in his mouth. Then he smoothed out the wrapper and held it up so he could read the message on the back.

"Follow the compass of your heart," it said.

Lance snorted scornfully. He'd already followed that particular compass one time too many. It wasn't worth following, any more than an ordinary compass was in this part of Minnesota. There was iron just below the surface of the ground everywhere in the Arrowhead region. The iron was an extremely magnetic type, so the needle of a compass had a tendency to point in all the wrong directions.

He caught sight of someone at the end of the long, winding road stretching out before him. A person was walking along the road. That in itself was a remarkable sight. Of course there was no law against walking down this part of Highway 61, and on rare occasions a tourist might choose to walk here instead of taking one of the many beautiful scenic paths in the area. But this person was different. Lance could see that at once. There was nothing the least bit ordinary about this man, who looked as if he'd stepped out of another era. It must have been his clothes that gave that impression. His jacket and pants seemed to be several sizes too big, and they were worn shiny. On his head he wore a round, wide-brimmed hat, which had also obviously seen better days. He looked like an old-fashioned tramp. Lance noticed that the face under the hat brim appeared to be covered in soot, as if he'd spent a long time sitting in front of a fire.

What a strange-looking man, Lance thought. As a police officer, he always noticed people who stood out in some way, and this man definitely seemed out of place. For a moment he wondered whether he ought to drive after him and warn him to be careful, because the traffic could be dangerous for a pedestrian. Just have a little chat with the man, as he often did with people if for some reason he had doubts about them. In the course of a brief conversation Lance was usually able to determine whether the individual was on the level or not. Most people were okay, some were not.

But he decided to keep heading south toward Two Harbors. There has to be a limit, he thought. And there was no reason to be overzealous about what the obligations of his job entailed.

Skunk Creek runs through Two Harbors. Large sections of the waterway now pass through pipes underneath the town, but in a few places it still flows in the open. When there's a heavy rainstorm, the creek overflows its banks, giving off a smell that matches its name. It's not really the smell of a skunk, but it's just as foul, and no one has ever been able to find a viable explanation for the smell. But some people think it's because Skunk Creek runs along the cemetery, so when it overflows it carries large amounts of soil from the graves. If this theory is correct, it means on certain days it's the stench of several generations of Scandinavians that makes it difficult to breathe freely in the small town of Two Harbors, on the shore of Lake Superior.

He turned in to the local Dairy Queen and approached his brother's house from the rear. The family's Ford Freestar was the only vehicle around. Andy's old Chevy Blazer was gone. It didn't look like he was home yet from work.

Lance parked, then got out and rang the doorbell. Soon he heard someone hurrying across the floor somewhere inside the house, and then the sound of the door to the hall opening. A moment later Tammy Hansen opened the door. She failed to hide her surprise at seeing her brother-in-law standing there. It took her a couple of seconds to muster a strained smile of welcome.

"Lance! Good Lord. Come in," she said, her voice loud and shrill.

He took off his shoes in the hall and followed Tammy into the kitchen.

He couldn't remember ever being in this house without the TV blaring. This time it was the game show *The Price Is Right.* The studio audience was howling with laughter at something the host had just said.

"Andy's not here," said Tammy.

Lance could barely hear her over the TV.

"Is he at work?"

"What?"

She seemed stressed.

"Is Andy still at work?" Lance repeated.

With a look of annoyance she went into the living room to turn down the sound. Lance followed her. "Did you want to talk to Andy?" she asked.

"Yes. Is he here?" Lance said.

He could hear a rhythmic thudding bass line coming from somewhere in the house.

"No, but he should be home pretty soon. Would you like a cup of coffee or something?"

He noticed that she was trying to play the role of hostess, though not very successfully. She just couldn't be anything other than what she was.

"Sure, thanks. A cup of coffee would be great," he told her.

Tammy went back to the kitchen without inviting him to have a seat.

He sat down in one of the two easy chairs. Hanging on the opposite wall was the usual collection of family photographs. And of course there was a picture of Jimmy as well, taken when he was two years old. Lance looked at the photo, thinking that he had been living in a different world back then. It seemed incredible that only five years had passed since that picture was taken.

Tammy soon returned with a mug of coffee. She set it in front of him on the coffee table and then sat down on the sofa. It was a U.S. Forest Service mug, the kind sent as Christmas gifts to the major logging contractors.

As Lance raised the mug to his lips, he noticed a couple of un-dissolved specks of instant coffee stuck to the inside of the mug, just below the rim. He blew on the hot liquid and then set down the mug.

"Need to let it cool off for a while," he explained.

Tammy took a pack of cigarettes from the newspaper rack underneath the coffee table. She shook one out of the pack and lit up.

"Well . . . ," she said and then took a long drag on her cigarette.

She exhaled a whole cloud of smoke. Lance watched as it rose in the sunlight that filled the room. He waited for her to say something more, but she didn't. The maniacally pulsating bass continued to thud.

After a while Lance said, "So, what's Andy up to these days?"

"He's logging over by Inga Lake," replied Tammy. "He should be here in half an hour. Is there something wrong?"

Lance laughed off the question. "Does there have to be something wrong for a man to visit his family?" he said.

He hardly ever came over to have a chat with his brother. He really never came into this house at all. The only exception was when deer season was approaching. Going out hunting on the second weekend in November was the only thing that the two Hansen brothers still did together. But today was June 30, and deer season was light-years away.

"Is it about that dead guy?" she asked.

"Er . . . yes . . . partially," said Lance.

Tammy gave him an expectant look. He remembered that at one time she'd actually been quite pretty. Now she looked like a person who had seen it all, even though she'd hardly seen anything outside of Two Harbors.

"I want to talk to him about Chrissy."

"What's she done now?" she asked anxiously.

Lance held up his hands to reassure her. "Relax," he said. "Chrissy hasn't done anything. But we've got a killer loose on the North Shore. At least, that's a possibility. We don't know for sure. But everybody needs to be cautious about where they let their kids go, how late they're allowed to stay out, and things like that. Not that I think there's any imminent danger, but you can never be too careful, right?"

He looked at Tammy. He had finally managed to get her attention.

The bass sound kept on thudding.

"My God," she said. "A killer on the loose!" She put her hand to her lips for a moment, as if to underscore the drama of the situation. "And Chrissy wasn't even home on the night of the murder! From now on, she's not going to be allowed to spend the night anywhere but here at home. At least until the murderer is caught."

"So where was Chrissy on that night?"

As soon as he asked the question, Lance wished that he hadn't. "I mean, she wasn't anywhere near the cross, was she?" he added.

"Of course not," said Tammy. "She was spending the night with a girlfriend in Duluth." She took another drag on her cigarette and blew the smoke in a thick stream out into the room. "And I was here all alone!" she said, as if she'd been in real danger. "Andy went out to the cabin to go fishing. I didn't hear about the murder until he and Chrissy came home later in the afternoon."

"He and Chrissy?" said Lance. "But I thought she was in Duluth."

"She was. Andy went to Duluth to pick her up before he came home."

"Oh, right. Doesn't she have a driver's license by now?"

"Sure. But we don't like to let her use the car. At least not the Freestar. It's okay for her to drive the Blazer, but Andy likes to have it available. He says it's perfect for driving on the forest roads around here."

"So he drove her to Duluth on Tuesday and then picked her up on Wednesday? Sounds almost like the old days when she was taking lessons . . . What was it? Ballet?"

"Well, dance lessons, anyway. But I was the one who always drove her there and back. And Andy didn't drive her to Duluth on Tuesday either. A girlfriend did. She came over and picked up Chrissy. Andy just went to get her in Duluth on Wednesday."

Suddenly she seemed to get suspicious, or at least found the situation a bit odd.

"So how are *you* doing?" Lance hastened to ask. He knew that almost everybody likes to talk about themselves. Especially people who sit home alone on a beautiful summer afternoon, watching game shows on TV.

"I'm okay," she said. "I just try to go with the flow. It's not that easy with a daughter who's seventeen, and a husband who's . . . well, who's . . . *Andy*," she said.

It didn't sound like a joke, but Lance couldn't help laughing, and this time his mirth was genuine.

"Sure. It's not easy for any of us," he said.

"But we're doing fine," she said. "I mean, we have our disagreements, just like everybody does, but we stick together. We're family."

Lance didn't know whether she'd intended to hurt him with that remark, but it made him think about Jimmy and Mary again.

"My God, you're the one who found the body. Isn't that right?" she suddenly exclaimed.

"Yep," said Lance. He had no desire to talk about that.

"Was it awful?"

"I could have done without the experience."

"Poor you," she said. "I would have been totally . . ." She held up her hands and pretended to be shaking all over.

"No, actually it didn't make me shake," said Lance. He instantly felt that he'd said something too personal. But Tammy merely raised her eyebrows in surprise.

At that moment the music stopped. The constant, monotonous bass notes that had been playing in the background were gone.

"Finally," she said, listening.

But after a few seconds it started up again, although the beat was different.

"Okay, that's enough." Tammy got up. "I'm just going to have a few words with that young lady," she said, and left the room.

Lance could hear her going out to the hall and then climbing the stairs to the second floor. He grabbed the mug from the table and took a few gulps of coffee. It was actually quite good. Then he heard a door open upstairs. After a few seconds the volume dropped. He thought about what he'd told Tammy, that she and Andy needed to look out for Chrissy. It was actually just the best excuse he was able to think of at the moment, to explain why he'd come over to talk to his brother. But now he wondered whether there might be some truth to it after all. Not that it was the reason for his visit, but they needed to be extra vigilant with Chrissy because there might be a murderer on the loose in the area. That wasn't something he'd thought of before. Up until now he hadn't really thought about the fact that the person who had killed the Norwegian might be a threat to other people. Not since he'd stood there in the woods, staring down at the naked corpse, the bashed-in skull. Not since he stood there in that swarm of flies. At the time, he'd had the feeling that whoever had done it presented an overriding threat to him personally. And he might be killed there and then. But a few minutes later the other Norwegian had turned up again, and Lance had taken charge of the situation. Then the sheriff had arrived with his team and taken over. And now the case was in the hands of the FBI and Inspector Eirik Nyland.

While this whole development was under way, it had never once occurred to Lance that he or anyone else might be in danger because the killer was still on the loose. But that was what he was thinking now. Because he didn't believe that Hauglie had killed his friend. At least, that was what he'd said when Nyland wanted to know his opinion. And if Hauglie was innocent, that meant a killer was still out there somewhere. So it would be best to keep an eye on all the kids. He decided that he needed to call Mary and ask her to be extra strict about not letting Jimmy go out alone. He was probably being overcautious, but better safe than sorry, Lance thought. And he decided to phone her later that evening.

Suddenly the music was turned up again. It sounded even louder than a few minutes ago. He heard Tammy slam the door to Chrissy's room and stomp down the stairs. When she came into the living room, she had calmed down a bit. She stubbed out her cigarette in an ashtray, meticulously grinding it out with her thumb, as she shook her head and tried to smile at the episode.

"Damn that kid!" she said. "You have no idea what it's like. Just wait. In a few years you'll have to go through it yourself."

"I know," said Lance, trying to sound sympathetic.

"But maybe boys aren't as bad," Tammy went on. She directed a scowl at the ceiling, as if she could see right through the wooden beams and into her daughter's room.

"It's probably just her age," said Lance.

Tammy sat down on the sofa with a groan. "It's more than her age, let me tell you," she said. "That girl is . . . I don't know . . ."

Lance thought she was going to cry. He'd actually never seen Tammy like this before. But then, he hadn't spent much time with her over the past few years.

She picked up the cigarette pack from under the table and lit up again. The bluish smoke curled lazily in the sunlight. In the background the game show on TV had started up after a commercial break. A middle-aged woman was ecstatically jumping up and down as she covered her face with her hands. Lance was glad that he didn't have to listen to her. He was trying to think of something friendly to say to Tammy when they both heard the front door open.

It took a few seconds before Andy was standing in the doorway. He looked from Lance to Tammy and then back again. "Hmm . . . ," he said.

Lance waited for him to say something else, but he just stood there, staring at them. He had on worn jeans and a T-shirt. On his head was an old Minnesota Twins cap. He looked exactly like what he was: a man who had just come back from working in the woods. Again his gaze shifted from Lance to Tammy and back. Lance noticed that this created some sort of connection between him and Tammy. As if it were them against Andy.

"Lance wants to talk to you about Chrissy," she told her husband.

He noticed a change in his brother's face, something that appeared and then quickly vanished. What was that? As if a wave of something had moved across his features. Tammy didn't seem to have noticed anything. Lance knew he'd seen that happen before, but he couldn't remember when or where.

"Since we might have a murderer loose on the North Shore, we need to keep better watch over our kids," he said. "That's basically what I wanted to say. Maybe you shouldn't be allowing her to go out in the evening right now. Not that I think there's any reason to panic, but you can never be too careful, right?"

Finally Andy stepped forward from the doorway and came into the living room. He sat down in the other easy chair, raised his cap, and ran his hand through his sweaty, thinning hair. Then he put his cap back on.

"Chrissy isn't going to be out in the evenings anymore," he said. He suddenly seemed to become aware of the music blaring from upstairs. He tipped his head back to stare up at the ceiling. "As you can hear, we'd know if she wasn't home."

Tammy was now perched on the edge of the sofa, her back straight as she fumbled nervously with her cigarette. Her eyes were fixed on the TV screen, which was showing a commercial for lawn-mowers.

"Does she have any plans for what she's going to do after she graduates from high school?" asked Lance.

"No. But you know how kids are." Andy threw out his hands. "I'm sure she'll find . . . her niche."

"She just needs to get a job," said Tammy. "It would be a waste of time for her to go to college."

Lance took a gulp of the now lukewarm coffee. He set the mug back on the table and looked at his brother. There was an alert expression in his blue eyes. Maybe also a slight wariness. Lance didn't look away, as he normally would have done. He felt that there was an opportunity here, in that look. An opening. Could he ask Andy what he was doing at the cross that night? What would happen if he asked the question? That much was obvious. He would deny it. Andy would deny ever being there, no matter how Lance pressed the point. If it were something Andy could have talked about, he would have already mentioned it. In any case, he wouldn't have come over to the ranger station the way he had done, to lie in the presence of the whole staff. And since he'd already started lying, he would keep doing that here. Besides, Lance would have played his best hand the minute he asked that question. Then Andy would know his brother had seen him that night.

"If she gets herself a job, then at least we'll know where she is. Right?" said Tammy. "You never know with college students."

Andy turned to look at her. "You don't know what you're talking about," he said. "Chrissy is sharp as a tack. Of course she's going to college."

Lance could see that the moment had passed. The opening that had been there between Andy and him was now gone.

"And what do *you* know about it?" said Tammy.

"About what?"

"What it takes to get an education."

"Just as much as you do," said Andy.

Lance didn't have the patience to sit there and listen to the two of them squabbling. He cleared his throat and managed to catch Andy's attention. "So you came from the north when you left work, right?" he asked.

"Yeah."

"Did you happen to notice a strange guy walking along the road?"

Andy frowned.

"My guess is that you would have run into him a little north of Silver Cliff."

"I don't recall seeing anybody along the road. What do you mean by 'strange'?"

Tammy got up, her back rigid with annoyance, and headed for the kitchen without saying a word.

"I don't really know, but he looked sort of like an old-fashioned tramp," said Lance.

Andy shook his head. "No, I didn't see anyone like that. I don't think there was anybody walking along the road at all. Is it important?"

"No, no. I was just wondering who he was. I've never seen him before. No, it's just the cop in me being curious."

The front door slammed again as Tammy left the house. The two brothers exchanged glances. Andy grimaced in resignation. Soon they heard her start up the car and drive off.

"So how's it going with the investigation?" he asked. "The homicide case, I mean. Everybody's talking about it. Have they found out anything yet?"

"I've got nothing to do with it," said Lance. "I'm just a witness, since I was the one who . . . who found the body." He looked his brother in the eye as he spoke these words. Andy looked away. "But as a cop, I can't avoid hearing rumors," he added.

"Really?" said his brother.

"Uh-huh. Police rumors. But of course you realize that I'm not allowed to discuss such matters."

"Sure, but . . . a murderer is on the loose, as you said, and a man has to think about his family."

"I understand that," said Lance. "But it's a strict rule . . . the vow of silence that I, as a police officer—"

"Did they find the murder weapon yet?"

"To be honest, I have no idea. But there's one little secret that I can tell you, as long as you promise to keep it between us."

Andy nodded.

"From what I understand, they now think there was a third person at the crime scene," said Lance. "Someone saw a car in the vicinity. At the parking lot near the cross, I think. But as I said, I've only heard rumors, and they need to be taken with a grain of salt."

Andy leaned forward, propping his elbows on his thighs. "A third person? I thought it was his friend who did it."

"In this case, apparently we can't be sure about *anything*," said Lance.

He noticed that his brother had that strange expression on his face again. The same one that had appeared and then vanished so quickly when Tammy said that Lance had come over to talk about their daughter. He knew he'd seen that look before, but he still couldn't remember where or when.

13

EIRIK NYLAND WAS SITTING AT A WINDOW TABLE in the South of the Border café in Grand Marais, gulping down his second cup of coffee of the morning. He had a dull headache, as he always did whenever he hadn't had enough sleep, and he'd forgotten the bottle of Excedrin in his hotel room. On the plate in front of him were the remains of an omelet. Across the street was the Grand Marais Liquor Store and Hank's Hardware. It was seven in the morning on Tuesday, July 1.

Just before five he'd awakened from a dream that he'd had many times before. The details weren't always exactly the same, but the dream always followed the same general pattern. Eirik's two daughters, Elsa and Marie, who are eleven and thirteen, respectively, are walking down the road toward the bus stop, and he's standing in the living room, watching them. He's home in Asker, and everything is completely normal. The two girls are headed off somewhere together. Sometimes to handball practice. Other times they're going to visit their grandparents in Drammen. Or they're going to a movie. This time they are going to band practice. Neither of them has ever played in the school marching band, but in his dream they do. So he is watching them walk to the bus stop, headed to band practice. As he stands there, a car slowly drives past the house, moving in the same direction as the two girls. A slow-moving car always appears in this dream. And always driving in the same direction as Elsa and Marie. Yet each time it comes as a complete surprise to him. He watches the car move slowly past. It's so quiet that he can hear dirt and gravel crunching under the tires. The driver looks up at the man in the window. Nyland meets his eye. It doesn't last more than a couple of seconds. Yet he knows that he has seen this man before. And just as the car has almost caught up with the two girls, he remembers where he knows the man from. He was a suspect in a homicide case, but the police never managed to find enough evidence to charge him. This murder case exists only in the dream, but in that context it is utterly real. It has to do with two girls who disappeared. Later they were found, sexually assaulted and killed. He runs out to warn his daughters. He has no shoes on. In the dream he is always standing in his stocking feet on the road outside their house in Asker, looking toward the bus stop. But the car and the two girls are gone.

He never woke up screaming or sweating from this dream. But he had the feeling that something inside of him had been destroyed. This was the only time when Eirik Nyland had the sense that his work wasn't good for him. Somewhere inside, it was taking its toll, as evidenced by the recurrent dream.

On this occasion, as usual, he found it impossible to go back to sleep. He lay in bed for a while, listening to the soothing sound of Lake Superior. He was so far away from Vibeke and the girls. But then he calculated that it was already noon in Norway, so he phoned home to talk to Vibeke. She and the girls were just about to leave for the cabin. He'd forgotten that they were going to Lillesand this week. He also spoke briefly to his daughters. After hearing their voices, he immediately felt better. Once again he felt connected to the normal world.

Then he got up, took a shower, and dressed before going down to the lobby to find out if it was possible to have breakfast. But it was still an hour until they started serving. The desk clerk suggested that he try the café in Grand Marais that opened for breakfast at 5:00 a.m., so Eirik got into his rental car, a red Subaru Forester, and drove over there.

Now he was sitting in the café, annoyed with himself for forgetting the Excedrin back at the hotel. The headache wasn't letting up, even though it wasn't really bad yet. If it didn't go away, he'd have to buy some more painkillers as soon as the drugstore opened. He thought he'd seen one on his way into town.

There was something slightly unreal about sitting here and

looking out at the street, nearly deserted at this hour of the morning, in a small town in Minnesota. Unreal, but at the same time pleasant. On the paneled walls all around him were old advertising posters and framed photographs of proud men holding up fish to show off what they'd caught. Most of the pictures must have hung there for decades. He guessed that the place had to be from the forties or fifties. He slid the palm of his hand over the worn vinyl of the booth as he thought about the steady stream of customers that must have passed through the café since it first opened. All those local residents who were now dead. A couple of generations of grouchy old men. Maybe young men had passed this way in the sixties and seventies, on their way to Canada, to hide out during the Vietnam War. He knew that many had fled to Canada for that reason, and he could easily picture this café as the place for one last American meal before they crossed the border, not knowing when they'd be able to return home. But criminals on the lam must have also passed through here, he thought. Men who had left their own lives and that of others in ruins. And that immediately got him thinking about who had killed Georg Lofthus.

He was leaning toward the idea that Bjørn Hauglie, overcome with jealousy and despair because of his lover's approaching marriage, had lost control and killed Lofthus. The extreme injuries that the dead man had suffered indicated that the murder had been a crime of passion. And so far they hadn't found any evidence of a third person being at or near the crime scene.

That was the present status of the case on this Tuesday morning, July 1, six days almost to the hour after Lance Hansen had found Georg Lofthus's badly beaten corpse near Baraga's Cross. They had spent much of the ensuing time obtaining information about the movements and activities of the two Norwegians. And even though Nyland's main responsibility was to handle anything having to do with Norway, he had gone out into the field several times along with Lecuyer and Fries. They went to cafés, motels, and various stores that the two canoeing enthusiasts might have visited. Nyland had the impression that the sudden appearance of a Norwegian police officer in the North Shore area was big news. Other than the motel clerk, Garry Yuhala, at the Whispering Pines, most of the people he'd spoken to were of Norwegian ancestry. And they were more than willing to talk to him. A few even seemed reluctant to let him go. Because of this local interest in all things Norwegian, there were a lot of people who remembered the two Norwegian tourists. But there was nothing in the information the FBI had gleaned that could move the investigation forward. At least not yet. No one had noticed anything special about the young men. Except that they were Norwegian, of course. And in good spirits. Several people had made a point of mentioning this. On the other hand, nobody could recall seeing the Norwegians with anyone else. It was always just the two of them.

On the basis of this information, Lecuyer and Nyland had formed quite a good picture of the Norwegians' movements. But not included were the hours after they left the Whispering Pines for the last time, and up until Georg Lofthus's death. For that time frame they had only Hauglie's own explanation to go on, and they didn't trust what he'd told them. On the contrary. Hauglie was their only suspect. They had agreed to arrest him and charge him with the murder if it turned out that the samples taken from the crime scene contained DNA solely from the two Norwegians. According to Lecuyer, they could expect to receive the results of the tests sometime during the week. No matter what, Nyland would have to stay until they had a chance to interrogate Bjørn Hauglie again. So far they had interviewed him only once. Before they talked to him again, they wanted to be one hundred percent sure that it was his semen they had found in the stomach of his friend. Apparently they'd know the results of that test by tomorrow. It was a simple test that would be done in Duluth. After it was determined that the semen belonged to Hauglie, they would confront him with this news, and then he'd have to tell them the truth about the canoeing vacation. And this was regardless of whether another person's DNA was found at the crime scene or not. No matter what, Bjørn Hauglie had withheld important information regarding the case—he hadn't reported the fact that the two men were lovers. Provided, of course, that it wasn't another man's semen that had been found in Lofthus's body. But they considered this possibility to be purely theoretical. So once this issue was resolved, Nyland had to see to it that Hauglie told the truth.

Later today he and Fries were going to the town of Finland, which was where the two Norwegians had stayed for a while before moving to the Whispering Pines Motel at the end of their trip.

In Finland they would talk to the manager of the Blue Moose Motel and the employees who worked in the area's only bar.

There wasn't much they knew with any certainty. But Lecuyer and Nyland did have a theory. They surmised that these two Christian young men had been lovers for a long time, although they were constantly filled with a strong sense of guilt for living what they thought was a sinful life. They may also have tried to end their relationship several times, but without success. In a desperate attempt to be "normal," Georg Lofthus had gone out and found himself a girlfriend. The fact that she also belonged to the same Christian group of young people—which mandated that everyone remain celibate before marriage—must have been advantageous for two reasons. First, Lofthus could claim her as his fiancée without being required to have sex with her. Second, the vow of celibacy guaranteed that she would want to get married as soon as possible, because then she could have as much sex as she liked—and with God's blessing.

Nyland thought about the Bible the clerk at the Whispering Pines had given them, with the inscription from the grandparents to the newly confirmed Georg Lofthus that invoked a passage from St. Paul: "For everything created by God is good, and nothing is to be rejected, if it is received with thanksgiving." Paul's first letter to Timothy. He thought there was a certain tolerance in those words that was completely lacking from the rest of the case. What was it Bjørn Hauglie had said to Lance Hansen? *"Kjærlighet."* Wasn't that it? Yes, Lance had reported hearing Hauglie say the Norwegian word for love, a word that he recognized. He knew what it meant in English. It was the first thing Hauglie said as he sat there next to the cross, in shock and covered in blood.

Thinking about Lance Hansen suddenly made Nyland remember something Bob Lecuyer had said. He was talking about the impression he'd had when he was interviewing Lance. A feeling that the Forest Service officer was holding something back. "I have no idea why. Sometimes you just get a gut feeling," he'd said. Nyland tried to think of anything suspicious that Lance might have said or done as they drove from Duluth to Tofte, but nothing came to mind. The man had made a solid impression. Nyland had liked him at once. But according to Lecuyer, there was reason to be suspicious of Lance Hansen.

Nyland took his notebook from the inside pocket of his jacket and then got out the business card that Hansen had given him before they parted outside the Bluefin Bay Resort that first evening. "If there's anything you want to know, just give me a call," Hansen had said.

The foremost thing Nyland wanted to know, of course, was who had killed Georg Lofthus. Even though he and Lecuyer had a theory about the homicide, they weren't positive that Hauglie had done it. Nyland also wanted to know if there was any credibility to Lecuyer's suspicion that Lance Hansen was holding something back. No matter what, Hansen was a man who possessed extensive knowledge about the area. Maybe he knew something important even though he might not be aware of its significance.

Nyland looked at Hansen's card with the phone number. He decided to call him later in the day.

The middle-aged waitress came over to ask if he wanted a refill. In one hand she held the coffeepot, and in the other a dishrag for wiping off the tables.

"Sure, thanks. Just half a cup," he said.

She filled his cup almost to the brim. "There you go," she said. And then, after a second's hesitation. "You're from out of town, aren't you?"

He gave her a smile. "You can certainly say that again."

"From Europe?"

"Norway."

"Are you kidding?"

"No, I'm not."

"I'm Norwegian on both sides of my family," she said.

Nyland leaned forward and pretended to be looking at both sides of her. "Amazing!" he said.

She snapped the dishrag at him with a coquettish grin.

"But apparently there's also some Swedish blood mixed in, way back in time somewhere," she added.

He laughed, but made no move to check out this additional information.

"Poor you, so far away from home," she went on. "Don't you have anybody here to look after you? To show you around and everything?"

Nyland shook his head.

"And it's going to be the Fourth of July soon. On Friday, you

118

know. Stars and Stripes and the whole shebang. You really *have* to see the parade and the fireworks. Have you ever seen a Fourth of July celebration before?"

Again he shook his head.

She patted him lightly on the arm. "You're going to *love* it," she told him. "Promise me you'll stay in Grand Marais for the Fourth of July. Promise?"

"I promise," said Nyland, holding up his hand, as if taking an oath. "What's your name, by the way?" he asked.

"Martha."

He was just about to say that Martha wasn't a Norwegian name, but he changed his mind.

"Martha Fitzpatrick. My maiden name was Vollum. That's a Norwegian name, isn't it?"

"Sounds a hundred percent Norwegian to my ears," said Nyland.

"I got the name Fitzpatrick because I married an Irishman."

"From Ireland?"

"No, from Duluth. He was originally from Chicago, but he lived in Duluth. Probably still lives there, as far as I know. Oh, here I go again, talking on and on about myself!" she said. "I apologize. I'll let you drink your coffee in peace."

"No need to apologize. It's nice talking to you," said Nyland. "I don't really know many people in Minnesota."

Martha Fitzpatrick laughed. "Well, I still better get back to work," she said. "Enjoy your coffee." Then she went back to the men eating breakfast in the other room. It was obvious that several of them knew her.

Nyland watched as she talked and laughed with the customers as she briskly and efficiently made her way among the tables with the coffeepot and dishrag. What a job, he thought. Starting work at the crack of dawn every day, serving these people breakfast, wiping off their tables, and laughing at their jokes. Always the same little café in the same small town. He wasn't sure whether he thought that was nice or depressing. Maybe it was both.

Through the windows in the larger section of the café he saw a police car pulling up to park in front. A moment later Bill Eggum, the sheriff of Cook County, came in. He nodded to a few customers, exchanged a few words with Martha Fitzpatrick, and then headed for a table.

Nyland raised a hand in greeting.

"Hey, good morning!" said Eggum. "Didn't expect to see you here. It's quite a drive."

"Yes, but I woke up too early, before they started serving breakfast at the hotel."

"Me too," said Eggum. "I mean, I got up before my wife was awake."

Nyland laughed briefly. It was still too early in the day for any sort of boisterous response.

"Mind if I join you?" said the sheriff. He was wearing his official hat and his sheriff's badge on his shirt.

With a wave of his hand, Nyland invited Eggum to sit down. The sheriff squeezed his stout body into the booth, then took off his hat and placed it on the seat next to him. His shiny bald pate looked sweaty. He glanced around and caught sight of Martha, who was already headed toward them. Nyland noticed that she wasn't carrying a menu.

"Morning, Bill. What'll it be?" she said.

"Two fried eggs, bacon, sausage, and hash browns," the sheriff immediately replied.

"Toast?"

"Rye."

Martha repeated his order and received an affirmative nod. "I'll be right back with your coffee," she said and went back to the other room.

"Okay, great," said Eggum as he stared vacantly out the window, clearly still trying to wake up.

The two men had met on a daily basis, but never without other police officers present. The sheriff had regularly stopped by the Bluefin Bay to see Lecuyer and Nyland and inquire about the latest developments in the case. Lecuyer thought he was a nuisance. Nyland had no opinion, one way or the other, about Bill Eggum. He thought the man seemed almost a parody of a provincial law enforcement officer, but otherwise he hadn't spent any time or energy thinking about Eggum. But now it was just the two of them, sitting here in a booth in a café called South of the Border.

Martha came back with the coffeepot and a cup, which she filled for Eggum. "All right now," she said. "Things are starting to look up. What about you?" She held out the pot toward Nyland, but he placed his hand over his cup.

"No, thanks," he said. "Otherwise I'm going to have to ask you for some Valium. That coffee is powerful stuff."

Martha laughed and was about to leave, but she suddenly thought of something. "So I guess you're not entirely without friends here in Minnesota, after all," she said, nodding to the sheriff.

"Sheriff Eggum and I are working together," Nyland told her.

"Oh?" she remarked, her eyes wide.

"This man is a famous homicide detective from Norway," said Eggum.

"Is that right?" exclaimed Martha.

"Only the part about being a homicide detective from Norway," said Nyland.

"Are you here because of that terrible thing that happened near Baraga's Cross?" she asked in a low voice.

Nyland nodded.

"I can't believe what some people can do," she said. "Just imagine killing a Norwegian!"

Nyland couldn't help laughing.

Martha looked at him in alarm. "But don't you agree? Don't you think it's simply unbelievable?"

He had no idea what to say.

"Don't go taking over the whole investigation, now," said Eggum.

"All right, but if it was up to me, the guilty party would end up getting a beating that he wouldn't soon forget."

"I have no doubt about that whatsoever," said the sheriff.

Martha Fitzpatrick pretended to give him a playful slap. It was obvious that they had known each other for a long time.

She went back to the other customers, leaving the two policemen on their own.

Nyland wondered if he might glean something useful to the investigation from this unexpected tête-à-tête with the sheriff. It was amazing what he could sometimes discover if he just let people talk.

"Eggum?" he said, as if appraising the sheriff's surname. "You must have Norwegian roots too. Am I right?"

The sheriff had, in fact, never talked about such matters before. In that sense, he was unlike all the rest of the Norwegian Americans in the region.

"Yep, you're right. Norwegian on my father's side, and that's where the name comes from. But I'm actually mostly Swedish. My mother's maiden name was Seagren."

"Must have been originally Sjögren in Swedish," said Nyland.

"I'm not sure about that," said the sheriff. "I don't speak Swedish. But I do remember the tale behind the name. It was one my grandmother's favorite stories. Three young Swedish emigrants sailed from Europe to America. I don't recall anymore what their names were. Anyway, it was a really difficult voyage, on board an old steamship. With stormy weather pretty much the whole way. The three young Swedes stuck together, through thick and thin. Worst of all was the seasickness. They threw up more than they'd ever thrown up in their lives. Before they were even halfway across the Atlantic, their stomachs were completely empty, but they kept on throwing up all the way to New York. At a certain point they actually thought their last hour had arrived, and so the three made a pact. If, in spite of everything, they managed to survive—and they didn't have much hope that they would—each of them would take a name in the New World that would remind them of the trials that they'd been through. They agreed to take names that included the word 'sea.' When they finally set foot on American soil, they had decided on the names Seaberg, Seaholm, and Seagren. Young Mr. Seagren was my great-grandfather. At least I think so. Or was he my great-great-grandfather? Well, no matter what, that's what happened. Do you think it's a true story?"

Eirik Nyland thought it sounded like a typical immigrant story, but he didn't want to say that.

"It sounds plausible enough," he said.

"Yeah, I think so too," said Eggum.

Nyland could hear from the tone of his voice that not everyone had the same faith in the tale.

"Are there some people who question whether it happened that way?" he asked.

Eggum uttered a resigned groan. "You know how it is. Some people read so much they end up all fuzzy-headed."

"Oh, really?"

"Have you met Lance Hansen, the man who found the dead body?"

Nyland nodded.

"Well, Hansen is a kind of local historian. And for the most part, his knowledge is impressive. But he thinks he knows everything about the immigrants who came to these parts, and that no one else has anything to contribute. If it hasn't been recorded and approved by Lance Hansen, then it's not worth knowing."

Eggum shook his head in dismay at the very idea.

"And Lance Hansen doesn't believe the story about how the Seagren name originated?"

"No. Do you know what he did?"

"No. What?"

"He laughed right in my face. Then he asked me whether I really believed in stories like that."

"That really doesn't seem . . ." Nyland tried to appear indignant.

"No, I agree. And the story isn't all that unlikely, is it?"

"Not at all."

"I personally know about stories that are ten times less likely, but they can still be verified as true. Stories in my own family."

Nyland had no desire to hear any of these stories. At least not right now. It was too early in the morning for more of Eggum's family anecdotes.

"This Hansen that you mentioned," he said.

"Yeah, what about him?"

"What's your honest opinion of the man? I mean from a professional point of view. Since he's our most important witness."

Sheriff Eggum seemed astonished by the question. He paused to think for a few seconds and then said, "Lance Hansen is a good man, both personally and as a police officer. That's something everybody knows. He might seem a bit eccentric when it comes to matters of history, but otherwise I can't think of a single reason to criticize him."

"Okay. That was the impression I had of him too."

They sat there for a few minutes in silence. The sheriff finished his coffee. Then Martha appeared with his breakfast. Fried eggs, bacon, sausage, and hash browns. The greasy smell coming from the plate made Nyland feel a bit nauseated. He declined yet another offer of coffee and then kept his eyes fixed on the window as the sheriff ate his breakfast. He thought the man ought to be able to enjoy the first meal of the day without somebody watching him.

As he stared out the window and listened to the sheriff chewing, Nyland noticed that he had started to feel quite at home here in Cook County. So far he'd been focused on getting up to speed on the case and establishing a good working relationship with Bob

Lecuyer and his assistant, Jason Fries. But now, on his fifth morning in Minnesota, Eirik Nyland had the distinct feeling that he liked it here. Maybe because of the lake. He saw it every day, both when he was driving around and from the windows of the conference room at the Bluefin Bay Resort, where the FBI had set up their central command post for the investigation. He could even see the lake from his hotel room. And it had been within sight the whole time he drove up here to Grand Marais early this morning. He had seen the sun come up over the quiet, smooth surface, which began right below the road and looked as if it continued on into space. Or maybe he had started feeling so comfortable here because of the people he'd met.

He let some more time pass before he glanced over at Eggum and concluded that it looked like the sheriff had finished eating. A few hash browns and half a piece of toast were all that remained on his plate.

"Good food?"

"Mmm," said Eggum almost reverently.

"There's one thing I've been wondering about," said Nyland.

"What's that?"

"Is there a drugstore nearby? I've got a headache."

Eggum nodded. "When you drive back to Tofte, there's one on the right-hand side, just as you're leaving town. The drugstore and souvenir shop are in the same building. Look for a sign that says 'Viking Hus.' By the way, my niece works in the drugstore. A great gal. I think they open at nine." He glanced at his watch. "It's five past eight right now," he said, and then downed the last of his coffee. "So I'd better get over to the office."

NYLAND STAYED UNTIL JUST BEFORE NINE O'CLOCK. Then he drove over to the drugstore, which, as far as he could tell, shared a front entrance with the souvenir shop.

He parked his car and went inside. The first thing he saw was a big poster in the hallway. It was a drawing of a man with a dripping red nose, and the text above read, "Ask your pharmacist!" In Norwegian. He'd seen the same poster at his own drugstore back in Norway, but he seemed to recall that it had been a few years since that particular advertisement was in use.

Could the thin, dark-haired woman behind the counter be Eggum's niece? She looked like she was almost the same age as the sheriff, so he doubted it. She wore a badge that told him her name was Deb Nelson.

"I need something for a headache," he said. "I've been taking something called Excedrin, and it works fine."

Deb Nelson got him a bottle of Excedrin. "Anything else?" she asked.

Nyland was about to say "no, thanks" but then he thought about Vibeke and the girls. He really should bring something home for them.

"Is it true that this is also a souvenir shop?" he asked.

"Through that door over there." Deb Nelson nodded toward a closed door at the other end of the drugstore. "I haven't had time to open the shop yet, but come with me, and I'll let you in."

Nyland put the pill bottle in the inside pocket of his jacket and followed her.

She stuck a key in the lock and unlocked the door. "Feel free to go in," she said. "I'll be back in a minute."

The first thing he saw was a bunch of hunched trolls wearing knitted tunics. On the walls hung decorative plates with pictures of the Norwegian king and queen, and others with pictures of the Swedish royal family. Coffee cups and serving platters with traditional Norwegian rosemaling designs. Cuckoo clocks with the same floral designs and an array of wooden moose. Decorated rolling pins, mangles, and cheese slicers. There was also a long row of rosemaling-painted wooden horses, which he had always thought were a Swedish tradition, not Norwegian. Weren't they called Dala horses? And of course there was a large selection of stickers, key rings, T-shirts, and other items bearing various messages. He read a few of them. "Pray for me, I'm married to a Norwegian!" "Being married to a Swede builds character." "Lutefisk: It separates the real Scandinavians from the bleached blondes!" "World's Greatest Farmor!" "Kiss me, I'm Swedish!" "Got sisu?" "Made in America (with Norwegian parts)." "How do you tell an extroverted Finn? He's looking at *your* shoes instead of his own."

Through the window he saw a logging truck slowly rumble past, making all the decorative plates and glass Viking ships rattle. He thought he ought to buy something. After all, he'd made her open the shop. But was there anything here that his daughters or Vibeke would like, if only as a joke?

He gave a start when he noticed someone come up behind him. Deb Nelson had come in. She was standing there without saying a word. She was evidently the sort of person who didn't speak unless spoken to. And her movements were constrained to the very minimum. It looked as if she rehearsed every gesture, as if she'd once taken a course in how to avoid drawing attention. Nothing should disturb a customer involved in considering an important purchase. It made Nyland feel very uncomfortable.

"I'd like that one," he said, pointing to a glass Viking ship.

"Certainly," said Deb Nelson.

"They're much cheaper here than in Norway," he explained.

"Ah, Norway . . ." The words seemed to slip out, but then she quickly controlled herself. "Sorry," she said, and disappeared out the door, presumably going to the storeroom.

Nyland picked up the glass object and peered at the price tag. It was a ridiculously expensive amount to pay for bringing home a Norwegian souvenir from abroad, he thought. But he didn't think he could change his mind. He was going to have to buy it, and the Viking ship was no worse than anything else in the shop. It was actually a nicely made glass Viking ship. Nothing wrong with that. It just seemed like a meaningless object to bring home from the States.

Deb Nelson returned with a small box. She took off the lid to let him see the glass Viking ship inside. It was nestled on a bed of soft tissue paper.

He nodded.

"Shall I wrap it for you?" she asked.

"That's probably a good idea," said Nyland.

He watched as she wrapped the box, soundlessly and with a minimum of movements, as if this too was something that she'd learned at a course in how to avoid drawing attention.

When she finally handed him the beautifully wrapped gift, he thanked Deb and bowed politely. He knew full well that he couldn't give Vibeke a glass Viking ship, but he was still glad he'd bought it.

They went back to the drugstore together. Behind the counter stood a tall, blond woman, whom he guessed to be about forty. Pinned to the left side of her ample and voluptuous bosom was a name tag: Cynthia Seagren.

He raised his eyes to meet hers. Cynthia Seagren smiled—the sort of smile offered by women who are used to being admired. He stood there with the Viking ship under his arm and thought about the story that Bill Eggum had told him, about the three Swedes who had crossed the Atlantic so long ago, throwing up the whole way. In front of him stood a direct result of that wearisome voyage. The three immigrants would have undoubtedly thought it was well worth the effort if they could have seen Cynthia.

14

THE SUN HAD COLORED THE LAKE an almost artificial-looking blend of yellow, pink, and violet. Soon the violet would darken and erase the other hues, until finally everything would turn to black. But it would be a while before that happened.

Lance was sitting at his desk at home looking at a photograph. He'd taken it out of a folder of old photos from the Soderberg archives. Each folder usually contained eight pictures, and he'd already gone through about twenty of these folders.

The photo he held in his hand showed a man standing in a small clearing in the woods. According to the accompanying text, he was standing on a path. He wore pin-striped trousers. They almost look like suit pants, thought Lance. His jacket might also pass for an old suit coat. Worn and wrinkled. He had his thumbs hooked in his suspenders and was staring truculently at the photographer, whoever that might have been. The text in the folder, written in Olga Soderberg's florid script, said, "Joe Caribou on the path leading to his mother's house, 1905."

There was no photo of Swamper Caribou in the archives. This picture of his brother was the closest Lance was going to get to the medicine man who had disappeared. Joe looked like someone who hadn't slept in a long time. The photo was taken thirteen years after his brother had vanished. The path to his mother's house, thought Lance. From the picture it wasn't possible to determine where the house was located. Somewhere in Cook County, he assumed. Maybe on the reservation, or near Grand Marais. Maybe somewhere else altogether. The path, which was barely visible in the picture, no long existed, of course. The house it once led to probably didn't either. The photo showed a long-deceased man standing on a path that had grown over ages ago, on his way to a place that no longer existed and would be impossible to reconstruct—the small home of an old Ojibwe woman in possession of old stories that had also been forgotten.

Thirteen years earlier this man's brother had vanished without a trace. It was this missing brother that Lance was searching for. He wanted to find out how Swamper had died—which was something no one knew. It seemed like an almost hopeless task, so many years after the man had disappeared. So far the only thing Lance had to go on was the information he'd found in the *Grand Marais Pioneer*. First and foremost, there was Joe Caribou's statement to the editor. He had said that his brother disappeared "from his hunting cabin near the mouth of the Cross River around the time of the last full moon, which was on the night of March 16." But this quote was not strong enough evidence that Swamper had vanished on that particular night. "Around the time of the last full moon" indicated that Joe wasn't exactly sure when his brother had gone missing. It might be give or take a couple of days, thought Lance. He also had the brief article from September 2 of that same year, which reported that a body had been found near the mouth of the Manitou River, but it had been impossible to establish the victim's identity. Lance assumed that the body of Swamper Caribou had been found. The current must have carried it the ten or so miles during the six months since he had died.

He put the photograph down on the desk and took another one out of the folder. This picture showed four young men in a photographer's studio. Two of them sat ramrod-straight on chairs, slightly turned toward each other. Behind them stood the other two men, their arms hanging straight at their sides. All four had big, workman hands that seemed much older than the rest of their bodies. They wore dark suits, and all of them had close-cropped blond hair. Under the picture Olga Soderberg had written: "Duluth, 1904. Four from Tofte visiting town. From left: Helge Tofte, Andrew Tofte, Thormod Olson, and Sam Bortvedt."

There sat Thormod Olson twelve years after he fell through the ice. If that was what actually happened, of course. Lance wondered whether the man staring at the camera knew the truth about Swamper Caribou. Or was the whole thing merely a coincidence? But it was the convergence of time and space that made Lance suspicious. The fact that both events—Swamper's disappearance and Thormod's night of terror, which, according to the family mythology, he should not have survived—took place around the time of the full moon in March 1892, near the mouth of the Cross River. But again he was confronted by the same lack of hard evidence. Because even though Thormod Olson was trekking through the moonlight, it didn't mean that he necessarily fell through the ice on the night when the moon was full. Here, too, there might be some leeway in the chronology of plus or minus a couple of days. And the fact that he fell through the ice "near the mouth of the Cross River," as Lance had always heard, didn't provide very exact information either. But it was impossible to tell anything from the face staring so resolutely at the camera in a photographer's studio in Duluth more than a hundred years ago.

Lance continued to study the two pictures. Three of the young men in the photo taken in Duluth had no role in the chain of events that he was trying to uncover. But Joe Caribou and Thormod Olson did. The one nicely turned out and blond, with big workman's fists, twenty-seven years old. The other with black bowl-cut hair and a solemn face. How old must he have been? If the photo had been taken recently, Lance would have guessed that Joe was about sixty, but presumably he hadn't yet turned forty. He looked as if he could have turned stone to dust, just with a glance. At the same time, he looked worn out. His face grimy and puffy. Was he an alcoholic? That was quite possible, considering how widespread alcoholism had been among the Indians back then. But it was impossible to determine from this one photo. Maybe pain made him sleep badly. He might have had rheumatism, for example. Or a plethora of other illnesses and complaints. Migraines. Nightmares. Or maybe economic worries were keeping him awake at night. Because as he stood there on that path that had long since been taken over by weeds, he looked like a man who hadn't had a proper night's sleep in a very long time.

Lance imagined Joe Caribou turning on his heel and continuing on his way through the woods as soon as the picture was snapped. Somewhere farther on was his mother's house. That was where he was headed. What had they talked about? Did they discuss

Joe's brother, Swamper, the medicine man? Who knows what they might have found out during the course of those thirteen years that had passed since he disappeared. Information could have come to the Ojibwe tribe via channels that were inaccessible to the newly arrived Scandinavians. But what could they have done if they thought someone had killed Swamper? Would the local police force even have cared? The truth was that a lost cow would have stirred greater interest than a missing Indian. Even one who had been well liked by the first editor of the local newspaper. A missing Indian was simply not something that required attention, thought Lance. Indians disappeared. There was nothing to be done about it. Besides, that chapter would soon be closed. He was fully aware that this was the general opinion of the times. But that wasn't how people thought anymore. At least Lance didn't. Swamper Caribou was entitled to justice.

At the same time, he knew that this was not the whole explanation behind his interest in the matter. There was something else, presumably even more important, although he wasn't fully prepared to admit it. He knew that he would never have started examining old murders in Cook County if not for the murder of the young Norwegian. "Has this ever happened before?" Mike Jones had asked as they stood there in the parking lot a few hours after Lance found the dead man. That was when it began. But now the mystery of Swamper Caribou's disappearance had become so interesting all on its own that he no longer made any effort to differentiate one motive from another. All he knew was that he would never have any peace until he found out what happened at the mouth of the Cross River in March 1892.

Again he looked at the two photographs. The blond Thormod, twenty-seven years old, staring with a steely expression into the camera lens in Duluth. Did he know what happened to Swamper Caribou twelve years earlier? Was he carrying around a big secret? Naturally it was impossible to tell such things from the picture. Just as it was impossible to guess what Joe Caribou and his mother had talked about when he arrived at her house in the woods.

There was one thing that Lance had wondered about ever since he found this photo of Joe. How did Olga Soderberg know that he was "on the path leading to his mother's house"? Somebody must have told her that. And who owned the original picture?

he wondered. All of these pictures were copies. Was there a list of who had supplied the originals? In the folder, each photo had been assigned a number. Underneath the empty plastic sleeve belonging to the Joe Caribou picture, the label said: "No. 0127: Joe Caribou on the path leading to his mother's house, 1905." What did these numbers refer to? Hadn't he once seen a list? It should have been included with the folders of photos, but it wasn't there.

He spun around on his desk chair and gave a kick to propel it over to the wall where the archives were stored. There was nothing to do but start looking. First he searched the spot where the photo folders belonged, although at the moment they were spread out haphazardly on his desk. When he didn't find anything, he got up from his chair and began a systematic search of the shelves. He kept finding things that he wanted to pull out and study more closely, even though he'd seen everything before. He never tired of looking through the archive materials. For instance, he had copies of all the annual reports of the Great Lakes Bank, which existed from 1911 until 1929. He also had minutes of proceedings and game results for the Cook County Timber Cruisers, a baseball team that was active between 1905 and 1951. He knew he'd find Norwegian and Swedish names mentioned everywhere, but almost nothing about those who had lived here before the Scandinavians arrived. The people who had been here all along.

For a moment he ran his fingertips over the worn spine of the diary belonging to his great-grandmother Nanette, the so-called French diary. He wondered what she had written about. Probably the weather, as well as her hopes for her children. Yet what sort of hopes could they really have had in the wilderness where they lived? That the children would not die too young?

Right above the French diary he found what he was looking for. A few sheets of paper inside a ledger, mistakenly filed among the folders containing handwritten recipes. He pulled the ledger from the shelf. The label said "Photo Index." The list began with the number 0001 and went all the way up to 0168. Next to each number was a brief description of the picture. For example, number 0019: "Duluth, 1904. From left: Helge Tofte, Andrew Tofte, Thormod Olson, and Sam Bortvedt." And under the text it said: "Photo credit: Palmer Stevenson, Duluth. Owner: Gus Tofte." Lance scanned a couple more pages until he finally came to what he was looking for:

"No. 0127: Joe Caribou on the path leading to his mother's house, 1905." And underneath: "Photo credit: Unknown. Owner: William Dupree."

The sight of his ex-father-in-law's name made Lance feel as if something had opened up inside him. Some sort of valve. Something opened, and then it closed again. It didn't last more than a second. It made him think about all the times he'd driven past old Willy Dupree's house and thought that he really ought to stop by for a chat. But after he and Mary got divorced, Lance had found it impossible to knock on Willy's door.

When he met Mary, he already knew her father through the historical society. Willy had never been an especially active member of the group. He would occasionally show up for a meeting or an excursion, although without making any contribution other than his presence. But if someone asked him anything about the Ojibwe and Grand Portage, he usually had a ready answer.

Lance looked at the picture of Swamper Caribou's brother. If there was anyone who might know something about the missing medicine man, it would be Willy Dupree. And this photo had come from Willy. But Lance couldn't recall his father-in-law ever mentioning Swamper Caribou or the ghost stories about him. Even though he didn't believe in ghosts, Lance thought it would be interesting to know more about those stories. They might contain fragments of actual occurrences, he thought. Details that might point to what really happened back in March 1892. Suddenly this all seemed quite plausible to him. Even though Willy, as far as Lance could remember, had never mentioned Swamper Caribou, he still had a feeling that Willy must be aware of the ghost stories that circulated among the Ojibwe. He was also curious as to why Willy owned an old photo of Swamper's brother, Joe. Maybe someone in his family had known the two brothers. That was not at all unlikely. On the contrary. The local Ojibwe band was not very big.

Thinking about his ex-father-in-law reminded Lance that he needed to phone Mary. That was something he'd decided yesterday, while he was visiting Andy and Tammy. It wouldn't hurt to take some extra precautions with our kids, he had thought. Now he glanced at his watch. It was just a little past nine. He grabbed the phone and was about to tap in her number, but then he hesitated. What was he really supposed to say? That she needed to take better care of their son? Oh, right. That was bound to go over well. Or should he say that there might be a murderer on the loose in the North Shore, and it was possible that he'd strike again? Like in some horror movie? He hung up the phone. I don't need to call her, he thought. But he felt a small pang of guilt, and wondered whether he should do it after all.

At that moment the phone rang.

"Hello?"

"Am I speaking to Lance Hansen?"

He could hear at once that it was the Norwegian policeman calling.

"Yep."

"This is Inspector Eirik Nyland."

"Oh, hi. How's it going?"

"Fine, thanks."

"Is there anything I could do to help?"

"I don't know whether I mentioned it when you picked me up at the airport, but I think I have relatives here in Minnesota," said Nyland.

"No, you didn't tell me that. Do you know where they live?"

"Well, not in this area. Minneapolis, I think."

Nyland speaks really good English, thought Lance. That was something he had noticed when he picked up the detective in Duluth. He had a distinct British accent, of course, but that was probably how they were taught to speak the language in Europe.

"Well, that's pretty common," he said now.

"I suppose so."

"There are as many Norwegian Americans as there are Norwegians."

"Good God . . . But I was just thinking that since I'm here in Minnesota anyway . . . well, it's tempting to have a talk with an expert on such matters. Maybe you could give me some tips on how to locate any possible relatives."

"I don't know about *expert*," Lance said, laughing, "but I do know how to go about a search like that. Of course I do."

"That's what I was thinking. Could we meet one of these days? At a café, for instance?"

Lance doubted that Nyland had learned to speak English so fluently in Norway. He wondered if the detective had studied abroad.

"Wait a minute!" he suddenly exclaimed.

"What?"

"This may sound strange, but . . . Do you happen to speak French?"

Nyland hesitated. "Well . . . I don't really *speak* French anymore, at least not much. But I do understand a little. Why do you ask?"

Lance used his feet to scoot his desk chair over to the shelves holding the Soderberg archives. Carefully he took down Nanette's diary.

"I've got a diary here that's written in French, and I can't understand a word of it. Do you think you could help me out with a little translation? Just for fun. A few sentences here and there. And in return I can tell you how to go about finding your relatives in Minnesota."

"A diary, you say?"

"Yes, it belonged to my great-grandmother. She was French Canadian."

"But I thought all of your ancestors were Norwegian," said Nyland.

"She's the one exception. The rest are all Norwegian. But what do you think? Maybe we could have a beer, over here at my place. If that suits you, I mean. You probably have a lot to do."

"No, that actually sounds very nice," said Nyland. "Let's see now. Today is Tuesday, isn't it?"

"That's right."

"Shall we say Thursday evening? Day after tomorrow?"

"That sounds great," said Lance. He had to restrain himself from sounding too eager.

"So where exactly do you live?"

"It's the easiest place to find in the world. A couple of miles north of Tofte is Isak Hansen's hardware store. A red wooden building right on the road."

"I've seen it."

"Okay, well, you take the road next to the store. The gravel road. Just follow it to the end, and that's where you'll find me."

After hanging up the phone Lance remained where he was, holding the old, leather-bound book in his hands. Cautiously he opened it and looked at the convoluted handwriting covering the pages. He couldn't read a single word. But one thing he did understand: the year on the first page was 1890, and somewhere toward the end of the book was the year 1894. He'd seen those two dates before, without giving them much thought. But while he was talking to Nyland, something had begun to dawn on him. Apparently a glimmer of an idea had already appeared while he was looking at the photographs of Thormod Olson and Joe Caribou. At last it seemed perfectly clear to him that somewhere in his great-grandmother's diary entries there must be a description of fifteen-year-old Thormod's dramatic arrival.

15

IT WAS THE MORNING OF WEDNESDAY, JULY 2, exactly one week after he discovered the murder. Lance was at the ranger station in Tofte. He was standing in the lobby, waiting for District Ranger John Zimmerman to arrive with some documents that the two of them needed to look at before Lance could get in his car and head out. But Zimmerman was busy with something in one of the nearby buildings. From what Lance understood, it had something to do with the firefighting crew.

He was leaning against the information counter, drinking coffee from the usual mug that he was always given whenever he came in. The receptionist, Mary Berglund, was standing behind the counter, talking on the phone. Lance let his gaze wander around the room without really taking anything in. He'd seen it all so many times before.

"All right. Would you like more coffee?" asked Mary when she was done with her phone call.

"No thanks," said Lance. "I've had too much already."

For a moment neither of them spoke.

Then Lance said, "So, what do you think about Zimmerman?" The remark was mostly meant just to pass the time. He'd been waiting a long time for the ranger, and he was feeling bored.

"Oh, Zimmerman," said Mary with both respect and admiration in her voice. "Now that's a worthy district ranger, let me tell you. I think we're extremely lucky. Especially the ladies," she added after a pause for effect.

Lance gave an obligatory smile. "If you say so."

"You don't agree?" said Mary.

"About what?"

"You don't think he's a handsome man?"

"Why would you think I'd know anything about that?" replied Lance.

"Hmm. But what a way to start off a new job," she remarked.

"You can say that again."

"It's been exactly one week today," she went on.

Lance nodded.

"I knew right from the start that it had something to do with sex," said Mary.

He gave her an uncomprehending look.

"The unnatural kind, that is," she continued.

"Oh, you mean . . . But we don't know anything about that," said Lance. "The fact that both of them were naked could have lots of different explanations."

"Like what?" asked Mary, wagging her head coquettishly.

"Well, for example . . ." But he couldn't think of anything. "Lots of different things."

"So you don't know about it?" said Mary.

"About what?"

"That they made an unusual discovery."

Lance had to laugh.

"It's nothing to laugh at," she told him. "And don't think I'm just spreading gossip."

"No, of course not," he said.

But Mary didn't notice the sarcastic undertone, or maybe she just didn't care.

"I have it on the highest authority," she said.

"Oh?" Lance was suddenly interested. "Who would that be?"

"I heard it from Zimmerman."

"Zimmerman? But he has nothing to do with the investigation."

"He heard it from Sparky Redmeyer. Whoops, I shouldn't have told you that," she added.

"Okay, but what is this discovery that they've made?"

Mary rolled her eyes, as if hinting that Lance ought to know, but she didn't really want to say it out loud.

"I don't get it," he said, confused.

Again she rolled her eyes.

"You know . . . ," she said.

"No, I don't," said Lance.

Then Mary leaned across the counter and put her face close to Lance's. He smelled chewing gum or toothpaste.

"They made a biological discovery in the dead man," she said.

"They've found some sort of biological evidence?"

Mary nodded solemnly.

"On the dead man?"

"No, *in* the dead man," she told him. "In his stomach," she added. And again she rolled her eyes, as if that would make Lance realize what she was talking about.

At that moment John Zimmerman arrived. "Hi, Lance," he said. "Sorry you had to wait. But Mary has been keeping you entertained, right?"

He winked at Mary, who immediately got busy with the ever-present coffee mugs.

"Mary tells me that they've made a discovery in the murder investigation," said Lance. "Some sort of biological evidence. What'd they find?"

"You must be talking about the semen."

"I am?" said Lance, startled.

"Yeah. They found semen in the victim's stomach," said Zimmerman. "I thought everybody knew about it by now," he added. "Especially after I told Mary."

He seemed completely nonchalant about discussing these matters.

"Good God," said Lance. "Does that mean they were . . . homosexual?"

"Well, it'd be hard to explain the discovery in any other way," said Zimmerman. "He couldn't have ingested it by accident, if you know what I mean."

Lance didn't know what to say. It was all so far beyond what he was used to discussing.

"What did I tell you?" murmured Mary Berglund. It wasn't really clear what she meant by that.

"Huh," he said, glancing around as if looking for something or someone. "The whole thing is dang strange."

Zimmerman chuckled. "But I wanted to see you about those

documents, Lance. Why don't you come in my office, and we'll have a look at them."

Lance followed the ranger down the hall to his office. Zimmerman leafed through some papers on his desk as Lance stood and waited.

"Do you know where Seven Beaver Lake is?"

"Of course," said Lance. "It's just north of Finland." He found the question ludicrous. As if he, Lance Hansen, wouldn't know where Seven Beaver Lake was.

After a moment Zimmerman found what he was looking for. "Here," he said, handing Lance a document.

The heading on the page said: "Complaint regarding use of campgrounds at Seven Beaver Lake." He quickly read through the text. It was a typical letter of complaint sent to the U.S. Forest Service. A man from St. Paul claimed that someone had put up "a permanent-looking structure" approximately a hundred yards east of the campgrounds. The site was covered with litter. "Empty liquor bottles, beer cans, toilet paper, and condoms," he read.

"Do you know which campground he's talking about?" asked Zimmerman.

"No. There are several at Seven Beaver Lake."

"It's campground number one-three-four."

"That's the one at the south end, right? Near the creek?"

Zimmerman consulted the large framed map that hung on the wall behind his desk.

"Yeah, that's right," he said.

"Okay," said Lance. "Then I guess I'll drive out and pay a visit to the Finns."

In the lobby he found Becky Tofte, who was the purchasing agent for the station, talking to Mary Berglund. Becky was married to Fred Tofte, whose great-grandparents had come over from Halsnøy in 1902 and were included in the group photograph that hung on the wall in Lance's home office. Becky was born and raised in Lutsen. Lance and Becky had been friends since childhood because his family had spent so many weekends and summer vacations in Lutsen.

"How's it going?" she asked.

"Back to the normal routines," said Lance. "Which is just fine, if you ask me."

Becky gave him her most dazzling smile. "Uh-huh. Routines are great, aren't they?"

"Actually, they are."

"That's the way I like things, at any rate," Becky went on. "Knowing exactly what I need to be doing. Not just today, but tomorrow and next week, and even next year, for that matter."

Lance nodded in agreement. That was the way he liked things too.

THE STRUCTURE turned out to be far less "permanent-looking" than the man from St. Paul had claimed in his letter. It was a rickety shack with a pitched roof covered with tarpaper and sod. Inside Lance found a bunch of candy wrappers, a couple of discarded potato chip bags, an empty Lucky Strike packet, five beer cans, an empty Jack Daniels bottle, and a copy of *Hustler*. Lance inspected the surrounding area as well but found only more empty beer cans. As usual, the complaint letter had exaggerated the situation. For instance, the man had stated that he'd seen condoms and toilet paper, but Lance didn't find anything like that. He figured a couple of teenagers had been out here, drinking and looking at porn.

Normal porn magazines, with pictures of naked *women,* he thought, and he felt his annoyance with John Zimmerman surge. He actually liked the new ranger, and he'd had a good first impression of the man, but when he thought about how he'd talked about the discovery . . . semen in the *stomach.* Lance didn't want to think about that. Zimmerman, on the other hand, had *joked* about it. He'd teased Lance for being so sensitive. And not just Lance, but seemingly everybody who lived here. People accepted Zimmerman for who he was, but in turn he needed to accept them, including their attitudes about what was right and wrong. He didn't have to agree with them, but there was a big difference between disagreement and scorn, thought Lance. And he'd felt the scorn in the way Zimmerman had laughed at his reaction.

Lance opened the porn magazine and took a quick look at some of the photos. He found them more surprising than exciting. What amazing inventiveness, he thought. None of it looked like it had anything to do with reality. At least not the reality Lance Hansen knew. But the fact that teenage boys enjoyed looking at these kinds of magazines seemed to him perfectly normal. Just as the rest of this place did. It was a typical teenage hideout. He couldn't even count the number of similar places he'd seen over the years. But it was still illegal, and he took his time pulling the little shack apart. He tossed the trash, including the big sheets of tarpaper, into the back of his pickup. He stuck the porn magazine under the floor mat on the passenger side so that nobody would see it. Then he decided to stop at the nearest café and have lunch.

FIFTEEN MINUTES LATER he drove into Finland, passing the twenty-foot-high statue of St. Urho, which had been carved from a single tree trunk and resembled an Indian totem pole. The saint of the Finns glowered from the dark-stained wood. The sculpture had been done with a chainsaw, which was a popular way of making works of art in the Arrowhead region.

St. Urho was described as "Finland's patron saint," and he had apparently been involved in driving out a pestilence of grasshoppers from the old country hundreds of years ago. At least that was what many locals believed, but in reality the whole St. Urho legend was just something that a bunch of Finnish American businessmen up in the Mesabi Iron Range area had dreamed up in the 1950s. They wanted to have something of their own to compete with the Irish festivities on St. Patrick's Day. And ever since, St. Urho's Day has been celebrated in many places in northern Minnesota, where a large segment of the population has Finnish roots—for instance, in the towns of Virginia, Hibbing, and Embarrass. But gradually the celebration caught on beyond the state's borders, and today the holiday is commemorated by many Americans who overtly want to honor their Finnish heritage. In the real Finland, few people have even heard of St. Urho. But in Finland, Minnesota, he is a legendary figure, and no one questions his status.

It wasn't until the 1890s that the first Finns settled in the beautiful Baptism River Valley. Until then, the region had long been uninhabited. By that time, the Ojibwe had abandoned their old hunting grounds in the valley, where they had once hunted moose. Like other immigrants, the Finns also wrote home to report on the excellent conditions they'd found in the New World. And this brought more

Finns, who soon discovered that the letters from America had not told the whole truth. In fact, many of those reports hadn't contained a single true word. In reality, the arable land along the Baptism River wasn't good for growing much of anything other than potatoes. In addition, all the goods that they'd brought with them had to be carried up from the lake. During the first couple of decades, this included everything they needed to eke out whatever living they could from the poor soil. Harrows, plows, and reapers—it all had to be carried, piece by piece, up the long, steep slopes from the lake. But they didn't give up. No matter what, they couldn't go back to the Finland that they'd left behind. There was now only one place in the whole world for them, and that was the new Finland, near the Baptism River in Minnesota.

In 1951, as a result of the Cold War, the Finland radar station was established. It was a complex of buildings, set up for the sole purpose of detecting Soviet jets as early as possible if the Big Invasion ever occurred. The 179th Fighter Squadron of the Minnesota Air National Guard was stationed in Duluth, and there the pilots were just waiting for word from the radar station up in Finland. In its heyday, there were 130 people employed at the radar base. A whole little village was built for them, just outside the old center of Finland. Of course, this generated both jobs and revenue for the local community. But in 1980 the base was closed. By then the fear had turned from planes to intercontinental missiles, and other, more modern, facilities were better equipped to detect them.

The community of Finland never really recovered after the radar station was closed. Over the next couple of years, nearly three hundred people moved out of the area, but the descendants of the original Finnish immigrants stayed on. Every year on March 16, strategically chosen to be one day before St. Patrick's Day, they celebrate St. Urho and the driving out of the grasshoppers from the old country. The local merchants organize a parade, people prepare Finnish food, and the children dress up like grasshoppers and leap around in the deep snowdrifts that usually still cover the Baptism River Valley in mid-March.

Lance parked in front of the Finland General Store, the area's only grocery store. He had decided to buy a ready-made sandwich and some potato chips, and then sit in his truck to eat them. It had been a long time since he'd been inside the store. In fact, he hadn't been out to Finland much at all in the past year. He'd driven through a few times, but that was about it.

Usually an old woman with arthritis in both hands worked in the store. Lance always had to look away when she rang up the prices of his purchases, using her claw-like fingers. But now it looked as if she'd finally retired. He hadn't seen this woman cashier before. He made a round of the aisles. He was clearly the only customer. It was an old-fashioned general store, selling everything from bread and beer to rubber boots and snowshoes. He wasn't very hungry, but he knew that he should eat something.

He was still annoyed with Zimmerman, and kept picturing his laughing face. What was it the new ranger had said? "He couldn't have ingested it by accident, if you know what I mean." When Lance thought about that now, he realized that Zimmerman must have had confirmed his own prejudices about the people up here when he reported on what had been found. That was why he had chuckled at the whole situation, because Lance had reacted exactly the way Zimmerman had expected. And that made Lance even more annoyed. But the ranger was entitled to his tired East Coast liberalism. It didn't really matter. Those attitudes aren't going to get him very far up here, thought Lance.

Out of habit he picked up a bag of Old Dutch potato chips, and put a handful of Dove chocolates in a paper bag. Then he chose a ready-made chicken sandwich and a Diet Coke and set all of his purchases on the old-fashioned wooden counter, which was worn smooth with age.

The cashier first picked up the bag of chocolates, but then stopped abruptly and put it back down. He looked at her. Judging by her expression, there was something that Lance had forgotten. Something completely obvious. And now she just sat there, waiting for him to do or say something about what he had so obviously forgotten. He didn't know what to say.

"So, how's it going, Lance?" the cashier finally asked him.

And that's when he understood.

"Debbie!" he exclaimed.

Because there sat Debbie Ahonen, twenty years older.

"Well, well, well," she said. She picked up the bag of chocolates, peeked inside, and started laughing.

For a moment he felt an inkling of something that was almost like love—a love that had been hibernating but had now burst forth somewhere deep inside him. It disappeared as soon as Debbie's laughter turned into the ugly cough of an inveterate smoker. He could hear the phlegm working its way up from the depths of her bronchial passages until it reached her throat and she was forced to swallow it again.

With the back of her hand she wiped away some invisible beads of sweat from her forehead.

"Always Dove chocolates," she said, punching in the price on the old manual cash register.

Then she quickly tallied up the rest of his purchases without saying anything more.

Lance remembered the day, twenty years ago, when she had beamed at him as she said those words: "Finally I'm in love too!" And again he felt the shame, almost as strongly as he had back then. The shame of having loved someone so much, or at least having adored her looks and her charm so passionately, only to find that his feelings had never been reciprocated. And even now, as she sat here looking as if she'd spent too much of her life indoors sucking on cigarettes, she was still able to make him feel ashamed.

"So, how's life been treating you, young Mr. Hansen?" she said then, looking up at him.

"Can't complain," said Lance.

"Are you married?"

"Divorced."

"Any kids?"

"A son. Seven years old."

Debbie smiled at the mention of his son.

"What about you?" he asked.

"Got divorced five years ago and moved back to Minnesota. Lived in Minneapolis for a couple of years. After that . . . well, you can see for yourself."

She waved her hand, as if to take in the whole dreary, outmoded, and virtually deserted store.

The place must have looked pretty much the same when she was a girl close to forty years ago, thought Lance. The same counter and the same shelves, just not as worn, and with far more customers back then. At the time Finland was filled with families connected to the radar station. More than a quarter century had passed since those people moved away. Now Lance and Debbie were the only ones in the store.

"How long have you lived in Finland?" he asked.

"Nearly four months now," said Debbie.

"Do you have kids?"

"Yes, one daughter. She's nineteen and lives in Santa Barbara. In California."

Debbie had put his purchases in a plastic bag, which she set in front of him on the counter. It was time to pick up the bag and leave unless he wanted to enter into a longer conversation, or maybe make plans to get together for a cup of coffee someday.

Lance picked up the plastic bag. "Well, I'd better get going," he said.

"Still a forest cop?" asked Debbie.

"Yep."

"You're the one who found the guy at Baraga's Cross, aren't you?"

"Christ, does *everybody* know about that?"

"What do you expect? This is Minnesota," said Debbie with a smile. "Are you on duty right now?" she added.

"Yeah. Some teenagers have been hanging out over by Seven Beaver Lake. So I had to go take a look at the place."

"Did you find out who they were?"

"No, I never do," said Lance.

"Never?" she said in disbelief.

"Not really. Very seldom, anyway. But I've got to go now," he said.

"Right. I guess you've got a lot of other cases to solve," said Debbie. Lance laughed.

He was already at the door and about to leave the store when he happened to think of something. He stopped and turned to ask her, "So what exactly brought you back to Finland?"

"Mom," said Debbie. "She's eighty now. Richie has been trying to take care of her, but it wasn't going to work out in the long run, so I needed to come back home."

She looked worn out. Lance tried to think of something pleasant to say but couldn't think of anything. "So you're staying with her?"

"No, I'm staying with Richie."

"Which Richie are you talking about?"

"Richie Akkola."

"You're staying with Richie Akkola?"

"Yes. We're living together," she told Lance, evading his eye.

"Okay," said Lance. "Well, tell your mom I said hi."

Debbie gave him a wan smile.

He opened the door and stepped out into the sunshine flooding the front of the Finland General Store. Richie Akkola, he thought. Richie had to be close to seventy. He owned the store and the gas station, and at one time he was considered quite well-to-do. And now he was living with Debbie Ahonen? Lance couldn't understand it. Beautiful Debbie, who had gone off with her policeman to sun-filled California twenty years ago.

Lance decided to drive to Our Place to get a cup of strong coffee and a decent homemade sandwich instead of eating the vacuum-packed one he'd just bought from Debbie.

OUR PLACE WAS THE ONLY BAR IN FINLAND. It was housed in a modern timbered building and was no more than ten years old. In the past there had been several bars in the community, but they had closed after the radar station was shut down. Then in the late 1990s, Ben Harvey and his wife had arrived from somewhere back east and opened a canoe rental business and the bar. It had been quite a while since Lance had last stopped by for a chat with Ben, who was such a friendly guy. As far as Lance could tell, his business was prospering. Tourism had made that possible. Canoeists, snowmobilers, sport fishermen, and hunters.

When Lance went in, he saw Ben standing in a classic bartender pose, leaning forward with his forearms resting on the counter as he talked to a customer straddling a bar stool. Lance could see only the back of the man sitting there, but he knew immediately that he wasn't from the area. It never took more than a brief glance for him to differentiate between a local and a visitor. There was just something about the way people held themselves, the way they occupied the space, from a purely physical standpoint.

Ben straightened up when he recognized Lance.

"Hey, long time no see!" he exclaimed. "The forest sheriff is back!"

Lance snorted.

The man sitting on the bar stool turned around and nodded a greeting. He looked like a typical sport fisherman, the type that spends more time fishing at the local bar than in the lake or streams. Fishing trips—the classic excuse to get away from home and do whatever you like for a few days. Lance returned the nod and then maneuvered himself onto another bar stool, taking care to leave one vacant next to the visitor. He glanced around. At the back of the room two middle-aged men were eating. Otherwise there were no other customers in the place. It was still too early in the day.

"Coffee, please," said Lance. "Black. Plus . . . let me see, now. What kind of sandwiches have you got?"

"Only chicken salad at the moment. I was just about to make some more, so if you want to wait a bit . . ."

"No, chicken salad sounds fine to me."

"Anything else to drink?"

"A Diet Coke."

Ben poured Lance a cup of coffee and filled a glass with Coke. Then he disappeared into the kitchen. Lance greedily slurped up the coffee. It was so hot that it almost burned his tongue, but he suddenly felt a great need for caffeine. As if he'd just woken up from his usual leaden and dreamless sleep. Am I really so exhausted from meeting Debbie? he wondered. At the same time he remembered other encounters with her, more than twenty years ago, when he'd also been exhausted afterward, but for entirely different reasons. Was it the huge gap between what she once was and what she was now that had upset him so much? Or was it the bizarre news that she was living with old Richie Akkola?

He finished his coffee. The other man at the bar was nursing the last of his beer.

"Feeling caffeine deprived today?" he asked.

"Can't deny it," said Lance.

"It's this heat. All the sunshine makes you feel tired and heavy-headed."

"You could be right."

Yet he wasn't feeling tired. When he thought about it, he realized that he felt *shaken*. As if someone had struck him, knocking him off his familiar path. Debbie, he thought again. Beautiful Debbie Ahonen. Maybe he could tell Ben about her. He heard about almost everything that went on in Finland, and he knew old Richie Akkola well. After all, the two men make up fifty percent of the business owners around here, Lance thought. And even though Ben had never known Debbie in her heyday, when she was so aloof and irresistible, he must have met the present-day Debbie long ago, since the Finland General Store was the only place to buy groceries. Lance wondered whether he could confide in Ben. As a bartender he must be used to hearing people's troubles. Maybe he could explain to Lance how exactly it had come about that Debbie was now living with Richie. Was it a relationship based purely on convenience? No, Lance couldn't bear to think about that. The whole thing was too sad, and he decided not to mention it. He felt that he owed it to Debbie to show her a certain respect. It was true that she had hurt him terribly, but they had also been very close and had shared a lot. In spite of everything, they had once been a couple. He couldn't start discussing her miserable fate with other men.

And Debbie Ahonen wasn't solely to blame for this feeling he had of being somehow off balance. He'd felt this way all day. Or had he? He paused to consider that question. And the longer he thought about it, the more convinced he became that he'd felt perfectly normal when he got up in the morning. Also while he ate breakfast. At least as normal as he could expect to feel these days, given everything that had happened recently. After breakfast he'd headed for the ranger station to talk to John Zimmerman. The new ranger had told him what had been discovered about the two Norwegians. Wasn't it after hearing what he'd said that Lance started feeling upset? Yes. He didn't like hearing about that sort of thing. He thought it was disgusting that men could be together in that way. But worst of all was the fact that Zimmerman had laughed about it. Because he *had* laughed, hadn't he? Chuckled, at least, thought Lance. And it had made him so angry that he now felt emotionally drained. Was that what had happened?

Ben reappeared with a freshly made chicken salad sandwich. "Here you go," he said. "Knock yourself out."

Lance started eating the sandwich, but even though he knew he should be hungry, he could swallow only a few bites before he'd had enough. "Could I get some more coffee?" he asked.

Ben refilled his cup.

Lance took a sip, but the hot coffee burned his lips.

"Well, I better see about getting back to the RV," said the other customer, dropping a few bills on the counter. "It's parked down by the river," he said, turning to Lance. "So I'll be *walking* there, not driving. Just thought it'd be smart to let you know."

Lance gave him an indifferent but polite smile. "That's fine," he said. "Have a nice day."

"You too," said the man and left.

Now it was just Lance and Ben at the bar. In the back of the room the two middle-aged men were still eating. The bartender went over to their table to pour them more coffee. Lance heard him talking to them about fishing for trout in Thunderbird Lake. Ben knew all the best fishing spots, which of course made his bar especially popular among sport fishermen. Lance didn't know Ben very well, but he'd stopped by the bar many times in the past ten years, to have coffee or eat lunch, and he often chatted with the owner. Everyone who spent any amount of time in the area would sooner or later stop by Our Place.

So when Ben came back, Lance asked him whether he'd heard about the murder at Baraga's Cross. It was basically a superfluous question, since everyone had heard about it. And besides, Ben Harvey was a man who undoubtedly heard about everything that went on in the region.

"Of course," said the bartender. "And I also heard that you were the one who found the dead guy. Is that right?"

"Yeah, that's right. I found the victim, and I arrested his companion."

Ben whistled, clearly impressed. "That must have been some day on the job, huh?"

"You can say that again. But it turns out that the two men spent a lot of time up here, including at the Blue Moose Motel. Did you ever see them?"

Ben nodded. "As it happens, I did," he said. "They were here at least twice."

"Nice guys?"

At that moment a new customer came in. Another sport fisherman apparently. He came over to the bar, near where Lance was sitting. Ben smiled and asked the man what he'd like to have.

"A cup of coffee. And could I see the menu?" he said, sitting down on the bar stool that the other sport fisherman had vacated a few minutes ago.

Ben served him coffee and handed him a yellowed menu.

"Sure," he then said, turning back to Lance. "They were pleasant folks. Very cheerful. And extremely polite. Didn't drink any alcohol, as far as I remember. Just coffee and mineral water. Real nice guys."

Lance wondered for a moment whether to ask Ben if he knew that the two Norwegians were lovers, but he thought it would be stupid to mention that. Besides, Ben was from somewhere back east, just like Zimmerman, and Lance had no desire to end up having a lengthy discussion on the topic.

The sport fisherman ordered a piece of rhubarb pie, then picked up his coffee cup and moved to a table.

When they were again alone at the bar, Ben leaned toward Lance to ask in a low voice, "Have you talked to that brother of yours lately?"

"Andy?" said Lance, as if he had lots of brothers.

Ben nodded.

"I talked to him a couple of days ago."

"Did the two of you discuss the murder?"

"The subject came up, sure."

Ben nodded knowingly.

"Why do you ask?"

"So what did he have to say about the two Norwegians?"

"Andy?" said Lance, and he could hear how his voice had gone shrill.

"Yeah."

"I don't know what you mean."

"He spent a whole evening sitting here talking to them. It must have been a couple of days before the murder. They sat over there for hours." He pointed at a table in the corner.

Lance felt something shut down inside himself. No picture or sound, as if a TV had suddenly turned off. As Ben went on, it sounded as if he were speaking from another room. He suddenly seemed far away.

"Looked like they were having a good time. Andy had a few beers, while the two Norwegians drank mineral water, I think. Have no idea what they were talking about. Fishing, maybe. Or the old country. It's none of my business, but I just thought he might have told you about it."

Lance still felt like he and the bartender were in two separate rooms. That he was listening to somebody on the other side of the wall.

"I guess he must have forgotten about it," Ben continued, but he clearly didn't believe that. He was just throwing out a lifeline to the silent man sitting on the bar stool.

Because Lance still hadn't said a word, although inside him things were starting to function again. Now he realized why he had felt so upset ever since Zimmerman had reported that the Norwegians were gay. He remembered the strange look on Andy's face two days earlier, and he now knew exactly where and when he'd seen his brother with that same expression before. He took a gulp of his Coke and then set the glass down on the counter so hard it banged.

"Is everything okay?" asked Ben.

"Tell me one thing," said Lance. "I assume the police have been up here to interview you, right?"

"Yeah. They interviewed me yesterday. An FBI agent and a Norwegian detective."

"Norwegian?"

"Uh-huh. Not a Norwegian American. He's from Norway."

"I know. And you told them about all this, right?"

"I told them the two Norwegians had been in here. I had to do that. But I didn't mention your brother. I know Andy. He does a lot of work around here, and I thought it would be stupid if he got mixed up in the case. He just happened to meet them here one evening, and sat and talked to them. But since you're a police officer too, I figure now I've reported it to the police," he said with a smile. "And if you think it's necessary, you can pass the information on to the FBI."

16

LANCE WAS SLAVING over a difficult math assignment he'd been given as homework. He was sitting in his room on the second floor, which had a view of a large section of downtown Duluth. A view he never bothered to stop and think about. That was just the way it looked from his window. Every day new ships would sail into town down there, and the old Aerial Bridge would be raised and lowered. It was a Saturday in September, his last year in high school, and he had pretty much made up his mind to become a policeman, like his dad. So he was trying his utmost to get the grades that were required for admittance to the police academy in Minneapolis. That was why he often stayed in his room to study on Saturday evenings, like he was doing now.

He had no idea where his brother, who was two years younger, was at the moment. And he didn't care. Andy had his own friends. Maybe they were over in Lester Park, on the outskirts of town, where the Lester River forms idyllic little pools and waterfalls. Lance didn't know what they would be doing there. Maybe playing music on those big boom boxes of theirs. Andy and his friends could spend a whole evening sitting on benches in Leif Erikson Park, down by the lake, apparently doing nothing at all. Other times they played baseball in the schoolyard at Duluth Central, which was the high school both brothers attended.

Lance could hear the sound of the TV from downstairs. His parents must be watching some boring sitcom. It was a typical Saturday night. So typical that he never would have remembered it if everything normal hadn't abruptly been shattered in the most violent manner.

The sound of a car door, someone running across the gravel in front of the house. Before Inga had time to poke her head out in the hall to see who it was, the person had bounded up the stairs to the second floor in three or four strides. Lance got up. At that instant Matt Johnson, who was one of Andy's friends, appeared in the doorway. He looked scared out of his wits.

"You need to come," he said. "Andy has totally flipped out!"

"What do you mean?" asked Lance.

But Matt just reached out toward Lance and gripped his arm so hard it hurt.

"You need to come now!" he said, and started pulling him out of the room.

Lance stuffed his feet in his running shoes and then followed Matt downstairs.

Inga was standing in the hallway, staring at them with a worried expression. "What's going on?" she asked.

Matt, who was usually such a polite boy, again grabbed Lance by the arm and tried to drag him out the door before he had time to answer his mother's question.

"I don't know," said Lance.

"Is it something to do with Andy?" she asked. "Has something happened to Andy?"

"I don't know!" Lance repeated.

Matt had already yanked open the car door. He turned around and yelled, "Come on, for God's sake!"

Lance ran over to the car and jumped in the passenger seat. As they sped off, he saw Inga standing on the doorstep with one hand raised to her mouth.

Afterward he could never recall what he was thinking as they drove much too fast through the streets on their way to the high school. Nor did he remember whether he and sixteen-year-old Matt Johnson exchanged any words, although Matt must have filled him in on the situation. Because what Lance did remember quite clearly was jumping out of the car and racing onto the big, blacktop area as he shouted his brother's name. He could even remember the way his voice resonated in the deserted schoolyard.

Over by the entrance to the toilets he caught sight of Clayton

Miller. He was on the ground, with his legs sticking out to the side, his back slumped. His long bangs hung down in his face. Lance could see that he was taking quick, shallow breaths, and he realized at once that the boy was injured. Andy was nowhere to be seen. Thin, black-haired Clayton Miller was the only person in the whole schoolyard.

Lance started running across the open space. Matt stayed near the gate, looking scared. Just as Lance had almost reached the tall, ungainly boy who was down on the ground, Andy suddenly came around the corner of the building. He was holding a baseball bat in his right hand. When he caught sight of his older brother, he stopped. Lance did too. His brother's face didn't look the way it usually did, and at that instant it occurred to Lance that Andy looked completely alone. Like somebody who is so alone he no longer knows what to do with himself. That was what Lance saw in his eyes and his face.

Neither of them spoke; they just stood there, staring at each other. The only sound in the schoolyard was the gasping, spasmodic breathing of Clayton Miller. Then Andy shifted his grip on the bat to hold it with both hands, ready to strike, and he started walking toward Clayton. But Lance knew he wouldn't do it. He could tell by the way his brother was walking. Andy had realized that everything was now under control because his big brother had arrived. He knew that he could approach Clayton with the bat raised, and Lance would find some way to intervene, to prevent him from doing more harm. Lance was not afraid of his younger brother. When he moved toward Andy, he didn't even consider the possibility that Andy might use that dangerous weapon against him. Lance simply went over and took hold of the bat. Andy stopped. Lance didn't try to wrest the bat away from him; he simply held on to it, passively.

"Let go," said Lance calmly.

And his brother let go.

The Hansen brothers stood there like that for a couple of seconds, looking each other in the eye. Lance saw that Andy wanted to say something. Maybe offer an explanation for what had gone on there.

"I . . . he . . . ," he said, but that was all.

He turned on his heel and headed for the gate. After a few yards, he started to run. Matt Johnson got into the car and drove off before Andy could reach him. Lance watched his brother run out the gate without looking back. Then he finally went the few remaining yards over to the injured boy, who was now curled up in a fetal position on the asphalt.

Lance put down the bat and squatted down next to Clayton. "How are you doing?" he asked.

"I think I've got a punctured lung," Clayton whispered.

Now Lance could see how pale he was.

"Are you his brother?"

Lance nodded.

"He tried to kill me . . ." Then Clayton started crying.

Lance, who now realized that the most important thing was to get help, told Clayton to lie still. Then he ran to the nearest public phone and called the medics.

It's not far from Duluth Central High School to St. Luke's Hospital, so when he got back to the schoolyard, the ambulance had already arrived. He watched as the medics carried Clayton away on a stretcher.

It turned out that he did have a punctured lung, which was blamed on two broken ribs. Lance found this out later from his classmates, who thought, almost without exception, that it was high time someone taught Clayton Miller a lesson. He'd also lost a tooth, from being punched or kicked in the mouth. Lance remembered that sometime later in the fall Oscar Hansen, their father, had held up Clayton's dental bill to show Andy, and he asked his younger son whether he had any idea how much overtime he was going to have to work to pay the bill. Lance didn't recall the details of how the matter was handled, and he probably never asked. Yet Andy suffered no consequences from this incident, which had to be because their father was on the police force. Oscar Hansen must have pulled some strings. Clearly he'd also had a talk with Clayton's parents and had come to some sort of agreement with them. The dental bill was not referred to an attorney but was dealt with directly and discreetly by the two families involved. Perhaps a doctor bill too, depending on what kind of health insurance Clayton may have had. But he must have had a good medical plan, since he came from a well-to-do family. Wasn't his father a professor at the College of St. Scholastica? It was something like that.

The only time Lance ever talked to Clayton was when he was lying on the blacktop in the schoolyard. But he still remembered a couple of things about the boy. For instance, the other kids claimed that knitting was one of his favorite hobbies. In the winter he wore long, multicolored scarves, which he had apparently knit himself. It was also rumored that he wrote poetry, which Lance could easily believe. Clayton was definitely the type. Later on, after high school, he was actually in a band that had a lot of success. Clayton Miller was the lead singer, wasn't he? But what Lance remembered most was that everyone thought Clayton was gay. Even before Andy beat him up, Lance had heard somebody say that Clayton Miller was gay. That was why Lance knew who he was, that gay kid who knit his own scarves. And later on Lance always assumed that had to be the only imaginable reason why Andy had done what he did. It had something to do with the fact that Clayton Miller was gay, or at least that everybody thought he was. Lance had always thought that Andy would have killed Clayton if he and Matt Johnson hadn't arrived in time. You don't just tap somebody on the head with a baseball bat; you use it to bash in his skull. And he'd already punctured the boy's lung, probably by kicking him as he lay on the ground. It was a true display of extreme violence. And from a boy who never hit anyone, other than when the two brothers used to play at fighting when they were younger. The teenaged Andy Hansen was a quiet, slightly withdrawn boy. If he changed at all after the incident with Clayton Miller, it was that he became even more withdrawn. It was as if he retreated into himself, even when he was in the middle of a crowd. But he never exhibited any sign of violence again. At least not as far as Lance knew.

What Lance remembered most from the whole Clayton Miller affair, and what he could never forget, was the look on Andy's face as he stood there, holding the baseball bat in his hands and staring at his big brother. It was the face of someone who was so alone that he had no idea what to do with himself. And that was the expression that Lance saw again twenty-eight years later when he visited his brother in Two Harbors and talked about the murder at Baraga's Cross.

17

EIRIK NYLAND HAD DELIBERATELY OMITTED telling Bob Lecuyer that he was going to visit Lance Hansen. You never know what might come up if you have a beer with a witness, he thought, and if you know something the others don't, it's a lot harder for them to fool you. Not that he distrusted Lecuyer. That just happened to be what he was thinking.

After eating an early dinner at the restaurant in the hotel, he got into his rental car and drove the couple of miles up to Isak Hansen's hardware store. He had considered getting a cab and bringing along a bottle of Gammel Opland, but he decided that would be overdoing things. It was only a Thursday evening, after all.

He was in a good mood. The workday had ended with useful, though not exactly surprising, news confirming that the semen found in Lofthus's stomach was from Bjørn Hauglie. Now they were just waiting for the results from the Chicago lab that was analyzing the evidence taken from the crime scene. If the results contained no trace of a third person, they would arrest Hauglie and charge him with the murder of Georg Lofthus. Either way, they would soon have to confront him with the fact that he had lied.

But at the moment Nyland was parking his rented Subaru next to Hansen's black Jeep. Then he got out. The house was painted the same shade of green used by the U.S. Forest Service. Several pieces of patio furniture and a barbecue stood on a covered deck. Farther out on the lawn was a hammock. A toy bulldozer lay toppled over on its side near the doorstep. There was a lovely view of the lake.

As Nyland began walking toward the house, the front door opened and Lance Hansen came out.

"Hi, and welcome!" he said, holding out his hand when Nyland was still a few yards away.

They greeted each other warmly.

"Nice place you've got here," said Nyland, casting a glance at the view.

"Can't complain."

Nyland looked around. "Does your family own the store down there?"

"One of my cousins. It was started in 1930 by my grandfather, the year after he arrived from Norway."

"Was he the one from Levanger?"

"Yep."

"Your father's father?"

"That's right."

Nyland again felt the sense of rapport that he'd noticed during their drive from the airport a week ago. He didn't know why, but he felt more at ease with Lance Hansen than with many people he'd known for years.

"Do you know when *your* relatives emigrated?" asked Lance.

"No, I haven't got a clue."

"So what was their last name?"

"I know this sounds ridiculous, but I don't even know that."

"Hmm . . . ," said Lance. "There's not really much to go on then."

"No, there isn't," Nyland agreed.

"If you want to come into my office, I can show you a few good websites, but if you don't even have a last name . . ."

"Well, maybe I'd better try to dig up some names when I get back home. Then I can e-mail them to you."

"Sure. You're welcome to do that."

They stood there, looking down at the hardware store that Lance's grandfather had started.

"I wonder what would make a man decide to emigrate and leave everything familiar behind," mused Nyland.

"It was hard to find work in Norway in 1929. Times were tough here too, but at least this was a much bigger country, with more opportunities. Plus, I think he must have had a certain thirst for adventure. He was young and single, after all."

"Do you think he ever had any regrets?"

"Hard to say. Especially since I've never cut the bonds the way he did, you know."

Nyland took this as an invitation to talk about personal things, about life in general.

"So do you think you could have done what he did?" he asked cautiously, trying to indicate that he didn't mean to pry.

Lance looked like he was giving the question serious consideration. Nyland noticed that an almost imperceptible smile appeared on his face for a moment and then vanished.

"Not in the past, but I'm not so sure anymore," he said.

"Oh? Any particular reason for that?"

"No, I guess I'm just getting old," said Lance.

That sounds like a retreat, thought Nyland. Maybe Lance felt he was getting too personal.

"And here I thought people got more and more set in their ways the older they got," he remarked. "But maybe I'm wrong."

"Set in their ways? Don't you think people *learn* more as the years pass?" said Lance. "And maybe they end up learning something that suddenly weakens the bonds to everything familiar."

Nyland wondered what he was really talking about now. Again it seemed like an invitation. He ventured another cautious question.

"And what would that be? What would weaken the bonds to things that are familiar?"

"People change, don't they?" said Lance. "People get older, and they change."

"The majority of people just stagnate in the image they've created for themselves, so to speak," said Nyland.

He thought the conversation had taken a peculiar turn. Not uncomfortable, but definitely odd. Yet he had purposely initiated a discussion that would be about more than just their jobs or the weather. That was the effect Lance Hansen had on him. The man had a seriousness about him that did not invite small talk. A certain weightiness that was not merely physical. Nyland thought this was one of the reasons why he felt so at ease in the company of this local policeman.

"All right, well, let's have a beer instead," Lance suddenly exclaimed. "Why don't you take a seat over there?"

He pointed to the patio furniture on the covered deck. "I'll go in and get us a couple of bottles."

Nyland sat down on a plastic lawn chair while Lance went into the house. Through a nearby window that was open Nyland could hear the clink of bottles and glasses. He wondered whether it was a mistake to have come here, at least if he was hoping to find out anything of value to the investigation. Would Lance Hansen really withhold important information? He seemed more like a man having a midlife crisis, the type who starts thinking about buying himself a Harley. People get older, and they change, he thought, and had to grin.

Behind him he heard a door open and close. A moment later Lance reappeared, carrying two glasses and two bottles of beer.

"Here you go," he said, sitting down. "Have you ever tasted Mesabi Red?"

"No. Is it a local brand?"

"From Duluth. One of my favorite beers."

He filled both glasses and offered a toast. Then Eirik Nyland took a sip of the reddish beer, holding it in his mouth for a couple of seconds, to allow his taste buds to savor the taste before he swallowed. Mesabi Red tasted fresh and bitter at the same time. He couldn't stop a sigh of contentment escaping from his lips.

Lance nodded. "Best beer in the world," he said. "But I don't drink it often. A man needs to keep a clear head. Especially in your line of work, I'd imagine."

"Hmm, well, I'm no teetotaler," said Nyland. "It's just a matter of keeping the job and your free time separate, in my opinion."

"Sure, sure," said Lance. "But doesn't the work demand . . . what should I say? A certain shrewdness? Being a homicide investigator, I mean."

"Mostly it requires an ability to combine a lot of information in many different ways," replied Nyland. "To see connections that others might not see. An ability to notice the little piece that does *not* fit the picture. That piece often says more about the case than all of the other pieces combined."

"Huh. And what sort of thing would that involve?" asked Lance.

"What do you mean?"

"The little piece that doesn't fit in the picture. What sort of thing might it be?"

"Basically it could be anything," said Nyland. "Something that points in a different direction than the other evidence and leads. Something that threatens to wreck an otherwise solid case. It could be as simple as a gut feeling. You might have a sense that somebody is holding something back. Somebody who shouldn't have any reason to withhold information."

Lance looked at him and smiled. "Well, if you think *I'm* holding something back, I'm afraid I'll have to disappoint you," he said.

Nyland laughed. "I'm sure you wouldn't do anything like that," he said. "You're a policeman, after all. Like me. We both take pride in our work."

Lance Hansen nodded. He nodded several times with a resolute look on his face.

"But I work for the U.S. Forest Service. I only have to deal with people fishing without a license, and things like that. Illegal campsites. While you . . ."

"But our jobs are essentially the same," said Nyland. "We enforce the law. And the law is more than mere words in a book. It's based on the fundamental idea that every society would collapse if there were no repercussions for wrongdoing."

"Yup," said Lance. "I'll drink to that."

They both took another swallow of beer, and then Nyland went on. "And for a law to have any value, somebody has to enforce it. And that means us, Lance. Even though there's no pleasure in issuing a fine to a hard-pressed family man who's fishing without a license. Am I right?"

Lance nodded.

"And there's actually no joy in making sure a killer ends up in prison, either. It's a thankless job, but somebody has to do it. It's of the greatest importance to society that these things get done. Both catching a murderer and issuing a fine for illegal fishing. And once a person takes on that sort of assignment, he has to prove himself worthy of the job."

Nyland took a sip of beer, settled himself more comfortably in his chair, and stretched out his legs in front of him. Then he cast a quick glance at Lance Hansen. He was stroking his chin, as if checking on the quality of his morning shave. Nyland hoped he'd given his colleague enough to think about, in case he was, in fact, withholding information. But he really didn't think he was. It was just something that Lecuyer had said. A feeling the FBI agent had got when Lance gave his statement. And then there was the fact that Lance was the one who had found the dead man, and also the one who had brought in Hauglie. There was no getting around it—Hansen had a central role in the case, at least so far.

They had talked to a lot of people, but no one had seen or heard anything suspicious. Two days ago Nyland had gone with Jason Fries to Finland. What a godforsaken place that was. Most of the residents were descendants of Finnish immigrants, of course. Nyland wasn't sure if that was the reason, but he'd sensed a different atmosphere there. More reserved. No one said more than was absolutely necessary. Maybe it would have been different if he'd been a *Finnish* investigator instead of Norwegian. The one person who had talked freely and easily was the owner of the community's only bar. He remembered the two Norwegians well. They'd stopped by a couple of times. Seemed like nice, polite guys. Drank only mineral water, he'd said. But not even the bar owner had told Nyland and Fries anything of significance.

Yet somewhere there had to be someone who knew something. There always was. Someone who, for example, might have seen Hauglie and Lofthus arguing earlier in the day. Or for that matter had observed a third person near the crime scene. Something like that. Nyland was convinced that person existed.

"Yeah, well, we just have to do the best we can," said Lance Hansen.

He seemed to be speaking more to himself than to Nyland. "But sometimes even that isn't good enough," he added.

"What do you mean?" asked Nyland.

"Oh, I'm just talking a bunch of crap." Then he seemed to pull himself together. He sat up straight in his chair and drank some more beer. "Mesabi Red," he said, studying the reddish liquid in his glass. "Named after the Mesabi Iron Range."

"What's that?" asked Nyland.

"The range is a chain of mountains and ridges seventy-five miles from here, off in that direction." He pointed behind him, away from the lake. "It once had the largest iron deposits in the world. Now they're mostly gone. The pits that were left behind are like huge wounds in the landscape. In some places the ridges have been obliterated with dynamite."

"Seems like a really shortsighted way to make use of a natural resource," remarked Nyland.

Lance nodded pensively. "Sometimes I think we seem like a gigantic swarm of grasshoppers that came flying across the sea and found this . . . this field that we call America. And we've kept on swarming and eating up the land. But I don't know . . . Other times it seems to me the most beautiful story that's ever been told."

Nyland thought Lance Hansen was not the average provincial policeman. Then again, he undoubtedly was that too. But he was also something different. As if part of him, but only that one part, had landed on the wrong rung in life.

"So what does 'Mesabi' mean?" he asked.

"It means 'giant.' The Ojibwe thought they could see the outline of a slumbering giant in the mountain chain. Most things up here have once had a different name. The lakes and the mountains and the streams. Lake Superior too."

Below them the lake stretched all the way to the horizon.

"Lake Superior is Kitchi-Gami. The big water. And Grand Portage is Kitchi Onigaming. The big portage place. You haven't been to Grand Portage yet, have you?"

"No," said Nyland.

"It's forty minutes north of Grand Marais, almost on the Canadian border. An Indian reservation. That's where my son lives."

"Oh, really? What's he doing up there?" asked Nyland.

"He goes to school. He's seven years old."

Nyland tried to put everything in place in his mind, but it felt like he was grabbing at thin air. He recalled that Jason Fries had mentioned the Indian reservation. One of the anonymous tips to the police had concerned somebody on that reservation. "A typical small-time crook," Fries had said.

"He lives there with his mother, my ex-wife," Lance went on. "I was married to an Ojibwe woman. We're divorced."

"Oh, now I understand," said Nyland.

But he didn't really get it. He no longer knew what to believe or think about Lance Hansen.

"Isn't that unusual?" he asked.

"To be married to an Ojibwe?"

"Yes. A mixed-race marriage, I mean."

"It's not exactly the norm, but it's not particularly unusual either. I think my parents would have had problems accepting it if I'd married an African American girl. But the fact that Mary was Ojibwe never really came up."

"Why do you think that is?"

"I think it's because the Ojibwe are a marginalized people. Not just the Ojibwe, but American Indians in general. So their cultures are not perceived as threatening. At the same time, many white Americans respect the Indian cultures, but it's a form of respect that involves no . . . what shall I say? That involves no risk, precisely because their traditional way of life was destroyed long ago. Not much of this is on a conscious level, of course. For instance, if you try to discuss these matters with people, they won't even know what you're talking about. Just as they'll deny that they have anything against marriage between whites and blacks. They'll deny it until the issue affects their own daughter or son. Then they'll suddenly find all sorts of excuses for why such a marriage shouldn't take place . . ." Lance waved his right hand as if shooing away an insect. "We may have a superficial respect for what we think their culture entails. Having a close relationship with nature, and all that. A form of spirituality. But, in fact, that doesn't count as respect."

"But it's different for you," remarked Nyland.

"Yes," said Lance. "For me, it's different."

Then, after a brief pause, "That's because of my son."

"And you must have friends and acquaintances among them. Among the Indian tribe, I mean."

"I have an ex-father-in-law who I'm extremely fond of, even though I haven't spoken to him in three years, not since Mary and I split up. Otherwise I don't have any real friends there. But my son does. And those friends have brothers and sisters and parents. It's a whole network of people. And even though I don't spend time with any of them, except for Jimmy—that's my son—that network is very important to me, because he's a part of it."

After a moment he added, "Do you have kids?"

"Yes, I do," said Nyland. "Two daughters. Eleven and thirteen."

Lance nodded and smiled.

A natural pause ensued, as if the conversation were taking a breather. Nyland sipped his Mesabi Red. Below them was Lake Superior, now displaying large patches of pink and gold on its surface, with an incredible number of different shades of blue. Off in the distance a few long, narrow streaks were almost turquoise. A fine mist floated over most of the enormous expanse of water. The light was soft and veiled, as if shining through millions of microscopic drops. Just like when he was sitting in the café with Sheriff Eggum, Nyland now thought that he was starting to enjoy being in this place. If everything fit together the way he and Lecuyer thought—meaning that Bjørn Hauglie had killed Georg Lofthus—would he want to go back to Norway as soon as Hauglie was arrested? He pictured in his mind Vibeke and their two daughters in the cabin out at Lillesand. Saw them eating at the table under the birch tree in the evening. The sunset over the archipelago. He thought about what it was like being Vibeke's husband. The girls' father. How good it was to be together like that, away from work and all the misery that he regularly encountered on the job.

Again he looked down and fixed his gaze on Lake Superior. Two SUVs with canoes fastened to the roofs drove past on the road. In his mind Nyland pictured a map of North America and thought about where he was on that map at this moment. It felt good to be here. Knowing that he was surrounded by such huge landmasses on all sides. Here he was, looking at the world's largest lake, yet in this place he had no sense of a *shoreline*, even though it was called the North Shore. He was definitely inland—that much he could tell. But not like in Norway, where being inland always made him feel slightly claustrophobic, confined and closed in. Here, on the other hand, he felt protected. And that was a good feeling. Way out there to the east was the Atlantic Ocean. Equally far to the west was the Pacific. And here he sat, drinking Mesabi Red with Lance Hansen, in the very middle of the continent. Maybe Hansen was another reason why he liked being here. The two of us would have been good friends if we'd lived in the same place, thought Nyland. He recalled that when he was young he'd had daydreams about starting over somewhere far away. With new friends, new routines, different interests. On this evening, here with Lance Hansen, he was experiencing something that resembled a distant echo of those daydreams.

But the feeling lasted only a moment.

"I was wondering about something," said Lance.

"What's that?"

"You've seen photos of the dead man, right?"

Nyland nodded.

"Doesn't that sort of thing ever make you feel . . . like throwing up?"

As a homicide detective, Eirik Nyland was constantly asked questions like that. How could he stand to see such brutal deaths?

"No, it doesn't really turn my stomach," he replied. "It did the first few times, but not anymore. I suppose you just get used to it. So, no, I don't feel like throwing up . . . but it's still . . . it does . . ."

"It does affect you, all the same?" Lance said, completing his sentence.

"That's right," said Nyland with relief. "Of course it affects me. That's only normal. It's not exactly the same thing as growing roses, after all."

He'd been on the verge of telling Lance his dream in which he was always left feeling so helpless in the end. Standing on the door-step outside their house in Asker. A man who assaults and kills little girls has just driven off with his daughters. A man whom Nyland had been investigating during a case, but he'd been unable to get the man convicted. And he'd almost told all of this to Lance Hansen. How, when he woke up, he felt something inside of him was about to be destroyed. This dream was the real answer to the question about how his job affected him. There was no other honest answer.

"Personally, I would never be able to handle it," said Lance. "This is the only murder case I've ever been involved in, but . . . well, not actually involved in, but . . . and I think it's completely . . . I don't know . . ."

"Have you been having problems since you found the body?"

Lance stared straight ahead, his face gloomy. "Nothing is the same after a murder, is it?" he said.

"What do you mean?"

"Nothing is ever the same."

"Not for the victim, at any rate," said Nyland.

Lance looked at him in disbelief.

"It was a joke," he said, raising his hands apologetically. "Not a very good one, but it was meant as a joke."

"Nothing is ever the same for anyone who comes in contact with the murder in some way. Don't you agree?" Lance went on. "For you and your colleagues, it's different. It has to be that way. But for everyone else who has a connection to the victim . . . or to the mur-derer . . . or to the crime scene . . . even a slight connection . . . for them something is forever destroyed. The time before the murder seems almost idyllic."

"Idyllic?" Nyland repeated in surprise.

"Yes. I don't know . . ." Lance sighed and rubbed his face, as if he felt worn out. "It's just that . . . this potential for violence . . . We don't see it, aren't aware of it. We notice it only after it's too late."

Nyland had a feeling Lance Hansen might know something about the murder after all. Something he hadn't told the police. Something he presumably hadn't told anyone. Nyland had encountered many people who lied during murder investigations. Lying about a homicide was not like lying about other types of crime. Having knowledge about a murder was an inhuman burden to carry. So when somebody did lie or withhold information in a homicide case, it was almost always for one of three reasons: The individual in question was the murderer and was lying so as not to get caught. Or he had something to do with the murder but couldn't report everything he knew because then he'd be forced to reveal something else that would prove to be vastly unfavorable, most often criminal, about himself. Or he was lying to protect others.

Nyland suddenly remembered what Lance had mentioned just a few minutes ago—that he had family on the Indian reservation. One of the anonymous tips had involved a man who lived there. Was there a connection? Lance had talked about a network. That a network existed and it meant a great deal to him because his son was part of it.

"Is there something about this murder that is bothering you in particular?" he now asked.

"Should there be something that *didn't* bother me in particular?" Lance replied.

"I mean . . . Is it possible that there's something you may have forgotten to tell us?"

"What do you mean by 'forgotten'?"

There was a sharpness in Lance's voice that Nyland hadn't heard before.

"When I say 'forgotten' I simply mean 'forgotten,'" he said. "Sometimes a person forgets a detail that later proves to be important to the case. You know what I mean?"

"Oh," said Lance, "and this detail is supposedly bothering me now? Is that what you mean?"

Nyland was just about to reply when Lance went on.

"Here's a detail for you. When I found the victim, he was lying on his stomach, so he was facedown on the forest floor. But even so, I could see his teeth."

"I remember that from the photographs," said Nyland.

"You've probably seen that sort of thing before, but for me, it was something out of a bad dream . . . a nightmare. I think about those teeth several times a day."

He picked up his glass and downed the rest of his beer in one gulp. Then he set the glass on the table and wiped his mouth with the back of his hand.

"So. There's your detail," he said.

"What about the diary?" asked Nyland. He was trying for a more cheerful tone.

Lance sat up straighter. "The diary? I almost forgot about that. Since I don't know French, I thought it might be fun to have you translate some of it. Just a few lines. I'd really appreciate it. Bring your beer, and we'll go into my office."

Nyland got up and followed Lance into the house. He noticed the shoes and boots that were lined up against the wall on the floor in the hallway. Jackets and caps hung neatly from a hat rack. Lance Hansen seemed to be an orderly sort of person. On the wall was a hunting photo: two men kneeling on either side of a buck. He couldn't be sure, but he assumed one of the men must be Lance.

As soon as he entered the office and saw the collection that covered one wall from floor to ceiling, he understood why Eggum had called Lance a local historian. The man had an entire archive at his disposal.

"Old newspapers?" he asked, pulling a binder halfway from the shelf. It was labeled: "*The Pioneer* 1891–93."

"The first newspaper in Cook County," said Lance.

"And these are your ancestors?" Nyland was studying a black-and-white photo that hung on the wall above the desk. It showed a group of black-clad people posing for the photographer a long time ago.

"A couple of them are, at least," said Lance. He pointed to a young man and a girl. "Those two later got married and became the parents of my maternal grandmother."

In the picture they stood far apart. Presumably with their

respective families, thought Nyland. They looked more like children as they posed for the photo.

"So that makes them your great-grandparents?"

"That's right."

Nyland leaned forward to get a better look, but up close the faces seemed no more than pale ovals atop the dark clothing.

He saw that someone had written "Duluth, October 3, 1902" in one corner.

"But it was the diary we were going to . . . let me see . . . ," murmured Lance behind him.

Now Nyland noticed that more pictures were lying on the desk. He picked up one of them to look at it. An old black-and-white photo of a man who seemed to be standing in a small meadow, or maybe a forest clearing. He had his thumbs hooked in his suspenders as he directed a hostile gaze at the camera. Nyland thought he looked like an Indian. And then it occurred to him that it was quite possible that was exactly what he was. He was just about to ask about the picture when Lance spoke first.

"Here it is," he said.

Nyland turned around to see that Lance had an old book in his hands.

"Feel it," he said, holding out the book for Nyland to touch, although he gave no sign of wanting to hand it over.

Nyland ran his fingers over the leather. It was so soft that it almost felt like the supple skin of a living creature.

"How old is the book?"

Lance placed it on the desk before cautiously opening it. At the top of the first page was the date 1890, printed in old-fashioned script.

"The entries go until sometime in 1894," said Lance.

"And who did you say wrote this diary?"

"One of my great-grandmothers. Nanette. She was French Canadian."

"Oh, that's right."

Nyland looked at the lines of writing that covered the first yellowed page. There was something untidy about the script, as if Hansen's great-grandmother had not had a steady hand. Or maybe she wasn't very skilled at writing, he thought. The diary entry was clearly old, but there was also something so personal and intimate about the handwriting that he had a very distinct sense of mortality and the passage of time.

"Where was this written?" he asked.

"In a little log cabin not far from what today is the center of Tofte. No more than a five-minute walk from your hotel."

"Did she write other diaries?"

"I don't think so. At any rate, this is the only one we know of."

"And you've never tried to have it translated?"

"There aren't exactly a lot of people in my family who have mastered French," said Lance with a smile. "And we don't know anyone else who speaks the language. Well, not until now," he added.

"But there are translation agencies that do this kind of work," said Nyland. "And I don't think they're particularly expensive." He placed both hands on the desk and then leaned over the old book, which was still open to the first page.

"No, wait a minute," said Lance. "Let's go farther in. There's something . . . something special . . ." He turned one page after another, apparently looking for something.

"What is it?" asked Nyland.

"Something special," Lance repeated. "She was sick . . . She had an illness that . . . I don't know what it was. That's what I'm trying to find. The name of her illness."

"Did she die from it?"

"No, she didn't. Although it almost killed her. Let's see now . . . I think it was in March 1892. At least that's what I remember hearing . . . let's see. *Here* it is!"

He pointed to a page on the right-hand side of the book. Nyland leaned closer. He could see that the entry was written on March 17.

"*Le garçon* . . . something about a boy," he began. "Let's see . . . This isn't easy . . . *Le garçon est . . . arrive . . . ce matin . . .*"

"But what does it mean?" whispered Lance, as if somebody were listening on the other side of the door.

"It means: 'The boy arrived this morning.'"

Hansen was standing close to Nyland, bending over the book.

"The boy arrived this morning?" he whispered. "Are you sure that's what it says?"

"Yes," said Nyland. "Do you think it means a birth? Maybe her illness had something to do with a birth or a pregnancy."

"I don't know," said Lance. "Keep reading."

"But I really can't make out much of it. It's been twenty years since I studied French. And besides, the handwriting is hard to decipher."

"Just do your best. Okay?"

Nyland scanned the page, looking for some recognizable word in the strange forest of old ink that seemed to have grown over the paper.

"God," he said. He saw the word *DIEU*, written in big letters. It practically jumped out of the sentence.

"God?" Hansen repeated.

"Yes, she's writing something about God. Let me see now . . . *la grâce de dieu* . . . God's mercy . . . *encore vivant* . . . something about being alive due to God's mercy, or something like that. Okay . . . *par la grâce de dieu, il est encore vivant* . . . Thanks to God's mercy, he is still alive . . . *mais à peine* . . . but just barely. Thanks to God's mercy he is still alive, but just barely. This must be about a birth, don't you think?"

Eirik Nyland could feel Lance Hansen's upper arm touching his own.

"Sure . . . a birth . . ." His voice sounded distant, as if he were thinking about something completely different.

"Well," said Nyland, "I don't know whether I can contribute much more. This was harder than I expected."

"Please try again," said Lance suddenly. "Just a little more? I may never have this opportunity again."

Nyland had to laugh at his eagerness.

"Okay," he said and went back to scanning the page.

"Deux profondes blessures," he read aloud. "Two deep wounds . . . That's what it says, but the rest is illegible."

"Two deep wounds?" Lance repeated.

There was something odd about his tone. Nyland no longer knew what to believe. Maybe this had nothing to do with an ill great-grandmother after all.

"I'm afraid that's all I can make out," he said.

"What about the next page?" said Lance. "Just a little of it?"

"You seem to be really interested in this sick great-grandmother of yours."

Lance laughed, but it sounded strained.

"She was my own flesh and blood, you know," he said.

Nyland didn't respond, just carefully turned the page. The entry for March 17 ended in the middle of the page, with only a few more lines.

"What does she write at the end?" asked Lance.

"Something about not wanting to say anything . . ." muttered Nyland as he tried to conjure recognizable French words from the scrawls on the yellowed paper.

"*Il ne veut rien raconteur* . . . he doesn't want to say . . . *de ce qu'il lui est arrivé* . . . Aha! It says: He doesn't want to say anything about what happened to him."

Lance Hansen straightened up and exhaled loudly, as if he'd been holding his breath the whole time they'd been examining the diary. He looked at Nyland.

"I'm never going to forget this," he said.

Nyland wanted to reply, but he had no idea what to say. He had a feeling that Lance's explanation didn't quite ring true. But there could be so many reasons for that. The diary was an old family heirloom, after all. Well over a hundred years old. Maybe it was linked to something shameful. Some extramarital scandal, for instance. It could be so many different things. But it had nothing to do with him, at least. Yet he still wanted to respond. There was something about Lance Hansen's attitude toward his ancestors that had made a deep impression on Eirik Nyland. He, on the other hand, knew the name of only one of his great-grandparents. He had to make a real effort to pull from his memory the full names of his four grandparents. In short, he knew next to nothing about his own ancestry. And had never cared to know anything either. While this man standing at his side had practically pleaded to have a few lines from a diary translated. His great-grandmother's diary. The thought of how deeply Lance cared about such things filled Nyland with admiration. And embarrassment. He still had no idea what to say. Whatever he came up with was bound to sound stupid.

To break the silence that had ensued, Nyland grabbed his glass of beer from the desk and finished it off.

"What did you say 'Mesabi' means?" he asked, setting the glass down again.

"It means 'giant.' The Ojibwe thought they could see the outline of a sleeping giant in the mountain chain that we call today the Mesabi Iron Range," Lance told him.

"Right . . . the Indians . . . that's what you said before."

On their way out, Nyland pointed to the hunting photo hanging in the front hall. He asked Lance if one of the two men was him.

"Yep. Twelve years ago and plenty of pounds lighter," he replied.

"So who's the other man in the picture?"

"That's my brother. Andy."

"Does he live up here too?"

"No, he lives in Two Harbors."

"Oh, that's right. The woman you waved to when we drove through Two Harbors was . . ."

"That was Andy's wife. By the way, would you like to see a picture of my son?"

"Of course," said Nyland.

He followed Lance into the living room, where one whole wall was nearly covered with family photos.

"So this is your whole family tree?"

"No, not at all. This is nothing. But there's my son, Jimmy, anyway."

Nyland saw a little boy holding up a tiny fish. The picture had been taken outdoors in the evening. Nothing was visible in the darkness surrounding the boy. His eyes shone red from the flash. There seemed to be something Asian-looking about his eyes. Then it dawned on Nyland that of course it had to be because he was half-Indian.

"A nice-looking boy. And is that him too? Sitting there?" He pointed to a photo of Lance seated on a snowmobile, holding a little boy on his lap.

"Yeah, that's us, all right," said Lance.

Eirik Nyland moved along the wall, peering at the photographs.

"Is that you?" he asked, pointing at the picture of a young boy with a haircut and shirt that had to be from the late seventies or early eighties.

"Yep. My high school picture."

"And that's your brother?"

"That's right. Andy in high school."

"So who's that sweet-looking girl?" He pointed to a picture of a young blonde.

"That's Chrissy. Andy's daughter. I don't think she's more than ten in that photo. She's seventeen now."

They both stood there for a moment staring at the picture of the fair-haired girl.

"Don't you miss your daughters when you're out traveling?" asked Lance.

"Yes, I do. I miss them terribly."

"Isn't having kids the best thing in the world?"

"Absolutely," said Nyland.

18

LANCE WOKE UP IN THE DARK. The first thing he thought about was whether he'd had any dreams. But of course he hadn't.

The alarm clock on the nightstand said it was one thirty. It was the Fourth of July, but there were many hours ahead before it was time for the parade and the fireworks. It was still night everywhere on the continent.

He got up, put on his bathrobe, and went into the living room, which was faintly lit by the streetlamp down near the hardware store. The dark outline of the building was visible on the left. A short segment of the road was also illuminated. Otherwise it was completely dark outside.

He thought about the lake out there in the darkness. The enormous expanse of water that went on and on, unseen by anyone, except as pictured in the minds of a few insomniacs. He wondered exactly how many people that might be. Regardless, he was one of them. One of the sleepless individuals who was thinking about the lake at this very moment.

Seven years ago he'd dreamed he was standing at the deepest spot in Lake Superior. He thought he was going to freeze to death. At the same time, it was beautiful. A blue landscape he was convinced existed only in his dream. Now he stared out at the darkness enveloping the lake. Once upon a time this was a place where dreams determined a person's path in life. The Ojibwe, before they became Christianized, were a people who interpreted dreams. No important decisions were made without considering dreams. Their names often came from dreams. They made dream catchers to protect themselves from nightmares, and they wore amulets that represented particularly significant dreams they'd had.

And now? Now there was a different kind of land out there.

My brother is a murderer, he thought. A dark chasm was contained in that thought, and it was in that darkness that he now belonged. Not out in the bright Fourth of July celebrations that would take over in a few hours. He would end up walking around like some sort of phantom. Like a dead man who had come back to wander among the living one last time, but without being able to share their warmth or participate in their laughter and conversation.

Andy had killed the Norwegian. He had done what he was in the process of doing to Clayton Miller when Lance had shown up at the schoolyard on that day so long ago. He had bashed in the man's skull the way he had planned to bash Clayton's skull. Those two young men, both of whom were gay. Because that has to be the reason, thought Lance. He hardly dared think about it, and yet he knew Georg Lofthus had been killed because he was a homosexual and just by chance happened to meet Andy Hansen in a bar.

Ben Harvey had neglected to tell the FBI that he'd seen the two Norwegians with Andy. Instead, he had pushed that burden onto Lance's shoulders. "And if you think it's necessary, you can pass the information on to the FBI," Ben had said. But he knew there was a connection between the Norwegians and Andy Hansen. And since Lance wasn't the only one who knew about this, he could never be certain it wouldn't all suddenly come to light. Maybe Ben would start having second thoughts, especially as time passed and no arrests were made in the case. And Andy had met the Norwegians in a public place, after all. It was true that the majority of customers at Our Place were sport fishermen and other tourists, people who were in the area for only a few days. But it was still possible that someone who knew Andy by sight had been in the bar in Finland on that evening. Our Place was a blind spot for Lance, and there was nothing he could do about it.

Moving slowly, he went into his home office and turned on the light. He paused to look around. Still lying on his desk was the photograph of Joe Caribou, standing on the path that led to his mother's house. Lying next to it was the picture of Thormod Olson and his friends, taken in the photographer's studio in Duluth. Lance picked up the picture of Thormod to study his face. What had he gone through on that night in 1892 when he was only fifteen years old? "Two deep wounds," he remembered. "He doesn't want to say anything about what happened to him." Falling through the ice was apparently not the only thing that had happened to the boy.

It was tempting to get more of the diary translated, three or four pages from the relevant dates. Then maybe he'd know the full story. Solving the mystery of Swamper Caribou's disappearance might be much closer than he'd dared believe. He decided to contact a translation agency first thing on Monday.

Based on the few fragments Nyland had translated, it seemed as if young Thormod had been involved in some sort of violent event. Lance again looked at the photograph. Did you meet Swamper Caribou? he wondered as he studied Thormod's face as it looked twelve years after his dramatic arrival in the North Shore. Even though he was twenty-seven and long since grown up, his face still had something boyish about it. That steely expression, which appeared well practiced, seemed to convey the message that this young man was not about to back down no matter who might stand in his way. Just try it! And it was exactly this defiant and stubborn expression that made his face seem boyish, even childish.

Was it possible that there were similarities between Thormod and Andy? Lance studied the obstinate face staring into the camera in Duluth on that day in 1904. The eyes. The lower lip, thrust out ever so slightly, like a little boy refusing to obey the wishes of an adult.

None of the other three in the photo had that hard-as-flint and yet childish expression. Sam Bortvedt and the brothers Helge and Andrew Tofte all looked like ordinary, hardworking young men, well scrubbed and wearing their best clothes for the occasion. None of them looked angry or defiant. Instead there was something steadfast and composed about their faces. Lance presumed they were men who acted with calm deliberation. Thormod Olson, on the other hand, looked as if he might leap from his chair at any second and give someone a punch. Had that face ever revealed the same sort of loneliness Lance had seen in his brother's face? Had someone—a brother or a friend, or maybe his wife—looked at him and thought: What's the matter with Thormod?

Lance had to admit there was no resemblance in the faces of

those two men. There was nothing he could point to and say: I recognize those features in Andy. His brother looked completely different. There was no physical similarity at all. Yet they were related by blood, just as Lance was also related to Thormod. And he couldn't get rid of the feeling that something about the well-groomed Thormod in the picture from 1904 reminded him of Andy. There was nothing specific, like the jawline or nose, ears or eyebrows; nothing he could put his finger on. Maybe it was just that Lance now believed both Thormod Olson and Andy Hansen were murderers. That was what they had in common, much more than any family connections. "That's the stuff we're made of," he remembered his father saying about Thormod. How ironic these words now seemed.

He sat down at his desk and picked up the other photograph. It was a copy of the photo owned by Willy Dupree. Maybe Willy knew where the path had led and where the house had stood. No matter what, his ex-father-in-law was the only person who might be able to tell him anything of value about Swamper Caribou. There was no getting around it. Lance was going to have to knock on Willy's door again, for the first time in more than three years.

Out the window he could see below his house the headlights of a car driving along Highway 61. For a few seconds a small patch of the lake was also lit up. Lake Superior. Kitchi-Gami. Then he thought about standing in the parking lot near Baraga's Cross, along with Sparky Redmeyer, Mike Jones, and Sheriff Eggum. That was after he'd discovered the murder victim. After he'd seen the crushed skull. The tufts of hair. The row of pearl-white teeth. Yet he now thought there was something innocent about the scene with the four policemen standing there and discussing whether this could be the first murder that had ever occurred in these parts. It wasn't on that day that everything changed, as he'd previously thought. It was first *now* that everything changed for Lance Hansen. That was what he realized as he sat there, slumped in his desk chair and staring out the window. His entire perception of his own history and sense of belonging had been turned upside down. He had thought of himself as a member of a hardworking and law-abiding North Shore family, but he now saw himself as belonging to a family of killers. Murder was suddenly at the center of his life. As long as he didn't tell the investigators what he knew, his actions were not much better than a murderer's. But could he do it? Could he expose Andy, send him to prison for life? His own younger brother? No. Lance knew that was something he could never do. From now on his role as a police officer was a sham. When he put on his uniform in the morning, he would know that he had no right to wear it.

And what about Jimmy? How could he be a father to the boy when he would have to carry around this secret forever? He suspected that the worst secret was not that Andy had committed a murder, but that he himself had failed when something of such magnitude was finally demanded of him. Because Lance knew exactly what that demand was. He knew what would be the right thing to do. He couldn't fool himself. Somewhere there was a mother and a father whose lives had now been destroyed. A young girl in love who was supposed to have gotten married. Maybe brothers and sisters. The fact that these people were Norwegian didn't really matter in this context. That was more of a curiosity. The important thing was that he sat here, knowing full well who had killed their son, brother, sweetheart, best friend. He knew who was to blame for the fact that they would never be happy again.

It was when Ben Harvey told him Andy had actually met the Norwegians that Lance became convinced his brother was guilty. The whole time Lance had thought it was a serious matter that Andy had been in the vicinity of the crime scene just a few hours before the murder, and had subsequently lied about it. That was something that had to be concealed at all costs, but he hadn't believed Andy's whereabouts had anything to do with the murder itself. Yet if Andy didn't kill Georg Lofthus, why hadn't he told Lance he'd met the two Norwegians at Our Place in Finland just two days earlier? There was no good reason to keep that fact a secret; but there were plenty of reasons *not* to hide it. Provided Andy was not the one who had killed the Norwegian. If he was the perpetrator, he would most likely just continue to keep his mouth shut and hope for the best.

All of this, added to the fact that Lofthus was gay, just like Clayton Miller, had convinced Lance. He no longer had any doubts about who the murderer was.

19

SMELLS OF FRIED FISH AND FRESH POPCORN were coming from the vendors' booths that had been temporarily set up along the harbor boardwalk in Grand Marais. The white paper sacks that people were carrying were stained with melted butter from the popcorn. Seagulls shrieked as they flew over the harbor, on the lookout for something to eat.

Eirik Nyland was sitting at a picnic table in front of the Trading Post. The shop sold sports equipment and vacation gear, Scandinavian sweaters and cardigans, Indian dream catchers, Norwegian trolls, wild rice from the lakes around the Iron Range, as well as books about traditional Indian foods, fishing lures, Swedish pioneers, and shipwrecks at the bottom of Lake Superior. Nyland had already handed over a few dollars in the shop. In a bag that he'd set next to the table was a little model canoe made of smooth, dark wood. It was a beautiful example of Ojibwe craftsmanship. But now he was sitting at this picnic table with Bob Lecuyer, Jason Fries, and Sparky Redmeyer. They'd been here for an hour. On the table stood two thermoses. One was already empty, while the other still held a few dregs of coffee.

Nyland had spent most of the morning on the phone with various people in Norway. He'd talked to three former teachers of Georg Lofthus and Bjørn Hauglie. All three had given the young men the best possible references. Nyland hadn't really expected to hear anything else. Of course teachers would have liked students such as Lofthus and Hauglie. There was never any trouble with Christian boys who were the outdoors type. When he asked—without specifically mentioning homosexuality—whether the two might have had a *very* close relationship, he noted that the teachers had no idea what he was hinting at. For them, the possibility that the boys might have been lovers was apparently as likely as Georg being killed by a Martian. From a police sergeant in the Norwegians' hometown, Nyland had also managed to obtain a brief statement from nineteen-year-old Linda Nørstevik, who was supposed to have married Lofthus in September. The sergeant had thought it better if he spoke to her instead of Nyland, since she was "in a state of shock and grief," as he put it. So Nyland had asked him to find out what Linda thought of Bjørn Hauglie. According to the sergeant, she had only good things to say about him. Bjørn and Georg were like brothers. That was how she'd described them. When Nyland asked the police sergeant whether he knew if Hauglie and Lofthus were gay, there was a long silence on the phone. Followed by indignation. The sergeant had known Georg Lofthus personally. He was also good friends with his father. And if that wasn't enough, he'd even known Georg's grandfather, when he was still alive. "There has to be a limit," said the sergeant. He said the words quietly, but his voice was smoldering with anger. Quite an emotional person, thought Nyland.

He ended up feeling annoyed after talking to all those people, and some of his irritation was still lingering as he sat outside the Trading Post. That surprised him a bit, because he didn't usually react this way. Yet he felt a similar vexation when he thought about Georg Lofthus's Bible. Or rather, when he thought about the Bible quote that the grandparents had chosen for the inscription in their gift to the newly confirmed grandson. Nyland knew the quote by heart: "For everything created by God is good, and nothing is to be rejected if it is received with thanksgiving." It made him both annoyed and a little sad.

By now it was almost eight o'clock in the evening. Since they'd worked all day, they hadn't had time to watch the parade. Sparky Redmeyer was the one who claimed the Fourth of July celebration in Grand Marais was something they all simply had to experience. So far they'd mostly just walked around looking at the people eating popcorn and fried fish. For the past hour they'd sat at this table in front of the Trading Post as they drank coffee and tried to find something to talk about that wasn't related to the case they were investigating. Sparky, who had quickly realized the other three men were not exactly impressed with the Fourth of July festivities in Grand Marais, now said it was the parade that made the day special.

"I think it's the coolest parade in all of Minnesota," he said. "The pharmacists, or maybe they're nurses, with their big hoses, spraying water on all the spectators. And the Sons of Norway with their very own Viking ship. And Sheriff Eggum dressed up like a sheriff out of the Wild West."

Redmeyer clearly regarded this as *his* day, and he wanted to show off his stomping grounds to the visitors who happened to be his bosses at work. So here they now sat at this picnic table, watching the people passing by and eating.

Eirik Nyland actually thought the very ordinariness of the whole scene was fascinating. Completely unlike the Norwegian independence day celebrations that he was familiar with, when the men wore suits and ties, the children were decked out in their best clothes, and the women donned national costumes that cost as much as a used car. Here most people had on T-shirts and shorts. The men all wore the ubiquitous visored caps. In that respect, the three law enforcement officers sitting at the table with Nyland were no exception. Lecuyer wore a Minnesota Twins cap. He had explained that this was the Twin Cities baseball team. Otherwise he was impeccably dressed in a newly ironed blue shirt, trousers with sharp creases, and shiny black shoes. Redmeyer had on a Hawaiian shirt, light-colored khaki shorts, and white jogging shoes. His cap said "Minnesota Timberwolves." Lecuyer's assistant, Jason Fries, wore a U.S. Navy cap to go with his light-blue jeans and striped T-shirt. Nyland had on a short-sleeved shirt and lightweight cotton trousers. All four men wore sunglasses, since the sun hadn't yet set. It was still low in the western sky, shining right into their faces.

They were actually waiting for the fireworks, which wouldn't start until ten o'clock, so it would be another couple of hours. But it was clear from the mood at the table that the other men would not be staying that long. Yet Nyland thought it was a fine evening. The Fourth of July celebration in Grand Marais was mostly just a big picnic, a casual summer gathering most notable for the sea of red, white, and blue—the Stars and Stripes in every imaginable shape and size. A ten-year-old girl with a sullen expression walked past wearing a T-shirt that proclaimed, "I'd rather be in New York."

"Can you see the other side of the lake from here?" asked Nyland, turning to Redmeyer.

"Not with the naked eye, no," said Sparky.

"But this isn't the widest part of the lake, is it?"

"No, not at all. It's much wider farther north, as soon as you get into Canada. Up there it's like an ocean."

Nyland noticed the hint of pride in his voice.

"So what exactly is on the other side?" asked Lecuyer in his matter-of-fact, slightly clipped voice.

"Wisconsin," Redmeyer told him.

"Oh. You mean cows," said Lecuyer.

Jason Fries's acne-pitted face crumpled with laughter. His complexion looked even worse when he laughed.

Nyland suddenly felt sorry for Sparky. No doubt he wanted to show them his hometown in a more positive light than what they'd seen so far in the investigation that had been occupying their days. It was a grotesque murder, after all, and that was the reason they were all sitting here.

"I really appreciate a good fireworks show," said Nyland, rubbing his hands in anticipation so that Redmeyer would know that he, at least, was not planning on leaving until he'd seen the undoubtedly spectacular finale to the Fourth of July celebration in Grand Marais.

"Oh, me too!" said Sparky happily.

"So you intend to stay here until ten o'clock?" asked Lecuyer.

Nyland nodded.

"Well, for my part, I think it's time to head home and digest all the impressions from the day." Lecuyer got up. "Shall we?" he said to Fries. It was an order, formulated as a question. Fries leaped to his feet. The two FBI agents said good-bye to Nyland and Redmeyer and then vanished into the crowd outside the Trading Post.

Nyland closed his eyes for a moment and leaned back. He didn't mind staying in Grand Marais for two more hours. Redmeyer might not be the world's most interesting conversationalist, but he was pleasant enough. Maybe they could find a café in a little while and get a bite to eat. That would be one way to pass the time. And he really did want to see the fireworks display over Lake Superior.

"So you were the one who was supposed to pick me up at the airport when I arrived, right?"

"Yeah. And I really appreciate that you haven't mentioned it before. In front of the others, I mean. I don't think Lecuyer would like it."

"Probably not," said Nyland. "So why couldn't you come and get me?"

"It was a family matter."

Nyland remembered now that it supposedly had something to do with Sparky's wife. Didn't Lance say that Redmeyer was scared of his wife? That's right. He'd made her a promise and would rather lie to the FBI than break his promise. That was it. Nyland had to stop himself from laughing.

"So where's your family today?" he asked.

That hadn't occurred to him earlier—that Sparky Redmeyer, who had a wife and two young children, was spending Independence Day with his colleagues instead of with his family.

"In Silver Bay."

Nyland knew that was where Redmeyer lived.

"And they're having a celebration there too?"

"Of course! The Fourth of July is celebrated everywhere. I usually spend the holiday in Silver Bay with my family. I just thought it might be nice for all of you, who aren't from around here, to experience a local Fourth celebration. But I was afraid our festivities in Silver Bay would seem a bit . . . hmm . . . what should I say? . . . *provincial*, maybe. So . . . well . . ." He threw out his hands and nodded toward the crowds, but there was something halfhearted about the gesture.

As far as Nyland could see, their table was the only one not fully occupied. That made the absence of Lecuyer and Fries even more noticeable. He was sure Redmeyer understood why the two men had left. They hadn't bothered to hide the fact that they were thoroughly bored. He thought it was a shame, since Redmeyer had given up spending the day with his family—especially since he was a man who was afraid of his wife.

"I think it's great," said Nyland.

"Really?" Redmeyer sounded skeptical.

"I've never been to a Fourth of July celebration before. It's something I'll remember all my life. I'm really grateful you took the trouble to bring us out here today."

"Oh, that's okay. It was no trouble," said Redmeyer. His face suddenly radiated genuine joy. "Really no trouble at all. Just ordinary hospitality."

Nyland turned around, pretending to study the people at the neighboring tables as he smiled. It was impossible not to smile. He couldn't remember the last time he'd encountered such a sincere response from an adult. And someone he didn't even know very well. It made him happy. At the same time, it struck him that Sparky Redmeyer would not have made a very good investigator. That job required being able to play a covert game with people, as well as the ability to expose the double-dealing and hidden agendas of others. An investigator constantly had to listen for what people were *not* saying.

"How about having something to eat before the fireworks?" he heard Redmeyer asking.

"Sure, why not? But I was wondering about one thing. How well do you know Lance Hansen?" As usual, his thoughts were still on his job.

"Hmm . . . I see him once in a while. This is a small place, and we're both in law enforcement. But we don't socialize, if that's what you mean. Why do you ask?"

"Oh, I just happened to be thinking about him. Probably because we were talking about that night when you were supposed to pick me up at the airport. I don't know. He seems like a nice guy."

"Sure, Lance is a good man," said Redmeyer. "But he knows too much," he added.

"And that's not a good thing?" asked Nyland.

"That depends on how a person . . . what should I say? . . . how somebody makes use of the knowledge that he has. Don't you agree?"

"What do you mean?"

"Lance is unique in the sense that he has all that knowledge about the region. He knows everything about everyone. Even the Ojibwe. But I've heard some people say—and quite recently too—that these days the local historical society is a joke. The same person said Lance no longer cares about the group; he just cares about the huge archive he's got in his house. Did you know about that?"

"About what?"

"That he has a huge historical archive at home?"

"No, I didn't know that."

"And it contains all sorts of information," Redmeyer went on.

"About everybody who lives up here. About the immigration period and our ancestors, what kind of jobs they held, who ended up in prison, *everything!*"

"And you think Lance just broods over this information, keeping it all to himself? Is that what you're getting at?"

"Heck, what do I know?" replied Redmeyer.

"Is he somebody that people gossip about?"

"Sure, of course he is. He's different, you know. People don't like the idea of him sitting there all alone in that house near the hardware store, with an archive containing so much information about their families and other people they know. Plenty of folks figure there's personal information about them in Hansen's archive. So, yeah—of course people talk about him."

"Is that what they call it?" asked Nyland. "Hansen's archive?"

"No, that's just something I happened to make up right now."

"But the impression I've got so far is that Hansen is well liked."

"And he is. Nobody has anything bad to say about Lance Hansen. I mean, what would that be?" Redmeyer gave Nyland a searching look. "Why are you so interested in Lance?" he said.

"Because he's our only witness. He found the dead man, and he brought in Hauglie. That means he has firsthand knowledge of the crime scene, which nobody else has."

"Except for the murderer," said Redmeyer.

"Right. Except for the murderer."

"But surely you don't think that Lance is . . . involved?"

"No, of course not," replied Nyland. "I'm just wondering whether he might have overlooked something of importance on that day. Some detail that might prove to be significant. That often happens. And in order to try and pinpoint what sort of thing he could have overlooked, I need to learn as much as possible about the way he thinks. And part of what shapes our thought processes is how other people perceive us. That's why I'm trying to form a picture of how folks up here regard Lance Hansen. Do you see?"

What he was actually trying to find out was whether Lance knew more about the murder than he had told the police. His son and ex-wife were Indian. They lived on the reservation. One of the anonymous tips in the case concerned an Indian who lived there too. Jason Fries had talked to this man and ruled him out as having nothing to do with the case. And yet . . .

The next day Nyland and Lecuyer were planning to go to Duluth to have another talk with Bjørn Hauglie. He'd been moved from the hospital to a hotel room, which the Norwegian consul in Minneapolis had booked for him. This time they were going to confront him with the discovery of the semen. If the lab in Chicago didn't find traces of a third person in the evidence taken from the crime scene, they would be arresting Hauglie very soon.

On the other hand, if there *were* traces from some unknown individual, Nyland was going to cut through the bullshit with Hansen, and try to make use of him to locate this third person. It wouldn't take much effort to dismantle Hansen's defense mechanisms, piece by piece, until he broke down and told them everything he knew. It wouldn't take much skill from Bob Lecuyer either. Or even from Jason Fries, thought Nyland. Hansen already seemed practically cooked. All they had to do was stick a fork in him to get him to talk.

"So what do you say we get us something to eat?" queried Redmeyer.

Nyland tore himself away from his speculations about the homicide case. "Okay, let's do that. Any suggestions?"

"Have you been to Sven and Ole's?"

"I'm sure I would remember it, if I had."

"Well, you can't leave here without having tasted Sven and Ole's pizza. They serve other things too. If we're lucky they might have fresh fish cakes. It just depends on the day's catch, since they buy their fish straight from the boats."

They got up and began slowly making their way through the crowds. Nyland carried the bag with the handmade canoe, carved out of smooth dark wood. The canoe was the same size as the Viking ship that he'd bought a few days earlier.

"Herring," said Sparky Redmeyer. "Freshwater herring. It makes the best fish cakes in the world. And of course it's Norwegians who make them."

"Of course," said Nyland. "And by that you mean Norwegian Americans, right?"

"But isn't that the same thing? We all come from Norway, after all."

There wasn't a single table free at Sven and Ole's Pizza, which was located smack in the middle of downtown Grand Marais. The two policemen were just about to leave when they heard someone yelling Sparky's name. And there, squeezed into the corner at the very back of the restaurant, was Bill Eggum together with a slender, petite woman. The sheriff gave the two men an authoritative wave, inviting them over. Nyland and Redmeyer made their way past all the other guests to the sheriff's table as they breathed in the aroma of pizza, which made them even hungrier.

"They've run out of fish cakes!" That was the first thing Eggum said to them.

"Oh no!" exclaimed Redmeyer.

"They sold the last of them right before you came in. We'll have to settle for pizza. Sorry," he said, turning to Nyland. "You really should try the fish cakes before you go back to the old country. But I'd like to introduce you to my wife, Crystal." The sheriff gallantly gestured toward the woman sitting on the other side of the table.

Eirik Nyland said hello to Crystal Eggum. She was stylish and soft-spoken—exactly the opposite of her overweight and sweaty husband.

"So pull up a chair, you two," said Eggum. "We haven't gotten our pizza yet. Why don't you have a slice when it arrives? In the meantime, you can order a pizza of your own. How does that sound? Instead of you sitting there and watching us eat, and then we'd have to watch you eat. What do you say, Crystal?"

"My dear husband, a Norwegian is always welcome at my table. You know that," she said.

So they sat down, and Nyland took a quick look around the room. At first glance, Sven and Ole's Pizza looked like any ordinary, rather rustic-style restaurant that could be anywhere in the world. Yet he soon noticed that the majority of objects decorating the walls bore an unmistakable Norwegian theme. He saw old wooden skis and poles. A copy of the first issue of *Birkebeineren.* An old coffee ad in Norwegian that said, "The best housewives choose Krone Coffee! Enjoyed from the North Cape to Lindesnes." A big black-and-white poster that looked like it was from the 1950s showed the bow of a Viking ship, and underneath the text read: "Oslo, the Viking Capital." There was also a photo of King Olav in full dress uniform next to an ad for a classic Saab: "Starts up like a rocket, even in extreme cold!" A big pair of deer heads hung on the wall, along with a number of old tools, which he assumed had been used for logging. Other objects looked like they might be gear for trapping, but he wasn't

entirely sure about that. Only a couple of yards away from their table, he saw three steps that led up to the small platform area that
held the bar, which bore the sign: "The Pickled Herring Club." A
couple of old geezers sat at the bar having a drink.

"So, what do you think?" asked Redmeyer. "Do you feel right at
home here?"

"It's almost like being in Norway," replied Nyland.

Bill Eggum raised his hand to wave at someone in the crowded
restaurant.

"Sid!" he yelled. "Sid, come over here!"

A moment later a thickset, middle-aged man was standing next
to their table. His brow glistened with sweat under the Sven and Ole
cap he wore.

"Your food is coming right up, Sheriff," he said.

"Good," said Eggum. "But look here, this is Eirik Nyland. He's
a policeman from Norway. Investigating the murder out at Baraga's
Cross."

Nyland said hello to Sid Backlund, owner of Sven and Ole's
Pizza.

"He says this place is practically like being in Norway," said
Eggum.

"Glad to hear it!" replied Backlund. "That's what we were aim-
ing for, you know. We just want folks to feel at home. Like they're
in Norway."

At that moment one of the employees called Sid from behind
the counter at the other end of the room. He excused himself and
hurried off.

"Backlund," said Nyland. "Isn't that a *Swedish* name?"

Sparky Redmeyer shrugged to show that he wasn't really sure.

"Yeah, but we don't pay too much attention," said Eggum. "I
mean, we don't really differentiate between Swedish and Norwegian.
We're all a hodgepodge, anyway. At least most of us are."

Nyland paused for a moment and then said, "But if Sid Backlund
is the owner, then who are Sven and Ole?"

That made the other three burst out laughing.

"Haven't you ever heard of Sven and Ole?" asked Eggum.

"No," Nyland had to admit.

"Then we'll have to tell you about them," Eggum went on. "Let's
see now . . ." He looked as if he were trying to decide on something.

"Okay," he said. "Sven and Ole went to see a ventriloquist who was performing in a tavern. The whole show consisted of jokes about how dumb Norwegians are, and finally they couldn't take it anymore. 'Hey, you!' shouted Sven. 'Stop making such derogatory remarks about Norwegians. We don't like it!' 'My good sir, they're just jokes,' said the ventriloquist. 'Shut up, you!' yelled Ole. 'We're talking to that little devil sitting on your knee!'"

Nyland laughed, and he noticed that his reaction immediately admitted him to the group. Because it wasn't just at Sheriff Eggum's table that everyone was laughing. No sooner had the laughter died down at one table than it broke out at the next. It was these rolling waves of laughter that formed the very pulse, the rhythm of the restaurant. The bursts of laughter rose from the tables to the ceiling, where they continued to roll around until they faded and left the air space to another volley of laughter that shot up from a different table.

"So I take it they're characters that appear in a lot of jokes. Am I right?" said Nyland.

"Yes," said Redmeyer. "Sven and Ole are the main characters in nearly all jokes about Norwegians and Swedes up here."

"That's not exactly true," said Crystal Eggum. "*Half* of the jokes about Norwegians and Swedes are about Sven and Ole. The rest are about Ole and his wife, Lena."

"Okay, you're right," admitted Redmeyer. "Sven and Ole, and Ole and Lena. Everybody has heard about them up here."

When the first pizza arrived, Redmeyer and Nyland ordered another one, and then all four began to eat. The pizza was okay, but Nyland had tasted better. As they ate, they talked about Cook County and its ties to Norway. Crystal said that many people in the region had visited Norway, and somebody was always going over there.

"They come back with stars in their eyes," she said.

"What about you?" Nyland asked her. "Do you have Norwegian roots too?"

He asked the question out of politeness, since that was obviously the most natural topic for conversation between a Norwegian and someone who lived in Cook County.

"Norwegian and Swedish," she told him. "The standard North Shore combination."

Only once did they touch on the murder at Baraga's Cross. That was when Nyland explained that he really should have been out at his cabin with his family right now.

"So I guess he's also guilty of wrecking your vacation," said Sparky Redmeyer. "The murderer, I mean."

"Whoever he may be," said the sheriff.

Nyland looked at Eggum. "Don't you think Bjørn Hauglie is the killer?" he asked.

Eggum was about to answer when his wife interrupted. "No talking shop!" she admonished her husband.

"Fair enough," he replied.

They ate in silence for a while, surrounded by loud voices and laughter. Outside the windows Nyland could see that people were still swarming the harbor area.

"But apropos the murder . . ." Eggum began as he wiped his mouth on a paper napkin.

"Didn't I just say no talking shop?" his wife reminded him.

"Yes, you did. But, as I was saying, apropos the murder . . . as far as I know there has never been a homicide in Cook County before."

"Is that true?" asked Nyland in surprise.

"Even Lance Hansen couldn't remember ever hearing of a murder taking place here. Not until now. And if *he* hasn't heard of it, then it didn't happen. Because that's how a lot of things are up here. If Lance hasn't heard of it, then it's not true."

Mrs. Eggum laughed. "Lance is a good man," she said.

"Sure," said the sheriff. "There's no question about that. But he won't listen to what other people say about things that have happened here. That's the whole problem."

"I think he just wants to have things verified," said Crystal.

Nyland thought about the story Eggum had told him, about the origin of the Seagren name.

"Verified?" said the sheriff, sounding a bit annoyed. "What about the lead bullet from Grandpa's skull? Shouldn't that be verification enough? But no, apparently not. Not for Lance Hansen, at least." He looked at Nyland. "Have I told you about my grandfather Jack Eggum?"

Nyland shook his head.

"Well, Jack was the first of the Eggum men to be born in the U.S. of A."

Crystal rolled her eyes. She'd clearly heard this story before.

"It was down on the prairie," her husband went on. "Near the Yellow Medicine River. That's where they lived in a little log cabin—Mr. and Mrs. Eggum, and a pile of young'uns. Including Jack, their firstborn. One day Jack had been out hunting—he must have been ten or eleven—and as he opened the door to come inside, there was a loud BANG! He had stumbled over one of the many babies crawling around on the earthen floor and shot himself in the head with his Winchester rifle. The shot went in here . . ."—Eggum pointed under his chin—". . . and continued through his mouth all the way up to his eyes. Then the bullet stopped. And this was in eighteen hundred and . . . hmm . . . when exactly was it? I'm not sure, but a long time ago, and you couldn't just phone for an ambulance. It would have taken a journey of several days to find a doctor. So of course everybody thought Jack was going to die. Nevertheless, his father rode off to bring back a doctor from the nearest town. When he returned . . . after . . . well, I don't know how long it must have taken, but no doubt at least a week, and when he got back, bringing a doctor along with him, there was a big surprise waiting. The first thing they both saw was the boy, whom they expected to find dead. He was out behind the house, doing target practice. After the doctor examined Jack, he said that the lead bullet from the Winchester hadn't struck anything of importance inside the boy's head. And now new tissue was in the process of growing around it. So it would be a greater risk to try to operate than to let the bullet stay where it was. And that's what happened. That's why Jack Eggum lived the next seventy years of his life with a bullet inside his head. And that's why it said in his obituary: 'Jack Eggum died with a bullet between the eyes, seventy years after the shot was fired.' But it didn't end there. Because after Jack died, one of his sons, my uncle, had the bullet surgically removed from his skull. He was close friends with the funeral director in town. Together they cut open the old man's head and took out the bullet from the Winchester. And since my uncle died childless, my father inherited the family treasure. And when he died . . . well, to make a long story short, I have the bullet from Grandpa's skull in a drawer at home."

"In the bedroom," said Crystal with a shudder.

"But do you think that's enough proof?" the sheriff suddenly shouted. "Do you think that's proof for the well-known local historian and forest cop, Lance Hansen?"

"Probably not," said Nyland.

"You're right about that. Do you know what Lance said when I showed him the bullet? This is years ago, now. He studied it for a while, and then he said, 'It'd be really interesting to know with certainty where this bullet came from.' He clearly didn't believe a word of what I'd told him. Not that I care anymore, but . . . verification, my you-know-what!"

"Now, now," said Crystal, trying to smooth things over. "That's just the way Lance is. And there's nothing anyone can do about it."

The second pizza arrived, and they devoured most of that one too. Afterward they all had coffee. Nyland could see from the light outside the windows that the sun was setting. It was a little past nine. They began making motions to leave. He picked up the plastic bag from the Trading Post.

"Nyland bought some Ojibwe handiwork," said Redmeyer.

"Oh, can I see?" said Crystal, her interest immediately sparked.

Nyland unwrapped the canoe, which took a few minutes, but at last it stood on the table amid a sea of blue tissue paper. A canoe made of dark wood. Maybe eight inches long, maybe two inches at the widest spot, carved from a single piece of wood, streamlined in form and polished smooth. In the back a little paddle rested against the edge, carved from the same piece of wood as the rest of the boat. The only thing missing was a miniature person, an Ojibwe Indian who could paddle off through the tissue-paper waves on the table.

"That's a beautiful piece of carving," said Sheriff Eggum appreciatively.

Both Crystal and Sparky reached out to touch the smooth surface that seemed almost unreal.

EVEN THOUGH THE FIREWORKS wouldn't start for another forty-five minutes, people had already begun making their way toward Artists' Point. It was a partially wooded promontory that stuck out into the lake over near the big white wooden building belonging to the Coast Guard. Nyland and Redmeyer crossed the parking lot in front of the Coast Guard station and headed down a path that led through the dense birch groves. When they emerged from the woods, they found themselves on top of a slope of bare rock that stretched off to their right and eventually formed a breakwater that continued, straight as an arrow, all the way out to the small white lighthouse at the very end. In the opposite direction, off to their left, was the promontory known as Artists' Point, with its pine trees and rocks.

"So, is this where they're going to shoot off the fireworks?" asked Nyland.

"Yes, from a raft on the lake," said Redmeyer.

Nyland noticed that a few people were sitting on part of the breakwater closest to land. Several small birds flew past the lighthouse. Over the harbor they wheeled about and came flying back, then landed on the breakwater right in front of the lighthouse.

"Come on, I want to show you something," said Redmeyer.

He made his way down the steep rocks until he was close to the water's edge. It wasn't more than a few feet below. Nyland followed suit. The rock was different down there. Darker and not as smooth as the bare surface they'd been standing on. Clearly a different type of rock, which stretched in a long, wide band along the edge of the lake, extending toward the breakwater. It was uneven, which made it a little difficult to walk, and in places puddles of standing water had collected in the deepest hollows.

"Do you see it?" asked Redmeyer, pointing at the rock in front of them.

Nyland looked but couldn't see anything special.

"What is it?" he asked.

"Look there." Redmeyer stretched out his foot and pointed with the toe of his shoe.

And now Nyland noticed that something had been carved into the stone. He squatted down. Redmeyer did the same.

Anton Pederson 1902. And a short distance away: *Mick Gallagher Duluth.*

"There's something special about this rock," said Redmeyer. "It's soft."

"So who are these people?" asked Nyland as he looked for more names close by. "Or rather, who *were* they?"

"A mixture of permanent residents and early tourists, I would guess," said Redmeyer. "I honestly don't know who any of these people were."

Nyland suddenly wished Lance Hansen were there. He could have undoubtedly told them who these people were.

"Except for one," Redmeyer went on. "Look over here . . ."

Nyland turned around and saw the name Sparky was pointing at:

Peder Rødmyr 1896.

"My great-great-grandfather," he said. "So now you can see where my family's name comes from."

"Oh. So Rødmyr became Redmeyer?"

"Yes."

"That means you really are Norwegian."

"Sure. Didn't you know that?" Redmeyer looked at Nyland in surprise.

"No, I didn't."

"Well, of course I'm Norwegian!"

"Where in Norway did old Rødmyr come from?"

"I don't know. Maybe somewhere on the west coast. The most important thing is not where he came from, but the fact that he came *here.*"

Nyland straightened up and took a couple of steps away, on the lookout for more names. They weren't that difficult to find. Some had dates, some did not. He walked around, stopping here and there to read a name:

Emil Mogren 23-4 1904

J. E. Parker Toledo Ohio 1900

Hilda Brekken 14-6 1901

John Hector 98

Thormod Olson 1895

Fanny Barber

Ben Aakre 1899

"Vanished, like ghosts," said Sparky Redmeyer behind him.

"Like smoke," said Eirik Nyland. He turned around and there, standing on the bare rock above him, was Lance Hansen, looking down at them.

"Hi, Lance," said Nyland.

Lance touched his finger to the visor of his Minnesota Vikings cap. He wore sunglasses, a blue short-sleeved shirt, and light summer trousers.

Redmeyer was already on his way up to greet him. Nyland followed close behind.

The three of them stood there, looking around uncertainly, as if none of them had expected to run into each other.

"What's happening out there?" Nyland finally asked. He pointed toward the breakwater, where a few youths were sitting. They seemed to be enjoying the sunset over the lake. But near the lighthouse, at the very end of the breakwater, some birds were making a commotion. Not seagulls this time—these birds were smaller and darker. They had a peculiar way of flying, with their wings held out stiffly and slightly bent.

Redmeyer looked at Nyland. "What do you mean?" he asked.

"The birds." He pointed again. "Don't you see them?"

Redmeyer pulled his sunglasses down and peered over the rims, shading his eyes with one hand. He stared hard at the breakwater. "No," he said. "No, I don't see any birds."

"Well, I can see them," said Lance Hansen. "In fact, I noticed them a while back. I was watching them as you were kneeling down and reading names and dates. I think they're a type of wading bird."

"Are they eating? What are they doing?" Nyland wondered.

Hansen shrugged.

"Would you like to join us out at Artists' Point to watch the fireworks?" asked Redmeyer.

"I don't know . . . ," said Lance hesitantly. "How about if we agree to meet again in ten or fifteen minutes? There's something I have to do first."

"Okay," said Redmeyer.

"So we'll see you out on the promontory?" said Nyland.

Lance nodded.

LANCE HANSEN DIDN'T LOOK BACK, just walked at a slow pace toward the glowing sunset. A quarter of the sun's disk had already disappeared. The sun was slowly sinking into the ridge above town. Kitchi-Gami was colored golden, pink, silvery-white, sulfur-yellow, as well as a number of hues for which no words existed.

The breakwater stretched out straight as an arrow toward the sunset and all the colors. He could still make out a vague figure beyond the foundation of the lighthouse. Even the white tower rising above the figure had almost disappeared in the light. It was this figure that had made him start to walk forward. He didn't know why, but there was something about it that he had to find out. When he met Redmeyer and Nyland, he was certain that they'd notice it, especially when Nyland began talking about the birds out there. But strangely enough, they hadn't seen it.

Some kids were sitting on the breakwater, not far from him. Lance was going to have to walk past behind them. He hoped he didn't know any of the teenagers. But it was possible. Maybe a son or daughter of one of his friends. They were sitting in a row, like birds in the setting sun. Five of them.

He could still see the figure at the very end of the breakwater. It looked like a seated person. A torso. Or could it be a big black sack? No, it was a person.

He had almost reached the teenagers now. One of them, a boy, cast a quick glance at Lance, then turned away to look at the water again. Lance walked behind them. Three boys and two girls. Fifteen or sixteen, he thought. One of the girls leaned back and looked up just as he walked past. He tried to give her a friendly smile, but she looked away, as if he had frightened her.

After passing the teenagers, he glanced quickly over his shoulder and noted that Redmeyer and Nyland were on their way toward the promontory.

The breakwater stretching out in front of him was completely swathed in light, all the way out to the lighthouse. But no one was sitting there anymore. The dark figure seemed almost to have dematerialized. The only way anyone could have slipped away was by walking past Lance, and no one had done that. The breakwater was only about six feet wide. Of course nobody could have passed by without him noticing. Yet he still turned around to look in the opposite direction, but he saw only the five teenagers, sitting there just as they had before. One of them, a boy, was now staring at Lance. The kids then put their heads together to say something, but he couldn't hear what they said.

What the heck, he thought, and started walking again. He didn't know what else to do. It seemed pointless to turn around and go back.

When he was almost up to the lighthouse, a flock of small wading birds rose up from the back of the tower, where they'd been sitting on the pavement. Since they were almost a cement gray themselves, Lance hadn't noticed them. They took off from the spot where the dark figure had been sitting. Now the birds were restlessly swooping around over the water in the harbor.

Lance went between the white-painted steel posts that supported the lighthouse, passed the steps leading up to the hatchway in the
floor, and came out on the other side of the tower. There the breakwater continued on for a few more yards before abruptly ending.

He walked all the way out to the edge and looked down, but
there was nothing to see. When he raised his head again, he saw a
canoe in the water, about sixty-five feet away. He noticed at once
that it was a birchbark canoe. The inner side of the bark gives canoes
like that a lovely yellowish color. This one seemed relatively new.
Lance knew birchbark canoes were still being made in places such
as Grand Portage. But they were sold for high prices as far as he
knew. He'd never seen anyone paddle one before.

A man was kneeling in the back of the canoe. He was using a
short, old-fashioned oar, which also looked new and beautiful. The
man wore a dark jacket and a big round hat. His clothes looked old
and tattered. He was paddling with slow, steady strokes, making the
canoe glide lightly and quickly through the water.

Lance had an urge to call out to the man. It wasn't unusual to
shout and wave to somebody in a boat. And this was a very special
kind of boat. He was just about to raise his hand when the man
stopped paddling and turned to look toward Lance standing on the
breakwater. His face was filthy, in a shiny sort of way, as if he'd spent
a long time sitting in front of a bonfire. And now Lance recognized
him. This was the man he'd seen walking along Highway 61 the day
he drove to Two Harbors to visit Andy and Tammy.

The man continued to glide away in the canoe as he held the
paddle just above the water. His speed decreased, and soon the canoe was almost motionless. But it was still moving just a little, carried forward by the current or the wind. The bow began to point
straight at Lance.

He waited for the man to say something. Surely he had stopped
because he meant to speak.

Lance thought his jacket looked like he'd found it in the attic of
a house that had been unoccupied since before World War II. Discovered in the attic and then put to use, without giving it so much as
a good brushing. At one time it had apparently been black, maybe a
suit jacket, but now it was so worn it seemed almost gray. And then
there was the man's hat with the wide, round brim that drooped a
bit, as if it had been in the water for a long time and lost some of its

original shape. The man in the canoe was truly a pitiful sight. And yet Lance felt nailed to the spot by the man's eyes. Because he wasn't merely looking at Lance, he had fixed his eyes on him. Lance felt his legs turn heavy and stiff while his heart hammered unpleasantly. He didn't know what there was about this man—all he knew was that he'd never experienced this feeling before. Never. To feel someone looking at him this way. A man like this.

At that instant the man lowered the short, old-fashioned oar into the water and began paddling again. He paddled without a sound, which was something only a truly experienced canoeist could do.

Lance watched him go. That broad, stooped back. A few tufts of dark hair visible between his hat and the collar of his jacket. Only now, when the man was no longer staring at him, did Lance realize he was an Ojibwe. And it wasn't because of the fine birchbark canoe or the skill with which he maneuvered it, but because he had an Ojibwe face. Only now did that occur to him. It was the face of a full-blooded Ojibwe.

Of course there were Ojibwe up here, just as there were birchbark canoes. Yet there was something unreal about this whole scene. As if it were a clip from an old documentary film about the Ojibwe Indians of Minnesota. He'd seen films like that, both in school and while working for the U.S. Forest Service. Black-and-white movies of unkempt Ojibwe wearing discarded clothing from white homes. From the worst period of all, around the beginning of the twentieth century, when they looked like a population of vagrants, bums, down-and-outs. The Indian in the canoe looked as if he'd stepped right out of one of those old films.

Lance stayed where he was, watching the canoe glide farther and farther out into the lake. The man had already put a considerable distance between himself and the breakwater. The sun had now almost completely disappeared. Sections of the surface had begun to darken, turning purple. Lance lost sight of the canoe as it crossed the border of one of these patches. He stood there on the breakwater, waiting for the boat to reappear, but that didn't happen.

When he turned to go back to shore, he saw that the five teenagers were no longer sitting there. He was alone on the breakwater. At that moment he heard a shrieking sound, and the first rocket exploded in a shower of green stars above the lake.

20

"I KNOW WHAT KIND OF RELATIONSHIP you and Georg had," said Eirik Nyland calmly. He was standing at the window, looking out. They were on the second floor of the Best Western Motel in Duluth. Outside was a parking lot that was almost full. It was Saturday, July 5.

"No, I don't think you do," said Bjørn Hauglie behind him. "It was a friendship that . . ." His voice broke before he could finish what he wanted to say.

"The two of you were lovers, weren't you?"

"What are you saying?" Hauglie sounded shocked.

"Do you think you're dealing with one of the teachers at your high school back home in Hordaland?" said Nyland, keeping his voice calm. "Or that I'm as naive as your family?"

Empty Coke cans that they'd just finished off stood on the little table between the two chairs in the room. The remains of two pieces of cake were also on the table. Nyland had told Hauglie that he'd gone into town to buy these items. In reality, he'd merely gone down to the lobby, where Bob Lecuyer was waiting with the cakes and sodas. It was at Lecuyer's request that Nyland was interviewing Hauglie alone. "I'm sure he's longing to speak Norwegian with someone. So you already have an advantage," Bob had said.

They had started off talking about inconsequential matters. The consulate in Minneapolis. This hotel room, which Hauglie wouldn't have to pay for, of course. His desire to fly home as soon as possible. Did he really have to stay here until the case was solved? What if it was never solved? Nyland had smiled and assured him that they were not going to detain him in Duluth forever. But after a while the detective stood up and went over to the window. He stood there for a long time, with his back to the room. And then he suddenly said that he knew what kind of relationship the two young men had shared.

Now he was standing in front of Hauglie, who was sitting on the chair, dressed in shorts and a T-shirt.

"The last time we talked, you lied to me. Now you need to tell the truth, no matter what it may be, or I'll make sure that you have much more serious problems than finding a cheap flight home. I can promise you that. You and Georg Lofthus were lovers. You can start there."

"My friend is dead," said Hauglie, a look of disbelief still on his face. "My best friend, and you . . ."

"I've been in contact with Linda," said Nyland.

"Linda?"

"She gave me her version of the story."

Suddenly there was nothing left of Hauglie's attempt at pretense. His expression had changed from feigned bewilderment to something that seemed genuine. He looked away.

"Linda . . . ," he repeated.

"That's right. Linda. What do you think of her?" Nyland pulled the other chair out a bit and sat down. His knees were almost touching Hauglie's. He leaned forward. "A nice girl?"

"Why did you talk to Linda?"

"She was Georg's fiancée, after all. They were going to get married, right?"

Bjørn Hauglie nodded.

"Naturally we had to talk to her," Nyland went on.

"So what did she say?" Hauglie's voice had faded until it was barely a whisper.

"What do you *think* she said?"

He merely shook his head.

"She said that she had started to wonder whether you and Georg were homosexual. That was the word she used. *Homosexual*." He saw how the young man shrank back, as if he'd been punched in the face.

"She said that?"

Nyland nodded.

"That damn . . . that fucking . . . that . . ."

Suddenly he slammed his fist on the table. One of the Coke cans fell to the floor. Nyland calmly leaned down to pick it up. He set it back on the table. He was prepared for this type of reaction. It was exactly where he wanted him. Hauglie was sitting there, gripping the armrests of his chair. For a moment Nyland wondered if the young man was going to throw up.

"Linda Nørstevik is a whore," said Hauglie. He was straining to keep his voice calm. "That's a nasty thing to say, but it's the truth. A slut who has offered herself to anybody and everybody, for as long as I can remember."

"But what about the fact that Georg loved her?"

"*Loved* her? You think Georg *loved* Linda? Are you crazy, man?"

"But they were engaged to be married. Of course he loved her. She was the one he loved."

"What do *you* know about love?" said Hauglie.

"I know at least that you and Georg were lovers. We found your semen in his stomach. Or maybe he swallowed it by accident?"

The young man turned bright red. Then he covered his face with his hands and bent forward. He remained sitting like that, with his face hidden in his hands.

"Take it easy," Nyland said at last. "Personally, I think you and Georg Lofthus had every right to be together. And in whatever way you liked."

Hauglie slowly sat up. He let his hands fall. When his face came into view again, it had changed color, taking on a grayish pallor. He looked at Nyland. *"Right?"* he repeated. *"No one* has the right to defy God's word. A person can't alter the meaning of the Word just in order to give free rein to his own . . . his repulsive . . . his—"

"For everything created by God is good, and nothing is to be rejected, if it is received with thanksgiving," Nyland said, interrupting him. "Do you remember that Bible quote?"

"Paul's first letter to Timothy. Chapter four, verse four. It's a sort of motto in Georg's family. Why are you asking about that?"

"We found his Bible. And the citation is inscribed on the first page, along with a greeting from his grandparents. A confirmation gift."

"Oh. Well, that sounds right."

"Don't you think there's something a bit grotesque about it

now? In light of . . . the relationship the two of you had? The way everything ended, I mean?"

Hauglie shook his head. He seemed totally perplexed.

"Okay, then, let's be a little more specific," said Nyland. "You had sex, and Georg said it was the last time. Right? He talked about Linda again. That he was actually going to get married very soon. To that slut Linda Nørstevik. In a way, I can understand why you did what you did. Or rather, I understand your rage. There's no doubt that you were badly treated."

"What exactly are you getting at?" said Hauglie.

"The truth," said Nyland. "And part of the truth is that you had sex with Georg Lofthus a few hours before he was killed. Lofthus was about to be married to the young woman who you just called a whore and a slut. So far there are no indications that there was a third individual at the scene of the crime. Don't you see where this is going?"

"But there's something I've remembered since the last time we talked. Something that I didn't mention before."

"I'm sure there is," said Nyland sarcastically.

"I think I said that we didn't hear or see any other people near the campsite . . ."

"That's what you said."

"Well, that's not entirely true. While we were out on the lake, we heard voices. Or maybe just one voice. And it happened only once. I'm not even sure where the sound was coming from. That's probably why I didn't mention it last time."

"No doubt," said Nyland, his tone still sarcastic. "And when did this happen, do you think?"

Hauglie looked as if he was giving it plenty of thought. "It was after we set up camp and ate dinner. We went out in the canoe, to paddle in the moonlight. So sometime during the first half of the canoe trip. Between ten and ten thirty, I would guess."

"I see. And what did this voice say, or shout?"

"It was impossible to tell. It lasted only a few seconds."

"So you didn't hear any words?"

"No, I'm afraid not."

"Was the voice talking or yelling?"

"Yelling, I think."

"Aggressively?"

"Maybe. And I think it was only one voice."

"Was it coming from somewhere near your tent?"

"I don't know. We were way out on the lake, you see."

"Did the two of you discuss this?"

"No. I don't even know if Georg noticed. It was just a voice. And only once. Nothing worth discussing."

"Was it a man's voice?"

"Yes, it was."

Nyland knew that while he and Hauglie were talking, the evidence from the crime scene was being analyzed in Chicago. The results would probably come in the following day.

"Did you kill Georg?" he asked.

"No," said Hauglie, his voice loud and emphatic.

"Then who do you think did it?"

"I've thought a lot about it, and I've come to the conclusion that it doesn't matter."

"What do you mean by that?"

"I just mean that whoever killed him was an instrument for something greater. It's actually quite obvious. Maybe not for you, because you're not a believer. You're blind. But for someone who can see, it's not difficult to realize that this was the punishment. The punishment for the way we were living. Georg and I. We brought this upon ourselves."

Nyland listened with interest. Was it himself that Hauglie was talking about as "an instrument for something greater"?

"But if it was God's punishment for how you and Georg were living," he said, "why are you sitting here while Georg is dead? Why would God punish only Georg?"

Bjørn Hauglie looked at Eirik Nyland. It seemed as though he couldn't believe what he'd just heard.

"So you think I've escaped punishment?" he said.

21

LANCE HANSEN had seen Willy Dupree only once since the divorce three years ago. It was at Nancy Dupree's funeral. Willy had been a widower for almost two years now. Lance hadn't talked with him at the funeral. He merely shook hands and offered his condolences.

For a few seconds as he turned onto the road that led to Willy's house, Lance could see a white wooden building that stood all alone down by the lake. Around it was a high palisade of pointed posts. That was the reconstructed headquarters of the North West Company, where Willy used to work as a guide during the tourist season after he retired. He had practically become a tourist attraction himself. An old Indian gave the visitors a feeling of authenticity. It was only two years ago that he had stopped being a guide.

When Willy's house came into view, Lance remembered what it had felt like to drive Mary home in the evening during that first summer, when she was still living upstairs in her parents' house. He glanced up at the window that had been hers. It was dark and there were no curtains.

He parked and climbed out of the Jeep. A moment later the door opened and there stood Willy Dupree.

The most noticeable change was that he'd become considerably smaller. Both shorter and thinner. As if someone had shrunk his body. Otherwise he didn't look bad, considering that he was now eighty years old. When he opened his mouth to speak, Lance could hear that his voice had also changed. It had lost all strength. As if it were coming from the other side of a wall.

"Lance . . . ," said Willy. "It's been a long time."

....

TWO OLD PHOTOGRAPHS in oval frames hung above the sofa. A
man and a woman with white hair and sunken, toothless mouths.
Under the pictures hung a dream catcher. It was the size of a person's palm, faded, gray with age.

Without thinking, Lance had sat down in the same easy chair
that he always used to sit in whenever they came to visit. When he
realized what he'd done, his first impulse was to get up and move.
But he stopped himself.

He heard the floorboards creak out in the kitchen. Willy came
in, carrying a plate of cookies. His hands shook, but he would have
been annoyed if Lance had offered to help. He set the plate on the
table and, with some effort, sank down on the other easy chair.

"Getting old is the shits," he said.

Lance had intended to ask how things were going, but now he
simply nodded, to show that he accepted Willy's pronouncement.

"At least my hearing is still good," he added.

"I'm glad. That must make it easier to talk to Jimmy," said Lance.

"He's over here every day. He's all I live for now."

Lance noticed that his ex-father-in-law's voice quavered.

"Do the two of you still go fishing?" he asked.

"Oh no . . . I can't . . . it wouldn't be safe."

Lance nodded sympathetically.

"Go ahead and have a cookie," said Willy.

Lance knew at once that Mary had baked them.

"I heard you found a dead man."

"Yeah."

"And they haven't caught who did it?"

"No."

For a moment neither of them spoke. Lance looked at the
dream catcher hanging on the wall over the sofa. He thought that it
was the opposite of what he needed. He could use something that
released dreams. Because it was as if all dreams, both good and bad,
got caught in an invisible dream catcher that was always hanging
over him when he slept.

"There's something I was wondering about," he said.

"What's that?"

"Earlier today I was going through some photographs in the archive. Soderberg's archive. And I happened to come across a picture

207

that was from you." He took the old photo out of his shirt pocket and handed it to Willy.

Willy put on his glasses and studied the picture. After a moment he shook his head. "I've never seen this before," he said.

"But it says 'Owner, William Dupree,' in Soderberg's list of photos."

The white-haired man slumped in the easy chair looked equally puzzled. "I can't remember ever donating photographs to the historical society. Can you?"

"No, not in my time. But this picture was apparently given to Olga Soderberg."

"When was it that she started collecting material?" Willy asked.

"Before the war, at least."

"She must have gotten it from my father." He nodded toward the two pictures on the wall above the sofa. "Dad was also named Willy Dupree. Or rather, William."

"Of course," said Lance.

"Do you know who the man is in the picture?" Willy handed the photo to Lance, who put it back in his shirt pocket.

"Joe Caribou."

He could see Willy soundlessly repeating the name to himself as he tried to make some connection.

"And who was that?"

"Swamper Caribou's brother."

"Ah, Swamper Caribou . . . now that's a name I haven't heard in a long time," Willy said. "'Don't go down to the lake alone, or Swamper Caribou will get you.' That's what the grown-ups used to say when I was a boy."

"Have you heard stories about him?"

"Sure, lots of stories. But most of them were nonsense, you know."

"Like what?"

"Hmm . . . like about the girl who disappeared. I remember that. Here in Grand Portage. Everybody knew she was a wild one. She didn't need a ghost to make her vanish, I can promise you that. But nevertheless . . . My mother made up a story. And she said the girl was lured into a canoe, and it was Swamper Caribou's doing. He paddled her out on the lake, and she was never seen again. My mother claimed to have seen this in a dream. Evidently the girl was actually pregnant and ran off to Minneapolis, or something like that."

"So you don't believe the story?"

"Stories." Willy rubbed his chin. "If you knew how many stories I've heard in my lifetime," he said. "And most of them will never be told again."

"Why not?"

"They'll die out with my generation. Everything the old ones told us when I was a boy."

"Are there any stories about Swamper Caribou that you *do* believe?"

"I don't know. One of my uncles told me about when he was out hunting near the lake. Suddenly he caught sight of a man sitting cross-legged on the top of a big boulder. A couple of inches of new snow covered the ground, so it was impossible to move without leaving footprints. But there were no prints leading to the boulder. My uncle said that the man just sat there, staring. Motionless. But then a gust of wind blew the stinging snow into my uncle's face, and he had to shut his eyes tight. When he opened them, the man was gone. My uncle went over to the boulder to look around. But the only footprints in sight were his own. According to my uncle, it was Swamper Caribou that he'd seen."

"And what do you think?" asked Lance.

"The man who told me the story was a trustworthy man. That much I know," said Willy Dupree.

"Have you ever heard any theories about what happened to Swamper Caribou?"

"No. He just disappeared. That's what I've always heard."

"Sure, but that alone must have stirred up speculation about what happened to him. From a purely factual point of view, I mean. Did he drown? Was it possible that he was killed?"

Lance could see that Willy was hesitating. The furrowed face of the old Indian was moving, as if he were chewing on something.

"Do you know what a windigo is?" he asked.

"Isn't it some sort of monster?" said Lance.

"A windigo is an ice giant. It looks like an incredibly huge human being, but it's made out of ice. You might ask: Where do windigos come from? Certain individuals become windigos. Then they hide in the woods and come out only when they want human flesh. Because they're cannibals. Ice cannibals."

"Did people think that's what happened to Swamper Caribou?" said Lance. "That he became a windigo?"

"No," replied Willy. "They thought that he'd *met* a windigo. And that it killed and ate him."

"An ice cannibal . . ."

"But the whole story is nothing but nonsense. It belongs to a different time. The old ones no doubt thought that it would take a supernatural being to slay Swamper Caribou. He was a powerful medicine man, you know."

"If someone became a windigo, could he ever become human again?" asked Lance.

"Yes. But first somebody would have to catch the windigo. And then a magic ritual was performed to melt the ice. The human being who had become a windigo still existed in a space inside the ice giant."

"A space?"

"Almost like a child in the mother's womb," said Willy, forming his hands into a protective hollow to illustrate what he meant.

Lance thought about how many times he'd seen those hands carefully taking hold of Jimmy to lift him up. The soft little baby body and the old leathery hands. And suddenly he knew that he could tell everything to Willy Dupree. *I can tell him about Andy!* he thought. Willy would never say a word to anyone. Nothing could make him do anything that harmed Jimmy. The old man *lived* for the boy. He'd said so himself: "He's over here every day. He's all I live for now."

"There's something I have to tell you," said Lance. "It's a secret. Something that you'll think about every day for the rest of your life."

"Something to do with Jimmy?" asked the old man.

"No. At least not directly. It's something . . . a secret that nobody . . . but I can't bear to keep it to myself any longer."

He paused for a moment.

"All right. What is it?" Willy asked, sounding like someone who expected the worst.

"It's . . . ," Lance began.

"What?"

"I know . . . I *think* I know . . ." He couldn't look Willy in the eye as he spoke. "I think I know who killed . . ."

Silence settled over them. He couldn't even hear Willy breathing. The old man had fixed his gaze on Lance's face. His lips were lightly parted. He was sitting there, waiting to hear what Lance would say next.

"I think I know who killed Swamper Caribou."

Willy looked bewildered. "Really?" was all he said.

"Yes. I'm not a hundred percent sure. It was a long time ago, after all. But it was probably not a windigo that did it."

"So who do you think killed him?"

"One of my ancestors. A relative on my mother's side."

"A Norwegian?"

"Yes. Thormod Olson. Have you ever heard of him?"

"No, but why do you think he killed Swamper Caribou?"

"Because of the convergence of time and place. Thormod came here from Norway in March 1892. That was when Swamper Caribou disappeared. In an article in the *Grand Marais Pioneer* from that same year, it says he went missing sometime around the full moon, which was on March sixteenth. Thormod Olson was on his way from Duluth to Carlton Peak, where his uncle lived. At night, he walked across the ice in the moonlight, heading across the bays. Near the mouth of the Cross River, he fell through the ice and almost drowned. That was also where Swamper Caribou had his hunting cabin. That was where he disappeared. It looks like these two things happened more or less at the same time, and in the same place. I wonder whether the story about falling through the ice was just something that Thormod made up. Maybe he met Swamper Caribou somewhere, and for some reason ended up getting into a fight with him."

"I don't understand this," said Willy. "How can you be sure that the Norwegian killed Swamper Caribou?"

"I'm not sure. And yet . . ."

"Lance . . . it happened more than a hundred years ago. Why are you letting an old story like this get you so upset?"

"Well, I . . . I don't know . . . I don't know what's wrong with me. Maybe I'm just in a difficult place in my life."

"You should get married again," said Willy Dupree.

"Why?"

"You're spending too much time brooding about things. It's not good for someone to live alone the way you do. Not a man of your age, in any case. A man needs a woman. Here, take another cookie."

Lance did as he was told.

22

HE WAS ON HIS WAY TO ANDERSON LAKE, where two men had been observed setting out nets. He suspected they were Ojibwe. If so, they had the right to be fishing with nets. On the other hand, if they were not Ojibwe, fishing was strictly forbidden, and Lance would have to issue fines and confiscate the nets. He'd done this many times before. It was a routine part of his job.

On the previous day, which was a Sunday, he'd gone into his small office at the ranger station and scanned four pages from Nanette's diary. Then he had faxed them to a translation agency in St. Paul that specialized in handwritten texts, often in the form of old letters from Europe. He started by faxing a single page so they could determine whether this was a task they could handle. A short time later he received a pleasant e-mail confirming that there shouldn't be any particular problems. They would send the translation to his personal e-mail address as soon as it was finished, just as he'd requested. They thought it would take about a week. Most likely he would receive the completed translation the following weekend.

As he drove to Anderson Lake, he thought about his visit to Willy Dupree two days earlier. His ex-father-in-law would have protected the secret as faithfully as Lance was doing, in order to spare his grandchild. But if Lance had told Willy, he would have made his own guilt even greater. That was what he realized at the last minute. He now knew that he couldn't share this secret with anyone. He would have to bear it alone.

"Don't give any more thought to Swamper Caribou," Willy had told Lance when he was about to leave. "He just disappeared."

But of course he was still thinking about Swamper Caribou. He was also thinking about the Indian he'd seen in Grand Marais. The man paddling the birchbark canoe. The same man he'd seen walking along Highway 61. It was as if a photograph had come alive. Or at least started moving. The image that should have been contained within the narrow white borders of a black-and-white picture had leaked out into the world and was now moving around like some sort of animated double-exposure.

HE FOUND A SUITABLE PARKING SPOT next to a pile of old logs that for some reason had never been picked up. Then he began making his way through bracken that reached almost to his waist. Up ahead was the edge of the pine forest that surrounded most of Anderson Lake. Between the tree trunks he could see the glitter of water. As he stepped in among the tall, straight pines, he paused to lean against one of them. He raised his binoculars to his eyes and quickly spotted two plastic jugs floating in the water, about a net's length from each other. Then he caught sight of two men sitting in a canoe close to shore, making ready a third net. They were no more Ojibwe than Lance was. They looked like they might be brothers. Two young brothers putting out nets. And it was Lance's job to punish them for that offense. Yet he was the person who was hiding the identity of a murderer. What right did he have to intervene with these two young men? Did their illegal net fishing really matter, compared with Lance's sins? No. That much he knew. And even though his job required him to confiscate the nets and fine the men, he still made no move to do any such thing. Yet this was one of his responsibilities. How would things end if he stopped doing his job? Then he thought about what had already happened. When he decided not to tell anyone that Andy was the perpetrator, he stopped being a real policeman. That was the moment when he became corrupt. Because that was what he was: a dirty cop. Not the type who took bribes, but the kind who looked through his fingers when it came to close family members. And that was basically just as bad.

As the two young men went about setting out a third net, Lance quietly returned to his vehicle.

He checked his cell phone, which was lying on the passenger seat, and saw that Sheriff Eggum had called his private number. For a moment he thought about calling him back, but changed his mind. Instead he simply sat in the pickup truck, staring straight ahead. He sat there motionless for maybe ten minutes. Then he remembered that he was only a few miles from Andy's cabin at Lost Lake. And according to his brother, that was where he'd spent the entire night when the murder was committed. Lance knew where the key was. He had permission to go inside and use the cabin for his lunch breaks whenever he liked. He hadn't used it in a long time, but there was no reason for him to think Andy had moved the key to a different hiding place.

HE PARKED IN THE USUAL SPOT, which was invisible from the road, and began walking along the path through the pine forest. He'd taken this path countless times before. But it was strange how seldom he'd been out here with Andy, even though the cabin belonged to his brother. He remembered that one time Chrissy was with him. She must have been about seven back then. But that was just a day trip, of course. Lance had never stayed overnight at his brother's cabin, either alone or with Andy, even though the place was equipped with its own generator.

As soon as the brown-painted walls of the building appeared between the trees, Lance had a feeling that the cabin was somehow connected to the murder. He stopped on the path. Stood still, staring at this place that everyone had overlooked. A small piece of the puzzle from the night of the murder. Every other place had undoubtedly been turned upside down and finecombed for evidence, but no one had been out here. He was sure of that. The police had no idea the cabin was even here, radiating a dark attraction over Lance, just as the body of Georg Lofthus had done while it was still lying in the birch woods and Lance was in the parking lot with the local police. But the FBI hadn't been out here to take photographs or record observations in little black notebooks.

For safety's sake he knocked on the door, but of course no one was inside the cabin. He pressed down on the handle, tugged at the door. Then he leaned down and pulled out a loose brick from the foundation. But there was nothing in the little hollow where the key was usually left. He peeked under the doormat and ran his hand along the narrow ledge above the door, but the key wasn't there either. What was the point of telling him that he could use the cabin for his lunch breaks if he couldn't find the key?

He tried peering through a window, but the curtains were drawn. The whole area was fragrant with the scent of sun-drenched heather and pine needles. Between the tree trunks he could glimpse the water of Lost Lake. An acrid smell came from an anthill somewhere close by. He heard insects buzzing, but otherwise it was quiet, with no sign of any people.

Lance was still holding the loose brick. Now he raised his hand and slammed the brick against the windowpane. With a crash the glass fell in and landed on the floor inside. He stood still and listened for a few seconds but heard only the usual buzzing of insects in the woods on a hot summer day.

After opening the window and removing as much of the glass as possible from the sill, Lance went to find an old barbecue grill from behind the cabin and brought it back with him.

Okay, now I can add this to my list, he thought as he climbed up on the rickety grill. Breaking and entering. A policeman at work!

With an effort he was able to haul his upper body onto the windowsill. It hurt his stomach and he was breathing hard. For a moment he was afraid he'd end up just hanging there, sort of like a down quilt hung up to air out, until somebody found his lifeless body. That thought reenergized him. Groaning with pain, he forced his heavy body over the sill until he could finally touch the floor inside with his hands. Then he let himself fall forward with a thud.

Scattered all over the floor were shards of glass, both big and small pieces, from the window he'd just shattered. He got to his feet and looked around. The room consisted of a nook for a sofa, coffee table, and TV. A worn easy chair stood in front of the fireplace. Under one of the two windows was a simple table with four spindle back chairs. To the right of the front door was a small refrigerator and stove, with a small kitchen counter and sink. A door led to the bedroom, while another one led to the minuscule bathroom. Both of these doors were closed.

Lance didn't notice anything out of the ordinary. An empty Coke can stood on the counter. He went over and picked it up, as if it might be a valuable piece of evidence. But it wasn't. Andy always drank Coke. Unlike Lance, who had to stick with Diet Coke, Andy could eat and drink anything he liked and never gain any weight.

There was nothing unusual in the cabin, as far as Lance could tell. He was just about to turn around when he caught sight of something that looked suspiciously like blood in the sink. Just a small drop. He touched it cautiously with his index finger. It was blood, all right. And it seemed very fresh. Lance held up his finger to study the blood. Then he noticed that he'd got a little cut on his ring finger, right at the tip. That was where the blood had come from. He touched it with his thumb. A sharp pain told him a piece of glass was still embedded in the flesh. He looked around, hoping to find a roll of paper towels, but he was out of luck. A new drop of blood fell from his fingertip onto the floor. It was a tiny cut, but since it was on his finger, the bleeding was relatively heavy. What should he do? He couldn't leave blood all over the floor of his brother's cabin. That was a stupid thought. He knew that, but he couldn't get it out of his mind. Those little drops of blood were too much for him. He held his hand over the sink again so the blood disappeared down the drain. Several dark drops were visible on the floor at his feet. He looked from the blood to the shattered glass and then back again, taking in a deep breath and letting it out with a shudder.

In the bathroom he found some toilet paper, which he wrapped around his finger. He stuffed some more paper in his pants pocket. Then he went back to the main room and looked around, as if still searching for some evidence to prove his brother's innocence.

Andy doesn't even know I'm protecting him, Lance thought. I'll never get a word of thanks for doing this. No one will ever know what I've done for my brother. It occurred to him that this was something he'd have to keep on doing for the rest of his life. It would never be over.

He thought of Clayton Miller on the ground in the schoolyard on that day when sixteen-year-old Andy came around the corner of the building, holding a baseball bat in his hand. With that completely lost look in his eyes. That lonely stare. That's where it all began, thought Lance. In the schoolyard on that day so long ago. That's why I'm standing here. That's why I broke into his cabin.

Why did you do it? Lance knew he should have asked Andy that question. Their parents should have asked him too. There had to be a reason. And Lance was convinced the motive was similar to the one that had made Andy kill the Norwegian tourist. There was a space inside his brother that was filled with cruelty. A space he might not ever visit voluntarily. But if someone happened to open the door by accident, Andy immediately became part of that cruelty. And then he was deadly dangerous. He must never suspect that Lance knew anything. Because then Lance's life would probably be in danger too.

He looked around. It wouldn't take long for Andy to discover the break-in. Was there anything that might lead him to think Lance was behind it? He hadn't taken anything. Everything was in its place, except for the pieces of glass on the floor.

Lance opened the cupboard above the sink, took out a glass, and dropped it to the floor, but it didn't break. Annoyed, he bent down and picked it up. Then he raised it high overhead, and with all his might he hurled it to the floor. Pieces of glass sprayed out over the room. He got out another tumbler and threw it against the wall. More shards of glass rained down over the room. In quick succession he broke four more glasses, three coffee mugs, and six big dinner plates. When he was done, he went into the bathroom and stuffed the whole roll of toilet paper into the toilet. Then he went into the bedroom and tore the bedclothes off all four bunk beds. He pulled one of the mattresses out of its frame and flung it into the living room.

He thought that at last it was starting to look as if some teenagers had vandalized the place. He was about to go back to the main room when he caught sight of a magazine. It was lying in plain view on the bedroom floor. He hadn't noticed it before because he was so busy throwing things around. At first he thought it was a porn magazine, but when he picked it up, he saw that it was a music publication called *Darkside*. He leafed through it for a moment. It was filled with black-clad people with edgy hairstyles. But there was something that didn't make sense. The idea of Andy buying a copy of *Darkside* was as likely as him starting up a rock band. He wouldn't have bought it. He wouldn't have brought it here. The magazine had to belong to a teenager, which meant it must be Chrissy's, thought Lance. At the same time, he couldn't quite believe that seventeen-year-old Chrissy would bother coming up here to the cabin anymore.

It was the June issue of the magazine. If Chrissy really had

brought it to the cabin, that meant she must have been here sometime during the three weeks before the Norwegian was killed. She
couldn't have been here after that, because Tammy was refusing to
allow her daughter to go anywhere after she heard about the murder. It was only a few days ago that he and Tammy had discussed
this very subject while they waited for Andy to come home. At that
time she told Lance she first learned of the murder when Andy and
Chrissy came home the next day. And in that context the "next day"
meant Wednesday, June 25, the same day Lance had found the dead
man. Andy had been out at the cabin, while Chrissy spent the night
with a girlfriend, and the next day they'd come home together. Andy
had gone to Duluth to pick up his daughter. Lance suddenly recalled
the look on Andy's face when Tammy said Lance had come over to
talk to them about Chrissy. It was the same hopeless, lost expression
that he'd had in the schoolyard, holding the baseball bat in his hands.

Had father and daughter been here together on that night?

Lance went into the main room and took one last look around.
He shook his head at the destruction. At least he wouldn't have to
crawl through the window again. The door had a latch that could be
opened from the inside. He was still holding the *Darkside* in his left
hand. From his right hand trailed a long piece of bloody toilet paper.
He tossed the magazine back in the bedroom, unwrapped the toilet
paper from his finger and dropped it on the floor. His finger had
stopped bleeding. It wasn't a bad cut, but when he touched it, he
could definitely feel the piece of glass was still in his finger.

LANCE DROVE STRAIGHT to his cousin's canoe rental place near
Sawbill Lake. He couldn't remember ever seeing so many customers
before. That was good for business, of course, but Lance doubted
Gary would have time to take a break and talk.

Finally he found a free parking spot between two other cars. He
got out, pulled his sunglasses down a bit, and peered over the rims,
squinting in the sunlight. Blue-clad teenagers were busy showing
inexperienced customers how to lift a canoe up onto their shoulders
with a few simple motions. Lance knew from experience how heavy
a canoe could feel if not lifted properly.

He went inside and saw Gary standing behind the counter, fill-
ing out paperwork. In front of the counter stood a small group of

tourists. But Gary wasn't working alone. Next to him stood the brunette, the one that Lance suspected his cousin was sleeping with.

As he stood there, studying them, he couldn't help noticing how at ease they seemed with each other. At one point the girl leaned close to say something to Gary, who merely nodded affirmatively as he continued to write down the information that the man standing on the other side of the counter was providing. At that moment, they seemed like a married couple. Lance saw it quite clearly. There was something about the way they were working side by side, something intimate, as if it were perfectly natural for them to be together. He had the same feeling as last time—he suspected then that Gary must be having an affair, and now he was more convinced than ever.

As Lance was thinking about all this, Gary suddenly looked up from the paperwork and let his eyes sweep over the room. He caught sight of his cousin standing there, watching him. His face lit up. He was pleasantly surprised, which made Lance feel happy. He was always a welcome visitor here. Gary gave Lance a wave to indicate that he'd be with him soon; he just had to take care of something first. Lance nodded. He saw his cousin whisper something to the brunette before he disappeared into the back room. A moment later he came out accompanied by a young man who took over his place behind the counter.

"So, how's it going?" said Gary as he came over to Lance.

"Good. What about you?"

"Can't complain."

"I was wondering if we could have lunch together, but I had no idea you'd be this busy," said Lance apologetically.

"I know. It's crazy, isn't it? But I've got to have some food sometime, no matter what. Let's see . . . If you sit down at one of the tables out back, I'll join you as soon as I can. I've just got a few more things to do."

"Could we sit inside?" asked Lance. "It's so hot today, and there's still one free table over there." He nodded toward the café area.

"Sorry, but we can't take up space at a table indoors. If you want to dine with the servants, you'll have to make do with a table out back. Go on and sit down. I'll bring some food when I join you. What would you like?"

"A grilled chicken sandwich."

"Diet Coke?"

"Sure. And coffee."

Lance went out the back door of the big log building and sat down at an empty table. This was where the employees usually ate their lunch, or just took a break, although there clearly wasn't much time for that today. Here too most of the tables were occupied by tourists.

Surely Gary has to realize there's no future in that sort of affair, thought Lance. He had to be at least twenty years older than the young woman. But he supposed the relationship had nothing to do with the future or plans to grow closer or anything like that. It was no doubt about an irresistible attraction. Even though Gary was putting his marriage at risk and probably knew the relationship couldn't last, he must feel alive in a completely different way than Lance felt. And he envied his cousin for that. The last time he was here he'd worried about Gary's wife, Barb. He thought he was going to have a hard time being around her, since he suspected Gary was carrying on an affair behind her back. But now he no longer cared. He wasn't happy about the situation, but the next time he saw Barb, he'd be the one hiding a much worse family secret than Gary's little fling with a summer employee.

"Here's some coffee while you're waiting," said a young voice.

Lance looked up. There stood the brunette, smiling at him. She set a coffee mug on the table.

"Gary will join you soon," she said.

"Thanks. That was nice of you."

He couldn't take his eyes off her face. He now saw that it wasn't just her youth that made her so attractive. There was something unique about her, or at least something that might make a person believe there was something unique inside of her. She also had a light dusting of tiny freckles across her nose. So this was the face that had captivated Gary. At least that was what Lance thought was going on.

She suddenly seemed embarrassed and lowered her eyes under his stare. Then she frowned. "You're bleeding," she said.

Lance looked down at his hands. The little cut had started bleeding again, although he hadn't noticed, and blood was now smeared over most of his palm and the inside of his fingers. It looked much worse than it was.

"It's nothing. Just a little piece of glass that's stuck in my finger," he told her.

"You should get it taken out. Wait here and I'll bring the first aid kit."

Before Lance could stop her, she dashed inside the building.

When she returned, she was carrying a first aid kit and a package of moist towelettes. The next instant she was sitting next to him, only a few inches away. She smelled of some sort of floral scent. Maybe from her skin cream, or was it her shampoo? When she took his hand and began cleaning it up with a towelette, the touch of her soft hands came as a shock to Lance. He couldn't remember the last time he'd felt anything like that. Maybe she sensed this, because she moved away a bit. Almost imperceptibly, just a slight shift in her center of gravity, but Lance noticed. She retreated a bit.

Then she took a pair of tweezers out of the first aid kit and held them ready in her right hand as she used the fingers of her left hand to squeeze the flesh of Lance's fingertip. The little cut opened between her fingers. "I can see the glass," she said. "Hold still now . . ." With a steady hand she inserted the tweezers into the cut.

Lance felt a slight tug as she pulled out the piece of glass.

"There," she said, holding up the tweezers to show him the tiny piece of glass, like a trophy. "Now I'll just clean it up."

She sprayed antiseptic on his fingertip. Then she carefully wrapped it in a Band-Aid. "All right. So, I'm sure Gary will be here any minute," she said, getting to her feet.

Lance watched her go back inside the building. There was something unreal about the thought that she and Gary were having an affair. Was it really possible?

Gary appeared in the door, carrying a tray. Cardboard sandwich boxes, paper cups filled with soda, and a thermos. He seemed younger.

"Here we are," he said as he set the lunch tray on the table. "Dig in. It's on the house."

The two cousins opened the boxes and started eating. For a while neither said a word. Then Gary asked, "Did you cut yourself?"

"Yeah. When I was cleaning up a campsite. On some broken beer bottles."

"Damn teenagers."

"But one of your employees helped me out. That young woman who was working with you behind the counter when I arrived."

"Jennifer. That was nice of her."

"Uh-huh. Not many girls would take the trouble to help an old man."

"Nope. You're right about that," said Gary.

He seems the same as usual, thought Lance. Could he be mistaken? But then he remembered the sight of the two of them behind the counter. It's hard to hide that sort of thing, he thought. It has something to do with the degree of trust between two bodies. It's noticeable when two people are used to being in each other's arms.

Under other circumstances he might have asked Gary about it, but not anymore. Lance had no right to an opinion about the morality of his cousin's actions. It was Gary who ought to take Lance to task and explain that he couldn't do what he was now doing. Protecting a murderer. Breaking into a cabin. Lying to the FBI.

"So how are you really doing?" asked Gary. He didn't look at Lance as he asked the question.

"Great."

"Sure?" Gary still didn't look at him.

"Yeah," said Lance, starting to get annoyed. "Why shouldn't I be great?"

Gary pretended to take a sip of his coffee. Lance had seen this ploy before. Whenever his cousin was feeling uncertain, he would always do something to divert attention. He would cough, for example. Or he'd suddenly have to blow his nose, as if he had a cold. Right now he raised the mug to his lips and pretended to drink.

"I don't know, but I was just thinking that . . . you found that dead Norwegian . . . ," he said as he slowly set the mug back down on the table. "I've been thinking a lot about it lately. That sort of thing doesn't happen every day."

"No, of course not," said Lance.

"So everything's okay, then?"

"Sure."

Lance realized that this was Gary's way of offering support. But he couldn't tell his cousin about what had happened. The moment he opened his mouth to say that Andy had killed the Norwegian, it would all be over. The world that he knew would be destroyed. Not just for him, but for everybody who was part of it. Andy, of course.

But also Tammy and Chrissy. And for Lance's own son, Jimmy. But it would be worst of all for Inga. Her son a murderer! She had undoubtedly long ago suppressed what happened to Clayton Miller. Did we ever talk about that? wondered Lance. Did we ask *why*? No. Of course it was a shock that Andy had almost killed a boy, but the thought of finding out why was even worse.

Lance sipped his coffee and took a bite of the chicken sandwich.

"I'm doing great," he repeated. "Working a little too hard, maybe, but who isn't?"

"Don't get me started," said Gary, making a show of looking at all the people surrounding them. "But I can't really complain. A man's got to be happy as long as he has plenty to do. And he has his health. How's Inga doing, by the way?"

"Really good."

"Do you visit her often?"

"You know I do. I've actually been thinking of taking her out for a drive sometime soon."

The truth was that the idea hadn't occurred to him until that very moment. It was just a passing thought. But now it seemed like exactly the right thing to do. He missed his mother.

23

THE PHONE WAS RINGING ON THE TABLE NEXT TO HIM. Groggy and only half-awake, he finally managed to pick it up. Peering at the display, he recognized the home phone number of Sheriff Eggum.

He cleared his throat. "Hello?" he said.

"Lance?" said Eggum on the other end of the line.

"Hi, Bill. Um, what time is it?"

"Ten to seven. In the evening. Did I wake you up? Your voice sounds a little . . ."

"Yeah, I must have dozed off."

The sheriff laughed. "Soon I'll be able to do the same thing. After I retire. Then I can sleep as much as I want. But you're just a youngster."

Lance was still so tired he was having trouble thinking of a response.

"You know what?" the sheriff went on. "I'm calling to tell you that the FBI has issued an arrest warrant in the murder case."

Suddenly Lance was sitting bolt upright on the sofa. "Arrest warrant?" he said. "Who did they arrest?"

"A man from Grand Portage. An Ojibwe. It turned out that an Ojibwe did it."

"When did this happen?"

"Today. This morning."

"Why did they arrest him?"

"Because they think he's the killer, of course."

"But as far as I know, there was no concrete evidence." Lance noticed that his voice was shaking.

"Oh, but there was. At the crime scene. Biological traces."

"Fingerprints?"

"DNA."

"Are you saying that they found this man's DNA at the crime scene?"

"Yes . . . or no, not exactly. It turned out to be impossible to get a complete DNA profile from the material they had. It was just a matter of a few microscopic drops of blood. But what they did find out was that the blood had to come from an Indian. Or rather, a man with a certain amount of Indian genes. Not necessarily a full-blood, in other words. Apparently it's a question of a mutation in a gene, or something like that. Something that only Indians have. So that led them straight to Grand Portage."

"But good Lord, there are Indians living everywhere in Minnesota," exclaimed Lance. "All over the country, for that matter. Why exactly Grand Portage?"

"Because early in the investigation they got a tip about a man who lives in Grand Portage. An anonymous tip. They even interviewed this individual, but decided that he didn't have anything to do with the murder."

"But now they've arrested this same man?"

"Yes. They managed to tear apart his alibi."

"But what's the motive?"

"Well, that's not clear yet, but apparently he's a drug addict, so I'm guessing that he must have snapped while he was on some sort of drug. But isn't it great that they've finally caught him?"

"Sure. Of course."

Lance still couldn't figure out how this had come about, but if the biological evidence proved that an Indian had killed Georg Lofthus, he didn't need to worry anymore about what Andy was doing that night. He could forget about the whole thing. Andy wasn't a murderer after all. Lance almost felt like crying.

"Are you still there?" asked Eggum.

"Yeah, I'm here."

"Are you okay?"

"I'm just incredibly relieved."

"So this has really been hard on you, huh?" said the sheriff.

"Much harder than I thought." Lance could hear that he didn't have full control over his voice.

"I can understand that. It was . . . what should I say? It was very *unfortunate* that you should have to stumble over . . . well, you know what I mean. Regardless, now we can all breathe easy and tell the women and children that the killer is under lock and key," said Eggum.

"Do you know what his name is?"

"Hmm . . . what did they tell me it was? I wrote it down, didn't I? But where? Oh . . . wait a minute . . ."

Lance heard Eggum put down the phone and walk around the room, muttering to himself. A moment later he was back on the line.

"Now let's see . . . ," said Eggum. "His name is Lenny Diver. Does that ring a bell?"

Lance paused to think for a few seconds.

"No," he said. "I've never heard that name before. But tell me one thing. Has he confessed?"

"Not yet, but they found a possible murder weapon in his possession."

"What sort of weapon?"

"A baseball bat. I think it was in his car. He claimed someone planted it there."

"Who would do something like that? The police?"

"Or the murderer."

"Do *you* think he's guilty?" asked Lance.

"A drug addict with a baseball bat seems to fit the bill for such a random and stupid act of violence—just like I've always thought it would turn out to be," said the sheriff. "The Norwegian was just in the wrong place at the wrong time. That must be what happened. A totally meaningless act. So, yeah, I think he's guilty."

AFTER TALKING TO BILL EGGUM, Lance went straight to the kitchen to get a Mesabi Red out of the fridge. He leaned against the counter and drank the whole bottle in four or five gulps.

Could it really be that simple? Just one phone call and the whole thing was over? If the biological evidence indicated that Georg Lofthus was killed by an Indian, then Andy couldn't possibly have done it. Plain and simple. Lance knew that no matter what, his brother had secrets that shouldn't, for all the world, get out, but he no longer believed that Andy had killed anyone.

Suddenly he remembered what it felt like to put on his running shoes in the hallway and go out running on the first springlike day of the year. Duluth, sometime back in the 1970s. A clear sidewalk after a long winter with lots of snow. The lake glittering in the sunlight. His legs feeling light, his feet practically flying over the cement. He had a similar feeling right now. An urge to run out of the house. Jump and kick like a ten-year-old. I can live with all the other questions, he thought. I can live with my own failure. The fact that I'm not a good policeman. Plenty of people live with much worse things. The only thing that Lance hadn't known if he could live with was the thought that his brother was a murderer. And having to hide a killer's identity. But now he'd been freed from that burden. Freed from having to find out whether he could have lived with that or not.

Then he happened to think about Inga. His mother was no longer in danger. Her world was not going to fall apart. She would leave this world without having been deeply hurt by one of her sons.

He went into the living room and called her at the nursing home in Duluth. When he heard how excited she was at the idea of going for a drive, he felt a pang of guilt at not suggesting it long ago.

"All the way to Grand Portage?" she exclaimed with enthusiasm.

"Yep. All the way up there. Does that sound good, Mom?"

Nothing had sounded that good to Inga Hansen in a long time.

After talking with his mother, Lance got another beer from the kitchen, opened it, and took it along to his home office. The window was open. He pulled a chair over and sat down, propping his feet up on the windowsill. He drank his beer. He still felt an urge to go running, but it was probably safer for a man of his age to sit here, comfortably leaning back and enjoying a Mesabi Red. He breathed in the cool evening air, the fragrance of flowers and grass. He could also smell the heat that had settled in the walls of the house, which had baked in the sun all afternoon. And the water. Underlying everything else was the clear scent of freshwater. He recognized it at once. It was the smell of the lake. In the wintertime the smell was sharper, rawer, with a tinge of iron. But he realized now that he hadn't noticed it in years.

24

EIRIK NYLAND was sitting on the flat rocks near Baraga's Cross, on a cream-colored blanket he'd brought with him from the hotel. Next to him was a red ice chest he'd just bought. Inside were a Viking ship, a bottle of Gammel Opland, and four bottles of Mesabi Red.

It's just so typical, he thought. When the breakthrough finally came, it turned out that the perpetrator was someone they'd already had contact with, but had decided was not of particular interest. Bjørn Hauglie had been of far greater interest the whole time. And the two men had actually been interviewed on the same day. While Bob Lecuyer and Nyland were in Duluth to talk to Hauglie for the first time, Jason Fries had gone up to Grand Portage to have a talk with a twenty-five-year-old named Lenny Diver. An anonymous man had called the police, claiming that it was Diver who had killed the Norwegian at Baraga's Cross. Diver had twice been indicted for possession of meth. He'd also served time for drunk driving. He was what the Norwegian press loved to call "an individual known to the police." Fries had called him a "typical small-time crook." But he seemed to have a solid alibi. So they had put him on the back burner and focused on Hauglie instead.

Then, two days ago, the results finally arrived from the lab in Chicago where the crime scene evidence had been sent for analysis. After that, everything happened very fast. Among the material sent to the lab was a tiny sample of blood that couldn't have belonged to the victim. Nor to Bjørn Hauglie, for that matter. Because it was determined that the blood had to have come from a man with Indian origins. A specific gene mutation was present that was found almost exclusively among Native Americans. It was true that the police did not have a DNA profile, nor was it possible to determine the percentage of Indian blood in the individual's genetic makeup. So it was possible the person in question was not a full-blooded Indian. This discovery might not have brought them any closer to finding the killer, except that they'd already interviewed someone in Grand Portage as the result of the anonymous tip.

On that same day Lenny Diver was arrested at his home. This happened after Lecuyer and Nyland paid a visit to one of the two men who had provided Diver with an alibi. The police were unable to get hold of the other one. Diver had told Fries he'd been playing cards and drinking with these two buddies all night long when the murder was committed. And both men had confirmed his account. They said Lenny hadn't been outside the house all night, so it would have been impossible for him to go out to Baraga's Cross and bash in the skull of some tourist. But when Lecuyer and Nyland went to see Mist, as the second friend was called, and brought it to his attention that he was about to be drawn into a homicide case, he quickly admitted he hadn't even seen Diver on the night in question. Nor had he been playing cards and drinking. Well, he did have a few drinks, but at home, and alone. Diver didn't call Mist until the following day. If the police happened to contact him, Mist was supposed to say he and Diver had been drinking and playing cards together all night. "You know how they always come down on me whenever anything happens," he'd told Mist. And Mist knew that was true. Lenny was the kind of guy who always ended up in the police spotlight, even if he'd done nothing wrong. And this time the only thing he'd done was to pick up some random chick and go back to her hotel room after some heavy drinking in a bar in Grand Marais. That was why he'd made up this story to tell his girlfriend—that he'd been in Grand Portage drinking and playing cards with two buddies all night long. Although the truth was that he'd been with another woman. But then he'd heard about the murder on the news. And he realized that if the cops came around, asking Lenny's friends if they'd seen him during the relevant time frame, they'd hear a whole different story than the one he'd told his girlfriend. And then it was only a matter of time before she found out what he'd really been doing. And if that happened, Lenny Diver would have hell to pay.

That was how he'd presented his case.

Mist assured Nyland and Lecuyer that he would never lie to cover up a crime. But this was about a private matter. Good God, it had to do with a woman, after all. And men are always rooting for tail, right? If he'd known that Lenny had anything to do with the murder, he would never have . . .

But Nyberg and Lecuyer had heard enough. They'd found out what they wanted to know. Georg Lofthus was killed by an Indian, and Lenny Diver had lied about his alibi.

Diver tried to run when he saw who was knocking on his door, but he was overpowered by two officers from the tribal police. Nyland had remained in the background, observing the scene. Officially he had nothing to do with the arrest. His job was to assist with the investigation. And in his opinion, that was what he'd done, to the best of his ability. Even though it now appeared that his contributions had not led to anything of importance. But that was often what happened in his line of work. Suddenly a breakthrough would occur in a case, and it was often something they least expected. It was impossible to predict.

Regardless, the case was now over for Eirik Nyland. His part of the job was done, and he was leaving tomorrow for Norway. In two days he'd be out at the cabin with Vibeke and the girls. He'd talked to them on the phone, and they were still there. "We're waiting for you," Vibeke had said.

Now he was sitting here at Baraga's Cross, waiting for Lance Hansen. It was almost seven o'clock in the evening, on Thursday, July 10, fifteen days after Hansen discovered the body. At first Nyland had planned to sit down next to the cross, but he changed his mind. He didn't know why. Maybe it was because of the withered flowers and burned-out candles he saw at the foot of the cross. At any rate, he'd decided to settle himself on rocks, about sixty feet away from the towering gray stone monument.

What a way to die, he thought. Struck down by a baseball bat in the woods near Lake Superior. A young man from western Norway.

Because the murder weapon was most likely a baseball bat. They'd found it under a pile of junk in Lenny Diver's car, wrapped up in a blanket. When they showed it to Diver, he said he'd never seen the bat before. Somebody must have planted it there. He pointed triumphantly at some initials that had been carved into the shaft a long time ago. They were not Lenny's initials. But it was later confirmed that his fingerprints were all over the bat. Nyland felt reasonably sure that closer analysis would reveal traces of blood from Georg Lofthus. And once they had both Diver's fingerprints and Lofthus's blood on the same baseball bat, Diver could say good-bye to Lake Superior for good.

What about the motive? Why had he killed Georg Lofthus? Maybe he did it in a drunken stupor. Diver had twice done time for meth. Or had he planned to rob the Norwegian tourists, and then something went wrong in the process? That was still an unanswered question. But Nyland was convinced that they'd arrested the right man—as convinced as he could be without having an eyewitness. Theoretically, at least, there was always a possibility that the individual in question was innocent. There were always other potential explanations than the one they had decided to go with. Not very likely, but still possible. For instance, someone might be able to come up with a plausible story for why Lenny Diver's fingerprints and Georg Lofthus's blood had been found on the same bat, even though the two men might never have met.

Nyland gave a start when he heard footsteps behind him. Lance Hansen was walking across the bare rocks toward him. He raised his hand in greeting before turning around again to gaze out at the lake. He listened to the footsteps getting closer until they stopped right behind him.

"It's great, isn't it?" said Lance.

Nyland looked up at him. He was wearing a short-sleeved blue shirt and light summer trousers. A Minnesota Vikings cap. And sunglasses.

"Yes, it's fantastic," said Nyland. "I'm going to miss this place. Have a seat."

Lance sat down on the blanket. The ice chest was between them.

"You can come back for a vacation with your family someday," he said. "Maybe you'll even get to meet your relatives who live here."

"Who's that?" said Nyland.

"You wanted me to help you find them. Don't you remember?"

"Oh, right . . ."

Lance looked at him. The silence lasted long enough for Nyland to realize that his ploy had been found out. Neither of them spoke.

Maybe it wasn't such a good idea to invite Lance Hansen out here, after all. He'd told Lance that he had a surprise for him. And he did. That stupid Viking ship that he'd bought in Grand Marais. Vibeke would never have allowed something like that in their home. That much he knew. So he'd brought the ship along in the ice chest, planning to give it to Lance as a farewell gift. But now he regretted bringing it, because he was simply trying to get rid of the thing. It was almost like using Lance Hansen as some sort of trash bin.

"So, let's see what we've got in here," Nyland said, opening the lid and making sure Lance couldn't see inside.

"Hmm . . . well, look at that." He dug two bottles of Mesabi Red out of the crushed ice and held them up. Lance smiled and nodded approval.

"But of course I forgot to bring a bottle opener," said Nyland. He hadn't thought about that until now.

"I'll open them," said Lance.

Nyland handed him the two bottles. Lance used a bottle opener that hung from his key ring. Then they drank a toast, taking a swallow of Lance's favorite beer.

Another couple of minutes passed in silence, so Eirik Nyland again opened the ice chest. But he still made sure that Lance couldn't see inside.

"Well, would you look at that!" he exclaimed. "Look what I found!" He held the bottle of aquavit up to the light. Beads of moisture had formed on the glass. "Norwegian *snaps*! Have you ever tasted it?"

"No, but I'm not really much of a drinker," said Lance. "To be honest, I can't even remember the last time I had hard liquor."

Nyland handed him the bottle. "We'll only have a little, since we need to get back in our cars and drive home safely afterward," he said.

"This is borderline illegal, you know," Lance muttered as he studied the label.

"But I got permission from the highest authority."

"Really?" Lance was still studying the bottle, trying to read what it said on the label.

"I had a word with the sheriff. He has, in fact, granted permission for a small taste test of Norwegian aquavit."

"He has?" Lance slowly unscrewed the top.

"Actually, he promised me that neither of us would be stopped by the police on our way home."

Lance laughed. "Good old Eggum," he said. He had the bottle open now. He held it up to his nose and sniffed. "Hmm . . . ," he said with interest. "And it's made from potatoes?"

Nyland nodded.

"Potatoes from where?"

"From Norway."

"But where in Norway?"

"My guess is they come from the area around Mjøsa, which is Norway's biggest lake."

"Perfect," exclaimed Lance. "That's great. And here we sit near Lake Superior, the biggest lake in the United States. Actually, in the world."

"From Mjøsa to Lake Superior," said Nyland dryly.

"Okay, then I think I do need to have a taste of these potatoes," said Lance. "Since the sheriff gave his approval, I mean."

"Wait a minute," said Nyland. "We need something to drink out of."

He opened the ice chest again and took out two plastic glasses he'd brought from his bathroom in the hotel. He gave one to Lance, who poured himself a small shot and then handed over the bottle. When they both had poured themselves a drink, they raised their plastic glasses for a toast.

"To big lakes," said Nyland.

"Yep," said Lance.

And they drank. Eirik Nyland closed his eyes and thought he could smell rib roast. He tasted gravy. And a special Christmas beer. "Ah," he sighed with reverence, and then opened his eyes.

Lance Hansen had also ingested his Norwegian potatoes. He shuddered as the liquor went down his throat.

"And now for some beer," said Nyland.

Both took a long swallow of Mesabi Red.

"So, what do you think?" he asked a moment later.

"I don't think you could get potatoes any better than that," said Lance.

"So you liked it?"

"Is there anybody who doesn't?" asked Lance in surprise.

"Not many, at any rate," replied Nyland. "At least *I* don't know of anyone. By the way, it was some of my colleagues who suggested that I bring along a bottle of aquavit. They told me, 'You can't show up in Minnesota from the old country without bringing aquavit.' They also thought I should bring some lutefisk, but I thought I'd spare you that. Do you know what lutefisk is?"

"Sure, and I happen to *like* it," said Lance. "There's a place called Sven and Ole's in Grand Marais where you can get it," he went on.

"I've eaten there," said Nyland.

"Really? I didn't know that. Did you have the fish cakes?"

"No, they were out, unfortunately. We had pizza instead."

"Well, Sven and Ole's serves seriously good lutefisk when it gets close to Christmastime. It's hard to find a table, I can tell you that. A lot of people up here love lutefisk. You should take some back to Norway."

"But what about security at the airport?" said Nyland. "Nowadays, when even deodorant is considered a possible weapon, I don't know what they'd say about lutefisk."

"You're probably right," said Lance, setting his plastic glass on the ice chest. It was empty. He'd understood the tradition and downed the shot in one gulp. That was the proper way to drink aquavit.

"Want some more?"

"Sure," said Lance, "but I think I should wait a bit. Those potatoes really pack a punch."

They both fell silent again, but this time there was nothing uncomfortable about the silence. Nyland was glad he'd invited Lance to have a drink out near Baraga's Cross. Of course there was something a bit morbid about choosing this particular location. They were very close to the crime scene, after all. But somehow it felt right. It was here that the case had begun, and now they were bringing it to an end. At least for Nyland's part.

"Tell me, why are there flowers over by the cross?" he said after a while. "Does it have something to do with the murder?"

He could see that Lance had been far away in his thoughts and had to make an effort to come back.

"No, people still honor Baraga's memory up here. Or at least some do. Occasionally church services are held out here in the open. There are almost always flowers at the cross."

Nyland thought the place seemed to change as Lance talked about it, taking on a new aura of meaning.

"I remember you telling me something about Baraga on the drive up here from Duluth. Wasn't he a priest who helped the Indians?"

Lance took a sip of his beer, then cleared his throat. "That's right," he said. "Frederic Baraga ran a mission on the other side of the lake. In La Pointe, Wisconsin." He nodded toward the horizon. There was nothing to see other than light and water and sky. "One day in 1846 he heard that the Ojibwe in Grand Portage had been stricken by the plague. And he saw it as his Christian duty to go up there to help. The problem was that it would take weeks, maybe months, to travel around the entire western part of Lake Superior. So he had to cross the lake by boat. And back then that was viewed as gambling with your life. Especially since the only vessel at his disposal was a flat-bottomed boat a local fur trapper had built. It wasn't designed for crossing the lake, and that's an understatement. But it was the only means available to Baraga."

Lance started to get up. Nyland watched the process with interest. It took some time, since Lance Hansen was a stout man. But finally he was on his feet. He stood next to Nyland, holding the beer bottle in one hand.

"Come with me and I'll show you something," he said. "Bring your beer."

Together the two men walked over to the big gray stone cross. Nyland looked at the withered flowers and the soot-covered tealight candle holders. Right across from them the river was calmly flowing into the lake.

"See that sandbank over there?" said Lance, pointing.

Nyland saw a ridge of sand and gravel stretching across the mouth of the river. The water level in the river was so low that parts of the ridge stuck up above the surface. A deep pool had formed close to it.

"The river carries all that sand and gravel here," Lance went on. "Most of it settles in place, and it builds up year after year." He leaned on the cross as he talked. "Baraga got hold of that fur trapper with the homemade boat, and together they set off across the lake. I assume that it was good weather or they would have waited. But you've seen for yourself how fast the weather can change around here."

Eirik Nyland nodded.

"And you have to remember that this was in 1846, which was

before there were any permanent settlements here. The area was Indian land; it belonged to the Indians. White people were not actually permitted to settle here. So imagine the kind of storm that we drove through on that evening from the airport. Plus a fierce wind. And no roads or houses. No light from a single lamp along the entire North Shore. The storm struck as Baraga and the fur trapper were about halfway between La Pointe in Wisconsin and Grand Portage, and soon they were at the mercy of the wind and waves, as the saying goes. The work was shared by the two men accordingly. The fur trapper fought for his life by bailing water from the boat. Baraga prayed to God. We might wonder why this fur trapper had allowed himself to be persuaded to go along with such a risky undertaking. Maybe it was a fear of God. I don't know. At any rate, they finally caught sight of land. And *this* was what they saw. This shore, but through the wind and rain, without any people or buildings. Nothing but forest. Big waves carried the boat straight for the rocks, right here where we're standing. It looked like the boat would be smashed to smithereens. But then a miracle occurred. An unusually big wave lifted the boat up and hurled it forward. When the two rain-soaked men gathered their wits, they realized they'd been saved. The boat had landed in the lowest, calm pool of a river, within the shelter of a sandbank that lay just below the surface of the water. The sandbank that the big wave had crashed over." Lance pointed to the mouth of the river and the sandbank in front of them. "Cross River," he said. "Nobody knows what it was called when Baraga and the fur trapper came here in 1846. But of course it must have had a name. An Ojibwe name that it had been called from time immemorial. Baraga believed God had intervened and rescued them. And so the next day they put up a cross on this spot before continuing on to Grand Portage. It was just a primitive wooden cross, made from two sticks. But it was still standing eight years later, in 1854, when the surveyors arrived to map the area, which in the meantime had been transferred from the Indians to the American government. They found the cross and gave the river its new name: Cross River. After that they erected a bigger cross that could better withstand the weather. It stood here for many years. The granite cross wasn't put up until 1932."

The two men stood there, holding their beer bottles and looking at the mouth of the river.

"The story is well known up here. It's part of the North Shore heritage, so to speak," said Lance after a moment. "And yet . . ."

Nyland looked at him. "And yet what?"

"Well, it's a nice story. The only thing is, it's not true."

"Really?"

"No, it can't be true," Lance went on. "At least not entirely. Baraga and the fur trapper did cross the lake in a flimsy boat. And they did come ashore and put up the cross. That's all true. But the key to the whole story . . . the miracle . . . the boat being lifted up on a giant wave and hurled over the sandbank and into the calm pool of water . . ." He pointed at the river and the sandbank as he spoke. "That couldn't possibly have happened."

"Why not?"

"Because there wasn't any sandbank here in 1846. Or a calm pool for the boat to land in after being flung over the sandbank. How do I know this? Well, because the sandbank is the result of erosion. Which in turn is a result of the big logging operation that the John Schroeder Lumber Company ran here between 1895 and 1905. They cut down all the trees along the entire Cross River. That was when the erosion started, when the virgin forest vanished during the course of only a few years. And it's still going on today, while the sandbank keeps growing, little by little. But it wasn't here in 1846."

Nyland looked at Lance in surprise. "How can you be so sure about that?"

"A lot of people noticed the erosion that suddenly started up after all the logging was done," said Lance. "After a few years some people also saw that a sandbank was appearing in the Cross River. It was a development that became very obvious during the period between the wars. So it's not a question of some sort of secret information. Don't think I'm the only one who knows where the sandbank came from or when. So that means the central part of the story must have originated at a much later date. At any rate after 1900."

"So what's the significance of that?" asked Nyland.

"It means the heart of the story about Baraga's crossing is not true. It might even be a deliberate lie. Who knows? Anyone who bothers to think about it will realize it can't be true. And yet nobody ever mentions that. We just keep on telling the same story. We hold church services out here and we burn candles—"

At that moment they heard someone shout from close by. "Okay, boys. Time to break up the party!"

Bill Eggum came walking out of the woods. Nyland shook hands with the sheriff, who was not in uniform. This was the first time he'd seen Eggum in civilian clothes.

"So this is where you are, hanging out and drinking beer," said the sheriff, shaking his head. "And here's old Eggum, without a drop to drink."

They went back to the blanket where Nyland and Lance had been sitting. Eggum kicked at the ice chest with the toe of his shoe. "And what do we have here, I wonder? Ice cream?"

"Have a seat, and I'll open the treasure chest," said Nyland. With a wave of his hand, he invited Bill Eggum to sit down on the side of the blanket where Lance had been sitting.

"I guess I can sit on the ground," said Hansen, settling himself in front of the sheriff.

Eirik Nyland sat down on the unoccupied part of the blanket. "All right. I assume this is the moment of truth," he said. "I don't want to hear any jokes about trying to hide something from the long arm of the law." He opened the lid of the ice chest to reveal the two unopened bottles of Mesabi Red and the bottle of Gammel Opland. "We were just going to have a little drink. But we've only got two glasses, so if you'd like to try some . . ." He unscrewed the cap from the bottle of aquavit and turned it over so it became a little cup between his thumb and forefinger. Then he mimed pouring a shot of aquavit into the cap.

"A little snort shouldn't do any harm," said Eggum.

Nyland filled it with a steady hand, not spilling a single drop. He held out the cap to the sheriff, who took it with an equally steady hand.

"Down the hatch!" said Lance.

Bill Eggum raised the cap to his lips, tilted his head back, and practically threw the liquor down his throat. Nyland took a bottle of beer out of the ice chest. He handed it to Lance, who quickly removed the cap and then offered the beer to the sheriff. Eggum grabbed the bottle and took a big gulp. Beads of sweat appeared on his flushed forehead. Finally both the beer and the aquavit managed to make their way down into his capacious system.

"Wow, that was great!" he exclaimed. "But it's probably not a good idea to have too many of those before driving home."

"Don't worry," said Lance. "We've only had one each. I was thinking about having one more, but that's all. And there's one more bottle of beer in the ice chest."

"Along with a Viking ship, I see," said Eggum, sounding surprised.

Nyland realized that he'd left the lid of the chest open.

Lance reached inside and took out the glass Viking ship. He held it up in the sunlight, turning it this way and that.

"Why do you have a Viking ship in the ice chest?" asked Eggum.

"It's a gift . . . to the local police force," said Nyland.

"But why is it in the *ice chest*?" the sheriff persisted.

"I was planning to give it to Lance and ask him to present it to you at the sheriff's office."

The two men looked at him, uncomprehending.

"Okay," said Lance. "Sure, why not do it the hard way?"

Eggum laughed. With a solemn expression, Lance handed him the Viking ship.

"Is it from Norway?" asked the sheriff.

"Well, I bought it here, but . . ."

"Where'd you get it?" asked Lance.

"In the souvenir shop in Grand Marais."

Lance and the sheriff burst out laughing.

"But it *is* from Norway," said Nyland. "I'm quite certain about that. I can tell, just by looking at the design."

Eggum turned the glass figurine upside down and peered at the bottom.

"Made in China," he read aloud.

That was the first time Nyland saw Lance Hansen laugh wholeheartedly. He completely surrendered to the laughter. Eggum clearly thought it was funny too, while Nyland felt crushed. Why on earth had he wanted to give Lance a present in the first place? Was there something special that he wanted to thank him for?

"But what difference does it make whether it came from Norway or China?" said Eggum. "A Viking ship is a Viking ship. Right?"

"A Chinese Viking ship, presented by a Norwegian police officer," said Lance. "Given to the sheriff of Cook County."

He poured a shot of Gammel Opland into the two plastic glasses, then into the cap from the bottle, which he handed to Eggum.

"I'd like to make a toast," said the sheriff. "Not to the United

States, or to Norway, for that matter. And definitely not to China. But to meetings between nations . . . meetings like this one."

"Absolutely," said Nyland.

"Hear, hear!" said Lance.

Then they all drank to the toast.

"In six weeks it'll all be over," said Eggum.

"What'll be over?" asked Lance.

"That's when I retire."

Eirik Nyland looked at the short, fat man wearing the Minnesota Twins cap. He thought about that early morning, with the professional truckers and retirees laughing in the next room. He and Eggum were having coffee together, and the sheriff had told him how the Swedish family had gotten the name of Seagren.

"Are you okay with that?" asked Lance.

"I'm counting the days!"

Nyland thought about the waitress, Martha Fitzpatrick. She'd been married to an Irishman from Chicago. But her maiden name was Norwegian. What was it again? No, he couldn't remember. He thought about the friendly mood she spread about her as she moved through the café. What a job, he thought. At the same time, he liked the idea of her continuing to work there. So in the future, whenever he thought about Cook County and Grand Marais, he could be reasonably certain that at least *something* was still the way he remembered it.

The other two men had started talking about fishing. He heard them mention words like "steelhead" and "walleye." He assumed these were types of fish.

"Did you know that?" said Eggum.

"What?" Nyland hadn't been paying attention.

The sheriff nodded toward the lake stretching out before them. "That we've got sturgeon out here."

Sturgeon? Wasn't that where caviar came from? "But those fish are huge," he said.

"Yeah," said Lance. "The biggest one ever caught in Lake Superior was well over six feet long. They can get up to two hundred and twenty pounds in weight. They used to be much more common, but the stock was heavily overfished by the Scandinavians who settled here."

"Big as a full-grown man. That would really be something to

catch on your fishing line," said Eggum, making motions to get up. "Well, I guess I'd better be heading home. Crystal is probably wondering what's happened to me."

All three got to their feet.

"Yeah, it's almost dark," said Lance. "I suppose it's time to be getting back."

"I think I'll stay here for a while longer," said Nyland. "I want to enjoy the view of the lake one last time."

"What time do you leave tomorrow?" asked Lance.

"Early."

They stood there, hesitating, not quite sure what more to say. Eirik Nyland knew he'd never see either of them again. Cook County wasn't the sort of place the Nyland family would visit on vacation. Rome was more their style. Or maybe Barcelona. There were so many places to choose from. But Cook County would not be high on the list.

"Well, well," Nyland said.

"You can say that again," said the sheriff. He straightened the cap he was wearing.

"Are you sure you've arrested the right man?" asked Lance.

"Yes," said Nyland. "His fingerprints were all over that baseball bat. If they also find traces from Lofthus on it, they'll have an airtight case."

There was nothing else he could say. Yet he thought for a moment about the uncertainty that both he and Bob Lecuyer had felt with regard to Lance Hansen. He still couldn't rid himself of that feeling. It might never go away.

"But didn't he claim that he'd never seen that bat before?" said Eggum.

"Yes, and there were actually somebody else's initials carved into the shaft. But that doesn't mean much since the fingerprints show that he'd had it in his hands."

"What was his name again?" asked Lance.

"Lenny Diver," said Nyland.

"And what about the initials?"

"A. H.," said Nyland.

"Sure, as if it's big news that a man like Lenny Diver would have in his possession something that didn't necessarily belong to him," said Eggum with a grin.

Nyland noticed that Lance had turned away slightly. He was gazing out at the lake.

"Well, have a good trip back to the old country," said the sheriff.

"Thanks. It's been a pleasure working with you, Eggum."

"Same here. And just so you know: I would have liked to see Bob Lecuyer sitting here having a drink with Lance and me!"

"He really missed out."

They shook hands to say good-bye.

"Don't forget the Viking ship," Nyland reminded him.

Eggum leaned down and picked up the glass figurine. "I'm going to put it in a place of honor in my office," he said. "And when I retire, I'm taking it home with me. Crystal loves this kind of thing."

Lance Hansen turned to face Nyland. "It was nice meeting you," he said, holding out his hand.

Nyland shook his hand firmly. "Nice meeting you too," he said. There was more he wanted to say, but he couldn't find the right words.

"Okay, so we're off," said Eggum.

Lance touched his finger to the visor of his Minnesota Vikings cap. Then the two men headed over the rocks toward the woods.

NYLAND WAS HOLDING A GLASS OF AQUAVIT IN HIS HAND. In front of him the Cross River flowed into the lake. The river water was visible a good ways out, making a faintly brown-colored fan shape. So this was where a miracle had supposedly occurred. But *he* knew better. He was one of the people who knew no sandbank had existed here in 1846. How strange that story would sound back home in Norway! He tried to picture himself recounting the tale at the dinner table one evening when he and Vibeke had guests. But in that setting it would be a story totally lacking in context. Here, on the other hand, it had a home. A place where it belonged.

It would soon lose all meaning, he thought. The minute he got home, all of this would seem as far away as a dream. Lance Hansen too. He tried to imagine Lance among their circle of friends. Tried to imagine his voice taking part in one of the numerous discussions around various dinner tables. But neither Lance Hansen nor the story about Baraga's Cross had any place in Eirik Nyland's world. They would lose all luster and weight. Both belonged here, in Cook County.

He held up the plastic glass toward the evening sun and admired the glow in the small shot of aquavit. Then he drank it down in one gulp. For everything created by God is good, he thought as he felt warmth spread through his body. Georg Lofthus's Bible. In spite of everything else, *he* was the one this case was about. A twenty-year-old Norwegian man who had been killed in Minnesota. That was how it all began. Nyland thought about how many things Georg must have had to keep secret over the course of his short life. All the lies. Mostly about himself, probably. And he thought about the Bible. He was going to make sure that it got sent back to the family. "For everything created by God is good, and nothing is to be rejected, if it is received with thanksgiving." A sort of family motto—wasn't that what Hauglie had said? If so, it was simply a meaningless convention. No matter what, "Grandma and Grandpa" couldn't possibly have meant that their grandson should receive with thanksgiving the love that he and Bjørn Hauglie had felt for each other.

That was the word Hauglie had said when Lance Hansen found him sitting here, leaning against the cross. *"Kjærlighet,"* he'd said in Norwegian. "Love." Nyland thought it was appropriate to end his visit to Baraga's Cross by thinking about the love between those two young men. Let's hope they also found happiness together, he thought. That it was more than just secrecy and shame. And it *must* have been. Wouldn't they have given it up long ago otherwise? He remembered Hauglie's response to the question of why God would punish Georg: "So you think I've escaped punishment?" Instead of giving up the relationship, they had come to Minnesota, spending time here as lovers. And yet Lofthus was about to get married. Nyland could only imagine what they must have endured because of the deep love they felt for each other. And if their love was so deep, then it must have included moments of great happiness.

That thought gave Eirik Nyland some consolation.

25

LANCE ALTERNATED between relief and uneasiness in the days following Nyland's departure for Norway. On the one hand, a man had been arrested and his fingerprints were found on the baseball bat that presumably had bashed in the head of the young Norwegian. On the other hand, Andy Hansen's initials had been found on that bat. Lance remembered quite clearly that Andy's initials had been carved into the bat he'd had ever since they were kids. The same bat Lance had picked up from the ground of the schoolyard after the ambulance had driven off with Clayton Miller. Clayton, the boy everyone thought was a homosexual, just like Georg Lofthus. But how could his brother have managed to get the baseball bat to Grand Portage, and with Lenny Diver's fingerprints on it? It didn't seem very plausible. And Andy couldn't be the only one in the world with the initials A. H. Besides, at the crime scene they'd found biological evidence that could only have come from an Indian. And this Lenny Diver had also lied about his alibi the first time the police had interviewed him. Andy couldn't possibly be the one who killed the Norwegian. Lance had no doubt whatsoever that his brother had been up to something that wouldn't bear the light of day. Otherwise he wouldn't have lied so blatantly when everyone was listening, the way he'd done at the ranger station. But he didn't murder that Norwegian canoeist. And the way the case had turned out, that was the only thing Lance cared about.

....

ON FRIDAY EVENING he drove to Grand Portage to pick up his son. He was afraid Mary might say something about the fact that he'd gone to see her father. She probably hadn't appreciated the way he'd shown up, unannounced and treading within the boundaries of her daily life. But nothing out of the ordinary happened. Mary kissed Jimmy when she said good-bye, gave her ex-husband a reserved smile, and then went back inside the house.

At eight o'clock father and son were having a late dinner. From their places at the table, they had a view of the lake and the weekend traffic on Highway 61. Just below the house was Isak Hansen's hardware store. That's where our story starts, thought Lance. But he immediately corrected himself. Because there was a whole series of different stories that had led up to them sitting here and eating pizza on this evening. There were stories that started in a land where no one had ever seen a white man before. The land of the Ojibwe. And stories that started in Norway long ago. Lance liked to think about all of this. The complex interweaving of stories surrounding them gave him an even stronger sense of connection with his son.

He looked at the boy, who was chewing on a mouthful of pizza. His cheeks were bulging. Hovering in the air between the table and his mouth was the glass of Sprite he was holding in his hand, ready to take a sip as soon as he swallowed enough pizza to make room for some soda. Lance had to laugh. Jimmy looked at him with big eyes. Then he noticed what he was doing, his cheeks bulging, the glass hovering, as if waiting impatiently for its turn. Lance saw the boy's cheeks get even bigger, as if they might burst. Then Jimmy couldn't stop himself. Out of his mouth sprayed chunks of pizza crust, pepperoni, peppers, and dissolved cheese. Some of the food landed on Lance's plate. That made Jimmy laugh even harder.

Lance looked down at his plate. "I think I've had plenty," he said. "How about you?"

"I'll have some more." Jimmy reached out his hand for the last piece of pizza. He was still laughing.

Lance shook his head, amazed at the boy's appetite.

While Jimmy finished eating, Lance began clearing the table. Out in the kitchen, he rinsed his plate in the sink, thinking for a moment about how things had been just a few years earlier, when all three of them had lived here. He wondered how much Jimmy recalled from those days. He was only four when his parents had separated and he and Mary had moved to Grand Portage. Did he even remember that they'd all lived here together? Lance would have liked to know, but he wouldn't ask. Things were fine the way they were.

When he turned around, he saw Jimmy standing in the doorway, looking at him. He was holding an empty plate in his hands. Lance had the feeling that he'd been standing there several minutes.

"Can I watch TV now?" he asked.

Lance took his plate and put it in the sink. "I don't think there's anything on for you to watch. It's almost eight thirty."

"Sure there is," said Jimmy. "Just for a little while. Please."

"Okay, let's see if we can find something suitable," said Lance.

They went back in the living room and sat down on the sofa. Lance zapped through the channels without finding anything for children. The closest he could get was the broadcast of a car race, and Jimmy seemed perfectly happy with that.

They sat there for a while without talking. Jimmy laughed loudly when a car slid off the racetrack. Finally Lance decided they'd seen enough. It was almost nine o'clock. The boy would have to go to bed soon.

But then the phone rang. He carried the phone into his office before taking the call. It was Sheriff Eggum. He said he'd just talked to Bob Lecuyer on the phone. They'd found biological material from Georg Lofthus on the baseball bat. There was no longer any doubt that the bat was the murder weapon. Plus, it had turned out to be impossible to find the woman whom Diver claimed to have been with on the night of the murder. And of course he couldn't remember her name. Or what she looked like. He said he'd been too drunk to remember anything. And none of the employees at the motel could recall having seen him there. "The case is all sewed up," said Eggum. "Lenny Diver is guilty and he's going to pay for what he did."

When Lance was done with the phone call, Jimmy came into the office. He looked bored. "Who was that?" he asked.

"The sheriff."

"Why was the sheriff calling you?"

"Just something to do with work."

"Was it about the murder?"

"Yeah."

Jimmy came over to Lance and leaned against the desk. "Do you think they're going to hang him?" he asked.

"*Hang* him?"

"Uh-huh . . . the murderer."

"No. He's going to be in prison for a very long time."

"How long?"

"Probably for the rest of his life."

"Were you scared he might kill *me*?"

"Sure I was," said Lance, pulling the boy onto his lap. "Of course I was scared of that."

Jimmy pulled out of his father's arms. "Who's that?" he said, pointing at the photograph of Joe Caribou that was still lying on the desk.

"That's a picture that belonged to your great-grandfather," said Lance. "Your grandfather's father."

"Is that him?"

"No, it's not. That's a man named Joe Caribou. He died a long time ago."

"Why did he die?"

"I don't know. I guess he just got old. When people get old, they die."

"Grandpa too," said Jimmy in a knowing voice that clearly indicated this was something his mother had discussed with him.

"Yes, Grandpa too," said Lance.

"But who's that?" Now Jimmy was pointing at the picture of the four young men who had posed in a photographer's studio.

"Oh, that's just . . . some other people."

"But who *are* they?"

Lance held up the picture so his son could see it better as he pointed to each man. "His name is Helge Tofte," he said. "And sitting here is his brother, Andrew Tofte. That's Thormod Olson. And the one on the right is named Sam Bortvedt."

"Are they all dead too?" asked Jimmy.

"Yes, they are."

Jimmy looked up at the photograph hanging on the wall over the desk, the picture in which the folks from Tofte had gathered on the desk of the steamship *America* in Duluth in October 1902.

"Those people too?" he asked.

"All of them."

"Do you only have pictures of dead people?"

Lance laughed. "Maybe in here, but otherwise . . . I do have tons of pictures of *you*, for instance."

"And I'm not dead," Jimmy said firmly.

"You certainly aren't. But I can tell by looking at you that you're getting sleepy."

"No, I'm not."

"Yes, you are. It's almost nine. Time to brush your teeth."

"Aw, come on, Dad . . ." Jimmy pressed closer to his father, making himself as heavy as possible. "Can't we watch a little more TV? Just a little?"

Lance held his son firmly and stood up. Then he hoisted the boy up onto his shoulder like a sack and carried him out. Jimmy laughed all the way to the bathroom.

When his father set him down and got out the toothbrush, Jimmy suddenly thought of something. "Dad, there's something I have to show you," he said.

"What is it?" asked Lance skeptically.

"Wait here . . . I'll go get it. Okay?"

"From your room?"

"Uh-huh."

"Okay," said Lance. "But be quick."

Jimmy ran down the hall to the room that had always been his. Lance heard him open the zipper on his bag. After a few seconds he came running back. He was holding a can of air rifle pellets. Has he already started shooting with an air rifle? thought Lance.

"Look inside," said Jimmy. He held out the flat metal container toward his father.

Lance took it and unscrewed the lid. Inside were Jimmy's baby teeth. They looked like tiny pearls or bits of porcelain. Behind him Lance heard his son saying something excitedly. Some of the teeth had reddish-brown specks on the roots. Probably dried blood. Nausea started swirling in Lance's stomach. He tried to force it back, but without success. It just got worse, and his forehead felt cold and damp. His son was tugging at him, saying something again. He sounded worried. But Lance knew that something inside him needed to get out. And he couldn't stop it. He dropped the container with the boy's teeth in the sink and threw himself down in front of the toilet. At first he retched loudly and painfully, but nothing came out. For a moment he pictured those teeth, gleaming white in the crushed skull. And then the nausea overwhelmed him. He instantly leaned over. Stomach acid and partially digested pizza sprayed out of him so violently, it was almost as if he had a high-pressure hose inside.

AFTER DRIVING JIMMY BACK HOME on Sunday afternoon, Lance went to see his mother at the nursing home. They agreed to go for a drive on the following weekend. He asked her if there was anything special she'd like to see or do on the North Shore, now that she had the opportunity. She said she couldn't think of anything. Lance was relieved that she didn't mention Andy or Tammy. He'd been afraid she might want to visit them.

Afterward he decided to take a little tour of Duluth. He drove up to the big shopping center on the plateau above the city, not far from the airport. He and Eirik Nyland had driven in the opposite direction on this same road just over two weeks earlier. How incredible that it was such a short time ago, he thought. Everything had happened within a span of a little less than three weeks. But now he had a feeling things were going to return to normal.

At the shopping center he turned onto Trinity Road, heading south, taking a road that goes in an arc back to town. He was still on the same plateau, but the road took him through well-tended, parklike woods. Between the trees he could see people taking a walk along the paths on this fine Sunday evening.

He thought about what happened on Friday night when Jimmy showed him those teeth. Afterward he'd spent a long time trying to reassure his son. Finally he'd managed to convince Jimmy that it was just an upset stomach.

Throwing up like that had actually done him good. Because each time he bent over to empty more from his stomach into the toilet, he felt as if the sight of the dead man faded farther away.

Now he was passing Enger Park on the right. He parked near one of the entrances and went in. When was the last time he was here? It had to be years ago. The paths were still covered with the same reddish gravel. The canal was still there too. It couldn't be more than a foot and a half deep. On the other side of the canal the path continued toward the hundred-foot-high tower, which offered the best view of the city and the lake, as well as over the flat plain in Wisconsin on the other side. Lance paused on the small bridge. He leaned on the railing and looked down at the canal. He remembered standing here with Debbie Ahonen. That had to be over twenty years ago. That might even have been the last time he was in Enger Park. They had stopped on the bridge and looked down at the water, just as Lance was doing now. Debbie had spit her chewing gum into the canal. Lance still remembered how it sank into the green water and came to rest on the sandy bottom. Somewhere in his mind the sight of that wad of chewing gum had been stored for more than twenty years. Forgotten until now. And as he thought about it, he also recalled her laughter, the way it had sounded back then. A warm laughter that hinted at what was behind her reserved expression. What he *thought* was behind there.

Now Debbie had come back from California and was living with Richie Akkola, a man who was close to seventy. Lance remembered her saying something that indicated Richie had been taking care of her aging mother. But was *that* the reason she was living with him? That can't be it, he thought. The world couldn't be that ugly. But he knew full well that it was even uglier. And that people had to adapt as best they could. No matter what, the past twenty years had erased any chance they might once have had to be together. That was the reality. Lance knew it. In real life people didn't find each other again after twenty years.

When he came back out of the park, he noticed a few people near a car at the other end of the parking lot. Some black-clad girls with black hair. Three girls, he saw now. They were talking to whoever was sitting inside the car. There was something about them that sparked Lance's curiosity, but he didn't know why.

He got into his Jeep and began driving toward them. The three girls were leaning down to talk to the person inside. As Lance slowly drove past, one of the girls straightened up and looked at him. For a few seconds their eyes met. She was wearing way too much eye makeup. It made her face look sickly pale. The dyed black hair was practically plastered to her head. Yet, he recognized her. And he saw that she recognized him too. It was Chrissy Hansen standing there.

....

THAT EVENING HE SAT FOR A LONG TIME, wondering whether he should call Andy and Tammy and tell them what he'd seen. Occasionally he would get up and restlessly pace the living room with his hands behind his back. But what did he really have to tell? That their daughter was with two of her girlfriends in the parking lot of Enger Park? That she now had black hair? Her parents must know what she looked like. It had been more than six months since Lance had last seen Chrissy. Back then she was still the blond "angel from Two Harbors." But she was seventeen now, and things changed fast during those teenage years. That was perfectly normal. Yet there was something disturbing about the sight of those three girls talking to someone in that car. He didn't know what it was. Regardless, it wasn't worth mentioning to her parents. But when he pictured in his mind his pale, black-clad niece, it suddenly didn't seem so strange that she might have been in the cabin at Lost Lake after all. He remembered how weird it had been to find a copy of *Darkside* there. Maybe she'd been out there partying with those black-clad friends of hers, he thought. Maybe they'd brought some boys with them. He hadn't even considered that possibility before. In general, he'd been thinking of Chrissy as a child.

But the thought of the cabin made him decide to call her parents after all. He tapped in the number. It was Andy who answered.

"Hello?"

"Hi, it's me."

"Oh." He sounded disappointed.

"How are things?"

"What's this about? I'm expecting somebody else to call . . ."

"Have you been out to the cabin lately?"

"Not since . . . Not for a couple of weeks, at least."

"I should have mentioned this before, but I've had a lot to do . . . and Jimmy was here over the weekend too . . . but, anyway, on Friday I went past the cabin, and it turned out that someone had broken in."

"Oh, shit . . . Did they break the lock, or what?"

"No, they broke a window. It looked real bad inside. A big mess. Blood and stuff. Broken glass. Must have been some kids, if you ask me. I just thought I'd better tell you."

"Thanks. I'll go up there as soon as I can. Did they steal anything?"

"Not as far as I could tell."

"What about the TV?"

"It was still there."

"Good."

There was a long pause. Lance could hear Andy breathing. There was something restrained about it, as if his brother knew he was listening. Maybe that was the same way he sounded to Andy.

"By the way," said Andy at last, "I heard they caught the murderer."

"Yeah. He hasn't been charged yet, but . . ."

"Ojibwe?"

"Uh-huh."

"A dope dealer?"

"He's been convicted of possession a couple of times. I don't know if I'd call him a *dealer*."

"So now they're going to lock him up for good, right?"

"Yeah, they sure are. If he's found guilty, that is."

"Good."

"Okay, well, say hi to Tammy and Chrissy for me."

"Sure. But tell me . . . What exactly were you doing out at the cabin on Friday?" said Andy.

"Oh, I just thought I'd stop there to have lunch. You've always said . . ."

"You wanted to eat indoors when the weather has been so great?"

Lance had the feeling his brother didn't believe his story. He tried to think of something else that would sound convincing, but his mind was blank.

"Well, anyway, thanks," said Andy. "I'll pop over to Lost Lake real soon and take a closer look."

26

WHEN LANCE GOT HOME FROM WORK on Tuesday afternoon, he found an e-mail from the translation agency in Minneapolis in his inbox. He'd almost forgotten about the diary and Swamper Caribou.

He opened the e-mail and read the brief message from the translator. She finished her message with the words: "This was unusually fascinating material to work with." Then came some practical information regarding payment. After that it was just a matter of downloading the attachment with the translation so that he could read it. Lance felt more uneasy than he had in a long time. He was actually feeling sick to his stomach. It reminded him of something from his childhood, but he wasn't sure what it was. Maybe having to appear onstage during a Christmas celebration at school? Or coming home with his report card on the last day before summer vacation? Right now he felt something similar to that combination of solemn occasion and doomsday. Then he downloaded the attachment and opened the document. Suddenly the text was there, right in front of him:

17 MARCH. *The boy arrived this morning. What a bitter cold he has endured! His face was like cold meat to the touch. His dreams are terrifying. He screams as we go about our daily chores. The children race anxiously past his bed every time they have to pass. My husband feels such great sorrow that it has not been possible for any of us to have peace in our hearts during this day. Thanks to God's mercy he is still among the*

living, but just barely. His thoughts merge with his dreams, and he speaks in delirium. Thank God that the children do not understand what he shouts in his dreams and feverish fantasies! Apparently he knows no English or French, but only the Norwegian language, which in my opinion can be learned only by a child who hears it sung at the cradle. A great and difficult task is now demanded of us. I promised Father François at the mission school that no lie would ever cross my lips. But when we removed all of his clothes, as we were forced to do, we saw two deep wounds in his right arm. I think that it is because of these wounds that he has lost most of his strength. My husband tried to ask him questions, but he would not tell us anything of what had happened to him.

18 MARCH. *My husband does not think that his sister's son will survive unless we can bring a doctor here or take the boy to a doctor. But every time he mentions this, the boy is seized with a terror that seems worse than his fear of dying. He still refuses to say anything about what happened to him, but it seems clear to us that he was in the cold water and nearly froze to death. But it is easy to see that someone stabbed him with a knife to give him those wounds. He refuses to talk about that, and we think that is the reason he does not want to be treated by a doctor. Because the doctor would ask how he had acquired those two wounds, and if he did not answer, the doctor might mention it to the authorities. It is clear to us that this is what he fears. But I have given this a lot of thought on my own, both last night and during the course of this day, and I am struggling to decide whether to tell my husband of my thoughts, because according to our beliefs, this is the work of the devil. What Nokomis taught me was not about the good, even though she was the most beloved, both then and forever. She lived in the darkness in which so many old people lived. But if I am now going to bring the boy back to health and save him from death, I will have to do as Nokomis taught me before I went to the mission school.*

21 MARCH. *Thanks be to God that we have managed to keep him on this side of death. He is past the worst of it now. I made*

*him a decoction to drink, as I remember Nokomis doing, and
something to spread on his wounds. I have also committed the
sin of making an asabikeshiinh for a person's dreams, because
he screamed and flailed so much that none of us could get any
sleep, not even the children, but now he is calm. May God have
mercy on me, for I knew not what else to do.*

24 MARCH. *Today he sat at the table and ate with us! When
we changed the bandages on his wounds, we saw that they were
clean and without pus, just as the wounds of Old Shingibis
were after Nokomis treated him when he was attacked by a
bear when I was a little girl. I clearly remember when they
arrived with Shingibis in the canoe. But even though this is a
good sign, and my husband is now lighter of heart than I have
seen him before, nothing can ever rectify what I have done.
For that reason my heart is as heavy as stone. My husband
says that we must never speak of this, just say that the boy
fell through the ice and almost died from frostbite, but that
we saved him with porridge and coffee. That is how we will
speak of it in the future, also when we talk to the boy. We will
never try to find out what happened to him. And here I have
promised Father François that no lie shall ever issue from
my lips.*

At first Lance's eyes merely took note of the text, but the meaning glanced right off. He didn't really take in what it said. He merely
saw the words. The sentences. There was nothing about these passages that distinguished them from passages in other documents
that he was constantly receiving. All sorts of reports, memos, personal e-mails. And even though he had known it might be like this, it
was still a shock. The whole thing seemed so trivial. He couldn't see
the connection between this typed text and the French scribblings
on the yellowed pages of the diary. So many times he had opened
that book and let his eyes glide over the incomprehensible words.
And he had thought about the fact that his great-grandmother had
held this very book in her hands. The diary became something that
reached from Lance back to that dark log cabin more than a hundred and twenty years ago. A time machine for his thoughts. He
often imagined he could see the cabin and the people inside. Smell

them, hear their voices. And the difference between that vivid experience and the modern, trivial text that now met his eyes when he opened the document caused him to read the words without fully comprehending what they said.

But then he read them again, and he understood.

One part was what she wrote about Thormod Olson. That confirmed what Lance had thought—that the boy's experience had encompassed more than just falling through the ice. Of course there was no proof that he'd encountered Swamper Caribou, much less killed him, but Lance still felt as if he was now closer to answering the question of what had happened to the medicine man.

But that was not the most important part. He was even more interested in what Nanette said about herself. Lance had always heard her described as the "French Canadian." But evidently it should have been the "French Canadian Indian." Maybe she wasn't French Canadian at all. Maybe she was a full-blooded Ojibwe from somewhere north of the border, and she had learned to speak French at a mission school. That would not be an unusual story. But what made it different was that it was about Lance's great-grandmother. At any rate, there was no mistaking that "Nokomis," who had taught Nanette to heal wounds by using plants, was her grandmother. The translator had erroneously assumed that "Nokomis" was a proper name, but Lance knew it was the Ojibwe word for "grandmother." He'd even heard Nancy Dupree use the word when she was talking to little Jimmy. "Come here to old nokomis," she had said merrily. In other words, Nanette had learned her skills from an old Ojibwe woman. Lance pictured a small, stooped figure in the dim light inside a birchbark wigwam. That was Lance's own great-great-grandmother.

Suddenly he felt as if he were being pulled away from the room where he sat. He grabbed hold of the edge of the desk with both hands and held on tight.

His maternal grandfather had died several years before Lance himself came into the world, but he'd seen pictures of the white-haired man. His face was marked by all the hard work he'd done outdoors in every kind of weather. But was there anything Indian about his features? It didn't matter. Because that was what he was. Half Indian. Or maybe one-quarter, depending on Nanette's own background.

Just as revealing as the word *nokomis* was the information that she had "committed the sin of making an asabikeshiinh for a person's dreams." Today "dream catchers" could be bought in all sorts of New Age shops, but in 1892 they were unknown outside the Ojibwe world. Lance knew what a genuine dream catcher looked like. The frame was made from a twig or other slender piece of wood that was bent into a circular or teardrop-shaped form. Inside this frame was a woven, interlacing pattern. It actually resembled a human-made spider web. And bad dreams were caught in the web before they could reach the slumbering person.

IT WAS ONLY SEVERAL HOURS LATER that the full significance of the diary entries occurred to Lance. He was sitting in front of the TV, trying to find some program that would interest him, but without success. The first shock had begun to wear off. Now he mostly thought the whole thing was exciting. He couldn't rid himself of the image of a small, stooped Ojibwe woman sitting in the dim light inside a birchbark wigwam. His great-great-grandmother. Every once in a while he had to laugh, but only because it was so surprising and new. And it would continue to feel that way for a long time. But it wasn't unpleasant. On the contrary, there was something about this discovery that suited him perfectly. He felt both conspiratorial and elated.

Was this something he could tell other people? Should Inga know about this? How would she react? It was difficult to predict, but, considering her age, it might be best to avoid giving her such shocking news. And what about Andy?

Andy . . . Lance discovered that he'd gotten up from his chair. On the wall in front of him hung all the family photographs. Faces smiling into the room. Andy's too. His high school picture. Lance remembered the look on his brother's face when he came around the corner of the building on that day. It was the expression of someone who could not be reached. Someone nobody could save. He stood there with the baseball bat in his hand, ready to start pounding Clayton Miller, the boy everyone said was homosexual. Lance went over to look at the photo of his brother. He had a strange feeling that no time had passed since they'd stood across from each other on that day in the schoolyard. He raised one hand to touch the picture but stopped when he saw that his hand was shaking. Surprised, he held up both hands. It was impossible to make them stop trembling.

At last I've started shaking, he thought.

Andy had Indian genes. That meant that the blood evidence could not rule him out. "A man with some percentage of Indian genes," he clearly remembered Eggum saying on the phone. "Not necessarily full-blooded." Now that discovery no longer pointed more strongly to Lenny Diver than to Andy. They both belonged to the group of men who could have done it. But Diver was the one who had been arrested and would have to spend the rest of his life in a prison cell. For a murder Andy Hansen had committed. Lance was now positive about that. Georg Lofthus had suffered the blows Clayton Miller had just barely escaped.

27

IT HAD TO BE MORE THAN TWO YEARS since Lance had called Mary to talk about something other than their son. He had no idea how she was going to react. She was the one who had wanted the divorce, after all. And that was also why she had been so skeptical about having any form of contact afterward, other than what was strictly necessary so that Lance could spend time with Jimmy every other weekend. Occasionally they would exchange a few words when he picked up the boy or dropped him off. Always about purely practical matters. Otherwise they hadn't talked to each other in over two years. And he had never tried to pump Jimmy for information about how his mother was doing. Or who might be coming to visit her. He was sure that if he did, sooner or later that sort of thing would come to her attention.

By now it was Wednesday evening. He hadn't slept at all last night. While he lay in bed, tossing and turning, he realized that from now on, each day represented another opportunity to rescue Lenny Diver from the nightmare in which he had landed. And each day he would decide not to make use of that opportunity. *Sin* was the only appropriate word he could come up with. He was a man who would have to commit a terrible sin every single day for the rest of his life. The same sin, over and over again.

Finally he decided he ought to call Mary. Not to tell her about the situation he found himself in. But Mary was a teacher. A teacher in Grand Portage. She'd held that job for more than a decade now. So he was thinking she must have taught Lenny Diver. Or at least a brother or sister of his. In other words, Mary must know something about the man who was now about to do time for a crime that Andy had committed. At the very least, she must know who he was. Maybe she could tell Lance what Lenny had been like in school.

As he lay in bed and watched the summer morning dawn outside the window, he felt a great need to hear someone talk about Lenny Diver. Tell a story about him, no matter how slight.

She picked up the phone after only two rings.

"Yes?"

Her voice was exactly the same.

"Hi. It's Lance."

A few seconds of silence.

"What is it?"

He didn't think he heard either a rebuff or a welcome in her voice.

"Uh, well . . . this isn't about Jimmy, at any rate. I was wondering if you'd heard that they've arrested somebody."

Silence again. He could almost *hear* her thinking.

"You mean Lenny Diver?"

"Yeah."

"I heard about it."

"Do you know him?"

"No, I don't."

Lance could hear from her voice that it wasn't that simple.

"Was he one of your students in school?"

She gave a brief laugh, but it wasn't a friendly sort of laugh.

"What *is* this? An interrogation?"

He could tell that things were about to take a wrong turn before he even got to the point.

"No, sorry . . . it's not . . . I didn't mean to . . . but you know I was the one who found the victim, right?"

"Yes. Yes, I know that."

Her voice instantly lost some of its edge.

"Well, the truth is that things haven't been that easy for me since then."

"Oh?"

"It was an unusually brutal murder. The body looked horrible. Did Jimmy tell you I got sick when he was here last weekend?"

"He said you threw up."

"That's right. I threw up when he showed me his baby teeth that he's been saving."

"Are you saying that it had something to do with . . . ?"

"Yeah, but I won't go into detail. I saw something that day. It was a shock, plain and simple. Please don't tell him I threw up because of his teeth."

"Of course not."

"This whole business has been a big shock for me. Much more than I thought at first. And now . . . maybe it's stupid, but . . ."

"What is it?"

"I don't know . . . I just feel a need to hear something about Lenny Diver. Now that they've discovered who did it. Maybe then I'll be able to put this whole thing behind me. If I realize that the murderer has a face and a past."

"But what do you want *me* to do? I really don't know Lenny Diver at all."

"But wasn't he in your class in school?"

"Sure, but that was a long time ago."

"When exactly?"

"Ten or eleven years ago. In junior high. But I don't remember anything in particular about him. I think he was a rather anonymous boy."

"Do you know anyone else in his family?"

"I'm not sure I should answer that question."

"I promise not to tell anyone that we've talked about this. Ever."

"Okay . . . His little sister is in my class. She's fifteen."

"So he has a sister. Have you ever met the parents?"

"Yes, his mother has come to some of the parent–teacher meetings. I think Bess is actually Lenny's half sister, by the way. Different fathers."

"Mary, I know this sounds strange. Maybe even weird. But I swear to you this has nothing to do with . . . *us* . . . or, well, you know . . . it's nothing like that, but . . ."

"What is it?" she asked, a bit impatiently.

"Would you consider meeting with me so you could tell me a little about Lenny Diver and his family? I need to know his story, I need to put a face on what happened. You have no idea what this whole thing has been like. I'm begging you, Mary."

"But I don't know anything about Lenny or his family except

what I've already told you. They're not the sort of people I socialize with. And I only know Lenny from his school days. So I don't think—"

"Please, Mary. And no one will ever hear about this. You have my word of honor."

"So where did you want to meet?"

"Anywhere is fine. We could have a bite to eat at the same time. But this is not about anything personal. It's not about us. It's just about the murder. I have to try to put the whole thing behind me once and for all."

He could hear her breathing as she weighed the pros and cons.

A LIGHT DRIZZLE was falling over the North Shore. The lake was a leaden gray beneath the low cloud cover. His windshield wipers were monotonously moving back and forth. Lance was on the road heading north toward Grand Marais. Even though the birch trees along the way were a leafy green, he felt as if it were fall. That must be because it had been so long since they'd had overcast skies and rain. He liked this kind of day, when he couldn't see more than a couple of hundred yards out over the lake. There was something comforting about that, something closed in, and he liked that feeling. Or at least he used to like it, before all this happened. At the moment it made him think of fall, which was still a couple of months away. And he didn't want to think about the future. Didn't even want to think about the fact that there *was* a future. Right now he just needed to make it through one day at a time. He glanced at the picture of Jimmy in the middle of his steering wheel. He would soon be starting second grade. And before long that toothless smile would be a thing of the past. Receding further and further into memory. Something that existed only in old pictures. And Lance himself would be an old man who sometimes took out those photos to look at them. An old man living with an old sin. No, a sin that had to be repeated each day, which meant that it would never grow old. Every single day he would once again have to condemn Lenny Diver to life in prison.

He crossed the Cascade River. In spite of the drizzle, tourists were out on the footbridge over the river. There they stood, admiring the series of foaming white waterfalls in the deep chasm the water had dug out as it flowed into the lake over thousands of years.

Lance knew that anyone who stood on the footbridge would feel the cold, wet gusts from the force of the water inside the chasm. Someone was almost always standing there. The waterfalls of the Cascade River were among the most photographed scenes on the North Shore. Only in the winter was the bridge deserted for long periods of time. That was when ice would practically fill up the chasm. Only a distant roar could be heard from deep inside the masses of ice.

A short time later he drove down the long, gentle slope toward Grand Marais, where it looks as if Highway 61 runs right into the lake. At the bottom of the hill, before he reached the center of town, he took a right and parked in front of the restaurant called the Angry Trout. It was in an old warehouse from the days when commercial fishing was done on a grand scale in the area. He saw that Mary had already arrived. There was no mistaking her old Toyota. It still had the bumper sticker that said: "Proud to be Anishinabe." As he walked past her car, he noticed a little dream catcher hanging from the rearview mirror. He didn't remember seeing that before.

There were always a lot of people in the Angry Trout, but he caught sight of Mary as soon as he stepped inside. She was sitting alone at a window table, with a glass in front of her, and she hadn't yet noticed him. She looked good. Her hair was cut in the usual tousled, boyish style, and she seemed just as slender as always. As Lance walked toward her, she turned her head and saw him approaching. She smiled, but it wasn't the big, welcoming smile that he knew. It was a brief, matter-of-fact smile.

"There you are," she said as he came over to the table.

Lance didn't know if he should give her a hug or not. It seemed so formal to offer to shake hands. He sat down without doing either.

"Have you been here long?"

"Ten minutes, maybe."

"What are you drinking?" He nodded at the glass on the table.

"Just water."

A young waiter came over and handed them menus, which they immediately began to peruse. Lance was glad to have something to occupy his eyes and hands. It also gave him time to think of something neutral to say to her. He glanced up from the menu. She was looking out the window.

"Some weather, huh?" he said.

"Yeah."

"But we need the rain, considering how dry it's been all summer."

"Sure, but this is nothing. We need a couple of weeks of steady downpour before it'll make any difference."

Neither of them spoke for a moment. Around them the hum of voices rose and fell from the other guests in the crowded restaurant. A sudden burst of laughter at the next table made their silence seem even more noticeable.

"So, where's Jimmy tonight?" he asked.

"With his grandfather."

He noticed a few tiny wrinkles at the corners of her eyes. They hadn't been there before.

"I went to see Willy a little while ago."

"He told me that."

"Is that okay with you?"

"You and Dad are both grown men. You make your own decisions," she said.

Lance wanted to have a nice, easy conversation, like they used to have, but Mary seemed wary and restrained.

"I noticed something when I arrived," he said. "You have a dream catcher hanging from the mirror in your car."

"And?"

"Well, it's just that I don't remember seeing it there before."

"Do you usually peek inside my car?"

"Of course not, but . . ." He didn't know what to say.

"Well, you're right, it's brand new. Why? Were you thinking of getting one for yourself?"

"No, I just happened to be reading about dream catchers the other day."

At that moment their waiter returned.

"I'll have the trout with wild rice and vegetables," said Lance. "And a Mesabi Red."

"I'll have a house salad," said Mary. "And ice water."

He felt a twinge of disappointment. A simple salad and ice water indicated that she wasn't planning to stay very long. Not that he'd had any expectations, other than hearing something about Lenny Diver, but it was still a letdown.

After ordering, they fell silent again. Lance watched the rain pelting the gray surface of the water outside the window. He remembered one time many years ago when they sat here and saw an otter diving for fish right near the restaurant. The place had been packed with people, and everyone was watching the otter. He remembered that they'd been so happy together back then. Now there was nothing to see out there. Just the rings made by the raindrops. It was starting to rain harder.

"So what about Lenny Diver?" she said. "Are they positive that he's the murderer?"

"That's what they're saying, anyway. What do *you* think?"

"I really don't know . . . It's hard to imagine anyone doing something like that, killing another person."

"I know what you mean," said Lance.

"And you were the one who found the dead man. Was it awful?"

"You'd better believe it."

It looked as though she was waiting for him to say more, but that wasn't what he wanted to talk about.

"You'd better believe it," he repeated.

"But I wonder what Diver was doing there," said Mary. "Do you think he went there with those two tourists?"

Lance shrugged. He was convinced Lenny Diver had never been anywhere near the crime scene.

"Don't you think that sounds more plausible?" she went on. "That all three of them went there together for some reason? What other explanation could there be? That the two Norwegians pitch their tent in the woods, and then Lenny Diver just happens to show up at that very same spot and murders one of them? It's a long way from Grand Portage to Baraga's Cross. Diver must have had a specific reason for going there." She frowned, the way she usually did whenever something didn't seem right.

"They found the murder weapon at his place," Lance said. "A baseball bat with Lenny's fingerprints on it, plus blood from the victim."

"So then there can't be any doubt that he's guilty," said Mary.

"No."

He gratefully eyed the bottle of Mesabi Red that appeared on the table in front of him at that moment. The waiter poured the beer into his glass and then handed Mary her ice water.

Andy must have found some way to get Lenny Diver's fingerprints on the bat, thought Lance. Maybe Diver was telling the truth when he said that he'd been with some woman that night, but he was so drunk he couldn't even remember her name or what she looked like. Could Andy have stumbled upon the dead-drunk Indian by accident and then planted the bat at his place?

Lance raised his glass and took a gulp of beer. His hand was shaking badly. Mary looked at him but didn't say a word.

"Is there anything you can tell me about Diver?" he said after he set his glass back on the table.

"I haven't spoken to him since he left junior high. And that was nine years ago. I've asked around a bit, but there's still not much to tell."

"What about his family?"

"His father was originally from the Leech Lake reservation. I have no idea where in the world he is now. Lenny's mother is from Grand Portage. His parents got divorced when he was a kid. Then she had a daughter fifteen years later. Bess is one of my students. I don't know who her father is. Bess and her mother live alone. Lenny rents a little house for himself. Or rather, rented. Now he's in jail, I suppose."

"Did he have a job?" asked Lance.

"No, he's never held a permanent job. But when he was done with school he actually spent a year apprenticed to Hank Morrison. Hank builds birchbark canoes in the old way. Lenny was supposedly a good apprentice."

"But he's been preoccupied with other things over the past few years, right?"

"Uh-huh. He started with methamphetamine. That's a big problem for us. But I think it was a bit up and down with him. Not continuous drug use over a long period of time. Not until last year. That's what I heard yesterday. I talked to a girl who was in the same class as Lenny. She said his drug use increased drastically about a year ago."

"Any special reason for that?"

"I guess it's just something that happens, sooner or later. They think they can control it, and then . . ." She shook her head sadly. "He earned a living partly by making little wooden sculptures that he sold," she went on. "Animal figurines. Little canoes. Standard Ojibwe handiwork. Apparently he's quite skilled at that sort of thing. His work is even sold in the souvenir shop at the casino. But his classmate thought that he'd stopped making anything about a year ago. About the same time as the meth began taking over."

"Do you remember anything about him from school?"

"When I got out the old class photos, I remembered what he looked like, but that's about all. Usually when I look at pictures of former students, I can instantly recall their voices. Their voices and their laughter. In many cases I can also remember what sort of clothes they wore. But with Lenny Diver . . . The only thing I can remember is that there was a boy named Lenny Diver. He sat at a desk in the middle of the room. That's basically all. He must not have been a troublemaker. Those are the kids who always stick in my mind. And he must not have been particularly bright, either. Or particularly slow. *Then* I would have remembered him. No, he was just there, without drawing special attention to himself. I wish I could tell you more."

"That's all right. Thanks for trying."

"Do you think it'll help you?"

"I think so. Maybe not immediately. But eventually it will."

Mary smiled and nodded. This time it was a smile that he recognized. She used to smile like that whenever he decided to follow her advice on some matter. Usually after they had started out by disagreeing. He noticed that he was feeling annoyed. Did she think this was all *her* idea now? That was how she made it seem, at least.

"What about his sister?" he said.

"Bess? What about her?"

"Well . . . how's she doing?"

"Come on now, I'm her teacher! How would you like it if Jimmy's teacher starting talking about him to some stranger?"

"Sorry."

The waiter brought their food. Lance breathed in the aroma of the dark, long-grained wild rice, which had originally been one of the mainstays of the Ojibwe diet. It smelled a bit like newly dried hay. The fish had been swimming around in the lake just a few hours earlier. The only way to get fresher fish was to go out fishing himself. For a short while he forgot all about why they were sitting there. He savored the food, glad that he'd come to the Angry Trout. It had been far too long since he'd eaten at this restaurant.

"So how's Jimmy?" he said. "Everything okay?"

"Absolutely."

"Is he doing well in school?"

"He's fine. He's doing just fine," she said.

Lance thought about the fact that he was protecting his family by ensuring that Lenny Diver spent the rest of his life in prison. His whole family. If he told the truth, the abyss would open up. Also beneath Jimmy. He would be the boy who had a murderer in the family. That would always be true, but as long as Lance didn't say anything, it would be like nothing had happened. And in that way, by protecting Jimmy, he was also protecting Mary.

"That's good," he said, picking up his glass to take a sip of beer and hide the lump in his throat. This time his hand didn't shake.

They didn't talk as they ate. Once, as she was busy trying to spear something in her salad with her fork, he took the opportunity to study her. Then he noticed that she had aged after all. Her beautiful face had lost some of the glow that had so attracted him in the beginning. It was as if an energy source inside her had been turned down a notch.

When they were finished with their food, they both sat there staring out the window. Lance knew she would leave soon. He tried to think of things he ought to ask her, but his mind was blank. Finally Mary took out her wallet.

"No, no," said Lance. "Let me pay. Please."

"Why? Can't we share the bill?"

"But I'm the one who asked you to come here. You've done me a favor. So it's only fair that I pay for the food."

"All right," she said.

Lance looked for their waiter but didn't see him. All the tables were occupied. The waiters were shuttling between the kitchen and the dining room.

"By the way, how's Inga doing?" asked Mary.

"She's doing okay. We're going to take a drive tomorrow. I thought we might go up to Grand Portage. See the whole North Shore. She hasn't been up there for a long time, you know."

Silence again. Lance regretted mentioning Grand Portage. Because they weren't planning on visiting Mary and Jimmy, of course. And Mary wasn't about to invite them to stop by. They both knew that.

"Well, it's getting late," she said, glancing at her watch. "I've got to pick up Jimmy. Dad gets easily tired these days."

Both of them looked around the restaurant.

"All right. You go ahead," said Lance. "I'll take care of the bill."

"Are you sure?"

"Of course. Say hi to Willy for me," said Lance.

"I'll do that." She picked up her handbag from the floor and got up.

"Good luck with . . . well, you know," she said. "And say hi to Inga."

Lance stood up, but before he could hold out his hand, she was heading for the exit.

He stood there watching her. I'm protecting both of them, he thought.

28

IT WASN'T YET TEN O'CLOCK when Lance turned the key in the ignition and started the Jeep in the parking lot behind Lakeview Nursing Home. Inga was sitting next to him, holding her purse on her lap. She'd dabbed on some perfume.

"All right, let's go," he said. "What do you think about this weather?"

It was a fine, dry day with high clouds, but on the other side of the lake, a big gray bank of clouds was hovering over Wisconsin, threatening rain.

"You brought the umbrellas, didn't you?" said Inga.

"Sure did. They're on the backseat."

"So there's no need to worry about the weather."

"No, I guess not."

They entered Highway 61 and began heading north.

Lance was glad his mother didn't know about everything that was now tormenting him, from the moment he woke up each morning until he fell asleep at night. The only thing she knew was that a Norwegian tourist had been killed near Baraga's Cross more than three weeks ago. And that Lance, her older son, had found the victim. Later a young man had been arrested for the murder. She probably wasn't thinking about it anymore. It had nothing to do with her.

"All weather is nice weather," she said.

"Sure. You're right."

He cast a quick glance at the spry old woman in the passenger seat. He thought he'd begun to notice something vulnerable about her in the past few years. Was it because Oscar was no longer here? In a sense she had been left all alone when he died.

"What is it?" said Inga. She had caught him looking at her.

"Nothing. Just wondering how you're doing. That's all."

"I haven't felt this good in a long time."

It would kill her if Andy was arrested and charged with murder, he thought. It's that simple. I can't kill my own mother. Then he remembered that Lenny Diver also had a mother. So Lenny was not the only one who was going to pay for Andy's crime. His mother would be subjected to the pain that Inga would be spared. She was living with that pain right now. Every second of the day. And it was Lance who had decided on this. He was the only one who knew, so he was also the only one who could put an end to it. After Lenny was arrested, it no longer mattered that Andy and the two Norwegians had been seen together at Our Place. Nobody was asking anymore, who killed Georg Lofthus? This applied both to Ben Harvey and to any customers who might have recognized Andy on that evening. Our Place was no longer a blind spot for Lance. There were no blind spots. The situation was simple and clear. All he had to do was keep his mouth shut.

"What about you, my boy? How are *you* doing?" asked Inga.

"Great," he said.

They passed the big white fiberglass rooster with the bright red comb and shiny yellow feet. Then the giant frontiersman who was leaning on a canoe paddle.

"Well, it certainly has been a long time," said Inga, as if she were greeting someone she hadn't seen in ages. "Two Harbors . . . turn right here."

He turned right onto Waterfront Drive, headed across Skunk Creek, and drove up onto the small hill with a view all the way down to the harbor, with its big, rusty shipping docks for taconite. On the right was the Lutheran church, built of dark, unhewn stone with a big gray cross on the roof. A seagull was perched on top of the cross.

"I think that seagull has been sitting there for almost fifty years," said Inga, pointing. "There was always a gull up there when we lived here."

Lance slowly drove along Waterfront Drive, past the library and the resplendent courthouse with its striking dome.

"That's where a concert was held every Thursday evening in

the summer." His mother pointed at the little music pavilion in the park. "Everyone went to it. There wasn't much entertainment available back then, you know. I remember we'd sit there on little folding chairs we brought along, enjoying the summer evening."

There was also a cannon in the park. A small, fat piece of artillery from the First World War that soldiers from Minnesota had captured from the Germans. One time Jimmy tried to climb on it, but Lance wouldn't let him. Not because it was dangerous but because he thought it would be disrespectful.

"Go left here," said Inga after they passed the park.

Lance turned onto Second Avenue. The sidewalks were full of cracks. Grass and weeds were pushing their way through. A lot of the houses looked empty. A few had signs out front with the name and phone number of a real estate agent. All of these small wooden houses had once been painted in bright, optimistic colors. Greens, blues, reds, yellows. Now they were in disrepair. The paint had flaked off. Tall grass was growing in front of the doorsteps. Here and there they saw an old flag, now so faded from the sun and rain that the stars and stripes were barely visible.

"Now take a right."

Lance turned onto a narrow side street.

"Stop here," said Inga. She began fidgeting with her seatbelt. "I need to get out and take a little walk."

Lance parked the car halfway up on the sidewalk. He turned off the engine and helped his mother release the seatbelt. Then he got out and went around to her side of the vehicle to help her out.

He looked around. There were no cars here. Only his parked Jeep. Insects were buzzing loudly in an overgrown yard on the other side of a rusty chain link fence. He saw a small, yellow house. Empty, with the windows boarded up.

"Willow Street," said Inga.

"Was that where you lived?" He nodded toward the yellow house.

"No, come on and I'll show you."

They headed slowly along the sidewalk. She stopped at the next house.

"Here," she said. "This was where we lived that first year."

And suddenly he remembered that he'd been here once before. He couldn't have been more than eight or nine. It was just him and his father that time. They had walked slowly past. He remembered that it looked different back then. And there was a dog.

"Have you been here before?" asked Inga.

"I think so. With Dad."

"Really?"

"A long time ago, if I remember right. Did the people who lived here have a dog?"

"I have no idea," she said with a laugh. "I'm sure lots of different people lived here after we did. It's a typical rental property. Not the sort of place where anyone would spend a whole lifetime."

It was a small, one-story wooden house painted green. The front porch was partially enclosed with a torn screen. Even though the lawn in the little yard had been mowed fairly recently, the place had a slightly abandoned air about it. Maybe because of the lack of curtains.

"Shall we?" he said, fumbling with the rickety wooden gate.

"Do you think it's all right?"

"Sure," he said, pushing open the gate. He noticed that it almost fell off its hinges when he touched it.

They slowly crossed the yard, which had three old apple trees. Daisies grew along the fence separating the lot from the neighbor's property. An empty umbrella clothesline stood near the back of the house. He grabbed one of the spokes and gave it a shove. The clothesline did a half turn. It hadn't been oiled in a long time, judging by the sound it made.

"You don't think that could be the same clothesline, do you? The one that was here almost fifty years ago?" said Inga, looking up at her son. "It stood in this very same spot."

"It's an old one, that's for sure," said Lance.

"You know what? I think it *is* the same one."

He thought to himself that the clothesline couldn't possibly be fifty years old.

"One morning I was standing in the kitchen watching Oscar," she said. "It was snowing. There was snow on the trees and the fence. He was standing right here . . ."

Again Lance noticed the perfume she was wearing. There was something familiar about it. Did Mary use the same scent? No, this was different. But he was sure he'd smelled it before.

"I could hardly believe my eyes," she went on. "He was feeding the birds, just as he always did in the winter. I'd seen him do that before. But then a little bird landed on his hand." She raised her arm, holding her hand palm up, as if testing for the first drops of rain. "It was eating out of Oscar's hand . . . a tiny bird . . . can you imagine that? I was completely . . . completely . . ." She laughed. She sounded surprised, as if she were once again standing at the window, watching her husband do something astonishing.

"Did the bird really eat from his hand?" said Lance in amazement.

"Yes. And soon there were more. They swarmed all around him. After that I saw it happen many more times. Do you remember?"

"I remember that he fed the birds. But did he always get them to eat out of his hand?"

"Yes," she said. "Didn't you ever see that? He did it often. But the first time I saw it was here."

Lance paused to think, but he couldn't recall ever seeing little birds eating out of his father's hand.

"No, I never saw him do that. Did he keep doing it even after I was grown up?"

"I think he did."

"Well, I don't remember. And I'm sure I'd have a memory of it if I'd seen it."

"Yes . . . well, I don't really know, but . . ."

"I must have forgotten," he hurried to say. He was afraid it would sound like he didn't believe her. And he wasn't sure that he did. Maybe she had seen something like that during the winter they lived here. It wasn't impossible to get little birds, especially chickadees, to eat from your hand. He knew that. Maybe Oscar, young and in love, had done it to impress her.

"What did you think when you saw Dad feeding those birds?" he asked.

"Oh, you know, I . . . It was . . . My heart was . . ." She put a hand to her heart. Then she shook her head and smiled. "It was special," she said. "He was special, your father."

Lance gently placed his hand on her thin shoulder. "Are you okay?" he asked.

"Of course I'm okay." She sounded a bit annoyed. And then, in a milder tone, she said, "Let's walk around the house and then go back to the car."

They went around the corner to the side of the house. Only five or six feet separated it from the neighbor's fence. On the other side of the fence a man about Lance's age was fiddling with an outboard motor that was propped up on a workbench. When he caught sight of Lance and Inga, the man grabbed an oil-stained cloth to wipe his hands. Lance nodded at him.

"Are you considering buying it?" asked the man.

"What?" said Lance.

"The house."

"So it's for sale?"

"Yeah."

"I didn't see a For Sale sign."

The man came over to the fence. He was still wiping his hands on the filthy cloth. The cap he was wearing said "Big Dog Fishing."

"They never last long around here. Lots of vandals, you know."

"That right? Well, we're not interested in buying. We're just taking a look at old properties."

"Oh, so you used to live here?"

"*I* did," said Inga.

"Were you the one who lived here before MacGuire?"

"MacGuire?" she said, bewildered.

"That's right."

"I lived here a long time ago."

"Before ninety-five?"

"A long, long time before that," said Inga.

"Okay, well, then I don't know." The man seemed to lose interest in them. "Well, well," he said, stuffing the dirty cloth in his pants pocket.

"We'd better head out," said Lance, giving him a nod.

They walked around the corner and found themselves back at the dilapidated gate.

"Who in the world is MacGuire?" said Lance's mother.

"I guess it's just somebody who used to live here. Shall we keep driving?"

Lance peered through the rip in the screen into the enclosed porch. There were two small benches set against the wall inside. He thought his parents must have sat there.

"So how long did you and Dad actually live here?"

"Oh, not long. Less than a year. From the fall until summer."

He turned to face her again. "Shall we?" he said and gallantly gestured toward the car parked on the sidewalk.

"You're a nice boy," said Inga, giving him a smile.

Lance closed the gate behind them and helped his mother into the car. Then he got in and was just about to turn on the engine when she suddenly said, "We moved because we were expecting a baby." She looked out the window, at the house where she had once lived. "That was you."

"Does that mean that it was here I was . . . conceived?"

"Yes."

"Good Lord."

He thought he heard a chuckle, but it was hard to know, since she was turned away from him.

"It was here that it began."

"Did you ever come back here? In later years, I mean?"

"Early on we drove past occasionally. I remember we talked about how much bigger and nicer our house in Duluth was, and how great it was that we actually owned it. But after that, I've never been back."

"I think Dad actually brought me here once. Just the two of us. I was probably eight or nine."

"Really?"

"Uh-huh. I remember walking past here."

"And then he told you that your mother and father had lived in that house long ago?"

"I don't know whether he did or not."

"I'm sure he did," she said. "And then he probably ruffled your hair. Do you remember how he used to do that?"

"Do you miss him?"

"Oh yes."

"Was he . . ." Lance tried to find the right word. "Do you think he was . . . content?" he said. "Did he die a contented man?"

"Suddenly there are so many things that no longer have any meaning," said Inga. "Things you may have struggled and wrestled with all your life. In the end he was thinking only about the good things. You and Andy. Chrissy, who wasn't more than ten back then. She was Oscar's only granddaughter, you know. And the fact that he and I had stayed together all those years . . ." Her voice was starting to sound brittle. "Let's get going," she said.

Neither one of them spoke as they drove through the narrow

streets of Two Harbors. Then Lance suddenly remembered that his mother was part Indian. That they both were. He'd forgotten about that for a while. Now it came rushing back to him. Does she know? he thought. The possibility opened up a whole new space around her, and around Lance too. Had he grown up with a mother who knew all along that she had Indian roots? If so, wouldn't she have told her sons about it? Not necessarily. It wasn't so long ago that such matters were considered shameful, as Lance well knew. Yet he had the feeling he would have sensed something if his mother had known. If not before, then at least after he found out the truth about Nanette. Now he could never again be completely sure about who his mother was. Before, he'd barely given it a thought. Inga was the person he thought he knew best. That was how it had always been. But now he might always have doubts—maybe she had lived among them with a big secret in her heart. And if so, then she was a different person than he'd always thought. Or was she?

No matter what, it would be unthinkable to ask her. Their brief visit to Willow Street had given him the feeling that she was enveloped in something terribly fragile that might shatter at the slightest prodding. It was something he hadn't noticed before. Maybe it was just a result of age. Maybe it was because of Oscar's death.

They came out onto Highway 61 again and left Two Harbors behind.

"How's Chrissy doing?" asked Inga.

"Pretty good, I guess."

"Really?"

"Sure. At least I haven't heard anything to the contrary," said Lance. He thought about that black-clad, pale-looking girl in the parking lot of Enger Park.

"You know she doesn't come to see me anymore. She's a young lady now, and I suppose she has other things on her mind," said his mother.

"I don't have a lot of contact with them," said Lance.

"You don't see your brother much?"

"No. Mostly just when we go deer hunting."

"Shouldn't you get together more often?"

"I don't know . . ."

"No, never mind. The two of you should do as you like. I'm not going to interfere in your business."

"There's nothing to interfere with."

"I suppose not. But he's your brother, after all."

"My brother, yes he is," he muttered.

Lance pictured the lost expression on Andy's face when he visited him in Two Harbors. The same look he'd had during the episode with Clayton Miller. He had seemed as alone as any human being could possibly be. Yet Lance had never asked his brother why he went after Clayton. And now, as he drove north along Lake Superior with his mother, he realized what it was that he feared most. It wasn't Andy's loneliness or the incomprehensible violence. Not exactly. What he feared was that the world would turn out to be different than he had always believed. That was what they all feared, he thought. His parents too. That their own little world would dissolve like a soaked piece of paper and reveal something else behind it. That was why no one had ever tried to find out why Andy had beaten up Clayton Miller.

They soon passed Silver Bay, with its landscape of black taconite mounds and big rust-colored shipping docks. A small group of men was standing outside the hangarlike buildings. They wore yellow hard hats and orange vests.

"Do you think the taconite will ever run out?" asked Inga.

"Of course it will."

"But in our lifetime, I mean. Or rather, in *your* lifetime."

"Hmm . . . I don't know," said Lance.

"And how will people up here make a living when there's no more taconite?"

"I'm sure it'll be fine. Not many people are dependent on taconite anymore. Besides, tourism is the future around here."

"You think so?"

"You should have seen how many people were over at Gary's canoe rental shop on Sawbill Lake."

"Oh, right. Gary. Are things okay between him and Barb?"

"Sure. Money is practically growing on the pine trees over there right now."

Inga laughed. "He's always been a go-getter, that boy," she said. "And then there's Barb, with those delicious cakes of hers. Do you remember when Jimmy ate all the cakes while the rest of us were watching TV? And how sick he was? Those were Barb's cakes."

"It wasn't Jimmy who did that. It was Chrissy."

"No, that can't be. Because Dad was there."

"That part is right. Oscar was there," he said.

Lance thought about the night his father died. Mary was six months pregnant. They were watching TV, and he was holding a plate of food on his lap, which meant that he couldn't get up to get the phone when it rang. So Mary did it. She got up with her big stomach and went over to the table where the phone was. She picked up the receiver. "Hello?" She listened for a long time. Then she said "okay" and "uh-huh" several times. Listened some more as she nodded. Finally she turned toward Lance, holding the phone in her hand. "It's Andy," she said, and he realized what his brother was going to say. He had known that his father was dying, but he was hoping that Oscar would get to see his grandchild before he passed.

They were now crossing the Manitou River. It was here, at the mouth of the river, that a dead body had been found in 1892. Lance figured he'd never find out for sure whether it was Swamper Caribou's body.

He got out a paper bag of Dove chocolates that he'd made a point of buying before he picked up his mother.

"My dear Lance, you didn't need to buy me anything," she said.

"It's just some chocolates."

Inga stuck her gaunt fingers inside the paper bag and took out a chocolate wrapped in thin silver paper.

"Make sure to read what it says on the inside of the wrapper," said Lance.

Both of them carefully took off the foil paper and stuck the little chocolate hearts in their mouths. Inga chewed cautiously. Then she smoothed out the wrapper and squinted her eyes to study the message.

Finally she laughed.

"What does it say?" asked Lance.

" 'You're only young once,' " she told him. "And unfortunately, that's so true. What does yours say?"

"It says, 'Live your own dream.' "

He heard his mother say something, but he didn't know what it was. Those four words on the silver wrapper had struck a deep chord inside him. Because that was how he felt. As if he were living in a dream. From the moment he discovered a naked and blood-covered man sitting on the ground and leaning against Baraga's Cross, his life had become less and less real. It was seven years since he'd had his last dream. That was when he was standing alone at the deepest spot in Lake Superior. In a shimmering blue landscape. For a long time afterward he'd hoped he would dream about that cold place again. But there were no more dreams. Not a single one for seven years. He thought that over the course of those years, a large number of undreamed dreams must have piled up, and that now they were starting to leak into his waking life. The dream material was seeping out and getting mixed up with tangible reality. That was what this banal message on the chocolate wrapper had made him think about.

"Are you listening to me at all?" asked Inga, annoyed.

"What did you say?"

"I asked you whether you're living your own dream."

"Whether I'm living my . . . That's just a bunch of nonsense, Mom."

"I happen to think it's a good message."

Lance didn't reply.

A little later they passed the sign that said "Baraga's Cross."

"Good thing they caught that murderer," she said.

"Uh-huh."

"Someone from Grand Portage?"

"Yeah."

"When I heard about it, I thought of Jimmy."

"Why's that?"

"I hope his family doesn't have any connection with that man."

"I don't think they do."

"None of them?"

"No. Mary had him as a student in school years ago. That's all. She barely remembers him."

"So you and Mary are talking?"

"We do have a son together. So of course we talk to each other."

When they arrived in Tofte, Inga wanted to find a restroom before they drove any farther. Lance drove down to the Bluefin Bay Resort and parked.

"We can use the bathroom here," he said. "I could use one myself."

He got out of the car and went around to the passenger side to assist his mother. He couldn't help noticing how little she now weighed.

"Oh, that feels good," she said. "I need to stretch my legs a bit." She gazed out at the bay, where a trim white sailboat was anchored, as usual. "Things are so different these days," she said. "That's for sure. When I was young, the old wharf was still out there." She pointed at the partially collapsed stone pilings sticking out of the water right across from the hotel.

"Wasn't it torn down in the early sixties?" said Lance.

"I don't know, but it was there when I was young, at least. Very young. I remember it well."

"Didn't you used to come up here before you met Dad too?"

"That's right. That was how we met. Your father was from around here, and we had relatives here that we came to visit."

"But your grandparents were dead, weren't they?"

"Yes, I never met them. They died before I was born. Knut and Nanette. But we visited my older brother who lived here with his family. I remember that Helga Aakre used to sit out there on the old wharf. She was my best friend up here. This must have been near the end of the war, I think. The wharf was no longer in use. And we really weren't supposed to be out there. The grown-ups said it could be dangerous."

"But you didn't listen to them?"

"Oh no, we sure didn't. Not Helga and I. No. But can you imagine what a big deal it must have been when the wharf was first built?"

Lance nodded.

"Do you know when that was?" asked his mother.

"In 1903, I think."

"Just imagine, finally the steamboat could dock here. What a difference that must have made. The modern world arrived in Tofte. It's really a monument to the hard work of the first generation," she said, as if the wharf was still standing, and not just the stone pilings. "A monument to their dreams."

"I guess we'd better go inside and find the bathrooms," said Lance. "By the way, is there anything you'd like to see or do before we continue north?"

"Yes, there is," she said.

THE CEMETERY IN TOFTE was a couple of hundred yards above Zoar Lutheran Church, at the end of a narrow road. It was surrounded by woods and difficult to find for anyone who didn't know its exact location.

It was here that the men and women were buried who had left behind everything they knew and headed for a land where dreams could become reality. Deep under the grass lay their crumbling bones.

On the headstones their names reappeared, like a greeting or a reminder to posterity: Anderson, Carlson, Larson, Bjerkness, Stenroos, Tveekrem, Engelsen, Olson, Tofte, Tveiten, Odden, Mattikainen, Tormondsen.

In some places a stone said: *Born in Norway,* or *Born in Sweden.* There were even a few inscriptions in Norwegian: *Hvil i fred.*

On the marker for Andrew and Sonneva Tofte was a little map, made of gold leaf, a simple outline of the land they had left behind. At the bottom left of this map was a star that represented Halsnøy, where both of them were born and raised.

Buried near a big fir tree, which couldn't have been more than a small sapling when they died, were Knut and Nanette Olson. They had died in 1925 and 1928, respectively. Approximately eighty years later one of their grandchildren stood at their grave. An old woman with white hair. And at her side stood a middle-aged man who was Knut and Nanette's great-grandson.

"This isn't a very big cemetery," said Lance, looking around.

"Oh, it's been plenty big so far."

"But it's starting to get crowded."

"Yes. I have a plot waiting for me in Duluth."

"I know."

"Next to Oscar."

"Mom . . . could we leave now?"

Inga looked up at him. "Are we in a hurry?"

"No, but . . ."

His mother began walking slowly toward the center of the cemetery. It took Lance only a couple of strides to catch up with her. Then they walked on, side by side. He saw that she was limping slightly. He hadn't noticed that before. Maybe she's already feeling tired, he thought. Had he been too optimistic to suggest driving all the way to Grand Portage and back?

"Look here," said Inga, pointing. "This is where Thormod Olson is buried."

The grave was marked with a big, almost perfectly round stone. It looked as if it had been brought straight from the shore, washed smooth by the waves over thousands of years. As if Thormod were resting under a small piece of the lake itself.

Lance squatted down to read the inscription. It said: "Thormod Olson, born in Norway in 1877, died in Grand Marais in 1953." He thought about what he'd recently discovered about the man who lay buried here. According to Nanette, someone had given him two deep wounds in his arm. He had lain in that little log cabin of theirs, having terrible nightmares. A fifteen-year-old who thrashed about, screaming in his dreams. Screaming in Norwegian in the dark, here on Lake Superior. Feverish and in pain. Beneath Lance's feet lay the moldering remains of the body that had fought for life on that March night in 1892. But Thormod Olson had taken his secret to the grave.

Lance knew that his mother was behind him, waiting for him to stand up. But he stayed where he was. He stroked the grass with his hand, as if he were tenderly stroking someone's hair. This was where he would one day be buried. And like Thormod, he would also be taking a secret to the grave. Only this time the victim would not be Swamper Caribou but Lenny Diver. For Lance the two almost seemed to merge into one. He realized that he would never be allowed to forget. This was how his life would be from now on.

"I remember the funeral," said Inga. "The pastor talked about how he had almost lost his life when he came here as a young boy."

"You were at the funeral?"

"Oh yes. I stood here with the whole family. In a way, Thormod was our hero."

"Do you remember him?"

"A little. An old man with white hair. Short and stocky. Walked with a cane. So would you like to stop by the cemetery in Lutsen to visit the Hansen graves too?"

"No, I think this is enough for today," said Lance.

They headed toward the center of the cemetery, where they saw more markers with newer dates. Inga stopped at one of them.

"Helga Johnson," Lance read. "Who was that?"

"Helga Aakre. I told you about her. She got married and spent all her adult life in Minneapolis. I went to visit her there a few times."

"You did?" said Lance. "I don't remember that."

"Well, I didn't go often. But there were a couple of periods when things were difficult and . . . that's when I went there, to see Helga."

Lance wondered when his parents had gone through difficult periods. He couldn't recall anything special. But he wasn't sure how much he could rely on his memory. He didn't even remember his father feeding little birds out of his hand.

ABOUT HALF AN HOUR LATER Inga Hansen asked her son to stop the car. "I need to stretch my legs again," she told him.

Lance pulled into a rest area with a view of Lake Superior. He went around to help his mother out of the car.

"Oh, these old knees of mine," she sighed.

"Should we turn around and go back?"

"Let me think about it." She leaned one hand on the car. "My goodness, it's so wonderful to get out for a drive," she said.

The lake spread out before them like an ocean. The sun had broken through the cloud cover. The vast body of water glittered. A slope led down from the rest area to the lake. Lance now noticed that a man was sitting down there, right at the water's edge. He recognized him at once. That hat and jacket were unmistakable.

Lance cast a glance at his mother to see if she'd noticed anything, but she was just standing there, gazing out at the lake. A gust of wind ruffled a few thin locks of her hair. Lance again looked down at the dark-clad figure. He could clearly see that the back of his jacket was shiny with age and that the brim of his hat drooped, as if it had lain in the water for a long time.

"It's strange," said Inga. "I've lived my whole life near the lake, but it's only seldom that I actually . . . notice it."

"Uh-huh," said Lance without taking his eyes off the figure.

He was looking at the man from the back. He seemed to be leaning forward, with his knees drawn up to his chin. Lance knew who he was. Maybe he'd known all along. He just hoped that the man wouldn't turn around and look at him, the way he'd done near the lighthouse in Grand Marais. He was afraid of meeting the man's eyes again. And yet, he was certain that it would happen. If not now, then another time. If not here, then somewhere else on the lake.

This is just the beginning, he thought.

VIDAR SUNDSTØL is the acclaimed Norwegian author of six novels, including the Minnesota Trilogy, written after he and his wife lived for two years on the shore of Lake Superior. *The Land of Dreams* was awarded the Riverton Prize for best Norwegian crime novel of the year in 2008, was nominated for the Glass Key for best Scandinavian crime novel of the year, and was ranked by *Dagbladet* as one of the top twenty-five Norwegian crime novels. The Minnesota Trilogy has been translated into eight languages and is the first of his works to be translated into English.

TIINA NUNNALLY is a translator of Danish, Norwegian, and Swedish literature. Her translation of *Kristin Lavransdatter III: The Cross* by Sigrid Undset won the PEN/Book-of-the-Month Club Translation Prize, and her translation of Peter Høeg's *Smilla's Sense of Snow* won the American Translators Association's Lewis Galantière Prize. The Swedish Academy honored her for her contributions to "the introduction of Swedish culture abroad," and she was appointed Knight of the Royal Norwegian Order of Merit for her efforts on behalf of Norwegian literature in the United States.